THE NEW HEROES
CROSSFIRE

MICHAEL CARROLL

MaxEdDal Publications
www.quantumprophecy.com

ISBN: 1517394473
ISBN-13: 978-1517394479

First published 2015

For our wonderful friends,
the Totally Excellently Awesome Evans family:
Julie, Izzy, Tom, Dan and Dave

Acknowledgments

I would like to extend my warmest, fuzziest and sweetest-smelling thanks to my agents; to the publishers; to my editors Matt Morgan, Nicholas Lake, Kiffin Steurer and Brian Geffen; to the copy-editors and designers and type-setters and marketing people and the countless others who work in the background and never seem to receive much credit; to my fellow writers, whose books you really should be reading instead of mine—er, I mean *as well as mine*; to the wonderful convention committees who somehow still keep inviting me to their events; to the noble librarians and stalwart teachers and courageous book-store folk who've promoted and supplied my books; to my friends and family for their continued support (even those who don't actually read the books but still believe that they're entitled to freebies...).

Special thanks as always to my old pal Michael Scott who started me on this road.

Super-special thanks to my darling wife, the utterly adorable Leonia; there isn't enough paper in the world to fit all the thanks she deserves.

And, lastly but not leastly, mega-ultimate-hyper thanks to the readers, many of whom have waited *very* patiently for this book!

Previously...

(AKA A Note from the Author!)

So, here we are in 2015, thirteen years after I first began working on the *Quantum Prophecy / New Heroes* series. We're not quite at the end yet, but we're getting there!

Crossfire is the eighth novel in the series. Yes, *eighth*! Some readers might be familiar only with the original trilogy, others only with the prequel series, so for those people the following will give you a taste of what you've missed! (But *just* a taste: for the full experience, you'll have to read the books themselves!)

The original trilogy (*The New Heroes*, published as *Quantum Prophecy* in the USA) opens ten years after a huge battle in which all of the world's superhumans disappeared. There have been no superhumans (heroes or villains) since.

The chief protagonists are young teenagers Colin Wagner and Danny Cooper, who discover that they are developing superhuman powers of their own. They soon learn that they are the offspring of some of the original superheroes: it is revealed that superhuman abilities develop at puberty, and the device that stripped the original heroes of their powers has not affected those whose powers had yet to manifest.

Danny develops incredible speed, while Colin has enhanced strength and senses, and—later—the ability to manipulate many forms of energy.

Colin and Danny come into conflict with twenty-one-year-old Victor Cross, a hyper-intelligent superhuman who has very much his own ideas as to how the human race should be controlled. Along they way, they also meet Renata Soliz, a fourteen-year-old girl who was effectively frozen in time ten years earlier, shortly before the other superhumans lost their powers, and Solomon Cord, formerly the non-powered superhero known as Paragon.

In book 2 they move to Sakkara, a fortified base near Topeka, Kansas, where they learn that they are not alone: the base is home to twin sisters Mina and Yvonne Duval (who are later revealed to be clones of the supervillain Ragnarök), and sixteen-year-old Butler Redmond. Cross realizes that these new heroes could be a threat to his plans, and so begins a power-struggle with Cross backed by his powerful, rapidly-growing organization, the Trutopians, which culminates in Colin being forced to choose whether to save the life of his friend Solomon Cord or Renata's entire family: he chooses the latter.

The last book of the trilogy sees Yvonne joining the Trutopians to spark a devastating world-wide war. They are eventually defeated, Yvonne is captured and Cross is seemingly killed: however, at the very end it is revealed that Cross has faked his death and is actually in the process of creating a number of clones of Colin.

Tied in with the original trilogy is the short-story collection *The New Heroes: Superhuman* which includes two novellas—*The Footsoldiers* and *Flesh and Blood*—that focus on minor characters; both novellas are also available as e-books.

The prequel series begins about twenty-three years before the original trilogy, before the older generation of superhumans lost their powers...

Super Human: The Helotry, a secret and very powerful organization, attempts to snatch the world's first superhuman—Krodin—from his own era some 4000 years in the past. They believe that it is Krodin's destiny to rule the entire human race, and they are willing achieve this at any cost. To aid their plan they unleash a devastating virus on the world which debilitates all adults. It's down to only a handful of teenage superhumans to stop them... Abby (super-strong and very fast), Thunder (able to manipulate sound), Roz (telekinetic) and Brawn (thirteen feet tall, invulnerable, immeasurably strong) work alongside would-be teen con-artist Lance McKendrick (no super powers) to stop the Helotry from bring Krodin out of the past.

The Ascension: The heroes suddenly find that the world has changed: they are in an alternate time-line where Krodin has taken control of the USA and is attempting to subjugate the rest of the world. With most of that reality's superhumans already dead, only our heroes are aware that this is not how the world should be. Ultimately, Lance is able to defeat Krodin by using one of his own machines against him: Lance uses a teleporter to take Krodin out of the past—*before* he could change history—and transport him to the airless deserts of Mars. With that done, the time-line returns to normal, with only the young heroes aware of the change.

Stronger: This is Brawn's story, detailing his life from the moment his superhuman abilities first appeared to his encounter, twenty-seven years later, with Colin Wagner (which occurs in the middle of the third book of the original trilogy).

Hunter: Lance McKendrick's life-story. Covering a period of about thirteen years, we see Lance grow from a rather selfish, arrogant teenager into a confident and compassionate adult, against the backdrop of superhuman conflicts and world-changing events.

For an overview of how the books fit together chronologically, here's the official timeline (it's based on the notion that the first book in the original trilogy is "year zero", which means that *Crossfire* takes place about two years after that)...

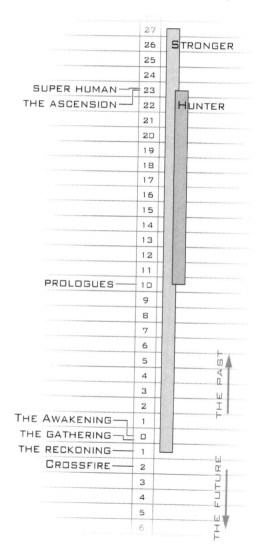

A few final notes... At the request of the publishers, the US edition of the third book in the original trilogy (*The Reckoning*, otherwise known as *Absolute Power*) contains an additional scene at the end of the book. For those who've never read that edition, I've included that scene as "Prologue 1" in this book.

The future of the series is, as ever, rather fluid. I do know exactly how it's all going to end, but I don't yet know *when*. Far too many different things can and do exert an influence on the best-laid plans... I can tell you that there will be at least one more novel in the series. And I'm not (yet) ruling out the possibility of "side" novels or novellas that are connected to the main series but work as stand-alone stories. You'll just have to wait and see! Do please check out the website (www.quantumprophecy.com) for the latest news.

But right now, this is *Crossfire*... The New Heroes are back!

What happened to Daniel Cooper after the Trutopian war? What about Renata Soliz, stripped of her powers? What new dangers will Colin Wagner face? And what on Earth is Victor Cross planning?

Keep reading, my friends... The answers lie within!

Michael Carroll

Dublin, Ireland, October 2015

Prologue 1

One year ago...

Danny sat by Renata's bed until he was sure she was asleep, then he gently pulled his hand free from hers and walked over to the window. Night was creeping over the horizon, the clouds orange-tinted from the fires in Topeka.

He knew he should be out there with Colin and the others, helping to restore some semblance of normality to the world, but they hadn't asked him and he hadn't felt inclined to offer.

The vision came true.

A sudden violent shudder rippled through him.

Oh God, it came true.

He realized now that he'd been scared ever since he'd seen the vision of his future self in the Californian desert.

Quantum had foreseen the deaths of billions of people, and had known—somehow—that Danny would be responsible.

That didn't happen, Danny thought. *Thousands died—maybe even hundreds of thousands—but not billions. So either we changed the future Quantum saw or his vision wasn't about the Trutopian war.*

What scared him most was that Quantum's visions had driven him almost insane.

Is that what's going to happen to me?

How long do I have before I can't take it any more?

He checked once more that Renata was sleeping comfortably, then silently left the infirmary and made his way to his own room.

As his bedroom door hissed open, the door to next room did

the same. Niall leaned out, grinned, and padded barefoot towards him. "Is she gonna be all right?"

Danny nodded. "Yeah. I think so."

Niall followed his brother into his room. "Can't you, like, see into the future and tell for sure?"

"Doesn't work like that," Danny said. "I can't control it."

"Dad said that the visions are like watching a tiny bit of a movie you've never seen before. You can see what's happening but you don't know exactly what it means. Is that right?"

"That's it exactly."

Niall climbed onto the bed and sat cross-legged, absently picking at his toe-nails as he looked at Danny. "They keep talking about how it's all your fault."

Danny stopped in the middle of pulling on his jacket. "They?"

"The news. They're saying that you forced everyone into going to Lieberstan, and if you hadn't done that then there wouldn't have been a war."

"The war has nothing to do with Lieberstan, Niall."

"Yeah, but they keep saying—"

"I know. They do that because if you tell the same lie over and over and don't give anyone a chance to hear the truth, then eventually you'll get enough people believing your story that the truth becomes the lie. Give me a hand with this, would you?"

Niall jumped off the bed and zipped up Danny's jacket. "Are you gonna get another robot arm?"

"Yeah. If they'll make me one. Thanks."

"But—"

Danny cut him off. "Sorry, Niall. But I don't want to talk about that now. OK?"

"Sure. But…"

"What?"

Niall looked away. "What about me, Danny? What powers am I going to get?"

"You might get the same powers Façade had. You know, being able to change your appearance." He smiled. "Be pretty cool that, wouldn't it?"

"I guess. But Dad was a bad guy. For a while."

"I know, but he did the right thing in the end. He's not a bad guy now. You just make sure you always do the right thing, and you'll be OK."

Niall looked up at him, unblinking. "*You* did the right thing, and look what they're saying about you."

Danny gave his brother another smile, showing a confidence he didn't feel. "Things'll work out all right in the end. Now go on back to your room. I've got to go out there and help Colin and the others."

He winked, then slipped into slow-time and left the room.

Seconds later Danny stood on the roof of Sakkara and looked out toward the city.

Quantum said that I would be responsible for a war in which billions of people are going to die. Well, I know I'm not responsible, but everyone is blaming me anyway. Is that what he was sensing?

The visions come without context.

I saw myself leading a group of kids away from an army, and that's what happened. But in the vision, when they fired at me, I raised my mechanical arm and the bullets bounced off an invisible shield.

I figured that was something built into the arm, but it was

Butler's force-field.

And I wasn't leading the kids, I was rescuing them.

He stepped up onto the low wall that skirted the edge of the roof, paused for a moment, then ran down the building's sloping side and through the now-deserted army base.

Despite everything that had happened, Danny was a little cheered up by this.

I can move so fast that gravity doesn't have enough time to take hold of me. It reminded him of a cartoon character running off the edge of a cliff. As long as the character doesn't look down, he's safe.

In slow-time I can do almost anything. I could—

He stopped himself in mid-speculation.

Slow-time. Why do I call it that? If anything it should be fast-time.

He couldn't remember when he'd first started to use the phrase, but it felt right.

He remembered his old teacher, Mr Stone, telling them that speed was "distance over time." "Thirty miles per hour," Mr Stone had said. "That means that in an hour the car would cover thirty miles. Obviously."

Danny skidded to a stop. He was now in the heart of Topeka, at north-east corner of Gage Park.

Time.

My powers are connected to time*, not speed. That's why I get visions of the future.*

He thought back to Max Dalton's power-damping machine in California. Colin had been trying to break through the machine's armor-plating, and Danny had placed his arm on Colin's shoulder in the hope of somehow imparting some of his speed to Colin, but it hadn't worked.

Why did I even think that was possible?

He shifted back into normal-time, and looked around. This part of the city had been relatively untouched by the war, but a few hours earlier it—like the rest of the world—had been completely crystalline.

Renata was able to extend her powers beyond herself, so maybe I can too.

Maybe I can alter everyone's *perception of time.*

He closed his eyes and tried to concentrate on his own future, tried to see what was coming.

There was nothing.

After the vision in California, all he'd had since were vague feelings.

But if it happened once, then it can happen again. Everything I saw came true. Does that mean that the future can't be changed?

Something moving through the night sky caught his attention. Danny looked up to see Colin drifting down towards him.

Colin was grinning, but looked exhausted. "Thought that was you! It's crazy out there, Dan. I saw a man stuck on the roof his house and when I went to help him he threw a brick at me. Then he panicked and fell off and I almost didn't catch him. So, how's Renata?"

"She was asleep when I left her. I think she's going to be OK. Apart from losing her powers."

Colin nodded. "Well, I'm glad you're with us now. Steph and Mina and Butler are out on the west-side trying to persuade a bunch of Trutopians to give up. They didn't hear Yvonne's message. There's probably a lot of them out there still fighting. Come on, I'll fly you over that way." He was already rising into the air, his hand out-stretched to Danny.

Danny reached out and grabbed hold of Colin's hand...

... And suddenly he was in a different place. A huge crater. Colin was at the center, lying on the ground, his entire body blackened and burned. He wasn't moving. He wasn't breathing.

Another flash, and Danny was looking at himself, about the same age as he was now, but with both arms intact. And there was another difference: this two-armed Danny had a look in his eyes that chilled him; a glare of pure hatred and ruthlessness.

Then a third flash. Danny was crouched on the ground, looking down at the dead body of a man he didn't recognize. But now, for the first time, the vision came with sound: A voice behind him said, "You didn't have to kill him."

Danny jerked his hand back.

"What? What is it?" Colin said.

"Nothing, I just... Maybe I'd better go back and get some armor."

"'Kay. I'll wait here."

Danny shifted into slow-time, and ran back toward Sakkara.

He couldn't let himself think about the visions now. *There's work to be done. People to be saved. That's what the good guys do, after all. And I'm one of the good guys.*

But he couldn't help asking himself, *Are you sure about that?*

12

Prologue 2

Kenya Cho paused half-way up the long straight hill. Ahead, the yellow glow of her home's downstairs lights surely meant her parents were still up. She took a deep breath in the hope that it would steady her nerves. *Be cool*, she told herself. *It worked last time, it'll work this time too.*

Kenya had spent the day with old friends who lived outside the community. That wasn't actually forbidden, but it was frowned upon.

The community—eight miles east of Fianarantsoa—was the first Trutopian establishment in Madagascar, and was home to almost two thousand people, more than half of whom had joined in the past six months.

Kenya's non-Trutopian friends constantly ribbed her about being in a "cult" but she didn't care—her family had been among the first to join the community, and it was plain to everyone that they were happier now than before. Her parents both had jobs, and she and her older brother Eugene were doing well in the community's high-school.

She liked the Trutopian ideals—they made sense. Work hard, obey the law, and you will be safe. Simple as that. There was no crime in the community, no one went hungry, you could always rely on your friends and neighbors for help.

Kenya understood the rules, and she believed in them. If she wanted to visit friends outside the community, all she had to do was ask her parents. They would put in a request with the local security office, who would look up Kenya's friends on their extensive computer database. It was an efficient system; if all went well, Kenya could expect a reply within a day. Two days at most.

So even though she knew she was breaking the rules and that could earn her family several demerits, she tended to just climb the fence, retrieve the old bike she'd hidden under a footbridge and cycle into Fianarantsoa to see Alarice and Mialy.

She'd been doing this every couple of weeks for months, and last time was the closest she'd come to being caught: Before she reached the front door she'd silently removed her jacket and boots and hidden them under the big bush on the front lawn. Then she'd opened the door as quietly as possible—it wasn't locked—closed it behind her and tousled her hair before entering the TV room.

"I can't sleep," she'd said to her father, who'd been hunched over the puzzle table painstakingly working on his three-foot-square, four thousand piece jigsaw puzzle.

Without looking up from her book, Kenya's mother said, "Have a cup of warm water. Not *too* hot."

Her father added, "And not a *full* cup, either. Otherwise you'll be peeing all night."

But tonight, even before she reached the house, she knew that wasn't going to work. Something was different. Something was *wrong*.

She pushed open the door and her mother shouted, "Kenya? Get in here! *Now!*"

Oh wonderful. How am I going to get out of this one?

The door to the TV room swung open before she touched the handle, and her brother Eugene was beckoning her inside.

"I was just out for a walk. I had a nightmare and I..." Kenya stopped, and looked around the room. Her parents were staring at the TV, which showed the Trutopian flag silently fluttering behind the words "Stand By."

"What's happening?"

"Where *were* you?" Her mother asked. "You *know* you're not allowed out on your own after nine!"

"Never mind that. Sit down, Kenya," her father said, eyes still on the TV set. "It's bad. Reginald Kinsella is dead. Murdered."

Kenya felt as though she'd been punched in the stomach. "No..."

Reg Kinsella was the leader of the entire Trutopian organization. A tall white man; bearded, slightly overweight, not exactly handsome... But there was something about him that Kenya had always liked. Sure, he was a politician, but he'd seemed honest, and passionate about his beliefs. When he'd taken control of the organization there had been only a handful of communities throughout the world, but now there were thousands.

Kenya dropped into her armchair and accepted the mug of coffee from Eugene without even noticing. "What happened?"

"His plane was shot down," her father said. "Yesterday. Somewhere over Poland." He turned to face Kenya, and the knot in her stomach tightened when she saw the fear in his eyes. "We... We don't live in Madagascar any more."

Kenya wrapped her hands around the hot mug and peered at her father through the steam. "What?"

Eugene said, "We've seceded. Broken away. From now on, the Trutopian communities are one nation." He shrugged. "I don't know how they're going to enforce that, but... The borders are closed. No one in or out. The whole world's going crazy—there's been attacks on Trutopian communities everywhere." He lowered his voice. "You were lucky to get back in, sis."

At that, their mother's head whipped around toward Kenya. "What? Where *were* you?"

"Nowhere! I was just—"

The image on the TV flickered. Now it was showing an empty podium that displayed the Trutopians' logo. A dark-haired, pale-skinned teenaged girl emerged through a flood of camera-flashes to walk up to the podium.

"Who's she?" Kenya asked.

"Shhh!"

On screen, the girl stood before the podium and was silent for a moment while she adjusted the microphones. Then the camera zoomed closer, and she began to speak. "The governments of the United States of America, Brazil, Germany, Australia and Poland have all declared their intentions to invade Trutopian territory. We will not allow this to happen. I have a message to all the Trutopians listening. You all understand that what we're building here is a utopia, a perfect world. But it's not logical to build a perfect world on imperfect foundations. The old world has to be destroyed before the new one can begin."

Kenya felt the flesh raise on her arms, the hairs on the back of her neck stiffened. "Oh no..."

Eugene dropped down next to her, put his arm around her shoulders. "It'll be all right."

The girl on screen said, "It's clear that the rest of the human race is not interested in living in peace. We've tried to make them understand, given them every opportunity to join us. They have refused. They have attacked us, time and again. No more. Now it's time to stop *talking* about peace, and start making it happen. Some people say that fighting for peace doesn't make a lot of sense… They're wrong. It makes perfect sense."

The girl stared into the camera, and Kenya—somehow—*knew* that the girl was speaking directly to her. "You will fight and kill anyone who is not a Trutopian. You will keep fighting until we are triumphant."

Three weeks later…

Kenya screamed, kicked and punched as the six burly soldiers threw themselves at her, forcing her to the ground. One of them managed to wrestle the now-empty pistol from her grip, but still she didn't stop. Another soldier, a woman—lying face-down across Kenya's stomach while her colleagues struggled to hold onto the girl's arms and legs—yelled out, "We need some help here!"

Others came running, some breaking away from their task of corralling Kenya's friends and neighbors.

Kenya jerked her left arm free and slammed her elbow into the side of the woman lying across her.

She grunted in pain, but held on. "You stupid little fool—we're trying to *help* you!" Another blow to the kidneys, and the woman screamed. "She's only a *kid*! How can she be this strong? Someone—get the tranquilizer gun!"

"I'll kill you!" Kenya screamed. "I'll kill you *all*!"

Kenya felt something sharp stab into her left calf, and the world began to swim. The pressure on her limbs and body seemed to ease, but she could barely move. Her eyes flickered closed, the noise around her suddenly seemed muffled and distant.

She knew she was blacking out, and tried to fight it.

A faraway voice said, "What's wrong with her *skin*? All those scars... How could anyone take so much damage and still be moving?"

The woman's voice: "No wonder she gave us so much trouble. We should have *known*. Get on to the base. Tell them we need help ASAP—we've got a superhuman prisoner. Tell them to contact Sakkara."

Chapter 1

Danny Cooper shielded his eyes against the early-morning sun as he looked up at the cracked, bullet-riddled statues mounted on the top of the Brandenburg Gate.

"Oh man... Look at that. Herlind said it's been here over two hundred years. Two world wars and it's still standing."

"*Three* world wars," a soft voice said from behind him. "If the Trutopian war doesn't count as a world-war, I don't know what *does.*"

Danny turned to see Mina Duval sitting cross-legged on the ground in the middle of the plaza, absently picking at a small scab on the back of her hand as she stared up at the gate. "Taking another break?"

Mina smiled back. "I'm conserving my energy, centering my focus. Or focusing my center. One of those."

"Don't take too long about it." He turned around slowly, surveying the damage, and the extensive repair work that had begun the day after the war ended and was still a long way from completion.

On the northern side of the street, a builder carrying a scaffolding pole on his shoulder turned to answer a shout from one of his friends. The rear end of the rusty pole swung around, on a direct path for the back of the supervisor's head.

Danny slipped into slow-time and walked over to them. He recognized the pole-carrying man as Wolfgang. He was tall, slim, permanently cheerful, and—Danny had quickly concluded—not the brightest. On their first meeting Wolfgang had extended his right hand to shake Danny's, then quickly pulled his arm back when he realized Danny didn't have a right arm of his own. Wolfgang had blurted an apology in German and then in English, and, when Danny told him that it wasn't a big deal, no harm done, the cheerful young man said, "So we're cool? Friends forgive friends, right? All is well." Then he'd extended his right hand again, and blinked happily and patiently at Danny while he waited for his hand to be shook.

Now, Danny walked slowly around Wolfgang. The man had his hi-viz jacket on inside-out, one of his bootlaces was untied, and when Danny passed behind him and ducked under the pole, he saw that Wolfgang's jeans were way too big for him: they had slipped down around his waist revealing to the world that he had tucked his t-shirt into the back of his underwear.

Danny slipped back into real-time and put out his hand to stop the pole from colliding with the supervisor's head. It thumped against Danny's palm, and Wolfgang turned his head around to see what the obstruction was.

"Hey-hey, Daniel Cooper."

"Hey-hey yourself, Wolfgang." Danny nodded his head back toward the woman as he led Wolfgang away from her. "You almost decapitated your boss."

The German man cringed for a moment. "Ooh. Danke. That would have been bad." He nodded and continued on his way across the street.

The crew's supervisor, Herlind, said, "Ah, Mister Cooper." She consulted her ever-present clip-board. "We are making fine progress."

"There's still a long way to go," Danny said. "I thought *London* was bad, but the Trutopians really did a number on this place."

"This is not the first time the German people have had to rebuild their cities." She shrugged. "But the Trutopians can't be blamed. They were under the control of that superhuman girl. They..." Herlind hesitated. "No. I should be honest, with you if no one else. We. Not they. *We*."

"You were a Trutopian?"

Herlind looked around, and, her voice low, said, "I can remember everything. Some people say they were in a trance, and have few memories of the war. Perhaps for some, that is true. Not for me. I wanted to kill everyone who was not a Trutopian. It was... a need so desperate that it consumed me. I was filled with fury and a madness that made sense at the time." Without looking at Danny, the woman added, "I was lucky. I didn't kill anyone. But I wanted to, and I *tried*. Then the message came that we should stop fighting. If it had come a few minutes later, I would have had the blood of many people on my hands."

Danny didn't know what to say to that.

"So now we work to repair the damage we caused. We can do no less." Herlind smiled, and tapped him on the shoulder with the edge of the clipboard. "You and your friends saved the world, Daniel. You should not have to also clean up the mess afterward. But we are grateful. Your friend Mina is very useful."

They looked over to where Mina was still sitting on the ground, and Herlind added, "Much of the time. Now, go. Back to work. You understand of course that what I have told you is private?"

Danny nodded. "Sure. We've all done things we're not proud of." He gave the supervisor a nod as she turned away.

He slipped into fast-time and returned to Mina.

21

"Got it!" she said as he approached. Mina had successfully removed the scab from her hand and was now holding it up on the tip of her index finger. "That hurt a bit, though."

"If it hurts, don't do it."

"Wise words. Saw you saving the dipstick from getting into trouble again. That's you all over, Danny." Mina rolled back heels-over-head and landed on her feet. "That's what Renata says about you. You can't *not* help people."

"So you and my girlfriend talk about me behind my back?"

"Yep. Well, we'd be stupid to do it in front of your face. She said that Colin said that you were like this back home, too. Always taking responsibility."

"Yeah, but what's wrong with that? If you can help someone and it won't cost you anything, but you choose not to, well, then you're just a jerk."

Mina spread her arms and turned around slowly on the spot. "Um, hello? I *am* helping people?"

"I don't mean you specifically." Danny looked at the civilians helping to clear the rubble and drag the burnt-out cars off the street. "Lot of them still blame us for all this."

"They blame *you*," Mina said. She shrugged. "Sorry, Danny, but you're just going to have to live with that. You can't change most people's minds. All you can do is, like, tell them the facts and hope they figure out the truth for themselves."

The radio clipped to Danny's ear beeped, and Warren Wagner's voice said, "Dan? You're needed. Gunfire. Kulturforum."

Danny hit the button on the radio's microphone. "Got it." To Mina, he said, "Now Warren needs help. Where's the Kulturforum?"

Without looking, the girl pointed to the left. "Potsdamer Platz. Southwest. About a kilometer." She jumped to her feet. "Go. I'll carry on here."

Danny nodded, and started to run. Some of the other members of the New Heroes didn't care for Mina, but Danny liked that she wasn't afraid to say whatever was on her mind.

Mina was fifteen, a little younger than Danny, and her ability to always be able to tell when someone was lying meant that a lot of the adults at the New Heroes' base kept their distance from her. It didn't help that Mina and her sister Yvonne were clones of a man called Casey Duval, who—using the name Ragnarök—had been one of the world's most dangerous superhumans.

Danny raced through the rubble-strewn streets so fast that the people working to clear them seemed as immobile as the statues on top of the Brandenburg Gate.

To his own perspective, he was moving at normal speed— barely a quick jog—but that wasn't how his powers worked. Speed is simply distance over time: Danny knew he wasn't actually running at hyper-speed, he was altering time around him.

In real-time, from anyone else's point-of-view, he covered the distance from the Brandenburg Gate to the Kulturforum in less than a second.

He spotted Mister Wagner crouching behind the mud-clogged tracks of a yellow bulldozer with three other adults—all businessmen wearing crisp dark suits that were now dusty at the knees and elbows—on the main plaza.

Danny shifted into normal time as he crouched down next to them, and three businessmen jumped back, startled, but

Warren Wagner simply glanced at him and nodded. He pointed to a three-story brick building. "Near as we can tell they're holed up there. The, uh, the Kupfer..."

One of the German men said, "Dem Kupferstichkabinett. The museum of printing."

"Right," Warren said. "Internal security is still down. We don't know how many, or what they're carrying. You can handle this?"

Danny nodded. "What do you want done with them?"

Another businessmen—short, with a heavy build and obviously dyed hair—said, "No, you cannot send this boy! He is..." The man looked sheepishly at Warren. "He lacks the... He is not the one to... We need the *other* boy. The one called Power."

"That's my son," Warren said. "He's back in the States. I promise you, Danny can take care of this."

The man didn't seem convinced.

Danny sighed, then patted the stump of his right arm—missing from just below the shoulder—with his left hand. "This bothering you? You don't think I can do it because I've only got one arm?"

The short man looked offended. "Certainly not! I'm saying that you should not be the one to take on these bandits! You are only a boy. You can't even grow a proper beard yet!"

Warren said, "Yeah, you might want to shave that off tonight at the hotel."

And that's another *couple of days*, Danny said to himself. He was so tired of people telling him to shave that he had secretly vowed to only shave when he managed to get through two whole days without anyone bringing it up.

The German man continued. "You don't have the necessary

training. This situation requires an experienced negotiator!"

"Yeah? Well, Colin's younger than me, and he doesn't have that much more experience than I do."

"But they are armed and your friend is bullet-proof, yes?"

One of the man's colleagues flinched at that. "Please, don't let there be gunfire!"

"Yes, the museum contains many, *many* priceless—"

Danny shifted into fast-time, and strode towards the building.

They just don't understand, he told himself. But he didn't blame them for that. Even some of his fellow superhumans couldn't fully grasp the extent of his powers.

When Danny was moving in fast-time, everything else was stopped, or moving incredibly slowly. He could pluck a bullet out of the air. He could switch off his bedroom light and read an entire comic-book before the room grew dark. Once, in Havana, he watched a flock of hummingbirds drifting with glacier-like speed through a field of flowers, each one seemingly frozen in the air as though they were intricate, delicate statues that were somehow exempt from the laws of gravity.

The main door to the print museum was open just enough for him to squeeze through, and for that he was thankful. At the speed he was moving, if he had to push open a door the impact might shatter the glass, warp the metal and possibly ignite the wood. Not that he would even notice—he'd be long gone before the effects became apparent.

Danny explored the museum at what was for him a sedate pace. He looked at the paintings and watercolors fixed to the walls, and attempted to read some of the plaques next to them. But the plaques were mostly in German, and his own grasp of the language was barely enough to enable him to buy a soda from a store.

He found the Trutopian soldiers in an office on the top floor. Four of them, each sitting on the floor with his back against the wall, weapons aimed at the door.

The men were in their thirties or forties, he guessed. They were thin, their clothing ragged and their hair long and untidy. Their eyes had the crazed look that he'd seen far too many times since the war ended.

The Trutopians had been ordered to fight and kill anyone who was not a member of their organization, and it was not an order they were able to resist. The order had come from Mina's sister Yvonne, a former member of the New Heroes who—they had discovered far too late—had been hiding her ability to manipulate other people's thoughts and emotions.

After the death of the Trutopians' leader Reginald Kinsella, Yvonne had made a televised broadcast that cut into every television and radio channel. Unable to resist Yvonne's instructions, almost every member of the organization who heard her words found himself or herself grabbing anything that could be used as a weapon.

Instantly, the world had erupted into war. Almost a million people died before Yvonne was captured and forced to reverse her order, but there were hundreds of thousands of Trutopians who were too busy fighting and killing to hear. So Yvonne broadcast the order to desist again and again, several times a day, for a month.

Then someone—the New Heroes had never learned who or exactly how—managed to get close enough to Yvonne to shoot her in the throat. She survived the attack, but could no longer speak.

Now, there remained thousands of Trutopian warriors—like the four men in the Kupferstichkabinett—who never received the order to stand down.

Danny moved through the men quickly, unclipping the magazines from their guns, stripping them of knives and grenades. He took extra care when removing their guns from their hands, aware that if he simply grabbed the weapons from them he would break their fingers.

He bound their wrists and ankles with the strong cable-ties he had tucked into his belt. The ties were already partly-closed, ready to be slipped over hands and feet: without a second arm, Danny couldn't easily fasten the ties.

The work done, he stepped back and looked down at the men. Though he knew that they had probably killed dozens of people, Danny couldn't hate them. They had no control over their actions, and unless someone found a way to reverse Yvonne's programming, they would never be able to break free of their murderous rampage, permanently wired to kill anyone who was not of their own kind. People like Herlind were the lucky ones, though Danny knew that they probably would be tormented with nightmares for the rest of their lives.

After checking that there was no one else inside the building, he returned to the plaza and again crouched down next to Warren, then shifted back to real-time.

The short businessman said, "and delicate artifacts that…" The man frowned at Danny. From his perspective, there had been nothing more than a flicker.

"All done?" Warren asked.

Danny nodded. "Four of them. Tied up, stripped of their

weapons." He gestured towards the building. "They're on the top floor. See that window, third from the right? They're in there."

"Good work."

"Listen, Mister Wagner... *Look* at this place. They—"

Warren raised a hand to cut him off. "I know."

One of the German men looked up. "Was ist er?"

"Nichts," Warren said. "Es ist nicht wichtig." He pushed himself to his feet, and led Danny away from the men.

"Colin and Cassie searched this whole area two months ago," Danny said. "No way those Trutopians were here then, and I don't see how they managed to get this far into the city with all the police and security cameras."

"I think it's pretty clear that they have help, Dan. I'm tempted to think that someone's deliberately trying to make our job harder for us, but it's more likely that it's a combination of bribery and incompetence. Same as everywhere else. Go back to the gate, help Mina. I'll see if I can get anything out of the prisoners."

Aside from the machine room, the gymnasium was the only place big enough in Sakkara to house Brawn. At thirteen feet tall, the blue-skinned giant could only make his way through the base's corridors by crawling on his hands and feet, so to accommodate him one of the gym's side walls had been removed, a huge door has been installed, and, outside, large steps had been constructed leading down the building's sloping sides and to the ground below.

The gym was where the New Heroes who were still in America tended to gather in the hour or so they had between going off-duty and getting the six hours' sleep on which the base's medics insisted.

Now, Warren Wagner's son Colin sat with his friends Cassandra Szalkowska and Butler Redmond as they listened to Brawn relating another of his adventures.

"And after Spain, where did you go?" Colin asked. "Because that was like only a few weeks before the final battle with Ragnarök, right? How did you get back?"

Brawn frowned for a moment. "Casey's people picked me up. He wanted me there for the battle. Though I still don't get why you keep calling it the *final* battle, Colin." He inclined his head towards the nearest window. "Haven't you been paying attention to what's been going on the past couple of years?"

Colin glanced toward the window. Though there was nothing to see of Topeka from this distance, he was all-too-aware of the damage the city had suffered.

Butler yawned and leaned back so that he was stretched out with his hands tucked behind his head. He appeared to be floating a good six inches above the floor. "Must have been something, though, to have that sort of strength. I mean, you threw a bus over a *hill*!"

A voice from the doorway said, "Forget that. Tell them about the time you held your own against me, Titan, Josh Dalton and Thunder."

They looked up to see Colin's mother walking towards them with Colin's baby sister in her arms.

"Paragon and Hesperus were there too, Caroline," Brawn said, and Colin noticed a look pass between his mother and the giant. The same look that all the adults had when their dead friends were mentioned.

"She's just not settling," Caroline said. "Cassandra? I hate to ask again, but..."

The fifteen-year-old girl pushed herself to her feet. "It's OK." She reached out her left hand and gently caressed the baby's forehead. "She's scared... But she doesn't know why. She's picking it up from you." Cassandra looked into Caroline's eyes. "Something happened... You were watching the TV news. You're worried about Danny and the others. She doesn't like it when you're worried, Mrs. Wagner." She leaned closer, pressed her cheek against the baby's forehead. "Shh, little one... It's OK. Everything is all right."

A few seconds later, the baby's eyes fluttered closed, and she was asleep.

Butler said, "Man, if you could bottle that..."

"*I'd* buy it," Brawn said.

"Me too," Caroline said. "She turned to her son. "Five more minutes, Colin, then go to bed. Even you need to rest from time to time."

Colin nodded. "Sure."

"You have no intention of sleeping tonight, do you?"

"Nope. Me and Razor are working on the new armor."

His mother raised her eyes. "Of course you are." She walked back toward the door. "Thanks, Cassandra."

As Cassandra sat down again, Butler asked, "What's it *like* inside a baby's mind? Is it much different than a person's?"

"Butler, babies *are* people too, you know," Cassandra said.

"Yeah, yeah, whatever."

Colin couldn't help liking Cassandra, even though—at first—he'd done his best to avoid her; he didn't like the idea of someone being able to read his thoughts. But her telepathy had proven to be a great asset to the team and now it was hard to imagine not having her around. It helped that Cassandra had what Razor had called "read-only" telepathy: she wasn't able to change people's thoughts or emotions.

A year ago, when the New Heroes rescued Cassandra and dozens of others from the prison camp in Lieberstan, she had been very quiet and nervous of strangers, but since then she had grown much more confident and was more than capable of holding her own against Butler.

Butler asked again, "So what *is* it like inside her mind?"

Cassandra shrugged. "Babies don't think in words the way we do. Just feelings, really. In some ways it's clearer than everyone else's mind, though. When she wants something, she *really* wants it, if you see what I mean. It's not all mixed up with other emotions."

Brawn said, "I know you can't read *my* mind, Cassie, but can you pick up anything at all?"

"Yeah, I can tell there's something there, but I can't make out any of your thoughts. That's just the way it is with some people: I can't read Impervia either. And Mina had problems reading your aura, didn't she?"

Under his breath—but still loud enough for the others to hear—Butler said, "Yeah, because there's no such thing as an aura and Mina's crazy."

"She's not crazy," Colin said. "Just different."

"We're all different. And *she's* crazy. Auras." Butler shook his head. "What a pile of new-age hippie garbage."

Cassandra said, "Whether or not auras are real, Mina can see *something*. You said it yourself, Butler: It could be that her power is a form of telepathy or empathy and it affects her vision. When I listen to someone else's mind I hear words. She sees colors. That might be the only difference."

"Aw, he's just jealous," Brawn said. "Mina's faster and stronger than him, *and* she can teleport herself short distances. All Butler can do is make a big bubble."

"It's a force-field!" Butler said. "Stop calling it a bubble. And what powers do *you* have? The power to be thirteen feet tall, blue and bald. Well, *that's* useful!"

Colin rose into the air. "All right, that'll do. It's nearly two o'clock in the morning, so get some sleep. We're leaving at eight." He floated over to the door, then out into the corridor.

A pair of weary-looking soldiers nodded a greeting as he passed them, no longer even remotely surprised to see a flying fourteen-year-old boy.

As Colin approached the base's machine room, the door opened and Razor peered out. "What kept you?"

The older boy held the door open as Colin drifted past him.

"Brawn was telling us about when he was in Spain." Colin looked around the room. "No one else on tonight?"

"Nah. Apparently someone's invented this thing call 'sane working hours.' They only work, like, twelve hours a day."

"Wimps," Colin said. He dropped to the floor next to Razor's workbench, and examined a blueprint on the over-sized computer monitor. "What's this? More new armor? You've got the scale wrong."

"No, I haven't." Razor grinned. "New idea."

"I love it when you have new ideas. What's this one?"

Razor combed his hands through his long dirty-blond hair. "This is the one that brings everything to a whole new level. We get *this* working, we're gonna be unstoppable."

Chapter 2

At the short but wide bridge that marked the Western end of Unter den Linden, Danny slowed to a stop and shifted back into real-time. "See?" He held up a paper bag containing three jelly donuts. "And here's the receipt. Charlottenburg, in less than ten minutes. That's six and a half kilometers there and back."

The young German man with the stopwatch looked at him with a raised eyebrow. "Hm."

"What?"

One of the man's two colleagues said, "Ten minutes?"

"There were other people ahead of me in the bakery. I wasn't going to push in line."

"But you moved too fast for us to see."

"That's the *point*," Danny said. "That proves I can do it."

"No, it only proves that you went from here to Charlottenburg and returned. We don't know that you *ran* all that way. Perhaps you teleported, like your friend Mina."

"Well I didn't. I ran," Danny said. "And you owe me two Euros and fifty cents for the donuts."

A voice behind Danny called out, "Hey!"

He turned to see Gerhard, the supervisor of this crew, staring at them.

"You are here to *work*, Daniel Cooper!" The man said. "You are not here to show off!" He beckoned Danny closer. "You're strong, right?" He pointed to the line of burnt-out cars on the side of the bridge. "We need the cars moved."

"Mina's the strong one, Gerhard," Danny said. "I'm the fast one. Can't you tow them out of the way?"

33

"The small truck is busy, and we cannot risk using the big truck until we're sure the bridge hasn't been weakened." Gerhard took off his hard-hat and scratched his head with the corner of his clipboard. "Some of the workers here are saying that this is *your* mess, Daniel. You learned of the governments' superhuman prison in Lieberstan and you told the whole world. You forced them to act."

Not this again, Danny said to himself. Aloud, he said, "Yeah, I did. But that had *nothing* to do with the Trutopian war. They're two completely separate events. The Trutopians had no connection with the prison."

Gerhard smiled. "Perhaps. But you are really as fast as they say, yes? Could you travel from here to Bremen and back in an hour?"

"Sure. How far is Bremen?"

"By road, almost four hundred kilometers. So you can do it?"

"I could do it in a couple of minutes. Why?"

"My company has some documentation to send here. Authorization to close the bridge for two days. My colleague was going to bring the documents by car, but she would have to drive through the night, so we won't be able to start until tomorrow. If you were to collect the documentation, we could begin this evening."

Danny nodded. "Sure. Which way is it?"

The supervisor pointed to the west. "Follow the signs." He scribbled an address on a blank page on his clipboard, and handed it to Danny. "Bremen isn't like your American cities with the roads in straight lines and at right-angles. It's more like Berlin—so you go here, to the stadium on the west of the city. It should be easy to find. I'll phone my colleague, ask her to meet you there."

"OK. When she gets there, let me know and I'll leave. Tell her to wait about five minutes. Just in case I *do* get lost."

Danny spent the next half-hour working with the young German men trying to clear the wrecked cars off the bridge, but he knew he wasn't much help. He was no stronger than an ordinary teenager, and having only one arm made everything a lot more complicated. In the end, the others told him to steer while they pushed.

Anybody could do this, he told himself. *They don't need me.*

As the Germans shouted instructions to him—"Links! Nien, Ihre *andere* links!"—he started to wonder whether he'd be better off going home. *I'm supposed to be a superhero, not a laborer! I helped save the* world*, and now here I am sitting in a burnt-out car trying to remember the German words for left and right.* "Links is left, yeah?" he shouted out.

"Ja! Left!" A voice called back, followed by a muttering that sounded very much like "idiot." Then, louder, "They both begin with L! It's not difficult!"

Not for you, Danny thought. *You're bilingual.*

Danny awkwardly steered the car as the others pushed, and as they reached the far side of the bridge Gerhard told Danny that it was time to go. "My friend is waiting for you in Bremen. Her name is Lenita. You'll recognize her—she looks a little like Nina Hagen." He unscrewed the top of his thermos flask and poured a measure of sweet-smelling milky tea into the cup.

Danny climbed out of the car. "I've no idea who that is," he said, brushing gray fragments of charred seat-cover off the backside of his pants.

The supervisor sighed, and sipped at his tea. "No one listens to the classics any more. She will be standing by her car. A white Toyota."

"OK. I'll be back in a few minutes."

Danny switched to fast-time mode—or slow-time, he was never sure which way to think of it—and began to jog back along Unter den Linden, heading west.

Though he was happy to help out, he sometimes felt that others took his powers for granted. More than once, he'd had to explain how they worked to the other New Heroes: "Look, guys... If I'm in fast-time and I travel thirty miles, it might only be a second from *your* perspective but from my point of view it feels like about four hours."

Now, with Bremen two hundred and fifty miles—or more—from Berlin, Danny faced a round trip of five hundred miles. To him, that was going to take the equivalent of about four days. He sometimes worried that by the time he reached the end of a long journey he might have forgotten what he was supposed to be doing.

After he passed through the Brandenburg Gate again he took a slight detour to the hotel in Tiergarten where he, Mina and Warren Wagner were staying. Seconds later he was back on the road, with his spare pair of sneakers stuffed into his backpack— he figured he'd worn out over eighty pairs in the past year—and his MP3 player on shuffle.

When he reached Helmstedt he left the autobahn and zipped through the town until he saw a public restroom, then, relieved and refreshed, he returned to the road.

In Bremen he followed the road signs to Weserstadion and spotted a middle-aged, dark-haired woman waiting by a white car. He checked that the car was a Toyota—Danny had never had much interest in cars and tended to categorize them by color and size rather than make—then shifted back to real-time.

The woman shrieked and jumped back when he appeared right in front of her.

Man, I've got to remember not to do that! "It's OK, it's me. Danny Cooper. Gerhard sent me, from Berlin. You're Lenita?"

She nodded. "The way you appeared like that... Unglaublich!"

That was one of the few German words with which Danny was familiar: he'd heard it often enough over the past few days. "I know. Sometimes even *I* don't believe it." Leaning against the side of her car, he pulled off his sneakers and put on his fresh pair.

Lenita took another step back, her nose wrinkling.

"Uh, yeah, sorry," Danny said. "My shoes can get a bit pongy after a few hundred miles." He pressed the velcro straps tight, then put the old sneakers into his bag. "Gerhard said you have some documents he needs?"

She handed him a large envelope. "Now, you must make sure that he get this, yes? Otherwise it'll be a whole mess trying to get replacements."

"No problem." He stuffed the envelope into his backpack next to his sneakers. "OK. I'll be back in Berlin in a few minutes. I'll get Gerhard to phone you so that you know he's got the documents."

He was about to slip back into fast-time when Lenita put her hand on his arm.

"Wait... You're the one from the news, aren't you? Shortly before the war, you were talking about that place in Lieberstan. The prison camp for superhumans."

"Yeah, that was me. But, look, the war was nothing to *do* with that!"

"I know. I just... You did the right thing. Places like that should not be allowed to exist. My grandfather was in Dachau during World War Two. It was a horrible, horrible place."

Danny wasn't quite sure how to react to that. "Did, uh, did he survive?"

"Yes." She stared at him, unblinking. "He was a guard."

"Oh. I see."

"When you spoke of the prison on television, you said that some of the people were there only because they had a connection to... How was it you put it? To someone the authorities considered to be a threat."

"That's true," Danny nodded. "They were the families and friends of known supervillains."

"Then you understand that people should never be punished for the actions of their ancestors."

Danny found his mouth had gone dry. "Of course they shouldn't." He fought the sudden urge to tell the woman about his own father. Or, rather, the former supervillain who'd spent eleven years masquerading as his father.

Finally, she seemed to relax. "That's good. Thank you. It is an honor to meet you." She reached out her right hand toward him, then pulled it back. "I'm sorry... Your arm."

"That's OK. I should go. It was nice to meet you." He moved into fast-time, and left Lenita standing by her car, aware that by the time she even noticed he was gone, he would be dozens of miles away.

Danny arrived back in Berlin to find Gerhard still standing in the same spot. He had his head tilted back as he drained the last of his tea from the thermos's plastic cup, and his bright yellow hard-hat was in the process of falling from his head.

Danny plucked the hat out of the air then moved a few feet back from the supervisor before he switched back to real-time. "Got it," Danny said. "You have to phone Lenita and let her know that I made it back."

Gerhard lowered the empty cup and smiled, then frowned when he spotted his hard-hat in Danny's hand. "What..?"

Danny handed it back. "It was falling." He slipped the backpack off his shoulders and crouched next to it on the ground as he opened it. "Got your documents here."

"Thanks. So, was I right?"

"About what?"

"Lenita. She looks like Nina Hagen, yes?"

"I dunno," Danny said, shrugging. "So, what next?"

Gerhard opened the envelope and as he flipped through the pages he said, "When we've cleared the bridge we need to strip the surface and then check the underlying concrete for fractures." He looked up. "Do you have any powers that can help with that? Can you see inside solid objects?"

"Yeah, but only if the solid objects are made of glass," Danny said.

Gerhard grinned, and returned to examining the pages. "Everything is here, I think… Yes. We can proceed." He led Danny to the iron fence and leaned over. "You see the stonework on the left, the scorch-marks? The Trutopians tried to destroy the bridge. They stole a boat and loaded it with canisters of propane, set it alight. But the boat sank before the heat was enough to explode the canisters. Still, we must check for damage." He straightened up. "You and your friends saved the world from those crazy people."

"They weren't crazy. They were just *controlled* by someone who was crazy."

"Perhaps. How many people died in the war, Daniel?"

"No one knows for sure. More than half a million, for certain. But it could have been a lot worse."

Gerhard leaned back against the fence and crossed his arms. "It is believed that one of your people was responsible for turning the world to crystal. The entire world. That level of power is frightening. My mother used to say that power should only be given to those who are too afraid to use it."

"It was the only way," Danny said, trying not to sound defensive. "If she hadn't done it a lot more people would have died. Billions, maybe."

"So you can move at impossible speeds, your friend Colin Wagner can fly and has great strength, Mina can transport herself instantly from one place to another. There's a young man who creates a... what do you call it? A force-shield?"

"Force-field."

"Yes. And there are others. It is said that the supervillain Brawn fights alongside you now. I remember him. A dangerous, evil man. A wild animal who rampages and kills at a whim."

Danny laughed. "Nah, Brawn never killed anyone. He's never even *hurt* anyone who wasn't trying to hurt him. Trust me on this. It was all fear and propaganda."

From the look on Gerhard's face, Danny knew that the man didn't believe him.

"Anyway," Gerhard said. "I don't know where your friend Mina has disappeared to, but we still have a lot of daylight left.

The work won't do itself."

Danny spent the next few hours helping the workers strip the asphalt from the bridge, though he felt that he was close to useless. His speed was of no real use in this situation, and all he could really do was carry away the chips of asphalt one bucket at a time. Without his right arm, he wasn't able to push a wheelbarrow.

Chapter 3

On the edge of the Appalachian Mountains, about forty miles west of Roanoke, Virginia, Colin Wagner darted through the air in pursuit of a sleek black aircraft.

With its wings swept back and over-sized tail, it reminded him of a Panavia Tornado, but it was smaller and appeared to carry no armaments.

Colin activated the microphone in his headset. "Sakkara, this is Colin. I'm tracking the craft now, staying in its wake, keeping my distance. It's heading sort of northish." *I really need a compass*, he told himself.

"Colin, we're not seeing anything out there apart from you. There's a lot of background noise on the radar—the UFO could be jamming us."

"Well, I can definitely see it. And I wish you wouldn't call it a UFO. I'm pretty sure there are no aliens on board."

"Is it an object that you can't identify and it's flying? Then it's an Unidentified Flying Object." There was a pause, then, "Colin, we're reading you at MACH two. Can you confirm?"

"I dunno," Colin said. "I'm going very, very fast, that's all I can tell you." *I need a compass with a speedometer built in.*

"An aircraft traveling at that speed shouldn't be unknown to us. Get closer, see if there are any markings."

"Will do." Colin increased his velocity, willing himself to slip faster through the air. He still had no idea exactly how his powers enabled him to fly, but he didn't question it too much. He sometimes had the feeling that if his brain realized that human flight was impossible, logic would suddenly notice him and he'd no longer be able to do it.

The aircraft's engines flared and it began to pull away from Colin.

"He's speeding up... I'm going to... *Whoa*."

Colin slowed to a hover. In seconds, the aircraft's speed had doubled, then doubled again. "He's gone. Man, that was fast!"

The radio voice came back. "Colin, we're getting the satellite feed now. There was definitely *something* there, but it was moving too fast for a clear image. You have no idea what it was?"

"The only time I've ever seen an aircraft that fast was Victor Cross's scramjet. But that was a lot smaller than this thing."

"All right... Regroup with the others—they're almost at the target. Three miles out you're going to want to rise up, high over their position, then wait until we give the command to proceed. Got that? We've no idea what to expect so keep your eyes and ears open."

Colin changed direction, heading west. The unknown aircraft had been spotted five minutes earlier by a commercial flight heading into Atlanta. Air Traffic Control had reported it to the air force, who in turn had contacted Sakkara.

And I should have a camera, Colin thought as he soared low over the Blue Ridge Mountains, his path contouring the land. Low and fast, his parents had taught him. That was the best way to avoid radar unless your enemy was specifically looking for you.

It was now close to noon, and for the past hour Brawn, Butler and Cassandra had been making their way through the mountains to a location believed to be the stronghold of a gang-lord known only as The Keeper.

In the weeks following the Trutopian war, when the country was in chaos and the forces of law and order had been spread wafer-thin, gangs had formed in every major city. Many were simply groups of ordinary people banding together for mutual help and protection, but some were opportunistic criminals taking advantage of the turmoil.

Some of the gangs waged war on their long-time enemies, murdering each other over shipments of food and supplies. Others, like The Keeper's gang, were far more cunning. They concentrated on scavenging the battlefields for weapons and ammunition, not caring whether the bodies they were stripping were those of Trutopian soldiers or the US military.

An air force base close to Lake Cumberland in Kentucky had been overrun by Trutopians during the war, and then abandoned by them as they spread north toward Lexington. The prohibitive cost of repairing and resupplying the base had meant that it had been left idle, but recent intelligence suggested that The Keeper and his people were now stationed there.

Sakkara's current controller was Amandine Paquette, formerly a superhuman called Impervia. None of the teenagers liked her, but they knew she was good at her job. "You hit them hard and fast," she had told them on the journey from Topeka. "Colin, they're going to be watching the sky—if they see you too soon, they'll tighten their defenses and that's going to make getting them out a lot harder. So Cassandra, you take point. If The Keeper's people are there, you should start picking up their thoughts from about four miles away. Or even sooner if there's a lot of them. Butler, you stick with her. Never more than a couple of yards behind. Be ready to raise your force-field at any time, got that? And Brawn, you take the rear. You'll be keeping to the forest so your blue skin is going to stand out. Your pack has two tubs of body-paint. Green and black. Camouflage yourself."

Brawn had argued that it would be a lot easier if they'd just supply him with camouflaged clothes designed for a thirteen-foot-tall man, but Impervia had come up with a simple argument against that: "We've already *got* the paint."

Colin crested a jagged-topped hill and shot straight up into the air. At a height that he guessed to be about a mile he slowed to a hover, and directed his superhuman sight at the air force base. At first it seemed to be deserted, but then he noticed fresh sets of tire-tracks in the dirt leading to a large hangar, and a glint of sunlight coming from a new padlock on one of the base's side gates.

He focused his hearing on the forest below: the snap of fallen branches, the rustling of leaves, Brawn's labored breathing.

Though the blue giant was still thirteen feet tall and extremely strong, he was technically no longer a superhuman. Over a decade ago, every superhuman—hero or otherwise—had been stripped of their abilities by a power-siphoning machine created by Ragnarök. Most superhumans—like Colin's parents—still looked normal, but there were some like Brawn who had been physically changed by whatever it was that made them superhuman. Their powers had been stripped, but their appearances remained unchanged.

Brawn was stronger than an ordinary person because of his size and bone-density, and while his extra-thick skin was no longer bullet-proof, it was a lot tougher than normal skin.

Façade, Danny's adopted father—also, like Brawn, a former supervillain—had explained that a normal-proportioned man who's more than twice the height of the average person weighed a lot more than two people put together. "Think of it like this," Façade had said. "You have a box ten centimeters on each side and it's filled with water, OK? That's ten by ten by ten centimeters. A thousand cubic centimeters, otherwise called a liter. A liter of water weighs a kilogram. But if your box is *twenty* centimeters on each side, the volume is twenty by twenty by twenty, right? Twenty times twenty is four hundred. Times twenty again is eight thousand. That's eight kilograms. So Brawn is at least eight times the weight of the average person."

Many of the adults in Sakkara had little time for Brawn, but Colin liked him. In the prison camp in Lieberstan, Colin had fought alongside Brawn against the Lieberstanian army. Long after the average person would have quit, Brawn had kept fighting.

The other prisoners had told Colin about Brawn's life in the prison, how at the hands of the prison's senior guard he had endured far more than anyone should ever have to suffer. Time and again, Brawn had been pushed far beyond the limits of human endurance, and still he'd kept going.

Colin could hear Brawn's massive heart now, pounding steadily as the giant followed Butler and Cassandra through the forest.

He could also hear Butler talking: "So, after this I figure we're way overdue for some R and R, y'know?"

"Rock and roll?" Cassandra asked.

"No, rest and recuperation. When was the last time we had a whole day off? It was, like, *ages* ago."

"But that's exactly what *I* was saying the other day! You never listen to anyone else, do you, Butler?"

"About a quarter past," Butler said, then grinned.

From behind them, Brawn's deep voice rumbled, "Quiet!"

"Who asked you?" Butler said, and continued talking to Cassandra.

Idiot! Colin said to himself. He knew what Butler was up to; he'd had a crush on Cassandra for months and was always trying to come up with a subtle way to ask her out. Even though Butler knew that Cassie was a telepath and could see straight through his tricks, he kept trying.

Colin's radio buzzed. "What can you see, Colin?"

"There's been some activity recently, so *someone's* definitely using the base, but from this distance I can't tell if anyone's there right now. If there *is*, they're not making a lot of noise or using much electricity. Can't see any signs of booby-traps or anything like that. How sure are you that The Keeper is using this place?"

"Sure enough to send you guys in. Stand by."

If I was The Keeper, Colin thought, *I'd know that sooner or later someone was going to come for me. So what would I do to defend my position?*

He's probably not dumb. We've taken down enough gangs like his that he'll be prepared for a superhuman attack. And if he figures I'll be here, he'll know that I can disable their electronic systems at a distance. So that leaves mechanical weapons. Guns, cannons, flame-throwers. And bows and arrows, if he has them. Colin grinned at that last thought. *Lot of good bows and arrows would do them. I'm bullet-proof, Butler's force-field can withstand almost anything, and they could stick Brawn with enough arrows to make him look like a porcupine and it wouldn't slow him down.*

So what'll he do? There's nothing he can do. He's out-matched. We're so far out of his league that he might as well throw out his weapons and surrender. He must know that.

The answer came a few minutes later. Colin was floating just above the treetops, trying to pick up the body-heat of the people inside the base. "I'm getting *something*," he said into his radio. "There's definitely people inside, but most of the heat-signatures are kinda weak. Maybe thirty-five, forty of them. Hold on…" He focused his hearing, concentrated on filtering out the sounds of the forest. "Sakkara, this is strange. There are forty or whatever people inside, but I can only hear the heartbeats of three of them."

He flinched when an amplified, feedback-drenched voice boomed out of loudspeakers set around the base: "We know you're out there. We know who you are. So let's make this simple. You back off right now, and you get to live."

"You get that, Sakkara?" Colin asked.

"We got it. Colin… Hold your position. This doesn't smell right."

"I know…" He shuddered. "The heat signatures are getting weaker. I think those people are dead."

Cassandra's telepathic voice suddenly screamed inside his head: "Colin! Get down here, now!"

Colin instantly dropped out of the sky, aiming for his friends. Thick branches splintered under him as he crashed down through the trees and came to a stop a few yards behind Brawn.

At the sound of his arrival Butler had automatically thrown up his force-field. Now, a dense shower of leaves and twigs settled on an invisible hemisphere around him and Cassandra.

"They've got superhumans," Cassandra said. "I'm not getting anything clear, but there are three of them. There's a lot of power there..."

There was a sudden blur, and something—it moved too fast for Colin to see—streaked toward them, crashing into Butler's force-field, pushing the flexible energy field deep enough that it slammed into the side of Cassandra's head.

Butler caught Cassandra around the waist before she collapsed. "Oh man, what *was* that? She's out cold."

"Brawn, go left," Colin said. "Keep out of sight until you have no choice. Butler, get Cassie out of here." He activated his radio. "Sakkara, you getting this?"

There was no response.

Butler said, "I should stay. Cover *all* of us with the force-field. At least until we have some idea what we're up against. You get up there, see what's coming."

Colin had to agree with that. Though he was their group's most powerful member, Butler's military-school training had given him a strong grasp of tactics. With Cassandra unconscious, Colin was their best early-warning system.

He rose quickly and silently through the trees, hovered a few feet above them and began scanning the horizon.

Then a dark object was racing toward him, approaching from the left at too great a speed for him to react. It struck him hard in the side, knocked him high into the air, tumbling head over heels.

Before he could right himself he was struck again, this time in the back of the head. From far below, he heard Brawn bellowing with rage—but he didn't have time to help his blue friend now: the two flying objects were rushing at him from each side.

Colin darted straight up for the count of ten, then immediately shifted direction, flying straight down. He saw the objects narrowly miss each other as they reached the point where he had been less than a second before.

They zipped away, curved and came back, zigzagging through the air, moving too fast for even Colin's superhuman eyesight to see exactly what they were, other than that they appeared to be human.

He picked the one on his left for no better reason than the sun was on his right: the light coming from behind him would—he hoped—give him some advantage over the attacker.

But the attacker was even more maneuverable than Colin had expected: he changed direction in mid-flight, instantly zooming out of Colin's path without decelerating. Then the other one was on him, coming down from above and crashing feet-first into Colin's back.

Colin whipped around, his fingers coming within half an inch of the attacker's black boot, but he was too slow.

The first one again struck him from behind, a vicious punch to the back of his neck. He pitched forward, straight into the swinging fist of the second attacker. It slammed into his stomach, his entire body convulsing with the force of the blow.

Another punch, this time to the left side of his face, followed immediately by a powerful kick that crashed into his right temple. He made another grab for the one on his right, and immediately the two broke away.

They hovered in place for a moment, watching him. They both wore matt-black suits that covered their entire bodies. Not even their eyes could be seen behind the black visors of their small helmets.

Ignore the pain! Colin told himself. *Grab hold of one of them and pound his stupid face into paste!*

Façade had once told him: "When going up against a more powerful enemy, your best approach is to catch him off-guard. Do something he's not expecting. If he wants you to run, don't. Stay and fight. If he puts something in your way, don't avoid it—go toward it."

He examined his attackers' uniforms. *Looks like cloth, but it could be some kind of lightweight armor.*

One of the attackers drifted away from the other, moving to the left but constantly facing Colin and keeping the same distance. A few seconds later, the other copied the action.

Colin turned slowly, trying to keep both of them in his field of vision.

They're not doing anything. What's this about? Are they testing me?

It was only when a third attacker struck, coming at Colin from the forest below, that he understood the truth. The first two had simply been keeping him distracted.

The third attacker was dressed identically to the others, and he moved with the same speed and grace, the same silent, lightning-fast approach as all three struck at once.

One crashed into Colin's legs and locked his arms around his knees. Another hit him from behind, pinning Colin's arms to his side. The third hovered in front of Colin as he slammed his gloved fists into Colin's face over and over.

Pain tore through Colin's body as punch after punch landed home, delivered with perfect accuracy and relentless force. He felt his upper lip split, a gash above his left ear tear open, one of his lower front teeth crack.

He concentrated on the ambient heat, soaked it into his pores, allowed it to build. *Let's see how these jerks cope with this!*

Colin released the heat in an air-scorching shockwave that ripped through all three of his attackers, searing their uniforms and blasting them away from him.

He knew that the time for playing fair was over. The attacker who'd been punching him had caught the worst of the blast— Colin threw himself at the tumbling, falling figure, putting as much speed as possible into his flight.

The others raced after him. Colin momentarily felt their gloved hands grab his arms and legs, but he was moving too fast for them to get a firm grip.

He caught hold of the falling man's leg and increased his speed as he held on tight, dragging the attacker behind him. They rocketed towards the treetops at a shallow angle, and Colin suddenly stopped, swung his arm forward and let go. The man recovered just in time to shout, "No!" before he crashed straight through the four-foot-thick trunk of a giant oak tree.

The remaining two launched themselves at Colin again, but this time he was ready for them. *Don't avoid the attack*, he reminded himself. *Go toward it.*

The one rushing at him from his left had his right arm pulled back, his fist tightly clenched. Instead of dodging or ducking to avoid the punch, Colin lashed out with a powerful lightning bolt and struck the man's fist full-on.

The attacker screamed, pivoting in mid-air as he clutched at his wrist, the white-hot armor now melting into a thick liquid that spewed smoke and sparks as it burned into his skin. He tried to drop down out of Colin's path, but instead of pursuing him Colin flipped over onto his back and—upside-down—launched himself at the last of the three.

The man saw Colin coming and shifted his stance, as though preparing to dive to his right.

Yeah, that's what I'd *do,* Colin said to himself. *Fake left, but go right.*

He threw himself to the man's left just as he was expected to do, but he lashed out to the right with twin lances of fire that struck the armored man square in the back.

For only the second time, one of them spoke: A cry from the man with the burning hand. "Abort!" He shot up into the air, followed immediately by his colleague from the trees below.

No you don't, Colin thought. *You're not getting away with this!*

But he knew he couldn't catch all of them. He raced after the third man, who was only now beginning to recover from Colin's fire-blasts. Colin crashed into him from behind and wrapped his left arm around the man's neck, held his right fist clenched in front of the man's visor.

"Who *are* you!?"

The man slammed his elbow back, aiming for Colin's chest, but Colin had been expecting this: still with his arm around the attacker's neck, Colin pivoted his body at the shoulders until he was lying parallel to the ground. He squeezed tighter. "I said, who *are* you?"

The attacker continued to struggle, squirming in Colin's grasp. It was all Colin could do to hold on. *Man, he's strong— might even be as strong as me.*

With his free hand he grabbed hold of the man's helmet and dug his fingers into the strong black material. He tore through the helmet just as the man broke his grip and spun around.

For a moment they both hovered in place, staring at each other.

The attacker wasn't a man. Not yet. He looked to be maybe a year or two younger than Colin, but taller and with a stronger build.

And he had Colin's face.

He grinned. "Hello, brother."

Chapter 4

In fast-time, Danny arrived back at the hotel in Tiergarten to see Warren Wagner frozen in the process of getting off the motorbike he used to drive around Berlin.

Danny switched to real-time, and walked up to Warren. "Another busy day, Mister W."

Warren removed his motorcycle helmet and hung it on the handlebars while he pulled off his gloves. "When is it ever *not* busy? Gerhard tells me you went to Bremen."

"Yeah, they needed authorization documents to close the bridge. What happened with the Trutopians?"

Warren led the way to the hotel's entrance. "The usual. Arrested and locked away." He held the door open for Danny.

"There can't be many more of them left," Danny said. "I was thinking about what you said about them bribing their way into the city... I don't think that's it. None of the Trutopians we've discovered have had anything on their minds other than killing everyone who isn't them. I can't see them collaborating with anyone."

"True. We should be done here in a couple of days," Warren said, "then we can start looking into it in more detail." He looked at his watch. "Way past dinner-time. Have you eaten?"

"Not since lunch. I'm starving."

"Gerhard told me there's a great Italian restaurant around here. Mina likes Italian, right? See if she's back. We'll meet back down here in, say, thirty minutes?"

"Sure." Danny shifted into fast-time and raced up the stairs to the fourth floor. It was a lot quicker than waiting for the elevator. Back in real-time, he knocked on the door of Mina's room. "It's me. You in there?"

There was no reply, so he dug his cell-phone out of his pocket and called her number as he walked to his own room. The call went to voice-mail. "This is Mina. I'm off saving the world or something. Leave a message and I'll get back to you when I feel like it. And if you're near a store, buy me a present! Thanks! Bye!"

"Yeah, Mina, it's Danny. Warren and I are going for dinner. Give us a call when you get this."

He unlocked his room and collapsed onto the bed, yawning and scratching at his thin beard. Not for the first time, he began to wonder why he didn't seem to be able to sleep in fast-time. *That'd be a real time-saver*, he thought. *If I was watching TV I could get the equivalent of a whole night's sleep during the commercial breaks.*

He showered and pulled on fresh clothes, then lay on the bed reading in fast-mode. Brawn had introduced him to the world of cold-war spy novels, and right now Danny was reading all of Ian Fleming's *James Bond* books in chronological order. He had a stack of the paperbacks beside his bed.

Reading was somewhat difficult with only one arm as he had to put the book down to turn the pages, but Danny was determined to master the art. In fast-time he also had to be careful not to turn the pages too quickly in case he ripped them to shreds, which had happened so often in the first few months after he lost his arm that no one in Sakkara would lend him their books.

He finished *On Her Majesty's Secret Service* and closed the book over, then made his way down to the hotel's lobby, where he realized that he still had twenty minutes to go before meeting Warren. *I could go back up and read the next one*, he thought, but then decided to leave *You Only Live Twice* for another day.

He dropped into one of the lobby's overstuffed armchairs and watched as the concierge attempted to explain theater locations to an overweight young man in cycling shorts who seemed to be particularly useless with directions.

He felt his stomach rumble. *Come on, Warren! I'm dying of hunger here! Wish I could slow myself way down as well as speed myself up. That'd make waiting a lot easier. Especially at the airport. Man, that was boring.*

Danny, Warren and Mina had taken a commercial flight to Germany, and their flight had been massively delayed. At ten minutes to boarding time, the passengers were told that there would be a short delay, another few minutes. They were "another few minutes" away from boarding for the next three and a half hours. By the time they were finally called to board the plane, Warren was sound asleep, Danny had read every article in the three newspapers Warren had brought, and Mina had explored every inch of the airport, teleporting herself from one location to another and always coming back to complain to Danny that if they let her, she could teleport them all to Berlin in only a few minutes.

Danny and Warren had not been taken with that idea: Mina's power allowed her to teleport herself or others over a distance of only a couple of miles. To get to Berlin from Kansas, she'd have to make thousands of jumps, and far too much of the journey would be over water.

Why can't *I just slow myself down?* Danny wondered. *If I can alter my perception of time in one direction, I should be able to do the opposite.* He concentrated on the baffled customer and the concierge, watched their arm movements as they tried to come to a mutual understanding of the concept of "south."

The concierge was waving his right arm toward the hotel's entrance, and making flicking movements with his wrist to indicate that the customer should turn left, then right. The customer was peering at a heavily-creased map and stabbing one finger at the same location over and over. Neither of them seemed to be listening to the other.

The thought occurred to Danny that he could offer to help—he'd come to know Berlin quite well over the past few days—but he was more interested in seeing if he could speed them up.

When in fast-time mode, from his perspective everything else seemed to slow way down. It often felt like all he had to do to make it work was relax and allow it to happen.

But the opposite effect didn't appear to be working. The noise from the concierge and the customer was too distracting, their arm-movements too erratic to allow him to concentrate.

The concierge was becoming irritated with the customer, his voice rising in pitch and his movements angrier and more dramatic.

Well, it was worth a shot. Danny turned to his left and looked out the window to see a car hurtling down the road at what had to be more than a hundred miles an hour. *Whoa, that guy's gonna kill someone!*

He jumped to his feet and shifted into fast-time, and that was when he realized that moving into slow-time *had* worked: he was in normal-time now, the car was traveling slowly and carefully, and the customer and concierge were having a normal, calm conversation.

Oh, that is cool! Danny grinned to himself and returned to the armchair. He tried again, and watched as people zipped through the hotel's lobby at three or four times the normal speed.

He saw the elevator doors open so fast they seemed to disappear, then Warren Wagner fast-walked over to him, his voice squeaking unintelligibly.

Danny switched back to normal time. "Sorry, what?"

"You OK? You were just sitting there like a zombie."

Danny stood up. "Yeah, I was experimenting. Turns out I can alter my perception of time in *both* directions. I can make things seem to move faster."

"Huh. Anyway, did you talk to Mina?"

"She wasn't in her room. I left her a voice-mail." Danny fished his phone out of his pocket. "Maybe she called back when I was... No, nothing yet."

"Right." Warren took out his own cell-phone, and keyed in a number. "Same here. Voice-mail." He strode over to the reception desk, and Danny followed.

"Hi," Warren said to the receptionist. "Can you tell me if Mina Duval has checked in?"

The young woman tapped at her computer keyboard. "Ms Duval last used her room key yesterday evening."

"OK, thanks." He turned back to Danny. "When was the last time you saw her?"

"I left her at the Brandenburg Gate, when you called to tell me about the Trutopians. She wasn't there when I got back. I thought she was with you."

"Well, I'm sure she's all right. She's more than capable of

looking after herself."

Danny knew that Mina could be a little flighty and had a tendency to go exploring and get distracted, but something about this didn't feel right. "Call Gerhard and Herlind. Get them to check with their crews and find out who was the last person to see her."

"Dan, she's just late, not missing in action. She probably spotted a cat or a puppy and got distracted again. She'll turn up."

Danny pulled out his phone again and selected a number. The call was answered instantly. "Razor? It's Danny."

"Hey Dan. How're things in Berlin?"

"OK. Listen, can you do something for me? Locate Mina's cell-phone."

"Hold on a sec." Danny heard the sound of rapid typing on a keyboard, then Razor said, "Satellite shows it's at fifty-five degrees, forty-one minutes, fifty-six seconds north, eighteen degrees, five minutes, forty-nine seconds east. Berlin's an hour behind Greenwich Mean Time... Twelve hours is a hundred and eighty degrees, and twelve goes into a hundred and eighty fifteen times. Which puts Berlin's longitude at roughly fifteen degrees east. So *eighteen* degrees would be about two hundred miles to the east of your position, at that latitude. The more north you go, the shorter the distance is between longitude lines. I could work it out—"

"Or you could just look it up on the Internet," Danny said.

"Yeah, that's a point." There was more typing. "Middle of the Baltic Sea. Two hundred and ninety miles to the north-east of your location. What's she doing there?"

"We don't know that she *is* there, Razor. Only that her

phone is. Now I *know* something's wrong."

Warren asked, "What's the problem?"

Danny shrugged. "Razor, who do we have that's closest to that location?"

"That'd be you guys. The nearest major city is Gdańsk in Poland. The cell-phone's about sixty miles north of the coast. You can't run on water, can you? Well, even if you could, the phone's probably not on the surface."

"OK. Send someone to find her phone. We'll check her room, ask the repair crews here who saw her last."

"Will do. Keep me posted."

Danny turned to Warren again. "Mina's phone is in the middle of the Baltic Sea, sixty miles offshore. She can't teleport herself that sort of distance unless she's making lots of jumps, and she can't easily do that over water. Someone's taken her."

Chapter 5

Lying flat and face-down in the ditch that ran along the edge of a cracked-concrete road, Kenya Cho spoke softly into the battered cell-phone she'd stolen from the men marching ahead of her. "What does it *matter* how I got this number? I need help, and it has to be your people."

The man on the other end of the call said, "Kid, do you have any idea how many people need our help? We can't just—"

"Put me on to Mister Miller. He gave me the number last year. Told me to call him if I needed him."

There was a pause. "I'm listening."

"I'm in Northland, Somalia," Kenya whispered. "I don't know the exact coordinates, but—"

The man said, "OK. Hold on... Got it. You're in luck—we have a team traveling west over Libya. Diverting them to your location now. ETA is fifty minutes. Stay where you are, understood? Don't put yourself in any more danger."

Kenya sighed into the phone. "Of course."

"All right. Now, you said that you took that phone from them?"

"They're moving single-file, on foot. I took the phone from the backpack of the last one in line."

"That was risky. They could have—"

"They wouldn't have heard me. I can move silently."

"What armaments are they carrying? Any insignia? Uniforms?"

"Rifles, handguns, grenades. No uniforms. These are the same men who ransacked four refugees camps in the past few days. They're *killers*. I counted at least fifty. Look, I'm fast. But not fast enough to stop them. And I don't have good night-vision—I'm almost *blind* at night. That's why I had to call you." Kenya raised her head a little over the edge of the ditch, and peered into the darkness for a moment before ducking back down. "I can hardly see anything now."

The phone suddenly beeped, loudly, and Kenya quickly glanced at the screen. "Battery's low."

"All right. Put the phone on stand-by—we can still track it. Our people will be coming in high, running silent. You won't know they're there until they reach you. It's vital that we maintain the element of surprise—we can't allow them enough time to bed down. So follow the targets but keep out of sight and do *not* engage. Understood?"

"Understood. Thank you."

"You're welcome, Kenya. Be careful."

"How do you know—?"

"I remember you. I *am* Miller. Put the phone on stand-by. We'll talk again when this is over."

Kenya shut the phone down, and tucked it into her pocket as she climbed out of the ditch. She hated moving almost blind like this, and had to resist the temptation to use the cell-phone's light.

Ahead, she could see a faint glow on the horizon, and began to carefully walk toward it.

She had been tracking these men for a week, and had finally come to the conclusion that—for the first time in months—she needed outside help. If the raiders kept up their current pace, by morning they would reach the village of Tukarodadhe. There, if they followed their established pattern, they would kill anyone who looked like he or she had the strength to fight back, and they would strip the village clean of supplies.

She'd seen enough death and destruction to give her nightmares for the rest of her life, but still she couldn't stop. She had a mission—self-appointed—and she would never rest. Never.

A year ago, when the irresistible order came for them to fight, Kenya and her family and fellow Trutopians marched on Fianarantsoa and ransacked the city.

Kenya had found herself almost burning with anger at the non-Trutopians. She wanted to kill them, to tear their heads from their shoulders and their hearts from their chests. They were evil, vicious, cruel things that didn't deserve to live. She would wipe them out—all of them—or she would die trying.

Kenya's older brother Eugene had found a set of swords in an antiques store. They weren't sharp, but they were heavy. She and Eugene raced through the city, smashing windows, torching shops and businesses, charging headlong at the city's small, terrified collection of police officers.

She didn't slow down—she'd known with a certainty like she'd never felt before that this was the right path. She and her brother and parents and friends charged the police lines. And the police—left with no choice—opened fire.

When the bullets tore through Eugene and showered her with his blood, Kenya's fury doubled. The second volley took down her parents, but Kenya still kept running, faster than the other Trutopians, much more agile. She easily vaulted the hastily-erected police cordon and landed among the scared, desperate men with her antique sword swinging.

There was a white-hot shock of pain in her side as a bullet

passed through, but still she didn't slow. She swung her sword directly into the face of the nearest officer, the blow strong enough to crush his skull.

At the last second, as the blade was only inches away from the man's face, she found herself thinking, *What am I doing? This will* kill *him!* And she realized that was what she wanted to happen. She allowed the sword to continue on its path.

Within an hour, every non-Trutopian in Fianarantsoa, Madagascar, was either dead or dying.

Kenya's colleagues—now scarred, encrusted with dust and blood and sweat, their chests heaving with exertion and their fists and teeth clenched, their eyes narrow with hate and murder—instinctively recognized that she was the one to lead them.

On her instructions, they plundered the city for food, weapons and ammunition, then they moved on to the next city, and the next.

For three weeks, Kenya's make-shift army slaughtered their way westward across Madagascar.

Then, only a day from the coastal city of Morombe, the soldiers from the United Nations finally caught up with them.

Kenya was the last to be subdued. When she finally regained consciousness, she discovered that she had been heavily chained to a massive concrete pillar, and was surrounded by a dozen or more soldiers, all of whom had their weapons trained on her.

Kenya had ranted and raged and screamed as she put every iota of her considerable strength to the task of snapping the chains, and all the while the UN Commander pleaded with her to calm down, to listen to reason.

"Fer cryin' out loud, kid—it's *over*! The war is over!" The Commander turned to one of his men. "How could they not know this by now? Duval's been broadcasting just about non-stop since they caught her!" To Kenya, he added, "You get that? Your psycho boss has been ordering you to stop fighting!"

The soldier replied, "Sir, her friends said they hadn't *heard* the order. They haven't slowed down long enough to watch TV or listen to the radio." The soldier removed a small, battery-driven radio from his backpack and set it on the ground, just out of Kenya's frenzied grasp.

Minutes later, she again heard the voice of the girl who had ordered her to fight: "To all Trutopians still fighting. Stand down. You will not fight, you will not resist. The war is over. Your minds are your own once again."

Kenya collapsed heavily onto the ground, the chains around her wrists and ankles suddenly feeling heavier than anything she had experienced before. Her mind had been cleared—the rage was gone, completely.

But she remembered. She remembered everything.

Even now, almost a year later, every time Kenya Cho tried to sleep all she could see were the anguished, blood-spattered, tear-streaked faces of the people she had murdered. Though she remembered them all, she didn't know exactly how many people had died at her hands: every time she tried to count them, the sense of horror and guilt overwhelmed her, left her sobbing and shaking.

The representatives from Sakkara—when they reached Morombe a month after Kenya's madness was taken away— had locked her up "for her own safety": though the fighting was over, and though the cause of the war was Yvonne Duval's mind-control and the Trutopians were not to blame, there was hardly a single person on the planet who had not lost someone in the war. And many—if not most—of those people wanted revenge. They directed their anger at the Trutopians.

Kenya and her fellow surviving Trutopians were held in a secure compound outside Andopitaly. Counselors and therapists were on-call at all times, and gradually, over the course of months, most of the Trutopians recovered enough to return to the world—or what was left of it.

Kenya, however, was watched more carefully than the others. She had been identified as a superhuman and that made her a special case.

Three months after the end of the war she was visited by a tall, slim white man who spoke with a faint mid-Atlantic accent. "They tell me that I'm the best person to speak to you, Kenya. You're a superhuman. So was I. And you... You've done some things that you don't think you can live with." A pause. "Me too. My name is Hector Thomas Miller. When I was your age, my friends called me Heck. You can call me that, if you like. But these days, everyone calls me by the name I chose when I still had my powers. Façade."

Kenya had looked up at that. "I've heard of you. You were able to change your appearance."

"Right. I was one of the bad guys. But that's where we differ. Sure, you've done some bad things—"

"Bad things? I *murdered* people. I don't know *how* many!"

At that, Façade had nodded. "I do. At least, we've made what we think is a pretty close estimate. Do you want to know?"

"Tell me."

"About six hundred and thirty."

Kenya had broken down then. For hours, she stayed on the floor of her cell, curled into a ball, sobbing, shivering, retching. And Façade sat with her the whole time, not saying anything, just watching her, letting her know that he was there.

Finally, she raised her head and looked at him. "I can't *live* with this. All those people..."

"It wasn't your fault. If I throw a rock and it breaks a window, who's to blame? Me or the rock?"

"It's not that simple! That's completely different!"

"*How* is it different? Kenya, you're as much a victim as the people who were killed. Yvonne was controlling you. Could you have resisted? No. You had no choice but to obey her orders. You're just a rock that can remember what it was used for—that doesn't change the fact that a rock cannot be held responsible for what happens when it's thrown. And you say you can't live like this? I say you *can*. And you *must*. You can't give those people back their lives, but taking your own life would do no one any good. Least of all yourself. If you want to make amends —and most of your friends do—then you have to get over this, or at least come to terms with it."

Façade crouched next to her, helped her to her feet. "You're not alone, Kenya. My son... My *adopted* son. He killed his real father in a fit of rage. He's superhuman too, and he didn't fully know how to control his powers when he lashed out at him. That's Danny Cooper—I'm sure you've heard of him. Danny's still going through a tough time because of what happened. He might never get over it. But he's trying. And his friend Colin? Under Yvonne's control he almost wiped out all of the New Heroes, plus hundreds of members of the United States' armed forces. But they keep fighting, both of them, to make the world a better place. *That's* how you can make amends, if you feel you must. Join the New Heroes."

Kenya told him that she'd think about it, but in her heart she was sure that wasn't the right path for her.

She knew she wouldn't fit in. Her own abilities were laughable compared to theirs. She was pretty fast, and twice as strong as the average teenage girl, but her eyesight was weak, and her skin even weaker: when injured, she healed quickly, but not flawlessly. Her body was covered in a network of white scar tissue. Even the slightest scratch resulted in a fresh, permanent scar.

Once, before the war, before her superhuman nature kicked in, she had been pretty. Everyone had told her so. Her first boyfriend, Lochlan, had said, "It's 'cos your dad's Chinese and your mom is African—mixed-race people are *always* good-looking." But now, from examining her body in the full-length mirror in the compound's bathroom, Kenya knew that she was ugly. She didn't want to join the New Heroes and be seen every day on the TV news.

Besides, the only ability she had that might be any good to them was her silence: she could move around without making the slightest noise. And she wasn't even sure that actually was a superhuman ability.

"I have to do this my own way," she'd told Façade.

A week later she escaped from the compound—a simple matter of scaling the high fence in the middle of the night. The fence was patrolled, but Kenya had been able to walk behind the guards and start climbing only a few feet away from them. They never noticed.

She used the same skills to hide out on a cargo ship to Mozambique, Africa, and since then she had traveled slowly north, doing anything and everything she could to repair the damage caused during the Trutopian war.

She worked on farms, and helped construction crews, and repaired power-lines. She accepted nothing but a small amount of food and water in return, and never gave her real name, never spoke to anyone unless it was absolutely necessary.

She traveled alone, but she was never lonely: she had her memories to keep her company.

Chapter 6

Colin Wagner stood with his colleagues on the edge of the forest. Brawn was hunkered down next to him as they watched the young man with Colin's face struggling to free himself from Butler's force-field.

"Anything?" Brawn asked Cassandra.

The girl shook her head. "It's like when I'm trying to read you or Impervia, like I'm listening to a radio station broadcasting in a foreign language. I can tell there's something going on, but I can't understand it."

"So what's the story here?" Butler asked. His voice was strained from the effort of keeping the double immobilized. "Your folks had another son they never told you about?"

"He's a shape-shifter," Cassandra said. "He must be. Like Façade."

Brawn said, "Then why pick *this* shape? Why make himself look like Colin? No, I reckon he's a clone. We know it can be done. Mina and Yvonne are clones."

Cassandra said, "Yeah, maybe, but... Who did it? Where did he *come* from? I mean, he looks about Colin's age, so he had to have been made when Colin was only a baby."

Colin slowly walked around the stranger, unable to stop staring.

Moments after he'd unmasked the young man, the fight had begun again, this time with even greater ferocity. The double was stronger than Colin, and faster, but he hadn't been trained to fight, and he lacked Colin's experience.

Colin had fled at first, dropping down to the trees, and the double had immediately followed, through the heart of a powerful fireball Colin had launched. But he was moving so fast that the fireball barely singed his uniform.

They clashed and broke free, over and over, equally matched, neither willing to back down. Colin had realized that he couldn't use fire or lightning to hurt the attacker, and he didn't have the strength to pummel him into submission. If he was going to win, he had to be smarter. Sneakier.

So again Colin fled, swooping and banking through the air as fast as he was able, constantly releasing large fireballs in his wake. The double flew straight through each one without pausing.

Colin spotted a concrete-surfaced road and dove down toward it at full speed, launching enough fireballs to obscure the double's vision. At the last second he shifted direction, dodging to the side just as the double slammed straight into the concrete road with an impact that left him semi-conscious and groaning in the center of a three-foot-deep crater.

Though his own energy supplies were almost exhausted, Colin was able to keep the double immobile long enough for Butler and the others to reach them. Now, they were waiting for the transport from Sakkara to pick them up.

Brawn said, "If he *is* a clone, then maybe whoever did it found a way to speed up the process. Man, he looks *exactly* like you, Col. I've seen some weird things in my time, but this is one of the weirdest. You said there were two others?"

"I didn't see their faces," Colin said.

"You think they were clones too? Makes sense, I guess. If you could make one, you'd make *more* than one."

"That's not what bothers me most. Why me?"

Cassandra said, "Because you're the most powerful superhuman ever, Colin. You're the perfect source material."

"I don't know about most powerful *ever*," Brawn said. "I reckon you'd have had a tough time against Krodin. But she's got a point. Someone made these guys for a reason." He shrugged. "I'm betting it's not a reason that'll be to the benefit of the human race. The good guys don't tend to make clones of other good guys."

"Maybe we should," Butler suggested.

The double—or clone, or whatever he was—continued to struggle. Butler's force-field was invisible most of the time, but now it had been in place long enough to collect a thin film of dust, revealing its outline. Butler had the flexible force-field wrapped lightly around the double's arms and legs, but left his head free.

He's not that smart, Colin thought. *Instead of trying to break free he could just fly straight up and drag Butler behind him.* Colin knew he couldn't say that to the others: there was no way of knowing how good the double's hearing was.

How are we even going to contain him when we get him back to Sakkara? And what if his two friends come back?

Then another thought struck him, and he fought to suppress a shudder. *How many more of them are out there?*

Chapter 7

Ahead of Kenya, and a little to the left, there was a campfire. She saw it as a bright patch against the blackness, but couldn't judge its distance, or see anyone around it—though she knew they must be there.

In the Andopitaly compound she and Façade had discussed the nature of her superhuman abilities. As they'd strolled around the compound, Façade had said, "It's not *always* a benefit, that's what most people don't realize. Whatever it is that changes us, sometimes it takes something away. Poor night vision isn't the worst disadvantage you could have. Do you remember Thalamus? No? He was superhuman, extremely intelligent—hadn't much of a clue about dealing with people, but he was almost unbeatable when it came to knowledge—but he was physically very weak. And there was no reason for that. He worked out as much as he could, he ate well, looked after himself, but he just could not develop his muscles much beyond those of a ten-year-old. It probably happens more than we know—there could be people out there who are superhuman without *any* positive effects."

That hadn't helped much. "Look at me," Kenya said. "Look at my face, my arms and legs... I'm going to be scarred like this forever, aren't I? How am I supposed to have a normal life?"

Façade had shrugged. "Who *says* you're supposed to have a normal life? Where is it written that everyone gets a fair shot? Brawn is thirteen feet tall and blue. Loligo—do you know of her?—has tentacles instead of arms. She has gills. Neither of them will *ever* be able to pass as a normal person. You get what

74

you get. Being upset about it won't help."

"That's easy for *you* to say!" Kenya had snapped. "You were able to change your appearance! You could always pass for normal. No one would ever know."

"Yeah, I was a shape-shifter. That was great. And then we all lost our powers and I couldn't change back. This isn't *my* face. This is the face of Paul Cooper, a good man whose life I helped destroy. I have to live with that. Just as you have to accept who and what you are. Because what's the alternative? Throw yourself off a bridge just because you have scars? End your life because you're not as pretty as you'd like to be? We only get one shot at life, Kenya. There is no reset button, no do-overs. Just one go, and that's it. You make the best of what you've been given and you don't whine about the things you can't change."

"Yeah, but—"

Façade leaned over and scooped up a small rock. "Oh good, it's rock-metaphor time again. You know, I *hate* this rock. I wish it was a banana. Every morning I will pray to Mighty Odin for it to become a banana. I will write letters to my congressman. I will start a petition on the internet for this rock to be transformed into a banana. I will do all of these things. I will cry bitter tears every night and scrawl in my diary about how life would be so much better if this rock was a banana. And guess what?"

"It'll always be a rock."

Façade bounced it in the palm of his hand for a second, then threw it over the fence. "Yep. One of billions. But you're not a rock. You're a person. If you don't like the way things are, and you can't change them, then you can either moan or you can get on with your life. Care to guess which of those two options is more likely to achieve a positive result?"

In the ten months since she arrived in Africa, Kenya had traveled more than two thousand miles, moving north along the east coast, through Mozambique, Tanzania, then Kenya—her mother's homeland, after which she was named—and then into Somalia.

She had helped hundreds of people, even though sometimes it was nothing more than giving their stalled car a push or finding an escaped puppy. But sometimes, she knew, her actions had a big impact on others. In Dar es Salaam, Tanzania, she'd chased down and caught a man who had savagely attacked another with a broken bottle. The following day she worked on a bucket-chain helping to put out a house-fire. She spent the day after that helping a young farmer dig holes for fence-posts.

In her mind, there was a set of scales, and she knew that even if she lived to be a million years old, she would never get the scales to balance. She had killed six hundred and thirty people. No amount of post-holes or found puppies was ever going to make things right.

But she knew she had to try.

Now, she crept closer to the mercenaries' camp, all too aware that her night-blindness put her at a serious disadvantage. They wouldn't be able to hear her coming, but she wouldn't be able to see them properly.

I should wait, she thought. *Whoever Façade is sending must be almost here by now.*

She almost regretted calling him. The raiders needed to be stopped, but if she had help did that count in the cosmic balance?

Ahead, the light from the campfire flickered as something passed in front of it, and Kenya dropped low to the ground. She could hear voices now, talking, laughing. A man was attempting to sing an old Roy Orbison song and getting the words wrong; Kenya's brother Eugene had been a fan of The Big O and had played his albums so often that Kenya knew all the songs by heart.

Something bright moved in the distance, dropping down so fast she thought it could only be a meteor, but she couldn't focus on what it was. Then another, off to the left, and a third.

Shouts, then gunfire, erupted from the campsite.

Flashlight beams bobbed and weaved as the raiders darted about, shooting at something Kenya couldn't see. Then the area was awash with light blazing down from above, and for the first time Kenya was able to see the scale of the campsite.

Thirty or more camouflaged tents, the same number of trucks and jeeps, and more than a hundred armed, frenzied men and women. The raiders were emptying their weapons at fast-moving objects that lay outside the beam of light. Some fired upwards, at the source of the light, uselessly—the light continued, and was now joined by others coming from the sides.

A series of rockets streaked down from the sky toward the vehicles, corralling the raiders in a ring of ground-trembling explosions—Kenya could feel a wave of warm air from her position two hundred yards away.

The sound of gunfire was mixed with screams of anger in a dozen languages. One of the flying objects smashed through a burning truck close to the heart of the camp, showering the raiders with red-hot debris.

Something heavy landed next to Kenya, and she rolled onto her side to see a bulky figure in red metallic armor looking down at her. The air was suddenly thick with a strong chemical scent that made Kenya think of gasoline mixed with alcohol.

"Kenya Cho, I presume?" It was a woman's voice, strong and confident.

Kenya nodded.

"Good. Stay down."

"I can help."

"We can handle it." The woman thumped her gloved fist against her armor. "Bullet-proof and bomb-proof. Stay here."

The woman's jetpack flared into life, and Kenya watched as she streaked toward the campsite and crashed into a cluster of raiders without slowing.

One of the raiders hurriedly lifted a rocket-launcher onto the shoulder of a colleague, but—before he could shoot—a blue-armored soldier zoomed out of the night and snatched the launcher from his arms.

The woman in red touched down thirty yards from the last group of raiders, and casually strode toward them, their bullets ricocheting uselessly off her armor as she walked straight through the campfire, scattering the embers into a cloud of red and orange sparks.

The roar of gunfire eased, and one-by-one the raiders dropped their weapons.

Another armored figure—this one male—touched down close to Kenya, crouched and offered her his hand. "It's over."

Kenya took his hand and climbed to her feet. "Who are you?"

"A friend. You're Kenya, right? My name's Grant. Façade sent us." He tilted his helmet toward the remains of the campfire. "Come on."

As she followed Grant, he pointed to another—still flying—figure and said, "That's Alia. She'll watch our backs. But we're safe. Looks like we've caught them all."

The red-armored woman turned as Kenya approached. "Watch them." She walked up to Kenya and flipped a switch on her helmet that turned its visor transparent.

"But you're only *my* age!" Kenya said.

"A little older, maybe. Façade spent *months* looking for you, Kenya. Why did you run?"

"I..." She shrugged. "I had to do things my own way."

"I understand that. You did good tracking these people. Their group has been terrorizing the region since the war. This is the first break we've had." She turned back to the raiders. Her voice, electronically amplified, called out, "Who's in charge here?" After a moment, she repeated her message in Spanish, then French, then German.

A tall, slim young man with ebony skin, cradling an AK-47 in his arms, stepped forward. "Who are you?" His English was crisp and clear.

"Who *we* are is not important. What is important is that as of now your operation is over. The supplies of food and medicine you've stolen will be delivered to their rightful owners, the refugees in the camps outside the Rift Valley. You have killed hundreds of people and you will pay for every life you took. Do you understand? This is over."

"No!" The slim man raised his weapon above his head. "No! We fight for our *freedom*, and we will never surrender!"

"You're a bunch of deluded thugs who are willing to murder and pillage just because you've got some dumb point to make. You want a fight, go ahead. Take us on. Your weapons are useless against our armor." She took another step closer to the slim man. "So you people will drop your guns and lie face-down on the ground. If you try to resist, you're going to be face-down on the ground anyway. But you won't be getting up. Ever."

The slim man spat on the ground between the girl's boots. "You call them refugees like that should mean something. They're parasites, swarming over our land like locusts! My father's father was—"

"I don't care who *any* of your ancestors were." The red-armored girl turned to one of her colleagues. "This is over. Call in the troops."

A voice from the side shouted, "No!" and Kenya turned to see another man approaching. He was considerably older than the others, his white hair and beard contrasting with his dark, wrinkled skin. "We will not submit to your rules! We fight because our government is corrupt and weak—they invite refugees from Ethiopia, take the food from our own children's mouths to feed them!"

The old man stopped ten feet away from them. "We fight for ourselves because no one will fight for us. Our cause is just and righteous and only God will judge us!"

"Yeah? You psychos attacked a UN supply convoy last month with grenade-launchers. You murdered five innocent people, and for what? For eighteen hundred mosquito nets. And when you realized what they were, you didn't just dump them on the side of the road. You poured gasoline all over them and set them on fire. You think God will look favorably on that?"

The old man bared his teeth, and swung a bony fist that cracked uselessly against bullet-proof armor.

Lights flickered on the northern horizon. "Troop carriers," the girl said. "I suggest you lay down your weapons because they're coming in armed and looking for a fight."

Cradling his injured hand, the old man said, "We will resist. We will never surrender. We will not rest until every Ethiopian —*every outsider*—is gone from our land! If that means they all must die, then so be it. Only then will we be free!"

"Free of what?" She leaned close to him. "You keep this in mind: we haven't fought back yet. Do you understand what I'm saying?"

He spat again. "Who are you to give orders to us?" He sneered. "A child, a *girl*. A pampered American girl pretending to be a soldier! You know nothing about the real world, nothing about the suffering my people have—"

"*Your* people?" She matched his sneer with a glare. "The same people you've spent the past year murdering? That's low. And you want to know who I am? Fine. My name is Renata Soliz. I used to be a superhuman called Diamond. Now I'm the leader of the New Heroes' armored division."

Renata pulled a web of strong-looking straps from a pouch on her belt, and before the old man could resist, she had looped the straps around his arms and chest. She turned to one of her colleagues. "Alia, keep this area locked down. I'm going to show this fool the consequences of his actions." As she clipped the harness to loops on her armor, she said, "Kenya might like to see this. Give her your backpack and helmet, link the controls to mine."

The young woman called Alia unclipped her pack and

stepped up behind Kenya. She quickly connected shoulder-straps and a belt, checked that they were secure, then removed her helmet and placed it on Kenya's head. It was a snug fit, but not uncomfortable. "You OK with the weight?"

Kenya nodded. "Sure... What is this?"

"Just relax, Kenya. You'll like this," Renata said. A soft whine emerged from her backpack, then seconds later Kenya felt her own begin to tremble a little.

Then Renata was rising into the air, with the old man dangling from the harness beneath her. And Kenya found herself being lifted up, following close behind them.

"This jetpack," Kenya shouted, "it's like Paragon's, right?"

"A more advanced version," Renata said. "Much quieter, greater range. And much faster if you're not wearing armor. Or carrying an old man beneath you."

For the first few minutes of the flight the old man screamed and kicked as he tried to undo the clasps that held him in place.

"I really wouldn't do that if I were you," Renata said. "We're eight hundred feet up. You wouldn't survive."

The old man roared at her: "You have no right! You have no right!"

"Shut up, or I *will* drop you!"

Full night had fallen by the time their flight slowed. Renata hovered in place for a moment before gently descending to the ground.

The old man had fallen completely silent.

Renata said, "Look around, Kenya. What can you see?"

"Nothing. Darkness. I don't have good night-vision."

"Oh, right. Façade mentioned that. Cover your eyes. I'm going to light a flare. You too, old man. *Do* it—this is going to be pretty bright."

Kenya placed her gloved hands over her helmet's visor, and heard a shark crack as something sparked into life.

"Now look."

Kenya tentatively lowered her hands from her face, and looked around. The red light from the flare showed that they were standing on a dry, flat plain punctuated by a dozen small clusters of boulders and a few parched-looking bushes.

Renata nudged the old man's shoulder and pointed to the boulder-cluster nearest to them. "You see that? You know what that is?"

"Yes."

"What is it?"

"A marker."

"Right. They arrange them in a pattern they hope they'll be able to recognize in the future. When things get better, and they're able to come back here and remove the bodies of their loved ones from their shallow graves."

The old man turned his head to face her. "I know this. Why have you brought me here?"

"Because every person buried here was killed by your men. Some of them you shot during your raids, others starved or died of malaria or cholera because you stole their food and medicines. Hold tight, Kenya, we're going up again."

Renata activated the jetpacks once more, and as they ascended the flare showed more and more of the landscape below. The dozen grave-markers became two dozen, then a hundred.

"*You* did this," Renata said to the old man. "The flare isn't bright enough to show you the true extent of your crimes... But

I've got something that is." She let the flare drop, then reached up and removed her helmet.

She placed the helmet on the old man's head. "The visors have thermal imaging. You know what that means? It allows me to see heat. Decaying bodies generate a lot more heat than you might realize. Now look down again. Kenya, there's a switch on the left side of your helmet, along the jaw-line."

Kenya saw the old man lower his head, and for a moment he was completely still, as though the fight had been completely drained from him.

She found the switch on her helmet, and flipped it. Instantly, the dark landscape below became a sea of glowing patches.

"Our satellites show over fifteen hundred graves here," Renata said. "Each one dug by hand. The smaller ones are children."

His voice weak, the man said, "This is a war. We're fighting a war."

Renata pulled the helmet from his head, and said, "You're butchering innocent, defenseless people. That's not a war. That's genocide."

He tried to twist around in the harness to see her face. "Who are you to judge us? Westerners with invulnerable suits and powerful weapons, forcing us to do your will! *You* are the aggressors here, not us!"

"Maybe you're right. Maybe we *are* the aggressors, this time. But we're not murderers. We're here to help the innocent, and we don't care which side of an imaginary border they were born on, or what their beliefs are. We are going to save the human race, and if that means we spend the rest of our lives taking down trash like you, we'll be happy to do that."

Renata clipped her helmet back in place, and glanced at Kenya for a moment. "Are you all right? Something like this can be pretty hard to take."

Kenya nodded. "Yeah. I… I've seen a lot of bad things. But this—"

The old man began to rant again. "If you imprison my people, we will break free! We will track you down and when we are done we will dance on *your* graves! You especially, girl. We will tear your head from your shoulders and—"

Renata interrupted him. "Yeah, right. Give it your best shot. But don't forget that three of us took down your entire operation, and not one of us is superhuman." They began to drift back toward the campsite. "You are under arrest for crimes of terrorism, mass murder, attempted genocide and anything else we can throw at you. You'll have a lot of time in prison to rant about your unfair treatment."

The old man fell silent.

As they approached the campsite, Kenya saw a convoy of vehicles converging on the raiders.

"The UN," Renata explained. "They've been trying to locate these jerks for months. They're probably going to give you a medal, Kenya."

"I don't want a medal. But I do want one of these helmets—I can't see well in the dark and this would make a huge difference."

"Façade still wants you to join us."

"I can't. I'm not like you and the others. I have my own mission. I have to do this alone."

"But you don't have to be an *idiot* about it. Take a few days off—you've more than earned them. Stick with us for a while.

We can give you food and equipment, drop you anywhere you want to go. Façade told me everything. I know what you did during the war. I understand that. But don't let your principals get in the way of the greater goal. You want to make amends? Fine. Allow us to make your task easier."

Two hours later, as they watched the last of the UN trucks take the prisoners away, Renata approached Kenya again. "So what do you say?"

"I can't... I don't want to be famous like you. I don't want people *looking* at me."

"Because of your scars?"

"Yeah, but not just that. The things I've done..."

Again, Renata thumped her armor. "If you were wearing one of these, no one would see your scars. Or your misplaced guilt."

Kenya looked from Renata over to the other two, Alia and Grant. "How many more of you are there?"

"Enough to make us an effective force, not so many that we get in each others' way."

"All right. I'm in."

Chapter 8

"Mina was last seen a few minutes after you left the Brandenburg Gate for Kulturforum," Warren Wagner told Danny as he put away his phone.

"I was only *gone* a few minutes," Danny said.

They were in Mina's hotel room, having searched through all of her things in the hope of finding something that would lead them to her.

Gerhard, the Berlin work crew's supervisor, told Danny that one of the other workers had asked Mina to teleport him to the roof of a fire-bombed building so he could evaluate the damage. After she dropped him off, she teleported out. That was the last time anyone had seen her.

According to Razor, Mina's phone had appeared in the Baltic Sea about thirty minutes later. That was more than enough time for Mina to teleport herself that distance, even if she was only moving a couple of miles with each jump.

Warren said, "What's really annoying is that Mina's the best one to *find* people who are missing. We don't have anyone else who can do that."

Danny flipped through Mina's diary. He'd been reluctant to even touch it at first, but as the hours passed and it became clear that Mina wasn't coming back, he'd snapped the weak padlock and checked the most recent entries. He was a little relieved to see that Mina hadn't been keeping her innermost secrets in the diary: most of the entries were no more private than, "Got up at eight. Had cornflackes. Played alot of Scrabble with Niall—beat him nearly every time! Hah! Looser!"

"Nothing useful," Danny said. "Except that her spelling is awful. I think I *should* search for her," he offered again. "I could take it street-by-street, house-by-house."

Warren shook his head. "That would take forever, even at your speed. Think of all the doors you'd have to open. Your father was able to pass through solid objects, but you've lost that ability."

"Yeah, but—"

"No, Danny." Warren moved to the window and looked out. "A long time ago Quantum covered pretty much the whole world in about a day of real-time. He visited practically every home on the planet." He turned back. "Not many people know this, so keep it to yourself, OK? The human race came so close to extinction... There was a plague, and your dad carried the cure—a sort of anti-virus. It could only be passed by touch. The scientists at the Center for Disease Control were able to create an airborne version of the cure, and me and a few others spread it wherever we could, but your dad was the real hero that day. He saved billions of people."

Danny sat down on the end of the bed. "Wow. That's... that's amazing. The whole world? From his perspective, it must have taken *years*."

"Yeah. And then some. He started in America, and went back and forth, visiting every city, every town, every home. Then he moved north to Canada, across the Bering Strait into Asia... He was moving so fast he was able to race across water. You ever tried that? Give it a go sometime. You're not as fast as he was, but it might work. He covered the whole *world*, Danny. Think about that. Not just the continents and islands. He tracked down ships, and submarines too. He said he spent a long time trying to figure out how to get to the people in airplanes before he finally concluded that the only way was to come back to each airport as the planes were due to land."

"But he couldn't have reached *everyone* on the planet!"

"He did, pretty much. Every adult, anyway—the virus didn't affect kids. I'm sure there were some he missed, but the airborne version of the cure caught them. There were very few reported deaths, and most of the world didn't even know it had happened." Warren held his breath for a moment. "Caroline worked it out... She sat down with a map of the world and a calculator and lots of sheets of paper. She figured that with all the trips back and forth, your father was on the road for the equivalent of about seventeen hundred years."

Danny shuddered. "Oh man... No wonder he..."

"No wonder he went crazy. Yeah, that and the visions of the future he used to get. I talked about it with him once. He said that the worst thing wasn't the loneliness. It was seeing the millions and millions of people that he *wasn't* able to help. The poor, the starving, the disease-ridden. The only consolation was that because of the virus almost everyone was sick. At any given time somewhere in the world there's a car about to crash, or someone being shot or dying from an accident. But most people were bed-ridden." Warren shrugged. "The irony is that probably far fewer people died that day than would have if there hadn't been a virus." He turned in a slow circle, looking around the room once more.

"Wow," Danny said. "I wished I'd known him." He tossed Mina's diary back onto the bed. "When she does turn up, best not to tell her I read that. Look, Mister Wagner, maybe I'm jumping the gun here, but this isn't good at all, is it? When Mina was under Yvonne's control she almost killed me. She's nearly as fast as I am and she's much more agile. And she can teleport. She's practically unstoppable. I mean, if she's gone bad..."

"If she's gone bad, then we deal with it. But that *is* jumping the gun. Let's assume that she's not been taken or turned against us. She's a teenage girl. Where could she have gone?"

"If it wasn't for her phone, I'd say she just went exploring. What are we doing about the phone anyway?"

"It's being picked up," Warren said, then looked at his own phone to check the time. "In fact, you should probably leave now. You need to get to Poland. Follow the signs for Gdansk, then head north and follow the coast all the way around until you reach the southernmost tip of the Hel peninsula." He tapped at the phone for a few seconds, then showed Danny the map. "Right there, on the beach. It's about sixty miles from Gdansk by road. Unless you want to try running across the ocean? That way it's only about twenty."

"I think I'll stick to the roads. Back as soon as I can." Danny slipped into fast-time, and went to his own room to collect his MP3 player and the large bag of potato chips he'd been saving.

Sometimes he found it strange that no matter how urgent something was, he didn't need to rush. From his point of view, he was strolling quite leisurely through Berlin, albeit a Berlin that seemed frozen in time.

As he eased his way through a large throng of late-night shoppers, he spotted a young girl reaching her hand toward the open purse of an unsuspecting woman. Danny snapped the purse closed and moved on.

At the German-Polish border-crossing he ducked under the barrier and sidled around a guard who was frozen in the act of tossing a peanut into the air to catch it in his mouth. Danny snatched the peanut out of the air as he passed, thinking, *That'll keep him wondering for a few minutes.*

He stopped for a few minutes on the road into Chojnice to examine a very expensive-looking open-topped sports car that was clearly traveling in excess of the posted speed limit, but he resisted the temptation to scrawl the message "Slow Down!" in the dust on the windshield as a punishment. He'd done that once before, in Canada, and was over ten miles away before he realized that the shock might cause the driver to crash. Instead, he pulled the keys out of the ignition and tossed them into the woods.

When he reached Gdansk he followed the coast road to the Hel peninsula. Here, the streetlights were few and he got lost trying to find the beach, so he shifted back to real-time until he heard the waves crashing on the shore, then he followed the sound.

He arrived at the beach just as a woman was emerging from the water.

She was dressed in a white one-piece bathing suit and looked to be about forty years old, and in place of her arms she had long squid-like tentacles. *That has to be Loligo*, Danny thought. Brawn had told him about her: she was one of the few former superhumans whose powers came with a physical change. Before she lost her abilities, Loligo had been able to move through the water at an incredible speed.

Though she was now—like Brawn—mostly human, she was still a remarkable swimmer, more at home in the water than on land. Brawn had said that she could even breathe underwater.

"Hi," Danny said, as he walked toward her, trying not to

stare at her tentacles or the gills on either side of her throat.

She smiled at him. "*Buonasera. Daniel, si?*"

"Yep. You speak English?"

The woman shrugged and shook her head. "*Non molto.*" She raised one tentacle toward him, and it uncurled to reveal Mina's cellphone. "*Io non credo che funziona ancora.*"

As he took the phone her other tentacle reached out and gently brushed his right sleeve where it had been cut short and folded over.

"*Il braccio. Fa male?*"

Danny shrugged. "Sorry, I don't know what you mean."

Loligo frowned for a moment, then asked, "The arm. Does it make… pain?"

"No, not any more. But sometimes I still find myself reaching for things with it. And I can't tie shoelaces or anything like that, which is really annoying. It's like…" He stopped himself. *What am I complaining about? At least I have an arm.* He wished that he could speak Italian, or that she was more fluent in English. He wanted to ask Loligo how she coped. Had the change come on all at once, like Brawn's, or had her arms become tentacles slowly over time? Had she been able to switch back and forth like some superhumans? How had her family and friends reacted when it happened?

He smiled again and tucked the phone into his pocket. "Thanks. I mean, gracias. No, wait, that's Spanish, isn't it?"

"*Grazie,*" Loligo said, returning the smile.

"OK then." He nodded back the way he had come. "I should get going. Thanks again. Grazie."

He felt it would be rude to just slip into fast-time and walk away, so he sauntered back up the beach at a normal speed.

Every time he glanced back, she was standing in the same spot, watching him.

Back on the coast road, he called Warren Wagner. "I've got Mina's phone. I think it's broken, though. Not sure what use it's going to be."

"Bring it back anyway," Warren said. "Maybe the data card is still intact."

"Will do." Danny ended the call and shifted into fast-time.

The journey back to Germany was not a pleasant one. He kept picturing Loligo on the beach. *What must it be like for her?* He wondered. *To have the ability to travel to any ocean and swim at incredible depths, but not have anyone to share that with?*

But she's alive, that's something. Brawn said she almost died in the prison camp several times. Alive is better than dead, no matter which way you look at it.

Is that the best we can hope for? That we get to live?

Once, back in Sakkara, Razor had jokingly described the superhuman abilities as a curse, but at times like this Danny feared that he might have been right.

Paragon was murdered by Victor Cross. Yvonne had betrayed the New Heroes and been shot in the throat. Brawn's friend Hesperus had been killed by Slaughter before Danny was even born. After he lost his powers, Ragnarök had taken his own life rather than be imprisoned.

And Quantum, Danny's own father, had been driven crazy by his experiences and his visions of the future. And then, years later, he had died when Danny—unable to control his new-found abilities—struck him in anger.

Danny looked down at the stump where his right arm used

to be. *One of the last things I did with that arm was kill my father.*

It was an accident. Everyone knows that. No one blames me.

No, they just blame me for causing the Trutopian war.

After the war, Colin's mother, Caroline, had tried to explain it clearly to the New Heroes in Sakkara: "What I tell you three times is true. That's from *The Hunting of the Snark*, by the Reverend Charles Dodgson. It means that if you tell a lie often enough, for a lot of people it *becomes* the truth. Everyone knows that back in the middle ages people thought the world was flat. That's common knowledge, right?"

Danny and some of the others had nodded at that.

"No, *wrong*," Caroline said. "Recorded history shows that people have known that the world is spherical for thousands of years. When *I* was in school we were taught that Christopher Columbus sailed west from Portugal to prove his theory that the world was round. That's just nonsense! Columbus—and every other sailor of his time—knew that it was round. The purpose of his expedition was to find faster trade routes. It was all about money, not exploration. The point here is that enough people *are* saying that there was a link between the prison camp in Lieberstan and the Trutopians. We could deny the lies until we're blue in the face—no offense, Brawn—but that wouldn't help. So we let it go. You can only change people's opinions when they *want* them to be changed."

Danny knew that Caroline was right, but that didn't make it any easier to take.

Chapter 9

The double of Colin Wagner struggled ceaselessly throughout the entire journey in the helicopter back to Sakkara.

Colin wasn't sure that taking him prisoner was the right decision, but the alternative was to let him go, and he was even less fond of that option.

After the copter set down on the former military base outside Sakkara, Colin and Brawn dragged him out of the copter while Butler, exhausted from the strain of maintaining his force-field for so long, was barely able to stand upright.

Colin had told the copter pilot to order everyone to stay away. "Until we know what we're doing with him, I don't want anyone else in the line of fire."

Now, the clone was face-down on the ground with Brawn kneeling on his back and holding onto his arms. "I can barely hold him! Stop squirming, you little punk!"

Colin crouched down next to the clone. "You better calm way down or you're *really* going to be hurt!"

The only response was a wide grin.

"What's your name?" Colin asked.

For only the second time, the clone spoke: "I'm Shadow."

Maybe he doesn't feel pain, Colin realized. *That's why he kept fighting.*

In his mind, Cassandra's voice said, "You could be right about that. Col, I don't think he's human. I mean, he's a person, but he's not like any of us. He's more like... Like a biological war machine."

We need him unconscious. Are you sure you can't tap into his mind?

"I don't even know where to begin," Cassandra thought. Aloud, she said, "How can we keep him prisoner if he's as strong as you are? Can you think of any place *you* couldn't escape from?"

Shadow suddenly spasmed violently, knocking Brawn to the side. Colin threw himself at the clone, and was met with a flurry of lightning-fast rock-hard punches to his chest and stomach.

Colin responded in kind, wishing that Danny was here to help, or that Renata hadn't lost her powers: her ability to turn anything into an immovable crystalline form would be ideal here.

Shadow rose high into the air, with Colin's arms locked around his waist. He kicked out, a vicious jab that collided heavily with Colin's left knee and sent waves of pain rippling through his whole body.

But the thought of Renata's power gave Colin an idea: he concentrated on the clone's body heat, drew it into his own body. In seconds Shadow's breath was misting in the air. Frost formed on his eyebrows and around his mouth.

Come on! Colin thought. *Freeze!*

The clone's movements began to slow. His cheeks and hands turned red with the cold, and Colin felt him start to shiver.

Can't freeze him too much—don't want to kill him. But if I can slow him down enough...

They were now several hundred yards above ground, and far below Colin could sense the others watching them. *They can't help—there's nothing they can do.*

Shadow twisted and spun in Colin's grip, slammed his left fist into Colin's throat then immediately formed the fingers of his right hand into a point. He struck out, aiming at Colin's eyes.

Colin barely twitched his head back in time: Shadow's fingers hit his cheekbone with enough force to send him sprawling.

He was trying to blind me! I've got to find a way to—

The clone brushed the ice and frost away from his face, then he looked at Colin and laughed.

"You think this is *funny*? What sort of a sicko are you?"

"I'm you. A better version. Stronger. Faster. Smarter."

Stronger and faster, maybe, Colin thought to himself*, but there's no way you're smarter.* "What do you *want*?" he asked.

"We want you dead, brother."

"Why? Who *are* you people?"

"We're the future." Shadow glanced down at Brawn, Cassandra and Butler. "You people… You're maggot-food. Max Dalton was right—the age of the superhumans *is* over. And so is the age of the *ordinary* humans. This is the age of a whole new race. We are better than you in every respect."

Colin drifted a little closer. "Where do you come from? Why do you look like me?"

"You already know. I was grown from a sample of your DNA. Improved, of course." Again, he grinned. "We were sent to test you, Colin. You failed."

"It was three against one. Your friends fled and you were captured. That's hardly failure."

"They didn't flee. They were recalled because they weren't needed." The clone arched his back, and flexed his fists. "If you have any gods, Colin, I'll give you a minute to pray to them now. Because this is the last chance you will have."

He's insane! Colin thought. *Cassandra, are you listening?*

"I can hear you."

Get everyone out of Sakkara. Right now. Get Butler and Brawn away from here.

"Colin, he wants to *kill* you!"

I know.

Shadow drifted closer, and glanced down. "Your friends are abandoning you. It doesn't matter. They're going to die anyway." He paused for a moment, then added, "I think I'll kill Cassandra first. She's trying to find a way into my mind, and I really don't want that."

"No," Colin said. "Your fight is with me."

"My fight is with *all* of you." He gave a sly smile. "And even if you defeat me, you'll never stop us all. We have something that will render *you* about as threatening as a kitten. I'd prefer to kill you when you're at your best—just to show that I'm better than you are—but either way I don't mind that much, as long as you're dead." He looked down at the others. "Yeah. The girl first. Stop me if you can." He immediately dropped down, flipped over and dove head-first for Cassandra.

Colin launched a fireball at the clone, then raced after him, moving so fast that he overtook the fireball.

Shadow's outstretched hands were inches away from Cassandra's neck when Colin snagged his ankle and wrenched him back into the fireball's path. The clone twisted, tried to break free, but Colin held tight, squeezing his right hand with as much force as he could muster. It was a grip strong enough to pulverize granite rocks, but the clone didn't seem to register any pain.

The fireball struck, engulfing Shadow and instantly evaporating the frost and ice from his body.

Colin swung him down hard into the concrete—Shadow's

head smacked off the ground with enough force to shatter the surface. Colin swung him again, and again, and his body went limp.

He's faking! Colin thought, but knew he had to take advantage of the clone's relaxed state: still maintaining his grip, he pulled him forward and lashed out with his left fist, burying it deep into Shadow's stomach.

The force of the blow pushed Shadow deeper into the ruined concrete, and Colin paused long enough to build up a thermal charge in his fist: it glowed white-hot as it arced through the air, aiming for the clone's chest.

The punch struck home and immediately burned a hole in the clone's uniform—and seared the skin beneath.

As the third strike was coming down, Shadow suddenly twisted and grabbed Colin's fist, wrapped his own hand tightly around it, oblivious to the fire.

His body bucked and spasmed, his limbs flailing with enough strength to break Colin's grip on his ankle. Still horizontal, he flipped over onto his stomach, kicking his legs out at the same time. His right foot cracked against the side of Colin's head, then almost immediately his left did the same.

Colin threw himself backwards to dodge the next powerful kick—but it didn't come. Instead, Shadow—still spinning—darted along the ground, aiming for Sakkara, following the path of Brawn and the others.

As Colin followed, he saw the clone snatch up two large, jagged slabs of concrete from the edge of the crater.

Shadow flipped his arms out, throwing the concrete ahead of him.

The first slammed into Brawn's shoulder, sent him spinning.

The second was aimed at the small of Cassandra's back, and Colin knew that if it hit her, she'd be killed.

He targeted the concrete slab with a lightning bolt—and missed.

No...! He knew he didn't have time to generate another one.

Less than a foot away from Cassandra, the concrete slab struck something invisible, and collapsed to the ground.

Butler's force-field! Colin realized.

Shadow abruptly changed direction. Still flying only a few feet above the ground, he was now heading for Butler.

The older boy threw himself flat on the ground as the clone reached him.

Good, Colin thought. *Now if I can keep that nutter away from the others—*

The clone flipped over in the air, doubled back and—upside-down—grabbed hold of Butler's arms.

He flipped again, throwing Butler high into the air.

He's doing that to distract me—he knows I'll have to go after him!

But Colin realized he was wrong when Shadow shifted direction once more, rising with lightning speed after Butler.

As Butler reached the apex of the arc, the clone lashed out with his fist, his arm moving so fast it was barely a blur.

Then he slowed, watched as Butler fell back toward the ground.

Colin darted after his friend, caught him in mid-air. Butler's body was limp, unmoving. His head lolled back so far that Colin knew his neck was broken.

"Huh," Shadow said from behind Colin. "Well, I was wrong. Cassandra *wasn't* the first."

Colin felt his mouth and throat dry up. "You..."

The clone began to drift backward. "Yeah. That's enough for now, I think. I'll be seeing you again, brother."

Colin stared down at Butler Redmond's lifeless eyes, at the blood slowly seeping from his mouth and nose. "He's dead. You... You just murdered him!"

Shadow shrugged, still moving backward. "What? Did you think this was just some sort of *game*? Your friend there is just the first of many. Tell the people of America to prepare themselves for annihilation. The Earth is ours now, and you are trespassing."

Chapter 10

Dawn was breaking in Somalia as Renata Soliz gathered Kenya, Alia and Grant. "I've called in the big transport. We're out of here. We, uh, we've got a situation. *Two* situations, maybe."

Beside her, Alia Cord pulled off her gloves, then removed her helmet and ran her fingers through her sweat-drenched hair. "Where are we going?"

"Berlin, first. Mina's disappeared. Danny and Warren are fine, but half of us will be staying behind to help them search for her."

Grant asked, "Disappeared? But isn't that what Mina *does*?"

"Not like that," Renata said. "No one's seen her for hours, and her phone was found in the Baltic Sea, hundreds of miles from where she should have been." Renata looked at Kenya. "You'll be coming with me back to Sakkara, and Alia and Grant will stay with Danny."

Kenya nodded. "Sure. What's the other situation?"

Renata almost couldn't bring herself to say it, but she knew that she had to. Being a leader wasn't just about issuing orders. It was about taking responsibility, making the hard decisions. She looked at the members of her team, knowing that if the enemy could kill someone as powerful as Butler, any of them would be a much easier target, despite their armor and experience.

On her left, Alia Cord, the twin sister of Stephanie, daughter of Solomon Cord, the greatest non-powered hero she had ever known. The twins had inherited their father's combat kills and courage, and their mother's intelligence, drive and compassion.

Stephanie and Alia were the heart of the team, always willing to help others despite any danger.

Next to Alia, standing so close to her that their armored legs touched, was Grant Paramjeet. He was still considered to be on probation with the team, and Renata wasn't sure of him yet. He was a nice guy, soft-spoken and often quite gentle, but was too much in love with the idea of being a superhero. He had the sort of enthusiasm that made him a liability.

They were a good team. Or at least they had strong potential. When Stephanie was with them, they were formidable, and Renata was sure that Kenya would be just as effective.

How do I tell them? She wondered. *Sure, Butler was a pain in the butt a lot of the time, but he was a good guy. He was one of us.*

Grant said, "Renata? What is it?"

She took a deep breath. "Colin, Butler, Brawn and Cassandra were attacked. An ambush. It was…"

Alia grabbed Renata's arm. "Is Colin all right?"

"He's fine. They were attacked by… Look, that's not important. Colin and Cassandra are fine. Brawn's been seriously wounded, but it's not life-threatening. He heals very quickly." She paused for a moment. "Butler's dead."

Kenya said, "I don't know who… Is he the one with the force-field?"

Renata related the story as it had been told to her, and when she was done, Grant said, "Clones."

"That's what they suspect, yeah."

"So if you guys get cloned, and the clones have powers, then…" He shrugged. "Maybe that means that there *is* something genetically different about superhumans."

Alia said, "We've already seen that with Mina and Yvonne."

"Yeah, but..."

Grant fell silent, and Renata was sure she knew why: Grant desperately wanted to have superhuman abilities, and if it was true that the powers were tied to genetics, then that might mean he'd never get powers of his own. Aloud, she said, "Right now finding Mina is our top priority—it could be that she was targeted by the same people who attacked Colin's team. Transport's coming in three minutes."

"What about the craft that brought you here?" Kenya asked.

"The Marlin's fast, but it doesn't have the range to get us to Germany." Renata looked at the others. "Are you all OK?"

Grant said, "I never really liked him, but still..."

"You can't *say* that!" Alia snapped at him, stepping away. "He was one of us!"

Renata placed her hand on Alia's shoulder. "Don't, please. Fighting amongst ourselves won't help. If the clone—or whatever he is—is that powerful, we need to be prepared. They've already given the order to evacuate Sakkara. Razor is the last non-superhuman there. He says he won't leave until he's finished his current project."

Grant nodded. "That guy's got lots of guts and no common sense. But I trust him."

"Has anyone told Butler's family?" Alia asked.

"Impervia said that it's being taken care of," Renata said.

"He is to be buried with full military honors, you got that?"

Caroline Wagner held the phone away from her ear and hesitated for a moment, thankful that Butler's father couldn't see the frown on her face. "Brigadier General, I'm not sure that would be permitted."

"My son was a hero. He fought for his country and as God is my witness he *will* be buried in a manner befitting his service."

"I do appreciate that, sir. But he wasn't a veteran—"

"My son was a hero," Butler's father repeated, his voice cracking. Then, much softer, he repeated, "A hero," and Caroline understood.

Butler had often spoken about his father, but the man had never once made contact with him after he joined Sakkara. He had been angry, Caroline guessed, that Butler had been expelled from the military academy in Alaska. A proud military man with an exemplary record, whose son had been discharged for constant insubordination and dereliction of duty.

They had fallen out over the incident and their relationship had never recovered. Sakkara should have been a second chance for Butler to regain his father's respect, but the Brigadier General had been too proud and too stubborn—or too embarrassed—to cross that bridge. And now it was too late.

"Yes, sir," Caroline said. "He was a hero. He was utterly fearless. And it was an honor and a privilege to teach him, and to work alongside him. Without him, we would never have survived the Trutopian attack on Sakkara. And..." She chose her next words carefully. "Your son's final act saved the life of a young civilian who recently came into our care."

"Thank you," Brigadier General Redmond said. "That's all I ask."

Chapter 11

In Berlin, Danny Cooper sat nervously in the bar of the hotel as Warren Wagner stared at the double-measure of whiskey in front of him.

"Mister Wagner, we have to *do* something."

"What *can* we do, Danny? Find whoever killed Butler and took Mina? Good idea. Where do we start?" Warren picked up the glass in his scarred left hand and held it for a few seconds before putting it down again. He sighed. "I don't drink any more, but this seemed like a good idea. Not so sure now." He slid the still-full glass away from him. It had been sitting on the table for so long that the ice had melted.

Danny said, "We're not doing any good here. We need to go back to the states."

"Why? Danny, the kid who killed Butler is gone. If Colin wasn't able to track him, no one else can. Not even you, fast as you are."

"So we just sit and wait until they attack again?"

"No, we wait until Team Paragon gets here. Then we figure out our next move."

For the first time, Danny realized that Warren Wagner was starting to look his age. The man was still only in his forties, but now, slumped in his chair and staring at a whiskey he probably wasn't going to drink, it seemed to Danny that Warren looked defeated.

It can't be easy to have been as powerful as he was when he was Titan, and then lose that power and have to become an ordinary person again.

Danny remembered what it had been like when his own powers temporarily abandoned him. The sense of loss, of helplessness, had been almost overwhelming. But Danny had only been superhuman for a very short time when that happened—Warren had been a superhuman for almost two decades.

"Have you talked to Caroline?" Danny asked, hoping to shake Warren out of his funk.

"Yeah, she's fine. The baby's still keeping her up at night, but she can cope." Warren grinned. "Colin cried non-stop for the entire first two years of his life. At least, that's what it felt like. One night my parents were staying with us, and at about three in the morning my dad went into Colin's room and said, 'All right. That's enough crying now.' And like *that*," Warren snapped his fingers, "Colin stopped. He's barely cried since. It's like he's got all the crying out of his system in one go."

"Any thoughts on what you're going to call the baby? You must have some ideas by now. You can't keep calling her 'the baby' forever."

"Oh, we do have a name. We just haven't announced it yet. We have to check with someone first." He sat back in the chair. "What the heck, I'll tell you. Just don't tell anyone else, deal?"

Danny nodded. "Sure."

"We're going to name her after an old friend, but we want to talk to her sister about it, make sure she's OK with it. She probably *will* be, but it's best to check."

"Go on…"

"There's a lot of things about the past that we don't talk about, Dan. Sometimes that's because Max zapped our memories or messed with our emotions, but sometimes it's because the memories are just too painful. You've heard of Hesperus?"

"Yeah. Brawn told us about her. They worked with Thunder and Roz Dalton for a while. She was killed by Slaughter, Brawn said."

"Her real name was Abigail de Luyando. Her sister was Vienna Cord. If she'd lived, Abby would have been Alia and Stephanie's aunt. So that's what we're calling our baby girl, if Vienna doesn't mind. And her middle name... Well, it's not traditionally a girl's name but then Abby would have liked that. She certainly didn't follow traditional paths. One of the things we all loved about her. Her middle name will be Solomon. Abigail Solomon Wagner."

"I like that," Danny said. "It works. Does Colin know?"

"Not yet." Warren looked down at his hands. "And neither does Brawn. He and Abby were good friends. I think he still blames himself for her death."

"He told us what happened. That he was working with Ragnarök... But he's a good guy, Mister Wagner."

"Good people sometimes make bad decisions. Look at what happened to Colin. He joined the Trutopians."

"He was under Yvonne's control."

"Not at the start." Warren sighed. "But he *is* a good kid. We're proud of him. Proud of you, too, and Renata. You've all been through a lot."

Danny moved the whiskey glass to the side and began running his finger through the ring of condensation left on the table. "We've been through more than we should ever have to face. We don't get to just *be* kids, do we?" He briefly looked up at Warren before returning his attention to the table. "All the things normal people do… They might not happen for us. And now Butler is dead—they'll *never* happen for him. He'll never have a girlfriend, buy a car, go to college…"

"I know."

"He never even had any friends, I think. I mean, none of us liked him all that much. He was a bit of jerk most of the time. He was always mean to Niall, always going on about how Niall might grow up to be a supervillain because Façade's his real father."

"Your brother's going to turn out fine," Warren said.

"Mina said that he's definitely going to be superhuman. She said he's got that same twist to his aura that the rest of us do." Danny sat back and wiped his damp finger on the leg of his jeans. "He desperately wants to be a superhero, but if I could change only one thing about the future, I'd change that. I'd make him a normal kid. Let him have the life that the rest of us can't."

"Nah, you're making the powers sound like a curse, Dan. That's the wrong attitude. We were chosen for this. How or why, I don't know. But we have been given abilities that most people can only barely imagine."

"But if we *were* chosen to have these powers, who did the choosing? And why are people like Slaughter or Victor Cross given powers too?"

"If I knew the answer to that," Warren said, "I'd be a much happier man. I've been wondering about that ever since my own powers first started to show up. Why me? Why any of us?"

"And what are the blue lights?" Danny asked.

"Yeah, well, I've never seen them myself, so you've got me there. Your dad talked about them—your real dad, I mean—but

I don't know if he really saw them, or if he just, you know, *imagined* that they were there."

"Colin can see them too."

Warren nodded. "So he says. I mean, I believe he thinks he sees them, but Mina sees auras and there's absolutely no evidence that any such thing exists. People see weird stuff *all* the time. Doesn't make it real. Remember that soldier in London a few months after the war, the one who turned out to be working for Torture? He was convinced that he had the ghost of a teenager haunting him." Warren's phone buzzed in his jacket pocket. He pulled it out and glanced at it. "They're here."

They left the bar and crossed the lobby, out to the mostly-empty parking lot at the rear of the hotel.

It was a warm night, but overcast, and looking up Danny could see only clouds tinted orange by the city lights.

Directly overhead a faint white glow appeared in the clouds. It broke up into eight bright discs, then the outline of the New Heroes' troop-carrier was clear against the sky, silently but rapidly dropping toward them.

The craft was the size of a school bus, but curved and elegant, only slightly wider than it was tall, its profile almost rectangular. The only noticeable features from this angle were the prototype gravity-nullifying engines that showed up as the glowing discs. The engineers at Sakkara, filled with pride at their ground-breaking creation, had voted to name it *The ChampionShip*. It annoyed them that Razor, who had designed the craft, insisted on calling it "The Big Fish."

Behind Danny, the hotel's lobby door opened again and some of the other hotel guests emerged, muttering to each other as they stared up at the craft.

It slowed to a hover at six feet off the ground in front of Warren and Danny, and its near side split open with a horizontal gash, the top half of the wide door raising to become a narrow canopy, the lower half unfolding itself as it dropped to form steps.

The wide doors on either side of the hull had been designed to allow the troops to disembark easily and quickly. Now, the three members of Team Paragon descended the steps in unison, though Danny knew that this time it was more for show than rapid deployment.

They were followed by another figure, a girl Danny hadn't seen before. Her face, neck and arms were covered with white scar tissue. The moment her feet touched the ground, the troop-carrier began to rise with much greater speed than its descent. In seconds, it was gone.

Warren said, "Let's go. I've reserved the hotel's conference room. We can talk there without all the lookie-loos getting an earful. Kenya, right?"

The scarred girl nodded, looking around. "I've never been to Europe before."

"Unfortunately you won't have time for sight-seeing. Dan? You've got ten minutes."

Danny and Renata held back while Warren led the others through the still-growing crowd. They stood side-by-side and watched as the hotel guests and staff reached out to touch the warriors' armor.

Some of the people followed them inside, but a few others remained, watching Renata and Danny.

"This isn't a good place to talk," Renata said. "Hold tight."

Danny put his arm around her shoulders and she activated

her jetpack as she put her own right arm around his waist.

She carried him up onto the hotel's roof, and they sat side-by-side on the low wall as she removed her helmet and gloves. "I talked to Col. He's... Well, he's trying to be calm but he's freaking out a bit."

"I don't blame him," Danny said. "How's Brawn?"

"He's recovering. His arm's in a cast and he's in a lot of pain, but you know him—he's not complaining."

Danny shuffled closer to Renata. "Missed you."

She smiled. "Missed you more."

They were in the middle of a kiss when a voice said, "Knock it off, you two."

Warren was walking toward them, the roof door swinging closed behind him.

"That was never ten minutes," Danny said.

Warren stopped in front of them. "Just got a call from Stephanie. She's back in Sakkara."

Renata said, "So now you're going to tell us what her secret mission was all about?"

Warren placed his palms on the wall and peered down at the street below. "It's something we've been talking about for a while..."

"When you say 'we' you mean you and Caroline and Façade and Impervia, right? The grown-ups."

"This is not the time for that, Renata. But Impervia wasn't involved. This is something that came from Brawn... When he was in Lieberstan he was visited by Victor Cross. That was three years ago. Around the time Cross started working for Max."

"So?" Danny asked. "Cross is dead."

"Brawn doesn't believe that. Cross out-smarted every one of

us—why wouldn't he be able to fake his own death?"

"They found his body," Danny said, "in the plane wreckage."

"They found *a* body. Badly burned, and in pieces."

"With Cross's DNA."

"Could have been a few lumps of flesh cloned from his own cells." Warren's eyes narrowed. "Brawn put it very simply. He said, 'Let's assume he's still alive. Let's assume that everything that happened—even the war—is part of some grand scheme.'"

"Mister Wagner, do *you* believe that's true?" Renata asked.

"Before we sent Stephanie to Puerto Rico, I was maybe half-convinced. Now I'm one hundred per cent sure."

"Why? What happened with Stephanie?"

"It wasn't that. When Cross ordered Dioxin's men to raid Sakkara they stole every single byte of data we'd taken from Ragnarök. That included all of his notes on the experiment that created Yvonne and Mina from his own cells. Now I'm thinking that's exactly what Cross was looking for. He's alive, and he's created a clone of Colin. Probably more than one. I pray that I'm wrong about that, because if I'm not, we're in more trouble than we have ever faced before."

In an annex of the hotel's conference room, Kenya watched as Alia and Grant helped each other out of their armor.

Clearly, there was a spark between the two, the way they were able to work together without needing to talk about it, but instead chat about something completely unrelated.

Not for the first time, Kenya wondered what she was getting into. In Africa, she knew how things worked. America would be very different. Renata had assured her that she was making the right decision: "You can do a lot more good with us than on your own. You don't have to suffer in silence. If you feel it's not working out, you can always go home again."

But Kenya knew that part wasn't true. She could never go home again. Home was a memory of her parents and her brother, of her friends and neighbors. All of that was gone forever. Almost every person she knew before the Trutopian war was now dead.

Alia looked up at her and asked, "You all right?"

Kenya nodded.

"OK. If you need anything, just let us know. I know you've been through a lot and, well, whatever we can do to help, all right?"

Kenya said, "Sorry, but you *don't* know what I've been through."

Grant said, "Hey, she was just saying—"

Alia put her hand on his arm. "No, Kenya's right. We don't know." To Kenya, she added, "And you don't have to tell us if you don't want to. But we're going to do what we can to make things easier for you, because, well, that's what we *do*."

Kenya nodded, and smiled. "OK. Thank you, I do appreciate that." And then she realized that she couldn't remember the last time she'd smiled.

"There's a question about Colin Wagner that has never been answered."

Evan Laurie put down his half-eaten toasted sandwich and looked at the teenage boy standing in the doorway. "And what is that, Nathan?"

Laurie was, as always, bundled up in a thick parka, with a hot-water bottle tucked inside his shirt. He'd removed his insulated gloves to eat, and already his fingers were pink from the cold.

He hated this place, with its artificial light and unappetizing food, and the sharp pain in his chest every time he took a deep breath of the freezing air. At night he dreamed of warm, earthy forests, and plush hotel rooms.

The boy pulled a chair over to Laurie's desk and sat down. He was wearing a t-shirt and a pair of shorts. His bare feet rested on the icy floor. "The others don't think this is important, but I do."

"Go on," Laurie said. He liked Nathan. The boy was smart and he asked a lot of questions. Sometimes those questions couldn't easily be answered, but that was OK with Laurie. An inquisitive mind was always more interesting than a blindly-accepting one.

Shadow, on the other hand, was a monster. The oldest of the nine surviving clones, Shadow was cruel and smug, and despite his intelligence he always followed Victor's orders to the letter. So far. But now that Shadow had made his first kill, Laurie feared that there would be no stopping him.

Nathan said, "Colin left America because the New Heroes recruited Max Dalton to help them fight Yvonne, right?"

"That's right."

"He made it to Europe and crossed it mostly on foot. The Trutopians picked him up in Romania. He'd been heading east for months."

"Yeah. So?"

"So where was he going?"

"The prison camp in Lieberstan. The platinum mine where the old superhumans were kept."

"Evan... Colin didn't know about the mine until Victor told him, and that was *after* the Trutopians picked him up. So... Where was he going? What was he looking for?"

Chapter 12

In the machine room in Sakkara, Colin leaned over a workbench as Razor pointed to a welded seam on the metal framework between them.

"And that one there," Razor said. "See? Fractures. You need to do it again."

"OK." Colin concentrated on building up the heat in his right index finger, then ran it along the seam. Under the pad of his finger the metal glowed red, then orange, then white. Tear-sized droplets spilled onto the heavily-scorched bench.

"We're losing too much. Hold on," Razor said. He picked up a thin titanium spar, and held its tip against the white-hot seam, drawing it slowly back ahead of Colin's finger. "Cool. That should do it."

They both stepped back, and looked at their construction. "Nice," Razor said. "And a lot quicker and neater than using an arc-welder. You could always get a job in the construction industry."

"How long before it's done?" Colin asked.

"A few more days." He picked up a small custom-built circuit board from the bench behind him and tossed it to Colin. "Check the power inputs on that, would you?"

Colin turned the board over in his hands. "What am I looking for?"

"The power's not getting to the processor—I think one of the tracks is broken, but I can't see it. Run a current through it, see what's up. I know the processor itself is intact—I tested each line in and out."

Colin touched a finger to the power connectors on the circuit board. He knew from the past few weeks working on the machine that he had to be very careful not to release too much electricity into the board. There was a growing pile of burnt-out microprocessors in the recycling bin.

He sent a tiny charge through the power-socket, and sensed rather than saw where the fault lay. "Ah. You can't find it because the tracks are fine." He turned the board upside-down and pointed to where the processor's pins protruded. "This one here's not supposed to be connected, right? But there's a tiny drop of solder in the hole. *That's* making the connection, and it's feeding the power in the wrong direction."

Razor pulled the circuit board from Colin's hand and peered it at. "Nice one, Col. I'd never have seen that." Again, he stepped back to examine the machine. "This is my last one, you know."

"You said that before."

"Yeah, but this time I mean it. I'm going home. I haven't seen my mom in, like, *forever*." He shrugged. "She always said I had to apply myself if I didn't want to end up like my dad. I have to show her that she was right. I'm not just a bum. Come on, let's go see how the big guy's doing."

"You almost never talk about your parents," Colin said as they walked toward the doors.

"There's not much to tell. Once, when they were fighting, Mom snapped and said he wasn't my real dad, but she never said anything else about that no matter how many times I asked her. But he's the only dad I ever knew. He left when I was about four, but he didn't *really* leave. He ran off with some woman and they broke up, so he came back. Then he did it again, and again. Eventually mom had had enough and she told him that was it: he was to get out and never come back. So the jerk moved in three houses down from our place. Can you believe that?" Razor entered a code on the keypad next to the doors, and they slid open. Since the attack Sakkara had been in total lock-down: every door was sealed and could only be opened by entering the correct codes.

"Maybe he wanted to be close to you?"

"Me? Nah, he didn't give a badger's bushy butt about *me*. The only advice he ever gave me was, 'Find something you're good at and stick with it.' What *he* was good at was drinking and getting into trouble. He stayed because he wanted to be near the bar across the street where his pals hung out." Razor shrugged. "So he was always around to interfere, but never there to help out, you know? I remember one time when the porch light went out and mom asked him to replace the bulb. She couldn't reach and I was still too small. She could have stood on a chair, but it was kind of a test, to see if he'd do it."

"And did he?"

"No. Kept saying he would, but he never did. It would have taken him all of about ten seconds, but he never found the time."

Colin considered this as they walked along the silent, empty corridors. "Yeah. Your dad was a jerk."

"Yep. Last time he actually spoke to me, I was fifteen. Me and Ritchie had got into some trouble. I won't say what it was. That's not important." Razor paused. "All right, we were siphoning gas out of the cars on the next street."

"What for?"

"To sell. I don't think we ever figured out *how* we were going to sell it. We weren't that smart. Anyway, this guy saw us and called the cops. We tried to run, but the guy also called a bunch of the other neighbors, because we'd been doing it for months. We figured that no one would notice if we only took a few pints at a time. There was a big old oil drum on the vacant lot next to Ritchie's house—we used to dump the gas in there. So anyway, there's cops everywhere, and all the neighbors out looking for us. We tried to hide in some other guy's back yard, but we got caught and dragged back out to the cops. Ritchie was all crying and everything, but I was saying that we'd never done it before and that we'd heard about other guys doing it so we thought it would be a good idea, but we were really sorry and we'd never do it again. And then my dad showed up, and said, 'That's my son!' and I thought, 'Great, Dad's going to get me out of this!' Then he came right up to me and said, 'Listen, Gar,'—he always called me 'Gar' because he didn't like the name Garland—he said, 'Listen, Gar, can I borrow ten bucks until tomorrow?' I told him I didn't have ten bucks on me, so then he just said, 'Useless' and walked away."

"And that was the last time you saw him?"

"No, but it was the last time we spoke. Last time I saw him was about a year later, outside the bar. He'd tried to rip off these four guys—hustled them in pool or something—and they were beating the snot out of him. Two of them were holding him up while the other two took turns to punch him. They were *really* laying into him."

"Did you help?"

"Nah," Razor said. "I could see that the four of them were doing a good job without me."

Colin laughed. "OK, how much of that is true?"

Razor was grinning. "All but the last part."

"Butler would have liked that one."

"Yeah."

They looked at each other for a few seconds, then Colin said, "Maybe you *should* go home. You'll be safer in Florida. If Shadow had wanted to, he could have killed all of us. He's stronger than I am. And he's a psychopath."

They stopped outside the door to the gymnasium, and Colin entered the code.

Inside, Brawn was lying on his bed—three double-mattresses joined side-by-side—with his right arm, shoulder and most of his chest covered in more bandages and plaster than Colin had ever seen in one go.

"Man, that's gotta hurt," Razor said.

"This?" Brawn said. "Well, it tickles a bit. How goes the latest invention?"

"It's getting there." Razor walked all the way around Brawn. "You're all blue already so I can't tell if you've got bruises or not."

"I do, but they don't show." Brawn turned to Colin. "You OK?"

Colin shook his head.

"He saved Cassandra," Brawn said. "Last thing Butler did, he saved her life. She's in shock, though. Impervia's taken her away. Wouldn't say where. So what are we doing? What's the plan?"

"Brawn, you're out of action until your arm recovers," Razor said. He dragged a chair next to the bed and sat down backwards on it, resting his folded arms across the back of the seat. "Renata, Façade and the new girl, Kenya, are coming back here. The others are going to help Danny and Warren look for Mina. Other than that, we don't really *have* a plan. We can't go after the bad guys until we know where they are."

"What about you?" Brawn asked. "You decided not to evacuate with the civilians. How smart do you think that was, on a scale of one to stupid?"

"Have to finish the machine first. Then I'm outta here. And I'm not coming back. Not for a long time, anyway."

"I don't blame you, kid. You've done more than your share."

Colin said, "If there are more clones like Shadow, if they're as tough as he is, we're not going to win."

"You definitely won't if you play nice," Brawn said. "Colin, you might have to *kill* them."

"That's never going to happen. I'm never going to kill anyone."

Brawn and Razor exchanged a look.

"What?" Colin asked.

Razor said, "You might not have a choice. Col, I understand your position, but don't make promises like that."

"My parents never killed anyone when they were superhuman."

"They never had to."

Brawn said, "They tried to kill *me*, once. But that was Max Dalton, using his mind-control on them. I've been thinking that maybe he's the man we need to talk to about this."

"Max is not exactly answering the phone these days." Razor said. "He went into hiding after the Trutopian war."

"That jerk is usually more trouble than he's worth, anyway," Colin said. "If I had my say, I'd—" He paused. A sound outside had caught his attention. "Something's coming. A helicopter...

Stephanie's flying it."

Brawn shook his head and muttered, "I don't know how they can let someone so young fly a helicopter!"

Colin flew over to the gym's external doors, entered the code, and stepped back as they slid open.

The copter set down on the grounds outside the gym's steps, and a few minutes later Stephanie Cord helped a man to climb out.

The man looked to be in his late thirties or early forties, heavily bearded with shoulder-length hair that whipped around his face in the down-draft from the copter's rotors. He was walking with a limp, leaning heavily on a wooden cane.

As Stephanie climbed back into the copter she greeted Colin with a wave and a smile. He returned the wave, and resisted the urge to go to her.

Once—before the Trutopian war, before Victor Cross had forced Colin to choose whether Stephanie's father or Renata's entire family would die—Colin and Stephanie had been close, always just on the verge of becoming boyfriend and girlfriend. Now, they were still friends, but that was all.

Not for the first time, Colin wondered whether he should ask Cassandra to scan Stephanie's mind, to find out what she really thought about him. But that felt wrong, like a betrayal of trust.

He'd almost asked her once, a few months ago, but even as he was trying to steer the conversation in a direction where he could make the request without it seeming too awkward, Cassandra had said, "Don't ask me to do that, Colin. You'll regret it no matter what the answer is. If she does still have feelings for you, you'll always be sorry you didn't wait to find out from her. And if she doesn't, you might end up resenting her for that. And resenting me for telling you. You have to let these things sort themselves out naturally."

Razor had given him almost the same advice, in a much simpler way: "Let it go, Col. If it was meant to be, it'll happen." Then he'd smiled and embarked on an out-of-tune rendition of The Supremes' song, "You Can't Hurry Love."

The stranger walked slowly toward the steps. He called up to Colin, "Hey, kid?" He tapped his left shin with the end of the cane. "Got a bum leg. I'm not great on steps. If you're not too busy being tragically heartbroken, you might want to offer some help."

Colin walked off the steps and drifted down to the man.

"Thanks. Let me lean on you, huh?"

"Uh, sure." Colin stepped close to him, and the man placed his left arm over Colin's shoulder.

Step-by-step, they ascended. By the time they reached the top, both Brawn and Razor had come to the doorway.

"Chair?" the man asked Razor. "No, you take your time, son. There's no rush. Maybe if you take long enough, my leg might grow back."

"Sorry, *who* are you?" Colin asked.

"Lance McKendrick. I'm your new boss."

Chapter 13

Victor Cross looked up from his computer screen when the small red light above the door began to blink. He immediately reached under the desk and turned off the fan-heater that had been keeping his legs warm.

The light told him that Evan Laurie was approaching down the icy corridor, and would reach him in a couple of minutes. For the past year Cross had worked hard to give his assistant the impression that he wasn't bothered by the cold.

Cross took the time to sit back and examine the eight other monitors on his desk. They were a mismatched collection of LCD panels and old CRT screens, all connected via a tangle of cables to the six networked PCs stacked next to the desk. A year ago the PCs had been top-of-the-range models, but now Cross was eager to replace them with newer machines.

The largest of the monitors showed the clones' life-signs in a grid of six across and four down. Fifteen of the boxes were grayed out, as they had been since shortly after the clones were removed from their artificial wombs. He knew that nine surviving clones out of twenty-four wasn't a bad rate, but he was still disappointed. Twenty-four would have greatly increased the odds of getting what he wanted.

He could always make more clones, but they took a lot of time and energy to maintain. Right now he wanted to see how this first batch worked out.

For the most part, Victor was pleased with them. Especially Shadow. He was immensely powerful and almost completely without ethics. He had responded perfectly to the neuro-linguistic programming that Cross had devised to give the clones the equivalent of twelve years' education in only six months.

The others, too, had responded well. Tuan wasn't as smart or as inventive as Shadow, but he had the most interesting ability of them all. He could increase his own size and body-mass by somehow stealing energy from the people around him. Victor was still trying to figure out exactly how that worked.

Likewise, Roman's ability to modify the atomic structures of simple base elements was invaluable. Though the effort left him exhausted and depressed for days, Roman was able to transmute ordinary graphite into any other form of carbon, from pure diamonds to graphene, a material so strong and durable it could be used to construct anything from thousand-story buildings to machines too small for the human eye to see.

That alone had promoted one of Cross's back-up plans from being merely an intriguing idea into a full-blown project that was now close to completion.

The rest of the clones hadn't yet fully developed their abilities. The artificial age-acceleration process—for reasons Cross had yet to determine—had been more effective on some than others.

Nathan seemed to be impervious to extremes of heat and cold, almost as much as his progenitor Colin Wagner, but in the months since that aspect was discovered, there had been no indication of any other abilities. He also appeared to have developed a resistance to some of the neuro-linguistic programming, specifically the parts that should have instilled a strong sense of loyalty to Cross. Nathan didn't like him and wasn't shy about making that known. But Cross kept him around anyway, because Laurie was fond of him.

The door to Cross's room opened, and Laurie entered. "I hate this place."

"Oh, really?" Cross said. "Well, you should have said something before now. Strange that you've kept it to yourself, instead of mentioning it every single time you talk to me."

"And the sarcasm really helps, Victor." Laurie picked up the room's only other chair and carried it over to the stack of PCs. Their fans exhaled a small amount of warm air and Laurie always took advantage of that. When Laurie left the room Cross would move the chair back again, just so that he'd have to pick it up and move it next time.

"It's time to schedule another round of tests for the boys," Cross said. "The works, this time. Blood, hair and saliva samples. And a spinal tap—let's see what's in there. Run everything through a full-spectrum genome comparison and flag anything unusual. And while you're at it, I want ultrasound, MRI and x-ray scans too."

"I don't know if we *can* do a spinal tap or take blood. Their skin's very tough. Soon it'll be impenetrable."

Cross pulled over his secondary keyboard and began typing. "Way ahead of you." He swiveled one of the monitors around. It showed a schematic of a hypodermic needle. "Get Roman to create these out of graphene; they should be strong enough. No sign of any other abilities? Aside from the usual flight and enhanced strength?"

"No. I figure they're fourteen now, almost fifteen. If any of them have any dormant powers, they're well hidden."

Cross sighed. "Disappointing. We might need to kick-start them into action. So. What do you want?"

"Me? I want to go home. I want to sit in the open air on a

warm day, with a cool drink in one hand and a great big bacon sandwich in the other. I want to meet people who don't have your face or Colin Wagner's. I'm beginning to forget what women look like."

Cross returned the computer screen back to its original position, and resumed typing on the primary keyboard. "Aside from all that, what do you want?"

"Nathan had a question that I couldn't answer."

"I'll set aside the obvious jokes, and assume that this is something important."

"It is, I think," Laurie said. "Our people picked up Colin Wagner in Romania, after he left the New Heroes."

"And?"

"Where was he going?"

Cross stopped typing, and straightened up in his chair. "Oh."

"Huh. Never seen *that* look on your face before."

"Shut up, Laurie. I'm thinking."

Victor ran through the current processes in his superhuman brain and one-by-one put all of them on hold, something he hadn't done in almost ten years. He scoured his memory for every conversation he'd had with Colin, for every piece of data he'd collected about the boy since his powers first appeared. He fed this information into each part of his brain, instructed it to examine the problem and return a plausible answer.

Cross's brain worked fast, and the answers came quickly. They were all discarded. He ran the process again, this time adding every piece of information that Dioxin's mercenaries had stolen from Sakkara's computers.

Still nothing viable.

In desperation, he included everything he knew, every piece

of data his flawless memory had gleaned in the decade since his own powers first appeared.

Finally, he came to an answer, the only possible answer his extreme intelligence could reach. He turned to Laurie to tell him, but Laurie was gone.

He glanced at the clock on the wall and saw that he'd been processing the problem for almost three hours.

Three hours to come up with this*? No way. I must have made a mistake somewhere.*

But he knew that couldn't be so. He didn't *make* mistakes.

He had his answer, and he mulled it over as he left the room to find food. The answer astonished him: it was not an answer he was used to encountering.

Where was *Colin Wagner going?*
I don't know.

Lance McKendrick sat in the chair with his good leg stretched out and resting on the edge of Brawn's bed. "So how have you been, Gethin?"

Brawn said, "Mostly in prison. You?"

"Only occasionally in prison. Y'know, it's hard to tell because you're so weird looking, but you haven't aged a day, man."

"*You* have. What's with the beard and the long hair?"

Lance pointed with his cane over to where Razor and Colin were watching from the long-unused bars on the far wall of the gym. "Long hair and a beard seems to be working for *this* guy."

"You lost your leg."

"I wouldn't say I lost it. We just had a parting of ways." Lance shifted in the chair. "OK, so this is the famous Sakkara, and the little dude is obviously Titan's and Energy's kid. Who's his hairy pal?"

"Calls himself Razor."

They both looked over toward Razor again.

"Ah, I love irony," Lance said. "So. I get a call out of the blue from Impervia. 'We need you to come and organize the team because you're so clever and handsome and sexy.' Those weren't her *exact* words, but I knew what she meant. My people tell me that *your* people picked up a new member in Somalia."

"So I've heard."

"Hmm. You've got one dead, one missing. How desperate is the situation?"

"Must be more desperate than I thought if they called *you* in. The kid who attacked us, the clone... Lance, I've only seen someone as fast and vicious as him once before, and that was Slaughter. If there's an army of them, we're toast."

"All right..." Lance reached into the pocket of his jacket and removed his cell-phone. "I know you've been briefed on Impervia's plan..."

"Yeah, some of it. She's taking Cassandra somewhere, but she didn't say where."

"That *was* the plan. I changed it. Ms Cord will be accompanying Cassandra instead. She's quite a pilot, I have to say. Can you imagine being able to fly a copter at her age?"

With a deep grunt, Brawn sat up. "Lance... Things aren't the way they used to be. These new heroes are good, but they're on their own. We had the older guys—Titan and Paragon and that lot—to back us up. They don't."

"They have *us*. And back in the day, we were pretty good at what we did."

"When you say 'we' you're including yourself? *That's* a stretch. You were never a superhuman."

"I know that," Lance said. He started keying a number into his phone. "Abby's dead, but we've got the next best thing—her nieces. Plus they have the added bonus of being Paragon's daughters. There's a chance that they've got the same thing that me and Cord did. Daedalus told us about it when we were in Krodin's pocket universe... There are three types of people, you see. There are ordinary humans, there are superhumans like you, and there's a very small number of us who were affected by whatever it is that makes you guys superhuman. We're not actually superhuman, but we're *changed*." Lance jerked his thumb over his shoulder in the direction of Razor. "I'd lay good money the hirsute kid has it too. He's got technical expertise way beyond his experience or education, right? Just like Cord."

"Yeah, but—"

Lance held up one finger as he raised the phone to his mouth. "It's ringing... Come on, pick up the phone!"

A man's deep voice said, "Hello?"

"Guess what, dude? This is your best friend in the world, Lance McKendrick. How's life in Reykjavík treating you?"

"What? Oh no. You're *kidding*."

"No kidding, James. I've got good news for you, man. Hope you can still fit into your old wet-suit, because we're putting the band back together."

"Lance, you're out of your mind. We don't have our powers any more."

"We *need* you, man. We... Huh."

Brawn asked, "What is it?"

Into the phone, Lance said, "Gotcha, dude. I see where you're coming from. Some supervillain attacked you and replaced your spine with jelly, right? Or maybe he spliced your DNA with that of a flightless bird, made you half-man, half-chicken?"

"Get stuffed, McKendrick! Maybe you're still drifting around without any cares or responsibilities, but don't assume that's true for the rest of us!"

"The New Heroes need us, Jimmy. I'm here in Sakkara now, with Brawn. Abby's gone but that leaves you and Roz, and she's already on the way here to join us."

Brawn frowned and started to say something, but Lance shook his head.

"Lance, I can tell from the tone of your voice that you're lying."

"No, you can tell I'm lying because you know Roz isn't coming here. And you know that because she's with *you*, right?"

James sighed. "How did you know?"

"I figured it out a while ago. Ever since Abby... I've been keeping tabs on all of you. Roz travels a lot, but always seems to end up in Iceland. Keeping it a secret from Josh and Max, right? I don't blame you. Is she with you now? Put her on."

"She's not here. Lance, you can't tell *anyone*. Seriously."

"I know, man. I won't say a word. Give her my best, huh? You know I was kidding about putting the group back together?"

"I figured. So... If you didn't call to recruit us, why *did* you call? And if you had my number all this time, why wait until now?"

"Because things are happening, James. *Bad* things. We're not all going to get out of this alive, and I might not get another chance to say good-bye."

Chapter 14

Alia Cord dropped onto the roof of the hotel in Berlin and shut down her jetpack. "Searching for Mina is a waste of time," she told Danny, who had appeared on the roof as she was coming in to land.

"You don't think she's worth finding?"

Alia removed her helmet. "No, I mean she's not here."

"Where else should we search? The Baltic? Your armor doesn't work underwater, and Loligo couldn't find any trace of her other than her cell-phone." Danny reached into the large styrofoam cooler and took out a bottle of water beside him. "Open this for me, will you?"

Alia opened the bottle and passed it back to Danny. "Did any of the cameras show anything?"

"Not so far."

Warren Wagner had instructed Grant and Kenya to help the Landespolizei—the state police—with the painstaking task of examining the footage from the city's CCTV cameras. Because of Mina's ability to instantly teleport herself from one location to another, the job was a lot harder than it would be for any other missing person. Many of the CCTV cameras had been damaged in the war: there were large areas of the city with almost no coverage.

Danny added, "Something might show up, though. Kenya had the idea that we don't need to check every face in every frame of video. If Mina materialized somewhere and it was caught on camera, there'll be a sequence where she's not there in one frame, and *is* there in the next. So right now the cops are writing software to compare each frame with the one before, and flag any major changes."

"Smart," Alia said. "But those films always have a little digital clock in the corner, right? So *that's* going to change every second. They'll have to mask out those bits."

"Yeah, Kenya already thought of that." Danny sipped from his water. "Plans have changed, Alia. The Big Fish is coming back in a few hours—we're going to leave you and Grant behind to continue the search. The rest of us are going back to Sakkara."

"But what can you do there? I mean, I want to go back but Mina disappeared from here. And there's no point searching for the guy who killed Butler. If Colin couldn't find him, we're not going to be any use."

"Impervia's working with this new guy to coordinate everything. Lance McKendrick. He's supposed to be some sort of genius."

Alia made a face. "Well, great. Working with geniuses has turned out real well so far, hasn't it? Victor Cross and Yvonne come to mind."

"This guy Lance is different. He's supposed to have a way with people." Danny shrugged. "I dunno. Warren trusts him, that's good enough for me. And he's got a plan, but they're not saying what it is."

Cassandra wasn't comfortable being alone with Stephanie Cord in the helicopter. She had been twelve years old when her ability to read minds developed, and in the four years since, she had become accustomed to casually scanning people's minds when she spoke to them.

She was aware that it was an intrusion into their privacy, but she couldn't stop herself. Besides, it saved time.

It didn't work perfectly with Stephanie—better than with many people, but not as well as she'd have liked. She could pick up some surface thoughts and emotions, enough to know that Stephanie didn't fully trust her.

Cassandra understood that: Stephanie's previous encounters with telepaths had not been positive.

She watched as Stephanie expertly manipulated the controls. "I still can't believe they let you fly this thing on your own."

Stephanie smiled. "Me either."

The copter was a reconditioned Alouette II, fast and small, and Stephanie handled it with ease, but Cassandra felt exposed inside the almost completely transparent canopy. Stephanie had assured her that it was bullet-proof, but Cassandra would have preferred a more solid-looking craft. This one looked like it had been built by someone who had heard of helicopters but never actually seen one.

Before they left Sakkara, Impervia had told Cassandra that when this was over she'd be given some time off. "A couple of weeks. You can stay with your mom in the Substation. How's that sound?"

"The Substation" was the name given to the large underground complex in which many of the former prisoners from Lieberstan were housed. Situated in the heart of Idaho, it had been designed as a particle accelerator but abandoned part-way to completion when the funding ran out. After the Trutopian war the US Government had purchased it and converted it into spacious living apartments. Cassandra liked the place a lot. It was practically a small city, albeit one with only a single circular street, and being underground meant that it was sheltered from the elements.

She had lived her entire life under the dome of the prison in Lieberstan, so not being able to see the sky didn't bother Cassandra, and she loved the fact that her mother liked the place. She had never seen her mother happy before.

Most of the inhabitants of the Substation seemed to enjoy their new lives. They were free to come and go as they pleased, each family had its own apartment, and there was always plenty of food. The government agent who oversaw the project—a short woman with gray hair and glasses, who always seemed to be wearing the same business suit—had told them that at some point in the future they would be expected to work for their accommodation, but right now everything was free, in return for a few favors.

The first favor had been for Cassandra's mother to allow her to join the New Heroes. Cassandra wasn't sure how she felt about that: she was now effectively supporting the whole community.

In the copter's cockpit beside her, Stephanie nudged Cassandra's arm. "Three minutes. You OK?"

Cassandra nodded.

There were advantages to working with the New Heroes, and chief among these was Razor. She liked him a lot, and she knew that he liked her. But he was four years older than her so he still thought of her as a kid.

Butler had liked her, too, but that hadn't been mutual. She'd been able to tolerate him because she'd always known what he was going to say, but he'd been too wrapped up in his own problems to allow himself to get close to the others.

And now he's dead, she thought. What bothered her most about his death was that it didn't really bother her *that* much: in the platinum mine sudden deaths had been quite common. Cassandra feared that she had become immune to death.

She wondered if she should tell the others what Butler had really thought of them, about how proud he'd felt to be working with them. How he had admired and respected them, and desperately wanted them to accept him. But he had always found himself saying the wrong thing, making comments that in his head had seemed clever and funny, but when they came out they sounded cruel.

She could tell them how Butler often despised himself for his selfishness, and how he had been overwhelmed with his jealousy of Razor, who had come from a broken home, had practically no education, no superhuman abilities, had been a borderline criminal, and yet the others loved him.

Colin and Danny's relationships with their fathers had been what hurt Butler the most. Cassandra knew that Butler's father had loved him, that wasn't the problem. The problem was that Butler had never learned how to return that love. He'd fought his father on almost everything, frequently fighting just because he didn't know any other way to behave.

And now he's dead, she thought again. *He's never going to have a chance to grow up.*

Ahead, Cassandra saw that they were approaching a large complex of stone-walled buildings completely surrounding an open courtyard. The buildings' roofs were flat, their edges rimmed with dense layers of razor-wire. A dozen large, automatic weapons had swiveled around to target the copter.

Into her radio, Stephanie said, "Base 228, this is kilo-niner coming in to nest. Clearance code zulu x-ray eight-zero."

The radio clicked into life. "Code acknowledged and verified, kilo-niner. Set down between the beacons and shut off your engines. Your transport will be secured when you disembark."

"What's that mean?" Cassandra asked.

Stephanie said, "They're going to attach really strong cables to the copter when we get out. Just in case something happens and some of the prisoners try to use it to escape."

The auto-guns continued to track the copter as it came in to land, and Cassandra looked around to see that every window facing the courtyard was occupied by two or more armed guards.

The copter set down with a slight bump in the middle of the courtyard, and Cassandra unclipped her seat harness as Stephanie shut everything down.

"All right," Stephanie said. "Here's the deal. There's a very specific prisoner in this place and you're the only one who can help. You probably won't see any of the others, but if you do, don't talk to them, and—if you can help it—don't scan the minds of the guards." She unclipped her own harness. "But you probably *won't* be able to prevent that, so I have to warn you that whatever you learn here has to stay secret, understood?"

Cassandra nodded. "OK."

"This place is home to some of the country's most dangerous criminals. Serial killers, rapists, terrorists, arsonists, poisoners... The very worst of the worst. Cassandra, you really don't want to see into *their* minds. So focus on the task, do only what I tell you, and you should be all right."

They climbed out of the copter to see a man wearing a doctor's coat approaching them. From the sides, four uniformed guards were dragging thick steel cables toward the copter.

"Miss Cord, always a pleasure."

As Stephanie shook his hand, Platt peered past her toward the copter. "Huh. When did *you* get your pilot's license?"

"I won't tell if you don't. Cassandra, this is Doctor Carter Platt. He's in charge here."

Platt smiled. "Well, I keep the place running, but I hardly think I'm in charge." He inclined his head back the way he had come. "I'm assuming that time, like always, is short."

As they strode toward the doorway, Doctor Platt said to Cassandra, "Welcome to The Cloister. A little place where we keep the bad guys away from everyone else. So you're a telepath? Excellent. You're one of a very small number. There's been a good number of *em*paths, of course, but genuine telepathy is rare." He held the door open for them. "A gift to be savored."

The inside of the prison was dark and damp. Cassandra saw Stephanie wrinkle her nose at the sharp stink of urine mixed with the cloying odor of mold, but the smell didn't bother Cassandra. She'd grown up in worse conditions than this.

They walked along the door-lined corridor and Doctor Platt put his hand on Cassandra's shoulder. "I'm sure Ms Cord here has already mentioned this, but—"

Cassandra said, "She did. I'm doing my best."

The thoughts around her, emanating from unseen prisoners behind the steel doors, seemed to be pressing against her mind. It reminded her of a horror movie they had watched in Sakkara a few months earlier. There was a scene in which the heroes were trapped in a bar as hundreds of zombies crowded around the doors and windows, desperate to find a way in.

The prisoners' minds were sharp and cold, venomous and barbed. She forced herself to block them out, to hold back the terrifying images and sounds.

As they passed a cell close to the end of the corridor, Cassandra stopped. "Wait!"

Stephanie and the doctor turned back to her. "What is it?" Platt asked.

She pointed to the cell door. "The man in there. He's innocent."

"You can read his mind even through the cell door?"

"Yes. He didn't do it. He was arrested for murder. Lots of murders. But he didn't do *any* of them! You have to let him go."

Platt gave her a wan smile. "I'm sorry, but you're wrong. He murdered fourteen people that we know of. Probably a lot more."

"No, he didn't! It was a set-up!"

"He *thinks* it was a set-up. He's insane, Cassandra."

"Then he should be in a hospital!"

"He was. That's where he murdered his three most recent victims. We have security film of him doing it. You don't want to see that. At first we thought that he had multiple personalities, but eventually we realized it wasn't that simple. He modifies his own memory. He can commit the most brutal of crimes and then erase his memories of them and replace them with memories of innocent activities. Trust me. This is not an ordinary prison where sometimes innocent people are convicted. Everyone here is absolutely, indisputably guilty." His voice a little softer, he added, "This is not like the prison in Lieberstan. I promise you."

She looked into Doctor Platt's own mind then, and saw that

he was telling the truth. *Or he believes it to be true, at least*, she thought. Then she touched on his memories of the prisoners, and pulled out as images of horrible crimes they'd committed came rushing at her. "OK." She took a deep breath and held it for a second. "OK. I'm sorry."

"No need to be sorry," Stephanie said. "Come on. We'll get this over with."

Cassandra took a last glance back at the cell door, then resumed following the doctor and Stephanie.

She forced her mind closed to all other thoughts until they stopped outside a heavy steel door that was at the end of a corridor all on its own.

Doctor Platt said, "The prisoner is extremely strong, and unbelievably dangerous. Behind the door there's a wall of transparent aluminum, eighteen inches thick, so you'll be safe. If anything does happen, the cell will be instantly flooded with enough halothane vapor to knock out an elephant. Ready?"

Cassandra already knew what she was going to find: the doctor's mind was now broadcasting it so loud that she couldn't block it if she tried.

Platt turned a large key in the door's lock, and grunted as he pulled the door open. Inside, behind the glass, a thin, pale, black-haired girl with dark-rimmed eyes was sitting on a bed, surrounded by plain white walls. She raised her head, and Cassandra saw that the girls' throat was covered in a mass of white and red scars.

"This is Yvonne Duval," Stephanie said. "I know you've heard of her."

Cassandra swallowed. Yvonne was Mina's sister, cloned by Ragnarök from his own DNA. She had grown up in Sakkara, where she discovered that she had the ability to control other people by simply telling them what to do.

Yvonne had sided with Victor Cross, helped him to infiltrate Sakkara, then fled with Solomon Cord as her prisoner. After Cross died—or *supposedly* died: people seemed to be less certain about that now than they had been a year ago—Yvonne had taken control of the entire Trutopian organization. In a live television broadcast watched by almost every Trutopian she used her power to order them to fight and kill everyone who wasn't a member of their organization. Because of Yvonne's actions, hundreds of thousands of people had died.

When she'd been captured by Stephanie Cord and Renata Soliz, Yvonne had been forced to make further broadcasts ordering the Trutopians to stand down. Then an unknown assassin had tried to kill her. The shot had torn through Yvonne's throat. She would never be able to speak again. Never be able to use her powers to force others to obey her commands.

Doctor Platt said, "Yvonne, this is Cassandra Szalkowska. You two need to have a little chat."

Yvonne looked at the doctor with one eyebrow raised, as if to say, "How?"

Stephanie said, "Go ahead, Cassandra. Tell her everything."

Cassandra looked at Yvonne, and projected her thoughts. *Your sister has gone missing. She was in Berlin, working with Danny Cooper and Warren Wagner. Helping to clear up the damage your war caused.*

Yvonne's thoughts came back: "You're a telepath. And you think that means we'll be able to communicate but I won't be able to control you."

143

I know your power worked through your voice, and you no longer have one. And I think we both know that if it looks like you can control me, the guards here would put a bullet in my brain before they let you force me to do anything.

Yvonne thought, "If they have questions, they could just give me a pencil and some paper. I can still write."

But you can write lies. You can't lie to me.

Yvonne shrugged. "True. So my sister's missing. I assume there's no trace of her, otherwise you wouldn't be desperate enough to come to me. How do you think I can help?"

You know her better than anyone. How could she have disappeared? She can only teleport a few miles at a time. Cassandra told Yvonne everything she knew about Mina's disappearance, and when she was done, Yvonne smiled and nodded.

"Seems to me that she didn't just vanish. And she's too smart to be taken by surprise. She was led away. Someone persuaded her to go with them. They fooled her at least long enough for them to disable her powers in some way. Which means that she's unconscious, because if she was awake she could teleport herself out of danger. So it's likely that whoever took her doesn't want her for her powers. They want her for something else. Or they just want her out of the way because they're planning something else and they really don't want to have to deal with a teleporter."

That makes sense, Cassandra thought. *If we can work out how they got her, we'll be further along the road to finding where she is.*

"I'm sure your people have already thought of this, but I'll say it anyway. Get a map. Draw a line between Berlin and the point where Mina's cellphone was recovered, then extend the line and see where it leads you. Their destination was somewhere along that path. Though you have to take into account that they'd be avoiding military installations and high-density population centers."

Cassandra nodded. *They've done that. It didn't help.*

"All right. If you plan to lead someone into a trap, it has to be baited with something they want. What did Mina want most?"

You tell me: you knew her best.

"It's tempting to think that what she wanted most was for me to return to her, but I doubt that. She had a major crush on Danny Cooper." Yvonne smiled again. "But I don't see how that helps. If someone disguised himself as Danny, it wouldn't fool Mina. Even the greatest shape-shifter in the world wouldn't know how to make his aura look like someone else's."

Cassandra thought, *Look, there's something else. Victor Cross. What if...*

"What if he's not dead? That thought has occurred to me. I was speaking to him on the phone when his plane was attacked. I heard the missiles strike. If he's not dead, then it means he deliberately betrayed me. He set me up. It means he knew exactly how I would react when I believed he was dead. And that means he wanted me to trigger the war."

Isn't that possible?

"Yes. It is. Cross is smarter than I am. And it could be true. I don't *want* it to be true, but only a fool would ignore a possibility just because she doesn't like it. If Cross did set me up, then we have to assume that everything that's happened since is part of his plan."

Do you know what that plan was?

"I thought I did. He wanted to control the world. He used to say that if the humans had spent their time and resources working together instead of fighting each other they'd have colonized a good portion of the galaxy by now." Yvonne shrugged. "I don't know if there's any truth to *that*. War drives technology forward. If we don't have enemies, there's no impetus for us to find better ways to kill them." She shook her head. "No, Victor *must* be dead. I was his strongest ally—I can't imagine any plan he might have had that would make sacrificing me the right thing to do."

What was that you just said about fools ignoring possibilities?

At that, Yvonne laughed silently. "If you do discover that Cross is still alive, get me out of here and I'll help you track him down. And I'll kill him for you, at no extra charge."

Cassandra watched her for a moment. *Why did you do it? Why did you betray the New Heroes? Don't you care that hundreds of thousands of people were killed?*

"No, I don't care. Call it solipsism, if you like."

What's solipsism?

"It's the belief that only oneself is real, that all others are... just background artists, playing their roles without any thoughts or agenda of their own."

Is that how you see things?

"No. But it's how people *think* I see things. I don't care about all those deaths because in the long run everyone dies. Everyone. They just got their buckets kicked for them a little early. I've saved them years of worrying about their jobs and families. They'll never feel pain again, never go hungry. I've given each of them their own utopia."

Cassandra looked away. *You're sick. Twisted. And you're never getting out of here. They should execute you for what you've done!*

"Yes, they probably should. But they won't. They're too weak, and I'm too useful." Yvonne raised her bare feet onto the bed and wrapped her arms around her calves, rested her chin on her knees. "I think we're done here, for now. But I'm sure you'll be back. Tell Platt I want more books. And a TV or a radio would be nice."

Cassandra turned to Stephanie. "That's all we're going to get out of her."

"Anything useful?"

"Maybe." To the doctor, she said, "She'd like more books, and a radio or TV."

"Of course she would." He looked in at Yvonne. "Would you like a zebra too? How about a hovercraft? Or a complete set of tools to help you break out of here? Consider yourself lucky you've got a bed."

On the walk back to the helicopter, Cassandra told Stephanie of Yvonne's theory that Mina had somehow been tricked into leaving Berlin.

They climbed on board as the guards were unlocking the copter.

"You think she could be right?" Cassandra asked.

"I think so. Mina's a bit flighty, but she's not an idiot. If someone attacked her she'd just teleport away." Stephanie clipped on her seat harness, and told Cassandra to do the same.

As the copter rose into the air, Stephanie said, "You can't tell the others that Yvonne is there, understood?"

"Sure. I'm a telepath. I understand the importance of

secrets."

"Good." She banked the copter to the left, heading south-east. "Because it *is* a secret, not a mystery. Mysteries are designed to be explored and shared. Secrets are meant to be kept. Now get some rest. Flight time's a good four hours."

Cassandra rested her head back against the co-pilot's chair and tried to fall asleep, but her thoughts kept returning to the meeting with Yvonne.

The coldness of Yvonne's mind disturbed her. The girl was almost totally selfish. The only concern she'd shown was for her sister, and even that had been mild, about as much concern as an ordinary person might have for a pet belonging to a distant relative that they'd never met.

How does someone get like that? Cassandra wondered. In the prison camp in Lieberstan, there had been many selfish people, but that had mostly been out of desperation and fear. Yvonne didn't seem to be afraid of anything. And she appeared to be almost without emotion. Aside from her slight worry about Mina, she had only become emotional at the thought that Victor Cross had betrayed her.

Fifteen minutes into the return journey, Cassandra was startled from her doze by Stephanie's panic-filled voice.

"Sakkara, this is kilo-niner! I'm seeing an incoming craft, no ID. It's moving fast and... We're under attack!"

Cassandra looked around wildly. "What is it? Where?"

"Directly behind us! Hold onto something—I've got to set her down. We've no armaments and whatever's coming is a lot faster than we are!"

The copter bucked and swayed, and Cassandra felt her stomach tighten as they suddenly dropped.

"Sakkara, come in!" Stephanie yelled into the radio. "No good—I think we're being jammed! Can you sense the thoughts of the pilot?"

Cassandra reached out with her mind. "No... Yes, there's something there. Two of them. They're men. Soldiers... Mercenaries. They've been ordered to capture us!"

The copter lurched again, a sickening drop that sent Cassandra's heart racing. Through the cockpit glass she could see the ground approaching far too quickly.

"Under your seat!" Stephanie said. "There's a survival pack. Take it out and hold on tight. It's got water, rations, a flare-gun, radio and a compass. If I don't make it, you find a way to get back to Sakkara!"

Cassandra pulled the bulky canvas bag out from under the seat, then glanced again through the glass. "We're crashing!"

"Just hold tight and don't panic. I've trained for this. Close your eyes if it helps."

Cassandra closed her eyes, and seconds later the copter slammed heavily into the ground.

Stephanie woke to find Cassandra dragging her across the ground, away from the crashed Alouette.

She didn't know how long she'd been unconscious, but was sure it couldn't have been more than a few seconds. A minute at most.

The copter had hit the ground hard enough that the landing struts on the port side had collapsed from the impact.

Its rotor blades had been sheered off, its engine was belching oily black smoke—it was not going to fly again.

"You're awake!" Cassandra said. "Are you hurt?"

Stephanie pushed herself to her feet. "Bruises, cuts. Nothing broken. You?"

"I'm OK. Steph, we need to *run*—they're coming!"

A gruff voice behind her said, "No, we're here."

Stephanie slowly turned around.

A large man wearing camouflage fatigues was staring at them down the barrel of an assault rifle. "Hands where I can see them. Where's the pilot?"

"*I'm* the pilot."

"Sure you are, kid. Shango, what do you see?" The man paused for a second, then nodded. "Got it." To Stephanie, he said, "My partner says it's a two-seater. You're both about fifteen? Sixteen? Got to say, this isn't what we were expecting."

Stephanie glanced toward Cassandra, who was frowning in concentration at the armed man. She muttered, "Can you read him?"

Cassandra nodded, and whispered, "He's confused. They were hired anonymously. Doesn't yet know where they're supposed to take me."

"Just you?"

The man lowered his gun a little and strode toward them. "Move apart. Slowly. At least five meters. Eyes on me at all times. No talking."

Stephanie moved to the side. *He's good*, she thought. *He's done this before.*

"Both of you, get down on your knees. Hands behind your head. Interlace your fingers."

The man stopped in front of Cassandra. "You. I know what you can do with that superhuman brain. My partner is watching you. Try anything and he will kill your friend."

As he slung his rifle over his shoulder Stephanie risked another glance at Cassandra, who was staring intently at the mercenary. *Trying to read his mind...*

The man turned to watch Stephanie as he clicked a set of handcuffs into place on Cassandra's left wrist, then pulled her arms down behind her back and cuffed her right wrist. "All right. Stand up, start walking. Don't look back."

"Where are you taking her?" Stephanie asked.

The mercenary unclipped a gun from the holster on his hip, and aimed it at Stephanie.

Her sense of relief that the weapon was not a pistol but a taser lasted less than a second before he pulled the trigger.

Chapter 15

The ChampionShip was half-way across the Atlantic Ocean when it suddenly surged forward. Renata knew what that meant; Façade, at the controls, had ramped the craft up to top speed by activating its rarely-used jets.

"What is it?" Warren called out.

"Gimme a minute," Façade called back.

Sitting next to Renata, Danny said, "This isn't good." To Kenya, he explained, "We never use the jets unless there's an emergency—the antigrav engines don't leave any trace someone could follow, but the jets do."

"What sort of a speed increase are you talking about?" Kenya asked.

"Four or five per cent, at best," Renata answered.

"That's not a lot."

Façade climbed out of his seat. "Autopilot's on. OK. Bad news. Stephanie took Cassandra out on a job. They were on their way back when her copter came under attack by an unknown aircraft. Steph was forced to land. Two men— mercenaries, Steph says. They took Cassandra, left Steph unconscious. She's OK, no major injuries."

The silence that followed was broken by Renata: "Three down. They're picking us off one at a time."

Danny asked, "Why did they send ordinary men to get Cassie when they could have sent that guy Shadow?"

Kenya replied, "Because they wanted her alive, maybe?"

Renata shook her head. "You don't capture a telepath— they'd be able to read all your secrets."

"Our ETA at Sakkara is three hours. Impervia called in the air force to pick up Steph. They're taking her back to Sakkara."

Kenya asked Renata, "Can your jetpacks get you there any faster?"

"No. We have greater speed than the Fish but we don't have the range."

"Then all of you who *have* jetpacks, I suggest you get out and push."

Everyone looked at her.

"I'm serious."

Façade said, "She's right. That's smart. And it'll help."

In Sakkara, Colin Wagner and Lance McKendrick sat in the machine room watching Razor at work. They looked up to see Stephanie Cord entering the room.

"Still with us?" Lance asked.

"I'm not dead yet," Stephanie said. She flexed her right arm, and grimaced. "It still hurts, though."

Colin said, "I was worried. A bit."

With a smile, Stephanie said, "I know." Then her smile faded. "There was nothing I could do to stop them taking Cassie."

Lance said, "But they didn't want you dead. That's something, at least. Cassandra's tracker blinked out about four miles north of the crash-site." Before the others could respond, he added, "Yes, I planted a tracking device on Cassandra. And on you too, Stephanie—that's how we got to you so fast. Your assailants either found Cassandra's tracker or they're blocking its signals."

Colin said, "You don't seem very concerned about her!"

Lance gave them both a reassuring smile. "We'll find her, I

promise. The fact that they took her alive is a good sign. And she's a telepath... That makes her far too valuable to kill. It's my guess that her captors just want her out of the way before they make their next move. Telepaths are notoriously hard to attack because they can see it coming. I've had some experience in that area." Lance nodded toward Razor. "The kid knows his stuff."

Stephanie nodded. "He does. Well, he was trained by the best. My dad. Solomon Cord. You knew him too, right?"

"Oh yeah. I knew him."

"You didn't like him?" Stephanie asked, her eyes narrowing.

Lance smiled. "Stephanie, I *loved* him. Sol was the coolest, greatest guy I've ever known. After my parents died I struck out on my own. *That* was a mistake. I should have stayed with your dad. Don't ever get to thinking you know better than your folks, kids. I know that's a trait that all young people have, but it's an illusion."

"What about you?" Colin asked. "Do you have children? Married?"

"There's been a good number of girls I've managed to avoid marrying. And one or two who've been lucky enough to avoid marrying me." Lance smiled, then swiveled in his chair to face Colin. "Joshua Dalton believes that Victor Cross is still alive."

"I know."

"What do *you* think?"

Colin shrugged. "If anyone was smart enough to fake his death and get away with it, it'd be Cross. Sorry, Mister McKendrick, but why *are* you here? You were never a superhero, were you?"

"What do I bring to the game? A little experience, maybe,

plus my innate skills. One of which I will tell you about in exactly three minutes. What time is it now?"

Colin looked at his wrist. "Don't know. I must have left my watch in my room."

Lance pulled back the sleeve of his jacket. "It's OK, I have mine here."

"But that's *my* watch!"

Lance unfastened the strap and held up the wristwatch. "Misdirection. A very simple trick. Most magic tricks don't take place when the audience thinks they do. The work is done before. The trick is practically over by the time the audience sees it. Here, give me your hand."

As Lance put the watch back on Colin's wrist, he nodded over toward Razor. "I'll teach you how to do it. You can try it on your friend."

Colin glanced at Razor. "I don't know. He's pretty smart. So it's like with card tricks, right? You have it all set up in advance so that you know exactly which card is going to be chosen?"

"Exactly. That's what Victor Cross is doing, you know. He knows the rules—or, rather, he's invented his *own* rules—and you guys are the audience."

Stephanie asked, "So *you* think he's alive?"

"I'm certain. There are only two ways to beat a shyster. Number one, you learn all the rules so that you know what's coming next. Number two, you force him to play *your* game. Cross is not only alive, but he and his pal Evan Laurie are, like, ten steps ahead of us. Are those three minutes up yet, Colin?"

Colin looked at his wrist again. "Oh come on! How did you do it *that* time?"

"You saw me putting the watch back on your wrist?"

"We both did," Stephanie said.

"No, you didn't. For a couple of seconds as I was closing the clasp the watch was completely covered by my hands. I pulled the straps tight enough that Colin felt like it was fastened. That feeling of pressure on the skin lasts for a little while. And just as he was putting his arm down I made you guys look over at Razor. Neither of you actually checked to *see* that the watch was still there."

"Because he thought he could still feel it?" Stephanie said. "I get it."

Lance grinned. "Yep. If our files on Victor Cross are accurate, the man has been playing you from day one. He gets himself noticed by Max Dalton, persuades Max to hire him. He learns about Quantum's visions of the future, and of Max's involvement in Ragnarök's power-stripping machine. It's easy for him to appeal to Max's vanity, because Max desperately wants to be the guy who saves the world. So Cross uses the money and resources he steals from Max to infiltrate the Trutopians, because he knows that with the right person at the helm the Trutopian organization will be *huge*. And bit by bit, all the pieces of Cross's plan fall into place."

"It can't work that way," Colin said. "There were things he couldn't anticipate. You can't plan for stuff if you don't know what's going to happen."

"Sure you can. You make big, long-range plans at the start, and then you work like crazy to make sure they come about. Cross seems to have the ability to work on a lot of different things at the same time. Look, this is how it goes... Stephanie, think of a number between one and six. Inclusive."

Stephanie shrugged. "Five."

"A good number. Now, turn around. On the bench behind you is a mug. Lift the mug and take a look. And be careful—the mug is full. You don't want cold tea spilling all over you."

Stephanie reached over to the bench and lifted up the mug. There was a small folded piece of paper under it. She unfolded the paper, and read the words aloud. "I knew you'd pick 5."

"Let's see how smart you are. How did I do that?" Lance asked. "Colin? You care to guess?"

Colin shrugged. Lance couldn't reach the bench from where he was sitting, not unless he had telekinetic powers. *No, that can't be it*, Colin thought. And then he remembered that when they entered the room Lance had asked Razor to explain exactly what he was working on. *He took notes*, Colin remembered. He smiled. *But he wasn't taking notes. He was setting up the trick!*

Lance had said, "The trick is practically over by the time the audience sees it."

Colin stood up and examined the bench. Next to where the mug had been was a slim folder. He opened it, and inside there was a note with the words, "I knew you'd pick 3."

"But that's cheating!" Stephanie said.

"No, it's clever," Colin said. "He hid a different note for each number. And he manipulated the conversation so that he'd have a chance to bring up the trick." To Lance, he said, "So you're saying *that's* how Victor Cross works?"

"For some of what he does, yes. At any given time he'll have one primary plan and several secondary ones. If the primary plan looks like it's not going to work out, he'll switch focus to the next most likely one." Lance sat back in the chair, and stretched out his good leg. "That's what we have to do, kids. So far you guys have been reacting, letting Cross steer this boat while you just follow. But we have to change that."

"What are you saying, exactly?"

"I'm saying that Shadow told you they had something that would... what was it you said? 'Render *you* about as threatening as a kitten.' And you're sure he emphasized the word 'you'?"

"That's right," Colin said. "Definitely."

"Cross understands how superhuman powers work. He knows how to wipe everyone's abilities. Since he hasn't done that we have to assume that he doesn't *want* to. Yet. But there's no doubt he wants you out of the way... And he knows you inside-out, knows exactly what it is that makes your powers work. After all, he's created multiple copies of you. Plenty of material for experimentation there. So I'm going to take a guess that Cross has figured out a way to strip only *your* powers and leave everyone else's intact."

"Oh man... I hope you're wrong."

"Me too." Lance tapped the side of his head with his index finger. "Need to let the old cauliflower ponder on that one for a while, see if there's a way we can turn that into an advantage. We'll certainly need all the advantages we can get, if we're going to take this to the next level."

"What do you mean?"

Stephanie said, "*I* know what he means. He's saying that it's time to stop reacting. It's time that we brought the fight to Victor Cross."

Chapter 16

Wearing a towel around her neck and with her hair still wet from the shower, Renata opened the doors to Sakkara's gymnasium and saw that she was the last to arrive.

Colin was carrying a steel bench over to one wall, while the newcomer—McKendrick—instructed him on exactly where to put it.

McKendrick leaned on Colin's shoulder as he stepped onto the bench. "Find a spot to sit, Ms Soliz. Quick as you can, huh?"

Brawn said, "Now you sound like a teacher."

"I was, for a while." McKendrick said. "Taught a semester of computer skills in a high-school in Oklahoma, until someone checked my qualifications and discovered that they were fake."

Renata sat on the floor next to Danny, then Colin came over and sat between herself and Stephanie.

McKendrick saw this and smiled. "Ah, young love! See how they blush and fidget—it's enchanting." He straightened up as he looked around the room. "We don't have time for 'enchanting.' We don't have time for young love or old love or the petty squabbles and grudges that inevitably form in teams this size. From this point on, I don't want to hear, 'But I miss my mommy' or 'I don't like the color of my uniform' or 'he's sitting in my chair' or anything of that nature. You people have been at war with Victor Cross and he's winning because, until now, he was the only one who knew that."

Warren Wagner called out, "That's unfair, Lance!"

Without looking in his direction, Lance said, "Warren, I'm sorry, but this isn't your show any more. Your days of being the big hero are over. That goes for *all* of the adults here, with one exception. But I'll get to that in time. We don't know where Cross is, because we haven't looked. Why *would* we look for someone we believed to be dead? But that's the crux of the problem. We believed him to be dead because a body with his DNA was found. Who shot down his plane? Who examined the wreckage to determine that it really was shot down and wasn't just a staged crash? How could someone as smart as Cross put himself in a position where he *could* be shot down? Cross is alive, and until someone can prove to me otherwise, I'll continue to believe that."

Renata took Danny's hand and gently squeezed it. He glanced back for a moment, and she could see that he was worried.

If McKendrick is right, Renata thought, *then we can't stop Cross. If he made one clone as powerful as Colin, he'll have made more. Could be hundreds, for all we know.*

Lance continued, "Last year Cross's people practically set the world on fire. Luckily Renata Soliz was there to put it out. What she did scared the heck out of everyone on the planet in the process, but it worked. So well done, Renata. Your prize is that you get a gold star, your photo up on the Employee of the Year board, and the chance to keep fighting. I know you don't have your powers any more, but you've shown you can operate the Paragon armor so you're still on the team. And that's another thing we'll be getting back to. Stephanie Cord? Front and center, Ms Cord. That means I want you to come up here."

Stephanie got to her feet, grumbling, "I know what it means." She walked up to Lance's bench.

"Your dad was my personal hero and my best friend. That

almost makes me your brother. And I had a crush on your aunt, too. So that nearly makes me your uncle, or something. Your job is to make sure that Uncle Lance doesn't get killed. Are you OK with that? Say 'Yes, Uncle Lance,' because you don't have a choice."

Stephanie nodded. "Uh, sure."

"Close enough. Now, you don't have your father's technical skills, but Razor does. You'll also be working with him. I want one of your fine suits of armor specially modified to fit me. Bear in mind that a large portion of my left leg is probably still in a landfill in Cambodia, so some sort of robotic replacement would be nice." He handed her a folded sheet of paper, and said, "Here are the specs I came up with. It's a bit rough, but you'll make sense of it." He nodded to Razor. "Time to get back to work, kid." He paused for a moment. "I don't mean, 'When you feel like it' or 'After this meeting is done.' I mean right now. And don't worry about losing progress on the big machine, because I'm recalling all the other techs from the Substation."

As Stephanie and Razor were leaving the room, Façade said, "The techs are civilians. You're putting them in harm's way."

"I know that," Lance said. He turned to Colin. "Col, you and Renata are going hunting."

"What will we be looking for?" Renata asked.

"Colin knows. We talked about it earlier. But don't go just yet. Danny? See me after class. I've got a job for you, too." Lance took a few deep breaths. "All right, folks. Here's the plan. The enemy has taken Cassandra and Mina. We don't yet know why, but we do know how they achieved it, which is because we were careless. I should not have sent Stephanie and Cassandra out on their own. My mistake. I won't make that one again.

Aside from Colin and Renata's hunting trip, from now on we do our best to stick together. It'll make it a lot harder for Cross's people to take us out. In the past, you've been spreading yourselves too thin. That's going to work in our favor now, because it's a pattern that you've established and people like Victor Cross love patterns. They make people predictable, and if you're predictable, you're giving your enemy an advantage. You know the old line about turning up for a knife-fight with a gun? That's what he's been doing. To continue that same analogy, next time Cross declares a knife-fight, we don't show up at all. Instead, we go to his house and burn it to the ground. Am I making myself clear?"

Façade said, "You are. We play dirty."

Lance grinned. "Spot on. We play dirty, because that's the only way the bad guy plays. If it comes to it, we will lie, cheat and steal to make sure we get the upper hand. In the past couple of days he's killed one of us, taken two, and seriously wounded two more. So we stand united against him. I know you're all concerned about putting the world to rights after the Trutopian war, and repairing the damage to your reputations. But that's peanuts. They're distractions."

He looked at Danny. "Yes, it's very, very sad that people are saying that *you* somehow caused the war. Time to get over it and grow up."

He turned toward Warren. "In Berlin, you encountered another band of Trutopians, right? They're another distraction. I know you want to catch them all, but you have to let it go for now."

Warren said, "Lance, they're killers. If we don't stop them, who will?"

"The police. The armies. You remember them? The people who are *paid* to stop killers. Your band of Trutopians infiltrated the city as far as Kulturforum because someone is letting them in. Someone paid by Cross, perhaps. You've been mopping up the water instead of plugging the leaks. And mopping up the water is not our job. We're superheroes, not janitors."

"If we don't keep going after the Trutopians, innocent people will be killed," Warren said.

"I know. I don't like it either. But stopping them is a task that others can and should be doing. Not us. We stick together, we train, we arm ourselves, and then we go after Cross."

Colin said, "Lance, you keep saying that we have to stick together, but you left Alia and Grant in Berlin!"

Lance looked down. "Yeah. I know that too."

Façade said, "Because they're the weakest, right? The least effective members of the team."

"Right."

Renata jumped to her feet. "No way. Seriously, you can't *do* that!"

"We have to, Renata. This is war. If we're going to stop Victor Cross, we're not all going to get out of this alive."

Danny stood up next to Renata. "What are you saying? That the others were left behind because you want Cross to focus on them instead of us?"

Lance nodded. "Yes. Don't say anything to Stephanie, but her sister and Grant are decoys. They're bait."

In his base in the Arctic, Victor Cross smiled. "Now, *that* guy's a challenge. I like the way he thinks. Wonder where they dug him up?"

Shadow cracked his knuckles. "This is all great fun," he said, his voice laced with sarcasm, "but we should be on the attack, not sitting around listening in."

"We have to wait until your brothers are up to speed. Besides, the New Heroes are a crackle on the soundtrack, nothing more. They're not actually important. And they're hardly a danger to us, now that we have you. You really think you can take them all on?"

"With Tuan, yeah. I've already beaten Colin, and he's the strongest. The others won't be a problem. Not even Cooper. He's faster than me, but fast is no good when you're dead. The other superhumans... There's the African girl, Kenya."

"*Chinese*-African," Cross said.

"Whatever. She's nowhere near a match for me. Maybe Cassandra could eventually learn how to read my mind and anticipate my moves, if she was still with them. Renata Soliz lost her powers, and the rest are just humans in body-armor. No danger at all."

"What about Brawn?"

"He's not a superhuman any more. He doesn't have the strength he once did."

Cross got to his feet. "He's still extremely strong, and he has a lot of experience, so don't underestimate him. Or *any* of them. Now let's go check on our prisoner."

Cross pulled on his padded jacket and walked out of the room, with Shadow flying behind him. At the end of the long, sloping tunnel they emerged into the base's main cavern, where Evan Laurie was serving the other boys their evening meal.

Laurie looked up. "Are you eating with us today, Victor?"

"Depends. What's in the pot?"

"Stew. Again. Made with re-hydrated vegetables and baby food that's well past its sell-by date. It's time we took a shopping trip."

Victor looked at the seven boys sitting around the long table. Apart from the length of their hair and a few inches in height, they were identical. Even he sometimes found it hard to tell them apart. If everything had happened according to the original plan, the boys would still be toddlers. Cross had known that the artificial growth-accelerants would help them to age more quickly than normal humans, but he hadn't anticipated it would work so vigorously, and for so long. *Not a mistake*, he told himself. *An unexpected opportunity.*

The biggest problem they faced was the shortage of supplies. Nine teenage boys consumed a lot of food, though that problem had eased a little when Shadow, Tuan and Roman came into their powers. Like their progenitor, they mostly fed off heat and light energy. *Solar-powered people*, Cross thought. *That would really simplify things.* "Shopping trip," he mused aloud. "Maybe that's not a bad idea. But not today. Today, you'll all be pleased to learn, we're doing another round of tests."

A chorus of "Aw no!" erupted from the boys.

"Has to be done," Cross said. He nodded to Shadow. "Let's go."

They left Laurie and the boys complaining, and passed through another corridor. They were half-way along when Shadow moved in front of Victor.

Victor smiled at that. Shadow's programming was so ingrained that he didn't even need to think about it. There was possible danger ahead, so Shadow automatically went into bodyguard mode.

The corridor led to a series of metal gantries and stairways that surrounded the second-largest cavern in the glacier. Shadow drifted ahead of Victor at all times as they descended, constantly watching the enormous pods below. The twenty-four pods were ten feet tall, six in diameter.

They had once served as artificial wombs for the clones. Now, all but one was empty.

They stopped in front of the occupied pod, and looked in through the glass at Mina Duval.

Strong cables around her upper arms suspended her in a thick, red-tinted fluid. A face-mask supplied a constant trickle of oxygen. Just enough to keep her alive, but not enough for her to wake up. Her black New Heroes uniform was torn in places, showing cuts and abrasions on her arms and legs.

Shadow said, "You know that she's the first real live girl I ever talked to?"

"I know. How do you feel about that?"

Shadow shrugged. "I'm not sure. I know that I *should* be interested in her, but I'm not. You changed us, didn't you? You made it so that we wouldn't have the same desires as ordinary people."

"I slowed that down a little. Just until the work is done. Can't have my boys unable to function because they're heart-broken over some girl."

"And she's a clone too, right?"

Victor nodded. "Yes. Ragnarök made her. She's one of two who survived out of a possible six. That we know of. I guess Ragnarök *could* have taken the others away and left Mina and Yvonne behind, but his notes are pretty clear that the others didn't make it. A shame, really. The girls have very different abilities. It would have been interesting to see what powers their siblings might have developed, if any."

"Why Colin?" Shadow asked. "Why did you make us from *his* DNA and not Cooper or Soliz?"

"Because Colin is the only one who's the product of two superhumans. I figured the odds were better that I'd get what I want."

"But you haven't."

"Not yet. We'll see what the tests show up." Victor moved away from the pod, back toward the stairs, and Shadow floated after him.

"Are you ever going to tell me what your super-secret plan is? I know it's something to do with that missile."

"Shadow, when the time comes you'll know all you'll need to know."

"But when is the time coming?"

"Soon, I promise." He looked back down at Mina's pod. "Very soon. Now come. It's time for your lessons. Languages again, I think. And then maybe tactics. Our enemies are gathering their forces. We need to be prepared."

Chapter 17

Colin checked the new computer fixed to his wrist and said to Renata, "Ninety-one kilometers per hour!"

Flying alongside him, Renata said, "Really."

"Yep. We're one thousand and six meters above sea-level, on a south-south-east heading. This thing is *so* cool! Let's see how long I can fly at exactly one thousand meters."

"What fun. Knock yourself out," Renata said.

"Ah, you're just jealous."

"I've already got all that stuff inside my armor. So what do you think of Lance's big plan to get us all killed?"

"It's not like that," Colin said. "I think he's right. We've been fighting Cross on his terms. If we're going to win we have to go on the offensive."

"We're kids. We shouldn't have to do any of this. I wish I was normal."

"You *are* normal, now." He increased his speed to bring himself level with Renata again. "You could quit."

"No, I couldn't." She sighed, then let out a groan of frustration. "We don't even know if this is going to work!"

"It's worth a shot."

"Colin, suppose we *do* win, supposed we capture Victor Cross... What'll you do?"

"You're asking me if I'm going to kill him."

"Well?"

"No. I'm not going to kill anyone. Ever. And I'm not going to let anyone else do it, either. Brawn said that the best way to deal with a criminal is to rehabilitate him. It worked for him, and it worked for Façade. It even worked for Razor. If we had someone like Victor Cross trying to help the human race rather than hurt it, just imagine what we could accomplish. We could save the world. If we do catch him, the first thing I'm going to do is ask him about the powers. How do they work, and why are only some people affected?"

"You think there really is an answer? Maybe it's just magic."

Colin laughed. "Yeah, well, I guess that's as good an answer as anything, until we know better."

"I'm more interested in where the energy comes from. You're flying, so what's keeping you up? It takes energy to defeat gravity, so where's it coming from? And when I had my powers, where did my strength come from?"

"The blue lights," Colin said.

"Yeah, so you say. But suppose they *are* balls of energy that somehow make us superhuman, then where did *they* come from? Why do they only affect a tiny number of people? And why is it sometimes hereditary, and sometimes not. I mean, my folks aren't superhuman, and neither are my brother or sister. So how come *I* am? Or was." She pointed ahead. "City."

Colin consulted his computer. "It's Shreveport. Man, I love this thing. Look, I can even link it into Wikipedia. It was founded in 1839, and population is about one hundred and eighty thousand. It was almost two hundred thousand before the war. There's tons of stuff here."

"What does it say about flying without looking where you're going?"

"I'm hardly likely to crash into a tree when I'm exactly nine hundred and eighty-nine point three-five meters up in the air."

"You could hit a plane."

"I'd hear it coming from miles away. Anyway, with this thing I can tap into the Air Traffic Control systems. Want to see?"

"Not especially."

"Well, what you do is hit the menu button, then..." Colin slowed down, and looked around. "Renata, we've got company."

Renata curved back to meet him. "What is it?"

"I don't know. Something coming in fast." He glanced at his screen. "It's not on the radar." He looked around wildly. "I'm not seeing anything, but I can *feel* it. Getting closer. Faster." Colin shuddered. "I don't like this. Why can't I *see* it? I can't hear anything either."

He spun quickly, scanning the horizon in all directions. "Nothing that shouldn't be there, just a plane coming in to Shreveport."

Then he realized he was still thinking in two dimensions. He looked up.

A dark object was rocketing toward them from directly above.

"Renata, *move!*" Colin shouted. "Go—get back to Sakkara!"

He focused his vision on the approaching object, and saw it split apart into three separate people. Each of them had his face.

Oh man, this is it! He concentrated on building up a charge, but he knew it would do no good.

Renata shouted, "Lance said we take the fight to them!"

She's right. They'll expect us to run, or stand and fight. They won't be expecting an attack. He grabbed her arm and soared upward, aiming directly for one of the clones.

The clone dodged out of the way at the last second, and

Colin immediately threw Renata off to the side with as much strength as he could muster, then he flipped around, angling toward another of the clones.

The first one had paused, and was now chasing him.

Colin stopped immediately, putting himself in the clone's path. He released a small bolt of lightning at the clone and followed it with a much more powerful charge aimed directly above him.

The clone arced up to dodge the first bolt, and the second struck him with enough force to knock him out of the sky.

One down, for now. Colin quickly looked around. *The others... No, that's the wrong approach. That's what they'll expect. Forget the others. Keep after the same guy!*

He threw himself after the injured clone, following the trail of thick smoke from his burning uniform.

A glance told him that Renata had followed his order: she was zooming from the scene. *Good—at least one of us should get away.*

He sensed the other clones racing after him, but he had a good lead on them, and the injured clone was falling at the pull of gravity: Colin's speed was at least five times that.

He reached out and snagged the clone's limp right arm, then immediately shifted his direction, heading straight for the other two. They broke off as he approached, darting away and circling him, clearly unsure what to do next.

As he flew, Colin pulled the injured clone nearer, clenched his fist and slammed it into the clone's blistered face. *Hitting a man when he's down,* Colin thought. *Definitely not my usual style.*

One of the other clones bellowed with rage, but Colin kept

hitting his injured companion, again and again, in the face, the neck, the stomach, leaving a trail of blood and scorched fabric behind him.

He felt sick, but knew that he had to do this. Another punch, and he felt one of the clone's front teeth crack.

The others were right behind him now, so Colin let go of the injured clone and immediately dropped down, heading feet-first toward the ground as he looked up to see how they would react.

Again, the clones split up. One went to help his colleague, the other came after Colin.

Now we're talking, Colin thought. *One-on-one.* "Come on!" He yelled. "Show me what you've got, you coward!"

The clone yelled back, "Learned a few tricks, I see!" and Colin knew then that this was Shadow. He glanced down—he was heading straight for the airport. *Can't go that way—too many people could be hurt.*

The sick feeling in his stomach grew when he realized that was exactly why he *had* to go that way. Shadow would be expecting him to protect the ordinary people, not put them in danger.

A 737 was taxiing to the runway, preparing for take-off. Colin put on a fresh burst of speed and flew directly at it, praying that Shadow would be focused only on him.

Two hundred meters above the runway he shifted direction again, aiming for the terminal building, then immediately switched back. A glance behind him showed that Shadow had been caught out—the clone had altered his course then lost precious seconds before he corrected it.

The moving plane was only meters below Colin now, and

Shadow was approaching fast from the side.

At the last possible moment Colin swooped below the plane, putting him temporarily out of Shadow's line of sight.

Without slowing down, he flipped his direction and soared back out the way he had come. He slammed head-first into Shadow's chest and wrapped his arms around him, forcing him back up into the air.

The impact had knocked the wind out of both of them. Colin's lungs felt like they were on fire, but he couldn't allow himself the luxury of stopping.

Shadow slammed his right fist hard into the side of Colin's head and Colin flinched with the force of the blow. He squeezed his arms together with all his strength, and Shadow groaned in pain.

He can't breathe! Colin thought. In the past, he would have let go long before now, would have allowed his enemy a chance to breathe before he suffocated. But this psychopathic doppelganger had murdered Butler in cold blood, had tried to kill Brawn and Cassandra.

Still squeezing, Colin lashed up with his right knee and slammed it into the pit of Shadow's stomach.

Shadow spasmed and—unable to scream without any breath in his lungs—emitted a short, low-pitched moan.

Colin felt Shadow's fists slamming into his back and head. He knew he was cut, his scalp above his ear had been ruptured, and blood was flowing freely, but he didn't care. He maintained his grip on the clone's chest as he continued to rise.

Behind them, the other clone was racing after them, gaining speed.

Have to get this over with!

He knew from their last fight that Shadow didn't seem bothered by heat or electricity, but there were other forms of energy Colin could use.

He closed his eyes and concentrated, knowing that he was going to hate himself for this. He allowed the ambient heat around him to build up, drew in heat energy from Shadow himself, and when he felt that he could take no more he quickly let go of Shadow, placed one hand on his chest and spun about to slam his other hand onto the other clone's face.

He released his stored energy into both in one powerful, sustained burst.

Finally able to catch his breath, Shadow screamed. It was a scream loud enough that it was heard on the ground, three miles below.

Twenty minutes later, on a large patch of undeveloped land close to Shreveport, the New Heroes arrived in the ChampionShip.

They found Colin and Renata sitting cross-legged on the ground, with Danny standing over them. Colin had torn the sleeve from his shirt and held it pressed against the wound in his head. The sleeve was soaked with his own blood.

In front of them, unconscious, were three of the clones. One was wearing a tattered, scorched uniform, his mouth and nose covered in blood, his teeth chipped and broken.

The other two looked to be merely asleep.

Stephanie Cord looked at Colin. "What did you *do*?"

"I did what I had to. I blasted their bodies with electrochemical energy, put their systems into overdrive, then I pulled it back out of them. The shock shut them down. Put them into a coma."

"Colin, that could have *killed* them!"

He rose into the air, then lowered his legs so that he was standing. "I know."

Chapter 18

"You've been having visions, on and off," Lance McKendrick said to Danny. "Just like your father did."

They were in Lance's office in Sakkara, and Danny was keen to be elsewhere. "Look, can we do this later? I want to check on Colin."

"There might not *be* a later. This new attack... Three at once. Could be that the end game is coming sooner than I'd expected, and we're not ready. I want to know everything you've seen. Every vision, every feeling about the future."

"Some of them are like dreams. You know how it is. You wake up and after a few seconds you can't remember them at all."

Lance shoved a pencil and a pad in front of Danny. "Just write everything you *can* remember, in as much detail as possible."

"That's going to take a while."

"Not for *me*, it won't. Go into super-speed mode or whatever you call it."

Danny sighed as he sat down, then picked up the pencil. "I need a pen—pencils snap too easily when I'm in fast-mode. And my handwriting still isn't very good. I was right-handed."

Lance passed him a ball-point pen. "Just do your best."

Danny bit the cap off the pen, leaned his head way back and spat the cap into the air, then shifted into fast mode and began to write.

It was slow going at first as he tried to remember everything in the right order, but then he gave up on that and just described each vision on a different page, figuring that since the visions were of the future, it didn't really matter much in which order he'd received them.

When he was done, he'd covered almost thirty pages, and his hand was beginning to cramp up.

He switched back to real-time, and caught the pen's cap before it hit the floor.

Lance smiled. "Nice work. And a cool bit of showing off, too." He reached over the desk and picked up the pad. "This is everything?"

"Yep. Near as I can remember."

"Thanks. If I've any questions, I'll call you. And if you want my advice, shave off that bum-fluff that's doing a very poor impersonation of a beard."

"Hah. You first."

"I can't shave mine off until my tan fades."

Danny rose from his chair. "Do me a favor? Don't tell any of the others what's in there, unless you have to. It might not all come true, but..."

"I get it. This is between you and me."

"And there's another thing. Go easy on Razor, will you? You're pushing him too hard. He's already planning to quit."

"You think I'm tougher on him than everyone else?" Lance asked.

"Well, yeah. Because you are."

"He can take it."

Inside a large, abandoned concrete grain-silo, two hundred miles west of Sakkara, Colin stood guard over the clones. None of them had regained consciousness so far, but he wasn't taking any risks. He was constantly listening to their heartbeats and their breathing—if they started to come around, he'd know. He just wasn't sure what he would do if that happened.

The wound in the side of his head was still aching, but it had finally stopped bleeding. His father had used superglue to close the cut; needles couldn't penetrate Colin's skin.

Danny appeared by his side. "Anything?"

"No. But this one," Colin said, pointing to the first one he'd beaten, "is just knocked out. The other two... Dad thinks they might really be in a comatose state." He looked at his friend. "What I did... I could have wiped their brains. But I couldn't think of any other way to stop them."

"It's not like you had any choice. They would have killed you and Renata, and then come for the rest of us."

"Doesn't make this any easier. What did Lance want you for?"

"Stuff. You?"

"Probably different stuff. You're not allowed to talk about it either?"

"No." Colin moved closer to Shadow. "Is that really what I look like?"

"Yeah. They're dead ringers for you, except for their haircuts. Hey, you know what we should do? We should shave their heads."

Colin grinned. "Yeah. And their eyebrows. And we could tattoo 'I love bunnies' on their foreheads."

"No, I'm serious. Say one of these guys recovered and managed to get rid of you, he could pretend to *be* you. But not if we shave their heads."

"That's a good point," Colin said. "I should have thought of that. We've all seen enough spy movies to… What? What are you looking at me like that for?"

Danny hesitated. "Just had a thought." He quickly looked away from Colin.

"I'm not one of them!"

"Yeah, but… How can we ever know that? I'm just saying. At some point in the future, one of them might show up claiming to be you. How would we know?"

"A password?" Colin suggested.

"No, that wouldn't work, because whoever it is might be able to read minds. Hey, you think that's how they got Mina? One of them went to Berlin and pretended to be you? She'd trust you, so he could persuade her to go with him."

"But she'd see from his aura that it's not me. Didn't she say something about herself and Yvonne having different auras, even though they're clones?"

"Yeah, I think she did."

"Wonder how many of them there are?" Colin said, looking down at the trio of unconscious bodies.

"The bigger question is what we do when they wake up. If they're all as strong as you are, how can we keep them prisoner? You could keep zapping them every time they wake, but that means you're stuck here."

Colin's shoulders sagged. "You're right. And if I'm here babysitting these guys, who's protecting Sakkara?"

In his base in Zaliv Kalinina, Victor Cross turned to Evan Laurie and said, "He's not dumb, is he?"

Laurie didn't respond. Cross knew that the man was still furious with him, but that wasn't a problem. He could put up with Laurie's moods.

The audio transmission from the grain-silo crackled and faded again, as it had been doing for the past few minutes.

"We're losing it," Victor said, rapidly typing on his keyboard. "I'd hoped we'd had enough transmitters planted on the kids that some of them would survive intact, but clearly there should have been more." He pushed the keyboard away. "And it's gone. Still, we've learned a lot."

Through gritted teeth, Laurie said, "You... You just threw the boys to the enemy! Just to see what would happen!"

"Yeah. Well, they're my toys, I can play with them however I like."

"But that's Shadow and Tuan and Roman—they're the most powerful of them all!"

"So far. But they're not what I need. Besides, we can get them back easily enough. Colin's idea is spot-on. If we attack Sakkara, he'll come running to save the day again. Then we get the boys out. If we want to."

"You really are an utter sociopath."

Cross slowly clapped his hands. "Wow. You deserve a prize for managing to get to the end of that *very* long word."

"Stop patronizing me, Victor. I'm not an idiot. My IQ is a hundred and eighty-nine."

"Well, aren't you the clever boy for spotting that he was being patronized?" Cross tapped his fingers on the edge of the desk for a moment. "Back to work. Roman's created enough graphene for us to finish construction on the rocket. The propulsion system is working, so all we need to do is complete the shell, install the guidance system, add in a few fail-safes, and start drilling the silo so that we can actually launch the thing."

"You're still not going to tell me what the payload is?"

"No. That's above your security clearance level. There are two levels. Zero and one. I'm at level one, everyone else in the world is at level zero. But get the rocket finished and I'll double that. Come on, it's only rocket science. How hard can it be? It's a little easier than brain surgery, and more fun because we get to blow things up."

In Sakkara's gymnasium, Lance McKendrick sat with Warren Wagner and Brawn.

Warren said, "We've had no luck getting in touch with Roz Dalton. But you talked to Thunder, right? He's not coming?"

Lance shook his head. "No. And I don't want him to. If *we* all get killed, there has to be someone left to tell the world how fantastic I am. Besides, have any of you been in contact with him since you lost your powers?"

"Have you?" Warren asked.

"No," Lance said. "But then I've only seen him a couple of times since that time in New Jersey when Brawn let Ragnarök go."

"That was the right thing to do," Brawn grumbled.

"Whatever. I'm not judging you, and I really don't want to have that argument again." Lance looked at Warren. "You didn't tell Grant and Alia why they're really in Berlin, did you?"

"No. But I think it's a bad move. They're just kids. They'll have no chance if Cross decides to move against them. Lance, if Stephanie realizes that her sister is just bait, she will hate you forever. She's already lost her father."

Brawn said, "I would not want to get on her bad side. Butler told me what she was like after Cord's body was brought back. She blamed Colin, and didn't speak to him for months."

"I can cope with sulky teenagers," Lance said. He stood, stretched, and walked in a slow circle around Brawn's over-sized bed. "I've been trying to see the big picture, to figure out what Cross is up to. I'm not getting it. If I could *talk* to him, I'd have a much better chance. But the only way I'm going to get to do that is if we've already captured him." He stopped walking and turned to face his friends. "If Cross simply wanted to rule the world, he would have stuck with the Trutopians. But he didn't. He abandoned them, and triggered the war. So what's he planning? It can't be that he wants to *destroy* the world, because he'd have done that already. Whatever he's up to, it's something beyond the usual supervillain megalomania."

"Right," Warren said. "But what's bigger than destroying the world?"

"I didn't say bigger, I said *beyond*. Maybe he's after something small."

"Such as?"

Lance shrugged. "I don't know."

"When I met him in Lieberstan," Brawn said, "he asked me about something he called The Chasm. He wanted to know what it meant to Ragnarök."

"Quantum talked about that too," Lance said, "in the video tapes Max recorded, but Danny's visions don't mention it. What does it mean? Maybe it's a mistranslation of another word. Maybe 'chasm' means something else in a different language. It could even be a physical place. Whatever it is, it seems to be important."

"We need to find Max," Warren said. "See what he

remembers."

The others exchanged a look.

"Come on," Warren said. "He knows stuff. We should use him."

Lance said, "Perhaps. But first, let's all put our heads together and try to think of a time when involving Max in something didn't make matters *worse*. I know where Max is. He believes he's safe, and as long as he stays hidden, he won't be getting in our way. He's more of a liability than an asset."

"Then what are our *other* assets?" Brawn said. He flexed his right shoulder. "I've almost recovered, but I wouldn't be anywhere near as strong as the clones. We've got half a dozen Paragon suits, and two spares. One now, because the other is being modified to fit you. And there's Colin, Danny and Kenya. She's really only starting out, and Danny's missing an arm. We just don't have the raw power we'll need to take on Cross."

"I'm working on it," Lance said. "I have a plan. It might not pay off, but if it does, we'll be able to put a stop to Cross for good."

Warren said, "In the parallel universe, in Krodin's world... You had to work alongside former enemies to stop Krodin, right? Slaughter and Daedalus. We should do the same now."

"You're talking about Yvonne," Lance said. "Her hypnotic voice was by far her greatest strength, and she no longer has that. Sure, she's smart, and from what Stephanie told us, she's furious with Cross... But I don't trust her. No, she stays where she is." He unclipped his radio from his belt, and hit the "call" button.

A few seconds later, Colin's voice said, "Yeah?"

"How are things, Colin?"

"OK. They're still unconscious."

"All right… I'm sending Renata to you. Danny's with you, right? Leave him there—if anything happens, he'll be fast enough to find you. As soon as Renata gets there, you both resume your mission."

Renata yawned inside her helmet. Dawn was breaking through the eastern horizon and she'd been up all night, drifting through the sky after Colin.

How does he *not get tired?* She wondered.

But she knew that even if their mission was called off and she returned to Sakkara, she probably wouldn't be able to sleep. So much had happened in the past few days.

She still couldn't quite get her head around the thought that Butler was dead, and wondered if that was because they hadn't spent a lot of time together since the war. After Impervia had split them into three teams, the groups had barely seen each other.

At least I got to go to Australia, she thought. She had already decided that when this was all over—if they won—she was going to move to Melbourne. Her parents still wanted her to finish high school and then go to college, but college didn't appeal to her. She knew that most of her friends had gone, and a few of them were even working in the same fields they had studied, but that seemed a lifetime ago. They were all in their mid-twenties now, many with families of their own.

They knew about her, of course. Everyone knew who she was, how she been lost for ten years when she was frozen in her crystalline form. There had even been a made-for-TV movie called *Diamond: the Renata Soliz Story*. That had been a source of great amusement to Danny and the others, especially since most of the movie had been completely fictional. Her entire background had been changed, because otherwise the movie makers would have had to pay her family to use their stories.

Butler had laughed so hard at one scene—in which an obviously plastic dummy of Colin's character was thrown off a roof in an attempt to make it look like it was flying—that he'd fallen back off his chair and smacked the back of his head on the edge of a table. He'd still been laughing while the others helped him to the infirmary so that Warren could sew up the wound.

Over the radio, Colin said, "Renata?"

"I'm here."

"OK. See that crossroads down there? A little to your left, right by that hill with the sticky-up bit?"

"Yeah, I see it. But where are *you*?"

"I'm about half a mile above you. Set down there and wait for me."

Renata eased the thrust on her jetpack, and steered herself toward the crossroads. The jetpack was controlled by sensors inside her gloves: by squeezing her fingers in certain patterns, she could adjust her height, direction and speed. It had taken a lot of practice to be able to use the armor without zooming off at a weird angle every time she made a fist, but it was second-nature to her now.

She set down with a slight bump in the middle of the crossroads, and looked up to see Colin rapidly descending toward her.

He came to a stop about fifteen feet overhead. "OK. Stay here."

Renata watched as Colin drifted toward the small hill. From

the air, the grass-covered hill had been barely noticeable, but here on the ground, now that she was aware of it, it was clearly artificial. Its peak was maybe twenty feet above the ground, and it was too round, too perfect.

Colin suddenly shot straight up, kept going until he was only a dot in the sky. Then he came back down, fast, head-first.

He slammed into the hill hard enough to send a shockwave that cracked the concrete under Renata's feet. A thick cloud of dirt and rocks began to erupt from the small hill, and Renata had to jump aside to avoid a flying boulder larger than her head.

By the time Colin was done, the entire crossroads was buried under three inches of dirt and stones, and the artificial hill had been reduced to a crater.

Colin drifted back to Renata, carrying a smooth metal sphere the size of a beach-ball under one arm. "I guess this is it."

"Yeah, but what *is* it?"

"You'll see." Colin set the sphere down, and they both slowly circled it.

"Looks like a wrecking-ball," Renata said.

"Trust me, it's not," Colin said. "According to Lance, we just crack it open. You ready?"

"Not really. I don't know what's supposed to happen."

"Lance said there's nothing to worry about. It can't hurt you. But you're going to have to ditch the armor."

"Aw, come on!"

He nodded. "I'm serious. Ditch the armor. All of it. We don't know what effect the metal will have."

"OK, but you can't look. I'm only wearing my bra and panties under it."

"Renata, I *have* to look. I have to be able to see what's

happening."

She groaned, and started unclipping the armor, helmet first, then gloves. "You'd better not be making this up!"

Colin pulled off his t-shirt and passed it to her. "Put that on if you're uncomfortable."

"Watch out for early-morning cars. I don't want anyone getting an eyeful and then running me over."

"There's nothing for miles around." Colin turned his back on her.

Renata unclipped her armor's chest-plate and let it fall to the ground, then the back-plate, and the flexible pieces on her arms. They were coated with an extremely strong steel and polymer mesh, bullet-proof and fire-proof.

"Well?" Colin asked.

"I'm doing it, I'm doing it!" She kicked off her boots, then her leggings, and pulled on the t-shirt. "Ew! When was the last time you had a shower?"

"I dunno. How long ago was Christmas?"

"All right. I'm done."

Colin turned back. "OK..." He looked down at the sphere, and ran his hands over it for a moment. "Here... This is where the two halves were welded together. Lance said the shell is about four inches thick."

She saw his fingertips glow red, then white, and took a step back as thin rivulets of molten steel began to run down the outside of the sphere.

"That should do it," Colin said. "Can't melt it all the way, but this should be enough for me to get a good grip on it." Almost instantly, the white-hot metal dulled and solidified as he reabsorbed the heat back into his body. "You get as close as you can. I'll rip it open."

Renata stepped up to the metal ball, so close that her knees were touching it.

Colin crouched down on the opposite side of the sphere, flexed his shoulders a little, then inserted his fingers into the now-cooled indentations on the surface. He pulled, the strain showing in the tendons on his neck.

The metal began to warp and buckled under his fingers. "This is part of your history," he told Renata, his teeth gritted. "Remember when you and my folks and all the others went after Ragnarök?"

"Like I'd forget *that*."

"Well, Ragnarök's plan was to siphon all the powers out of every other superhuman. Except himself, of course." The metal sphere split, and Colin jumped back.

Renata peered down into the cracked sphere. "So what's supposed to happen now?"

If Colin responded, she didn't hear it. Her entire body was instantly wracked with a tidal wave of pure agony. She felt as though her skin was burning, melting, sloughing away from her muscles, while a million poisoned darts plunged into her body from every direction.

She collapsed to the ground and her stomach heaved, her eyes streamed with thick tears, her ears ached like they had been skewered with railroad spikes.

Another wave of agony washed over her even before the first had subsided, and she felt every muscle in her body twitch and jump as though she was being electrocuted. Her hands slammed palm-down onto the dirt-covered road, and she felt her nails splintering on the concrete surface as her fingers curled into fists.

Then, instantly, the pain was gone.

Colin was kneeling at her side, and she held onto his arm as she pulled herself up into a kneeling position.

"Are you all right? I didn't think it would hurt—Lance *said* it wouldn't hurt!"

Renata wiped the back of her left hand across her mouth, and it came away streaked with mud, saliva and blood.

"It's OK—you just bit your lip," Colin said.

She turned her hand over, and looked at her nails, expecting to see bloody stumps where they had been ripped out of her fingertips. They were intact. "What? I felt them..." And then Renata looked back down at the ground, and saw two sets of four long, thin gouges in the concrete. "Oh wow."

"Can you stand?"

"I think so." Leaning on Colin for support, she got to her feet, then stepped away from him as she arched her back and flexed her muscles. "I'm OK."

Colin said, "So... Ragnarök's machine stole all that energy from all the superhumans." He gave the metal sphere a kick. "And inside *this* is where that energy was stored, kind of like a giant battery. Max's people had buried it, just in case it ever got into the wrong hands. At least, that was the official story. The truth is that he didn't know how to make use of it. But Lance figured it out... Remember how Danny lost his powers, but he got them back after he ran into one of those blue lights? Well, they're hard to find because only very few of us can see then, but Lance guessed that the energy in the sphere was the same stuff." He grinned. "So, some of that was probably *your* energy to begin with. Well? Want to give it a go?"

She nodded, and took a deep breath as she concentrated. An almost forgotten sensation rippled over her skin, and her body became transparent and crystalline.

After a few seconds, she returned to normal, and smiled at Colin. "I'm back."

Colin stared at her. "Yeah..."

"What?"

"Before you lost your powers you could turn yourself crystal, and then you learned to change other things, right? And then you learned how to change only *some* parts of your body... But those parts couldn't move."

"So?" Renata allowed her left hand to turn solid, then held it above her head and watched the refracted image of the clouds rippling through it. *Never thought I'd see this again! But Mina sounded so certain when she said that my powers were gone for good, and that I was an ordinary human.*

I know she's a bit jealous of me and Danny but...

And how did Mister McKendrick know that my powers weren't gone forever? For someone we've never heard of before, he knows way too much about all of us.

"Renata," Colin said. "Stop day-dreaming for a second... I'm trying to tell you something!"

She lowered her hand. "I'm listening."

He stepped closer to her. "I thought I saw... Look, just turn solid again."

She turned herself completely solid, then flinched as Colin threw a punch at her. For a moment she thought that it wasn't him, that it was one of the clones, but then she saw him grinning at her and she realized what he was trying to demonstrate.

Renata looked down at her crystalline hands, and flexed them into fists.

She returned Colin's grin. "I've never been able to do this before!"

Colin nodded. "Yep. You can *move.*"

Chapter 19

When Colin and Renata returned to Sakkara they found Lance waiting for them on the roof. Before they could speak, he put his finger to his lips, and slightly shook his head.

He passed a hand-written note to Colin. It read, "Don't speak. Do you know what an electromagnetic pulse is?"

Colin nodded.

Lance passed him a second note. "I'll have one of those. Right here, right now. Extra-large, please. Enough to blanket the entire building. Everything important inside is shielded."

Colin started to speak, but was handed a third note: "No, Renata will be fine as long as her armor's not active."

He showed the note to Renata, who immediately powered down her armor.

Two more notes came next. The first read, "Well?" and the second read, "I refer you to note number 2."

Lance looked at him with an expression that said, "What are you waiting for?"

Colin had read about electromagnetic pulses, how they could disrupt electronic circuits and even burn out microprocessors. But he figured that if Lance said it was OK, it was probably important. Even though Lance had been wrong—or had lied— about the energy in the metal sphere not hurting Renata.

Lance took hold of Renata's arm and pulled her away from Colin as he drew the energy around him into his body.

Colin felt the charge building inside him, growing stronger, itching to break free. Lance nodded, and Colin let it go.

The pulse was invisible, and completely harmless to humans,

but Colin sensed it surge through the building beneath his feet, racing through electricity cables, along metal water-pipes, through dozens of free-standing pieces of electronic equipment.

"Done?" Lance asked.

"It's done. It's zapped a few computers, though. Better check for fires."

"Everyone's been warned about that already, thanks to good old pencil and paper."

"I'm guessing the purpose was to destroy any bugs that the bad guys might have planted in there."

Lance motioned that they should follow him toward the stairs. "Correct. I'm not saying that there *was* anything, but just in case. Now you know why we couldn't discuss the plan out loud. So, Renata, I can see that you're eager to tell me that it worked."

She grinned. "It did. I haven't really tested it yet, but look..." She pulled off her glove and held up her hand, and transformed it into crystal.

"Are we back to the stage where you can only transform yourself?"

"Only me, so far. And my clothes and my armor. But check *this* out!" She waggled her crystalline fingers. "I can move!"

Lance led them along the corridor toward the machine room. "Good. That gives me hope that one day you'll regain the ability to change other objects. That would come in handy for keeping our clone friends prisoner."

"Yeah, but I can *move*! I was never able to do that before!"

"Sure you were. You just hadn't learned *how.* Takes a while for some of you to learn the extent of your powers." Lance nodded toward Colin. "Like this guy. It was nearly a year before he learned how to fly."

Colin began, "Mister McKendrick..."

"Lance."

"Lance. How did you know that Renata's powers weren't gone forever? Mina said that her aura was perfectly human. She said it wasn't even like when my folks and the others lost *their* powers."

"I wasn't completely sure. I just had a hunch." Lance shrugged. "In this world, especially when it comes to superhumans, it's never wise to close your mind to any possibility, kids. We live in the age of miracles. Well, maybe not *miracles* exactly, but it's certainly the age of really weird stuff."

In the machine room, they saw that the room was once again swarming with technicians. Razor was at his bench, fitting components to the large framework, and he looked up as he saw them.

"No major damage from the EMP, Mister Mac."

"I told you before. Call me Lance, or boss, or sir, if you don't want me to call you Garland."

"Yeah, whatever. If there were any bugs in this place, they're toast now. Col? Give me a hand, would you? Take the big end and hold it up against this. Have to make sure it'll fit."

Renata said, "*I* can do that. I'm stronger than Colin, after all." She walked around the bench and lifted the framework single-handed. "Where exactly do you want it?"

"Nice," Razor said, smiling. "So what happened? How'd your powers come back?"

Lance said, "We can't say, yet."

"OK. But Mina said your powers were *never* coming back, that your aura was normal. Perfectly human."

Colin said, "Yeah, that's what *I* said."

"Enough," Lance said. "Seriously, this isn't the time for that. Razor, how much longer before this machine is ready?"

"Four days, maybe."

"You have one day."

"What?! Are you crazy?"

Lance sighed, "Son, you don't kid a kidder. Engineers always want to buy some more time, so they double how long they think it'll really take. But you guessed that *I* know that, which means that you doubled it twice. So you have twenty-four hours." He looked at his watch. "This time tomorrow."

Razor threw a wrench across the room. "I quit."

"Oh, really? You're going to run out on your friends now, when they need you most?"

Razor stormed up to Lance, and glared at him, face-to-face. "Yes. Do you have a problem with that?"

"Whoa, hey," Colin said, approaching them. "Come on. We have to work *together*." He looked from Razor to Lance and back. They were staring each other down, bearded faces so close their noses were almost touching. "Razor, we *need* you to..." He frowned for a moment. "Aw, no way."

Beside him, Renata asked, "What?" She looked around wildly. "Did you hear something? Is something coming?"

Lance and Razor broke their staring contest.

"What is it?" Lance asked.

Colin looked away. "No, nothing. I just... For a second I thought you were going to thump each other. Look, Razor, you have to stay. We need you. And Lance, you back off. Let him work at his own pace. There's no one in the world who understands machines like he does."

"All right," Lance said. He turned back to Razor. "Your friend is talking sense. We'll call a truce, for now." He held out his hand. "Agreed?"

Razor stepped back, and turned away. "I've got work to do."

"Twenty-four hours," Lance said. "Razor, this is not me just being a jerk for the sake of it. I'm being a jerk because this work is important. You *know* that. Whatever you need to get it done, it's yours. Except that you can't have Colin and Renata at the same time. They have to take shifts watching the prisoners. Speaking of which..." He looked back at Renata. "Your turn. Danny's been there for hours."

"But I've been up all night!"

"So have I. Go on. Colin will relieve you in two hours. He doesn't need much sleep."

As Lance followed Renata out of the room, he said to Colin, "My office, ten minutes."

"Yeah, sure." Colin lifted up the framework for Razor. "Soon as I'm done here."

"Steady," Razor said. "OK. Closer, left. Bit more. Up a tiny bit. Hold it there." He climbed up onto the bench and spent the next few minutes using a marker to indicate on the framework where the two pieces matched up. "Got it, cool, thanks."

Colin said, "Aaaand... He's gone."

Razor looked over toward the doors. "Good." He jumped down to the floor. "That guy... Drives me *crazy*. I thought it was bad under Josh, then Impervia, but he's *way* worse. Everything has to be done yesterday. You know I still don't get paid for this?"

"Who does?"

"What do you think of him?"

"Solomon Cord liked him. They were good friends."

"Yeah, well. Go on, have your secret meeting with the new boss. Teacher's pet. Why don't you bring him an apple?"

Colin closed the door to Lance's office and said, "You're not going to tell him?"

"Nope. Not yet, anyway."

"You should. If it was the other way around, wouldn't you like to know?"

Lance said, "Colin, right now we've all got more important things to worry about. Ten points for figuring it out, by the way. So far, you're the only one."

"Is that why you're here?"

"It's one of the reasons." Lance nodded to the chair on the other side of the desk. "Sit, please." When Colin was sitting, he continued. "OK, so this is how it goes... My parents and my brother were murdered by Slaughter because the old crew and I foiled her plans to bring Krodin out of the past and into the present. Well, it was the present back then, twenty-five years ago. After that, Max took me in for a while, but he and I never did get along. I set out on my own, which was stupid because I was just a kid."

"Where did you go?" Colin picked up a pencil and began to twirl it around his fingers.

"Everywhere. I ended up working with a carnival. Changed my name, lied about my age... All because I wanted to stay hidden from Max. At the carnival I met this girl. She was pretty amazing, but I couldn't see that at first because... Never mind. Lots of reasons. Anyway, Max found me and dragged me back into his ongoing fight with Casey Duval. I never saw her again.

Colin, will you cut that *out*? It's distracting."

"Sorry." Colin stopped twirling the pencil. "So when Impervia asked you to..." He stopped. "Hold on a second. How did she even know you? Impervia, I mean."

"Oh, she and Max had a little thing going for a while. Secret lovers, and all that. I knew her from back then. Impervia wanted someone she could trust, and who had a knack for lateral thinking. Which is nicely ironic because I don't really trust *her*. You know what lateral thinking is?"

"Remind me," Colin said.

"The ability to think around problems. To come up with solutions that aren't obvious to most people. It's a handy skill when people try to catch you out with logic problems. Like... OK. Here's an example. John's teacher has only five children in her class. Going by age, the youngest is Susan, then there's Peter, then David, and the fourth is Mary. So is the fifth student, the oldest, a boy or a girl?"

"There's no way to tell... Is there a pattern? It goes girl, boy, boy, girl. Susan, Peter, David, Mary. SPDM. Number of letters in their names? Five, five, five and four. That's not helpful. Oh, wait, they're the names of people in a famous band or something like that, right?"

"Nope."

Colin frowned. "Wait a second... Just because someone is called, say, David, that doesn't mean they're a boy, does it? Names are just labels—they could be applied to anyone no matter what their sex is. So there's absolutely no way to know."

"No, that's not it. Good thinking, but you're way off-track. Let's assume that the names go with the usual genders. David's a boy, Mary's a girl, and so on."

"Then I give up."

Lance reached out and picked up the phone. He entered an extension number and a few seconds later the call was answered. "Razor? Lance. Here's a puzzle for you…" He repeated the puzzle, then said, "Hold on, I want Colin to hear this." He put the phone on speaker.

Razor said, "Well, duh. The oldest is a boy. Why? What's this about?"

"Not important. Thanks, kid." Lance hung up the phone.

"You gave him the answer earlier?" Colin said.

"No, I didn't. He worked it out. Lateral thinking. You have to examine the question, Colin. Consider what I said, not what you *think* I said. You've heard it twice now. How did it start?"

"The teacher has only five children in her class—"

"That's not what I said."

"All right, *John's* teacher has only five… Ah." Colin grinned. "That's a good one."

"That's why I'm here. Whatever it is that causes some people to become superhuman is connected to the blue lights. But very few people can see them. In fact, as far as I know, only you, Quantum and Krodin have ever had that skill. What did you see when you cracked open the sphere?"

"A *lot* of blue light. It only lasted a second, though."

"That's what I thought. We don't know where they come from, or what their connection really is to the superhuman abilities. Are the lights the actual energy you use? If so, would it be possible to generate them artificially? Casey Duval probably knew, and I'm guessing that Victor Cross does too. After Danny lost his abilities you saw one of the lights pass right through him, and shortly after that his powers returned. I believe that he burned himself out, you see… He used up all his energy in one go, sent the superhuman part of him into a dormant state. The blue light either recharged him, or just woke up the superhuman part."

"Same with Renata, after she froze the world."

"Right. She had just enough energy left to restore everything to normal, then—zap!—she'd burnt herself out."

"Then why was it different for the two of them? When the light hit Danny, it didn't seem to have any effect. With Renata, it looked like she was in a lot of pain."

Lance shrugged. "Search me. Different people, different powers. But Danny never *fully* recovered his powers, and I suspect that Renata won't either. She'll never be able to freeze the world again. Might not even be able to freeze other objects. But right now, I'll take whatever we can get."

"So… Do you think that the blue lights are the *only* cause of the superhuman powers? If an ordinary person gets hit by one of them, will they get powers too?"

"No. There's something different about you guys. I think it's in your DNA. Some people have a genetic peculiarity that makes them susceptible to the blue lights."

"But they've searched for that, and they've never found anything." Colin realized he was twirling the pencil again, and stopped.

"Absence of evidence is not evidence of absence… Just because you haven't found something doesn't mean it's not there. But maybe I'm wrong. Maybe it's something else entirely. Whatever it is, we know it *can* be passed from parent to child, but isn't always. Same with people like Solomon Cord and Razor and me. We're not superhuman, but we're not quite human either. And we know *that* can be inherited genetically, too."

"Would the blue lights work on someone who *used* to be superhuman, like Façade or my parents or Brawn? If you'd sent Brawn out with us, maybe he would have got his powers back."

"No, that's different. I believe Ragnarök's machine *destroyed* the thing that makes them superhuman. Now, listen... I have a job for you. It's not going to be easy, but you're the only one who can do it."

For the next five minutes Lance explained his plan, and when he was done Colin had a tight knot forming in the pit of his stomach. He felt like he was going to throw up. "Lance... I don't want to do this."

Lance gave him a thin smile. "I understand. I'm open to suggestions, but unless you come up with something brilliant, this is the only way to do it. You have to be fully committed to this, Colin. Once we start down that path, there's no going back."

Colin swallowed, and nodded. *He's right*, he thought. *This is the only way.* Aloud, he said, "Lateral thinking, yeah?"

"Exactly." Lance picked up his cane and pushed himself out of his chair. "Break's over. I have to go and shout at people now." He winked at Colin. "Because he's your friend, I'll leave Razor alone for a few hours."

"And you're not going to tell him?"

"I'll tell him one day, maybe. But not today. Right now, he hates me, and that hatred is spurring him on to work harder and smarter than ever before. We need that a lot more than he needs to know who his real father is."

Chapter 20

In the grain-silo Renata saw one of the prisoners start to moan and twitch. Into her radio, she said, "They're waking up!"

She glanced toward her armor piled up in the corner. *Do I have time to put it on?*

The answer came sooner than she'd expected. The clone's eyes opened, and he jumped to his feet, threw himself against her, slamming her back into the wall, his right fist pulled back, ready to strike.

Renata shimmered, became crystal just as the clone's fist cracked into her face.

She pushed him away as he was staring at his bloodied knuckles, then swung her own fist at him.

He threw his head back to dodge the punch, then carried the movement through, falling back onto the ground and kicking up with one foot. His boot struck Renata's arm with enough force to throw her off-balance.

The clone, now flat on his back, flipped over onto his stomach, facing away from her, and launched himself forward toward the silo's sealed door. Renata threw herself at him and locked her right arm around his neck, willing it to become solid and immovable.

Struggling to get free, he raised his legs and kicked out at the door, pushing himself and Renata back into the center of the silo.

"No you don't!" Renata said, her teeth clenched. She squeezed tighter on his neck. His left elbow shot back and cracked uselessly against her diamond-hard stomach. She knew she could solidify her entire body and he'd never break her grip, but he'd still be able to fly. He'd just carry her away.

Can't let him think of that—have to keep him on the defensive!

She jabbed her left fist hard into his kidney, and as he squirmed in pain she solidified her entire skull, then lashed her head forward, cracking it against the back of his head.

He immediately went limp in her arms, and collapsed to the floor as she stepped back.

A sudden movement behind her—Renata whirled around to see another of the clones darting straight up, crashing through the roof. Shattered bricks cascaded down, and Renata automatically crouched over the unconscious clones to shelter them. *What am I doing? They're the bad guys!*

The once-dark interior of the silo was thick with dust, and Renata covered her mouth as she pushed the fallen bricks off the clones' unconscious bodies. She was still in her invulnerable crystalline form, but didn't want to breathe in too much of the dust. It couldn't harm her, but even though she wasn't sure how her lungs could possibly work in this form, they did seem to be taking in air. She didn't like the idea of turning back to normal with her lungs still clogged.

Danny suddenly appeared next to her—a tunnel in the dust cloud was slowly closing behind him. "What happened?"

"Two of them woke. One got away."

"Are you hurt?"

"No, but I—"

"Keep watch on these two. If they start to wake again, grab hold of their wrists and turn yourself solid. That'll slow them down." As abruptly as he arrived, Danny vanished, leaving a fresh tunnel in the swirling dust.

Moments later, a voice on her radio said, "Renata, maintain your position. We're on the way."

"Will do, Steph."

She hauled the clones from under the bricks, and carried them out into the farmyard. *If I could change* them *to crystal, the way I used to be able to do, that'd make this a lot easier.*

She put them on the ground and knelt down between them. The one who'd attacked her in the silo looked slightly older than his companion. *I think this is the first one, Shadow. We should have put labels on them.*

The older clone's eyes flickered open, and Renata grabbed his arm. *Can't let this one get away.*

In a weak voice, Shadow said, "H... hh... help me."

Renata shifted back, her eyes wide. "What?"

"He's controlling us... We don't want to fight. He makes us do it."

"Who are you talking about, Shadow? Who's behind this?"

"Ragnarök."

Despite being in her crystalline form, Renata shuddered. "No. He's dead."

"Not dead." Shadow tried to sit up, but Renata put her hand on his chest and pushed him back down. "He's not dead. Not really. His *first* body died. Cloned himself, transferred his mind."

Renata put her hand to her mouth. "Is that even *possible*?"

Then Shadow said, "No." He lashed out with his right fist, slamming it up into Renata's jaw. She tumbled through the air and crash heavily back into the curved wall of the grain-silo.

She jumped to her feet, expecting to see that he had gone, but he was still in the same spot, standing over his clone-brother.

"You hurt Roman."

"So he has a name too. Good. The guy inscribing the gravestones will want to know."

"Rule number one," Shadow said, a slight snarl on his lips. "You keep the enemy off-guard. Of *course* Ragnarök is dead. He killed himself when he realized he'd lost everything. Those clones were his last chance, and when they were found, he knew that it was all over for him."

"What does that mean? His last chance for what?"

Shadow tilted his head to the side a little as he peered at her. "Your powers have evolved."

"I know." Slowly, Renata walked toward him. She was sure Shadow couldn't actually hurt her, but he could simply fly away as his companions had done. "What's rule number two?"

"Never take on an enemy you can't defeat."

"You think you *can* defeat me? In this form I'm stronger than you, and I'm invulnerable. What do you people hope to accomplish?"

"We do what the boss tells us. Simple as that."

"And who's your boss?"

"You know who he is."

"Victor Cross."

Shadow nodded. "He offered you the chance to join him. You turned him down." Still watching her, he began to move to the left.

"Cross is a coward, and a murderer. He's a power-hungry madman. And you people are his pets. No, worse than that, you're his puppets." Renata also moved to her left, the two of them slowly circling around Roman's unconscious form, then she thought, *No, this is what he's expecting. I have to out-think him.*

"Victor prefers to think of us as his toys."

"Toys? And you're OK with that?" She stopped moving.

Shadow seemed to hesitate for a moment, then he stopped too. "Sure. Why not? We know who we are, how we were made."

"Cloned from Colin's DNA, grown in an artificial womb. Victor Cross is playing God."

"If so, then he's winning." Shadow smiled. "You people still have no idea what Victor's planning, do you?"

"Enlighten me."

"Oh, please. Give me more credit than that! But I will tell you this... He *is* going to win. He's the smartest person I've ever met." He shrugged. "Well, not that I've met many other people. I'm only a few months old. Victor made a lot of improvements to Ragnarök's cloning technology."

"How many of you are there?" *Come on*, Renata thought, *do something!* She knew that the longer he talked, the more information she'd be able to get out of him. But useful as that information was, she'd rather he was gone before Stephanie and the others arrived.

"Nine. I'm the oldest. By two days."

Renata deliberately allowed herself to relax. "Hey, do you all have the same powers?" *Have to let him think I've let my guard down.* "Yvonne and Mina don't, so I guess you guys don't either."

"Ah, Mina..." Shadow's smile grew. "She *is* cute. She's prettier than you."

"Cross didn't teach you manners, then?" *So they* do *have*

Mina. "It's not polite to say stuff like that. And what about Cassandra? Do you think *she's* pretty, too?"

He shrugged. "I only saw her for a few moments. I was too busy killing your friend Butler to check her out."

"Well, Mina and Cassie had better be still alive, because if they're not, if you've killed them too, we are going to tear you apart. Though we're going to do that anyway."

"We know where your brother is, Renata. We can get to him just like *that*." Shadow snapped his fingers. "He's not superhuman. How many punches do you think it would take me to cave in his skull?"

She glowered at him. "If you go anywhere near Robbie I will..." She caught herself. *He's trying to get me riled up—I should be doing it to him!* "What if your artificial aging hasn't stopped? How long before you and Roman and the rest of you die of old age? You look about fourteen or fifteen now. How long ago were you born?"

"Six months ago."

"So by the time you're three, you'll be the equivalent of about ninety years old. Wow. That's not a lot of time to save for a pension."

"Yeah, but the artificial aging *has* stopped."

"How do you know?"

Shadow's gaze flicked away for a moment.

Got him! Renata thought. "You know what I could do? I could freeze the world again. Just keep everything except you guys frozen for, say, five years. Then I turn everything back to normal, and you'd all have died of old age. How do you like the sound of that?"

"You're bluffing. You might have some of your powers back,

but not all. If you *could* solidify anything other than yourself, you'd have already done it to me and Roman and Tuan."

"OK, so I was lying about that. But I'm not wrong about your rapid aging. Victor Cross has built a time-bomb into your systems, and it's ticking away the seconds of your short life. Tick, tock, tick, tock. You don't believe me, get Cassandra to read Cross's mind."

"We're not stupid enough to let a telepath anywhere near Victor."

"So why did you take her?"

"We don't want *you* to have her either. Telepaths are dangerous."

"And what do you want *Mina* for?"

"She's..." Shadow stopped. His body stiffened, and he said, "Next time we meet, I'm going to kill you." He darted toward Roman, arms out-stretched.

Renata did the same: she grabbed Roman's ankle at the same time Shadow caught his wrist.

Shadow soared into the air, dragging Roman behind him. It was only when Renata screamed, "Let him go!" that he looked back and saw that he was towing her too.

"*You* let go!"

Renata pulled herself up, reached out and grabbed Roman's other wrist before letting go of his ankle. She jerked on his arm with all of her strength, and swung her body around enough to lock onto Roman's throat with her free hand. "Let go or I'll crush his neck!"

She didn't want to think about how high up they were right now. All she allowed herself to focus on was Shadow. She had to stare him down, make him believe that she really would kill his clone-brother.

Shadow glared back. And then let go.

In seconds, he was gone.

The wind whipped at Renata as she and Roman began to plummet toward the ground. She knew that she could survive the fall, but wasn't sure about the clone. *What have I done? If he dies, it'll be my fault!*

Still holding onto Roman's arm, she twisted around, spread her limbs in the hope that the increased wind resistance would slow her descent.

The ground was rushing toward her now—close enough that she could see the abandoned farm below. Shadow had dragged them straight up: they were going to come down within yards of the grain silo.

At the last second she flipped over onto her back, throwing Roman upward, hoping that it would help reduce the speed of his fall. She turned herself solid and crashed into the ground.

Even before the dust had settled, she was on her feet, scrambling out of the crater she'd made, running to where the clone had come down.

He was alive, moaning softly. His eyes were flickering wildly.

His left leg and left arm were shattered, twisted at sickening angles no human being should ever have to see, let alone suffer.

He's not going anywhere for a while, Renata thought. She ran for the grain silo and tore through the rubble until she found her armor. Beneath it, shielded from the falling bricks by her chest-plate, was a small computer similar to the one Colin wore on his wrist.

She tapped at the controls for a moment, bringing up a map of the world

On screen, two bright dots were rapidly heading north. "Flying home to Daddy. Good. *Now* we've got you."

And then the dots disappeared.

Chapter 21

When he could no longer see the two superhuman figures racing through the air, Danny slowed to a stop.

After he left Renata he'd caught up with the clone and been able to keep pace, but he was stuck on the ground while his quarry was hundreds of feet above.

Then another of the clones approached from the south, fell into place alongside the first.

Danny had kept up with them for hundreds of miles, but in the past few minutes they'd increased their height, and disappeared into the clouds.

He shifted back to real-time and switched on his computer screen. *Why can't they build me one that works when I'm in fast-time?* But he knew the answer to that: Razor had explained that it didn't matter how fast or slow Danny was moving: the signals from the GPS tracking devices they'd hidden in the clones' boots would come in at the same speed.

The on-screen map showed that the clones were approaching the Arctic Circle. *So their base is definitely up north. Unless they know we're tracking them.*

The computer told Danny that he was in Alberta, Canada, forty-two miles west of Edmonton. "Oh great," he said aloud. "Thirteen hundred miles from home." He looked down at his boots. *Another pair about to wear out. I've got to find a better way to do this. Maybe I need roller-skates. Oh,* that'd *be cool!*

The radio built into the computer beeped. "Danny, you there?"

"I'm here, Lance. In Canada, apparently."

"Good. Bring me back a maple-flavored moose, or something. The clones' GPS signals just stopped—I'm guessing that they discovered the trackers. Or maybe Cross figured we'd plant something on them if they were caught, so they have a standing order to destroy their clothes before returning to base. Either way, we lost them."

"But they were going in a straight line, so just follow that path until it intersects with the other one. You know, the one from Berlin to where Mina's phone was found."

"Right. Like they're dumb enough to fly back to their HQ in a straight line. They must have known we'd track them, so we have to assume that wherever their base is, it's *not* on this path."

"Yeah, but it they knew *we'd* know that, then—"

Lance interrupted. "Stop. We could go back and forth all day on who knew what. Just get back to base."

In Sakkara, Lance and Colin watched the monitors. "Danny's right, of course. North," Lance said. "But *where* in the north?" He tapped on his computer's keyboard. A globe of the Earth appeared on the screen, showing a straight line from the farmhouse to the clones' last confirmed location. "Cross would have made it very clear to them not to fly straight home. But maybe we can make a few guesses. We extrapolate their vector. That takes them into Alaska... OK, now they're not going north any more, the line's starting to drift south... Across the Bering Sea, over Kamchatskaya... And down into Japan." He sighed. "Even a few more minutes and we could narrow it down a lot more."

"What about if we trace a line from Berlin through the point where Mina's phone was found?" Colin asked.

"Already done that... It extends into Russia."

"And then the two lines cross in Japan. That's where they are."

"It's not. That's too simple. Like I said, Cross wouldn't let them fly home in a straight line. So we can assume that Japan is the one place they're *not*."

"Unless that's what he *wants* us to think."

"Didn't I *just* have this conversation with Danny?" Lance angrily pushed the keyboard away. "This isn't telling us anything useful. Colin, we're going to have to go with the earlier plan. What do you say?"

Colin swallowed. "They might just *kill* me."

"I know. You ever play chess? Sometimes, to get the better of your opponent, you have to do what he's not expecting. You have to put your most powerful piece in danger. The queen. You're the queen."

"Oh, great. Thanks."

"I know it's asking a lot, but can you do it?"

"Yeah." Colin nodded. "Yeah. I can do it."

Lance crouched down in front of the injured clone. "So. I'm told your name is Roman. My name is Jason Myers, and you've already met Renata. You seem to be in a little bit of pain, yes?"

Roman nodded slightly, and groaned.

"Well, without the anesthetic we've given you, it would be a lot worse. A thousand times worse. And this particular anesthetic is expensive stuff. I'm not going to waste it on you unless you're willing to talk. It's already starting to wear off so if you clam up, no more pain relief. You are really *not* going to like that, believe me. So you'll tell me everything I need to know, right?"

"I'll talk. But it won't do you any good."

"We'll see. How many clones are there, including you?"

"Nine."

"Have they all developed their powers yet?"

"Yes, mostly."

"Where is Victor Cross's base?"

The clone looked away. "I can't tell you."

"Oh, I think you can. And you *will*."

"No, it's... It's hidden from us. We don't *know*. Victor modified our brains... All we know is that it's somewhere north. When we get closer to it, we remember the location more accurately. He did this to stop anyone from using us to find him."

We could load him onto a plane, Lance thought. *Head north and scout around until he remembers... No, that would make us sitting ducks.* "Roman, what is Victor Cross planning?"

"There's a rocket. A missile. Very big. It's almost complete. Please... The pain."

"Payload and destination?"

Roman groaned. "The pain...!"

"Payload and destination?" Lance repeated. "I won't ask a third time."

"I don't know! Victor wouldn't say. But I know what it's *for*. He's going to crack open the world."

Lance leaned on his cane as he stood up. "Administer another dose," he said to Renata. "Ten milliliters should do it."

He walked over to Stephanie and Kenya. "Get back to Sakkara. Tell Razor to prepare Brawn and ready the ship."

Kenya pointed to Roman. "What about him?"

"We'll be taking him back to Sakkara."

"Are you crazy? He's dangerous!"

"Not as dangerous as Renata, and I think he knows that by now."

Stephanie said, "Lance, we need Colin. Where is he?"

"Colin's busy. Now go." He watched them depart, then he returned to the clone's side. "What do you mean when you say Victor's going to crack open the world?"

"And I, behold, I do bring the flood of waters upon the earth, to destroy all flesh, wherein is the breath of life, from under heaven; everything that is in the earth shall perish."

Lance rocked back as though he'd been slapped. "No..."

"What *is* that?" Renata asked.

"The Bible," Lance said. "The book of Genesis. The flood."

"Yes," Roman said. "We will crack open the world, shatter the tectonic plates and trigger a dozen supervolcanoes that will release enough magma to drown the Earth. All that you know will be destroyed. A flood. Not of water, but of fire."

Chapter 22

In a small, well-hidden fortress in western Oregon, Antonio Lashley rushed out of his office, pulling on his jacket as he ran.

In the long corridor outside, one of base's guards caught up with him. "It's coming in *fast*, sir, on a vector that brings it right to us."

"No arrivals on the schedule?"

"No sir. Everyone's on alert. Nothing is getting in or out. I'd stake my job on that."

"You already have." Lashley slowed to a quick walk, already out of breath. Once, he'd been able to run for miles with a fifty-pound pack on his back and barely break a sweat, but those days were gone. Now he'd reached the age—and attained the status—that meant he shouldn't *have* to run anywhere, that there was always a subordinate to do his running for him.

He'd recovered a little by the time they reached the main corridor leading to the fortress's concrete landing-pad. "Check the usual channels for authorization. We shoot first. I want whatever it is atomized before it gets within two miles."

"In range of the auto-guns in fourteen, sir."

"Fourteen minutes... Thought you said it was moving fast?"

"Fourteen *seconds*, sir!"

Overhead, the fortress's automatic weapons burst into life with a sustained, deafening barrage of gunfire. Lashley cowered back, covered his ears with his hands. For half a minute the landing-pad was showered with a heavy rain of brass shell-casings.

"So what *was* it?" Lashley yelled, the noise still ringing in his ears.

The guard next to him shouted back, "Uh, sir, 'was' isn't the right word. 'Is' would be a better choice."

A teenage boy stood in the center of the courtyard, slowly looking around. He spotted Lashley and began to walk toward him.

A trickle of cold sweat ran down Lashley's back. "It's Wagner. Titan's kid." Louder, he called out, "How did you find this place? We're not on any maps, there are no records—"

"We have our ways," Colin replied. "I want Cassandra Szalkowska. Now."

Antonio Lashley ran a trembling hand across his mouth. He knew there was no point in denying that they were holding the girl. "Son, I can't authorize that. We were hired by appointed representatives of the United States government to seize and hold—"

"No, you weren't. You were operating on bogus orders."

"We received the correct authorization codes. They're *impossible* to fake."

"Impossible for a normal person, maybe," Colin said, "but we're not dealing with a normal person. I know who you are, Lashley, and what you do. You sell your skills to the highest bidder. *And* I know who you used to work for—that gives me another reason to dislike you. So I know you understand what I can and will do if you don't hand Cassandra over to me."

Lashley shook his head. "I can't do that. Maybe if you give me a half-hour to check, I'll be able to—"

"No, you'll bring Cassandra to me right *now*, or I will tear this whole complex apart, stone by stone."

Lashley turned to the guard. "Get the girl, Shango." To Colin, he said, "She's on the way."

Less than a minute later, the guard and a colleague returned, carrying Cassandra between them.

"We had to sedate her," Lashley said, "but she's unharmed. She'll be out for another couple of hours."

Colin took Cassandra in his arms, and rose into the air. In seconds, he was gone.

Lashley turned to Shango. "I want the weapons checked and reloaded."

"Yes, sir. You think he's coming back?"

"No. But whoever really issued those orders might not be too pleased that we lost their prize."

Danny arrived at Sakkara to see the ChampionShip docked on its roof. He raced up the building's sloping sides and returned to real-time. On the roof, Kenya and Stephanie were helping Renata into her armor.

"Hey," Danny said.

Renata turned around. "Hey yourself. Are you ready?"

"Ready for what, exactly?"

"We're prepping to go. We know that Cross is based somewhere in the north, so we're moving out. We're bringing the war to them."

"Oh man… Where's Colin?"

"Lance has sent him out. He won't say where."

"But what about Alia and Grant in Berlin? Lance wanted them to be the bait to attract Cross."

"A double-bluff," Stephanie said. "He was sure that Cross had Sakkara bugged, so he knew they'd be safe."

Renata led Danny into the ship, and Kenya and Stephanie

followed. She slapped Danny on the shoulder as she moved toward the cockpit. "I'm taking her up. Two minutes."

Inside, it was more cramped than usual, and Danny grinned when he saw Brawn. "So *that's* it."

The giant rumbled, "Yeah. And there's a present for you, too." He reached out and pulled the top off a large packing crate. "In here."

Inside was a suit of armor similar to those worn by Team Paragon, but painted green rather than blue or red. "This is yours," Brawn said. "You were able to use your mechanical arm when you were at top speed, right? Well, now you've got a new arm built into a whole suit. You got a jetpack and everything. And you'll be bullet-proof."

"I thought you were modifying the armor for Lance?"

"Another lie," Stephanie said. "Remember that note he gave me with the specifications? It was this." She reached into the crate and pulled out the helmet. "Are you ready to go to war?"

Danny looked around at his friends. "Yeah. I'm ready."

Colin sat on a bed in Sakkara's infirmary as his father again used superglue to seal the wound in his temple. "Ow!"

"Sorry, son. I know it stings but needles just won't do the trick."

Nearby, Lance stood leaning against the wall, watching them. "You understand what you have to do, Colin?"

"I do. How's Cassie?"

"She's recovering. Still a little groggy, but that'll pass. Her anger at being taken, though, is going to take a lot longer to subside."

Warren said, "I don't like this, McKendrick. Not one bit." He tilted Colin's head to the side and peered at the wound. "That'll hold for a while. Maybe long enough to heal properly, if you don't take any more damage."

Lance said, "Doesn't matter whether you like it, Warren. This is Colin's choice."

"But it's your idea, so I'm holding you responsible." He rested his hand on Colin's shoulder. "Just... Just remember to stay low."

"Sure, Dad. I'll be all right." He tried to sound braver than he felt, but wasn't sure that the act was fooling any of them. *Lance is right—this is the only way.*

"Do you want to talk to your mother before you go?" Warren asked.

Colin slid down off the bed. "Yeah, but I won't. She'd only panic." He smiled. "If I never make it back, you'll tell my little sister all about me, right?" He'd meant that as a joke, a lighthearted comment to break the tension, but no one was laughing.

"Still in a lot of pain, huh?" Lance said to the injured clone, Roman.

Weakly, Roman nodded. He was lying on a small camp-bed inside the tent Lance had ordered to be erected on the roof of Sakkara.

"We're not monsters, kid. It's not that we're leaving you in this state just because you're the enemy. We've given you the strongest painkillers available but you're practically immune to them." Lance took a step back and looked at Roman from head to toe.

Earlier, before they'd carried Roman to the copter, Lance

had watched as Renata did her best to force his broken bones back into place. It had been a futile effort. Whenever the clone coughed or his muscles twitched, the bones shifted, their shattered ends grinding against each other. There wasn't a needle and thread in the world strong enough to sew up his wounds. In the end, Lance had asked Renata to twist a series of steel bars around his arm and leg to act as splints.

And then they had left him there, alone. Renata and Colin were the only two strong enough to detain him, and Lance wasn't going to risk leaving anyone else with him.

Now, the steel bars were warped, some of them split, and the jagged broken end of Roman's femur was again pushing through the skin.

He's going to die in agony because he's so strong, Lance thought. *We could sedate a normal person.* Aloud, he said, "Roman... I'm sorry about this. I truly am. But there's nothing more we can do for you. Your body will have to heal itself, and I don't know whether that's even possible. But... bad as this is, it's still better than being dead. Do you understand what I'm telling you?"

Very slightly, Roman nodded. "You think I... deserve this."

"Maybe you *do.* You attacked us without reason. Your friends have already killed one of us, and taken two others. My people are about to launch their counter-attack on Victor Cross's base. If they fail, that's it for life on this planet. Everything will burn. Do you want that?"

"We... *We'll* survive. We can withstand any amount... of heat. One of the reasons Colin's DNA was chosen."

"I see. And what about Cross? He doesn't have superhuman strength. He'll die. A single supervolcano would discharge enough lava to swamp the United States. It would cover the entire world in an ash cloud so dense that every air-breathing creature would suffocate. It would block out the sun, global temperatures would plummet. Within a year, all the plants would be dead. There are forty or more dormant supervolcanoes on the planet. You said Victor Cross intends to trigger a *dozen* of them. And you want to live in a world like that?"

Roman didn't reply.

"Physically, you're almost identical to Colin Wagner, but morally... He's by far your superior. You're a weak copy of him." Lance turned away, hesitated, and turned back. "If you don't die of infection, or blood-loss, you'll have the privilege of watching the world burn. The lava will wash over this world, boiling the seas, setting even the air on fire. And you and your fellow clones might well be tough enough to survive that. But I've done some calculations, Roman. This area, right here,"—he tapped his cane on the floor—"will be buried under a thousand feet of lava. And you're *weak* now because of your injuries. If the weight of the lava doesn't crush you, if you somehow live long enough for it to cool and solidify, you'll be stuck. Buried alive. You won't be able to scream for help, because your lungs will be filled with solid rock. Your friends will never find you. You'll be stuck here, alone, in agony, deformed because we're not strong enough to properly set your bones."

Lance paused for effect, then added, "And while you're pondering that, throw *this* thought into the mix... What if you're immortal?"

After a moment, Roman raised his good arm to his face and brushed the tears from his eyes. "All right... What do you want me to do?"

Lance faked a look of surprise. "What do you mean? I don't want you to do anything. I just came to let you know what you're in for. It's not like you're in any position to stop Cross's plans, is it? Even if you had the strength, he'd set your brothers against you. No, you're no good to me. You're no good to anyone, now." Again, Lance turned away, and again he stopped. "I can't do it. Even though you're beneath contempt, I can't leave you to suffer forever. There is something else we can do to ease your pain."

"Please. Anything..."

"You have to let Cassandra into your mind. She can't heal you, but she can take the pain away."

"Yes... I'm begging you. Do it."

The tent flap was pulled open, and Cassandra stepped in. She knelt down beside the bed, her face close to Roman's. "I want you to relax, as much as you can. This will be uncomfortable, but not painful."

Lance stood back and watched as Cassandra stared, unmoving, at the clone. *Come on. This has to work. If she can get through to him, we just might have a chance.*

Chapter 23

"They'll have tracked you, of course," Victor cross said to Shadow. "I've no doubt they're on the way even as we speak."

Shadow floated around the base of the missile's launch pad. "Yeah. Man, this is *big*." The cylindrical rocket towered over them. Far above, working on a flimsy-looking gantry, Evan Laurie was instructing two of Shadow's brothers how to attach a bulky fuel-line. "We left Roman behind."

"I know. When this is done we'll get him back."

"What if he talks?"

"He won't."

"They might *force* him to."

"They're the good guys," Victor said. "They're not going to resort to torture."

Shadow completed his circuit and drifted back to Victor. "Renata said something that got me thinking. Are we going to keep growing older at the same rate?"

"No, it's pretty much stopped now. You'll age like everyone else. Unless you're one of those lucky few superhumans who happen to be immortal."

"Like Krodin."

"Right. He's immortal because his body constantly repairs itself, but I'm sure there are other ways to achieve that wonderful state."

"I don't like the idea of living forever. You'd get to see everyone you know die, and then in a few billion years the sun will explode, and you'd be all alone in space. Forever. Until the universe comes to an end. And after that... Well, there *is* no after that."

"When the universe ends, it'll be replaced by another one," Victor said, looking up at the missile. "It's happened before, it'll happen again. It keeps happening." He looked back at Shadow. "Of course, when I say 'before' that's not really accurate. There was no 'before' the universe because time is one of the aspects *of* the universe. The next one will certainly have different aspects. Time might not be among them." He shrugged. "It's hard even for *me* to get my head around that one. How can a universe exist with no time?"

"Other universes," Shadow mused. "Like when Krodin changed the past?"

"No, not that like. That was an alternate reality to this one. That's like... Suppose that the universe is a page in a book. Krodin's reality was on the other side of the same page. But the other universes are different books. Understand?"

"Not really."

"Well, I don't care. Now, go help Evan. Time is short. For now. The heroes are coming and they'll no doubt have a few surprises for us."

"How dead do you want them?"

"Dead as you can, thanks." As Shadow began to rise, Cross called out, "Actually, hold on a second... They're going to want to rescue Mina. If they achieve that, we could be in trouble. Better kill her first."

Cross's radio beeped, and he held up a hand to tell Shadow to wait. "Yeah?"

Evan Laurie's voice said, "Victor... We've got activity on one of the monitored locations. It's the New Heroes. They're, well, I don't know *how* they found out, but..."

"Get to the point."

"They're going after your father."

"I see."

Laurie said, "Victor, it's your *dad*. He's your only living relative!"

"So they found him... Or maybe they've always known where he is." Cross pursed his lips and tapped the corner of the radio against his chin. "Shadow, forget what I just told you. Take Tuan, Zeke and Warwick out to find Colin Wagner—he's coming here. Bring the extractor with you. Their telepath must have found a way to break through Roman's defenses. She could have figured out our location from his memories."

"But you have the location blocked from us!"

"They're smart enough to put the clues together."

"Then, what about your father?" Shadow asked.

"Hmm? Oh, right. No, he'll be fine. They're not going after him. It's a trap. Go get Colin."

"You want him dead?"

"Only if you have no choice, but I'd prefer you to use the Extractor. I've got a lot of questions for that young man and I'd like him to be in a condition to answer them."

Colin flew due north, hoping that he was going in the right direction. Or at least close enough.

He wondered how many of his clones he'd have to face this time. *Three weren't enough to stop me. They might send four or five. Or all of them.*

At times like this he wished he had Renata's invulnerability. His skin was strong, but he could be hurt, and his guts churned with the thought of what he knew was coming. *I don't want to do this. It's dangerous and crazy and it might get me killed.*

Maybe I'll get lucky and Cross will send them one at a time. I could deal with that. Probably.

He was within sight of Hudson Bay when he sensed them coming.

Four of them in a tight cluster, rocketing toward him at least as fast as he was traveling.

In seconds, they had surrounded him, and Colin decelerated to a stop. He turned around slowly. The clones were keeping their distance, but watching him.

"Tell me, do you guys all have names, or did Cross give you numbers to make it easier?"

The clone on his left said, "We have names. You've met me before. Shadow. On my left is Zeke. Then Tuan and Warwick."

"Pity you're all so ugly," Colin said, and all of them, including Colin, laughed. "So… We all have a big fight now and those of you who survive go home to nurse your wounds, right?"

Shadow said, "We could do that. Or we could beat the snot out of you and leave you broken and dying, like your people did with Roman."

"He's not dead yet," Colin said. "But he's definitely out of the fight. So that's one down and eight to go. Who's next?"

"You are," Shadow said. "If it was up to me, we'd pulverize you into paste, but the boss has other plans for you."

Here it comes, Colin thought. He braced himself. "What plans?"

"He didn't say. But he did give us *this*." Shadow held up a device that reminded Colin of a child's toy ray-gun. "You can try to zap it with that thing you do to control electricity, but this was designed especially for you. It's shielded."

"A gun. Not very original."

"It's not a gun. Remember Ragnarök's power-damping machine? Remember the one Victor made for Max Dalton? Similar technology, only instead of wiping out everyone's powers, this Extractor only works on *you*. Won't even work on us, and we're almost identical to you."

Colin said, "An Extractor. You're going to try to take away my powers." He narrowed his eyes. "You think you're a good enough shot to hit me?"

Shadow lowered the weapon, held it by his side. "Like I said, it's not a gun. Victor put it inside this toy only because it was a handy casing for it. I don't need to be a good shot, because it's omni-directional. Doesn't matter *where* you are, as long as you're in range—"

Colin darted up into the air, racing away from the clones as fast as he could move. His path took him in a wide arc, brought him low, almost to the ground. He didn't waste time looking back to see if they were following—he knew they would be.

In the woods to the east of Hudson Bay he rapidly zigzagged between the trees. He darted across an old road that cut through the forest, zoomed down a hillside and rocketed across a wide lake.

Wish he'd said what the range is *on that thing.*

He entered another forest and slowed, extended his hearing to concentrate on the sounds of the forest, listening for anything that shouldn't be there.

Flying is silent, but if they talk to each other I'll be able to pin-point their location.

He stopped, hovering a couple of feet above the forest floor. *Don't know if they can see me here... One of them might have infra-red vision.*

Then all the sounds of the forest faded away, and Colin fell to the ground.

Above him, Shadow dropped through the trees. "And just like that—zap!—Colin Wagner is no longer a superhuman."

Colin shuffled backwards on his hands and feet.

The leaves rustled as Shadow landed softly on the forest floor, and began walking toward him. Behind him, the other three clones were descending.

"Still want that fight?" Shadow asked. "Seriously. Go for it. I *want* you to."

One of the others—Colin thought it was Zeke, or maybe Warwick—said, "Just grab him, Shadow. Victor wants him alive."

The four superhuman clones advanced on Colin. In his entire life, he had never felt so helpless, or so scared.

In Sakkara, Lance McKendrick looked at the tall man standing in the doorway of his quarters. "Yeah?"

"You sent the kids in without us," Façade said.

"This is true. You'd get in the way."

"That's not how this is supposed to happen. They're *our* children!"

"Technically, Danny's *not* your son. But I do understand. And I sympathize. But if you were there, Danny would be worried about protecting you. There's nothing you can add to the fight that would make any difference." Lance stepped back from the doorway. "Come in." He pointed toward the sofa with the tip of his cane. "Have a seat."

"Razor said that Colin's been captured."

"This is also true." Lance sat down in his armchair. "Believe me, I'm as worried about him as you are. For now, all we can do is wait. Renata knows not to break radio silence until they've been spotted."

"What's your back-up if this doesn't work?" Façade asked.

"There is no back-up. This is a one-shot, all-or-nothing attack."

"According to Shadow, there are nine clones in total. We've got one of them, but we don't know what other defenses Cross has." Façade stood in front of Lance's chair and glowered at him. "You've just sent my son to his death."

Lance looked away, shaking his head. "You don't know that," he said quietly. "He's resourceful. They *all* are—you trained them well. And they're the only hope this world has."

Façade began to speak, but Lance cut him off: "Just listen. Cassandra was able to get inside Roman's mind. It was tricky for her to decipher because he's still just an infant in many ways, but she saw a lot. Most of the clones have very simple powers. Flight, strength, speed. They also have a pretty high tolerance for variations in temperature, but nothing like Colin's. Cross was disappointed with that. He was hoping for something else, something special—Roman doesn't know what that *is*—but he didn't get it. This tells me that Cross is no longer working on his A-plan. He's moved on to another one."

"How does *that* help us?" Façade asked.

"That I don't know. Yet. Now… There's transport coming to take everyone back to the Substation. The rest of the civilians are already there. We're abandoning Sakkara. If the kids fail, this place will be Cross's first target. So you go to the Substation, be with Rose and Niall. Because if the world is coming to an end, that's where you're going to *want* to be."

"And you?" Façade asked.

"I'm staying. Someone has to be here to liaise with the kids, and to make the place seem occupied if their mission fails and Cross comes here. Of course, if *that* happens, if that vermin comes within a mile of here, I'm going to nuke the building off the face of the Earth."

Chapter 24

Victor Cross watched as Evan Laurie draped a blanket around Colin's trembling shoulders, then handed him a mug of warm tea. The boy was standing in the center of the ice-walled room and had barely moved since his clone-brothers had brought him to the base.

"Cold out there, isn't it?" Cross asked.

Colin was shivering too much to nod. He raised the steaming mug to his mouth and just as it touched his lips Cross reached out and pulled it from his hands, poured the tea onto the frozen floor and handed the mug back to Laurie.

"Yeah. I'm not one for the cold, really." Cross said. "Or the heat. I prefer a more moderate climate." Cross placed his hand on Colin's shoulder and kept it there as he walked around to face him from the front. "The good news is that your powers aren't gone forever. This isn't like when Danny's powers were wiped out, or Renata's. The energy that gives you your abilities has been drained, that's all. Drained right down to *almost* zero. It's going to take a long time for the energy to build back up to a level that's useful."

Colin began, "H... How..."

"How long? I'm not sure. It'll be different for everyone." He smiled. "I'm not talking hours or even days, Colin. It'll be months, maybe even as much as a year. That's not going to be much use to you, because you'll be dead long before that happens. So. There's no escape, waste of time trying, blah, blah, blah. You know how it goes. When you've warmed up a little, we'll talk. I have *lots* of questions for you. I'll give you a taster so you'll have enough time to come up with clever lies that won't fool me for a second because I'm too smart for you. First one... What were you doing in Romania when my people picked you up? You were going somewhere. Where and why? Here's another one. What is The Chasm?" Victor smiled. "I'm sure you *don't* know the answer to that. No one does. Not even me. But I'll find out one day. It has to be important—it cropped up so many times in Quantum's visions. Third question: How—"

His entire body still trembling from the cold, Colin whispered, "I know."

"What?"

"The Chasm. *I* know."

Victor Cross took a step back, and raised a hand to his chin, stroking the day-old stubble. "*You* know. Colin, you *can't* know. I'm a hundred—a thousand—times smarter than you. I've been studying Quantum's visions for *years* tying to understand what The Chasm is." Cross turned to Laurie. "Get this young man a seat. He looks like he's about to collapse."

Laurie darted to the side of the room and came back with a chair, and helped Colin into it.

Cross knelt down in front of him. "Tell me."

"Let Mina go."

"I can't do that."

"Then I can't tell you what The Chasm is."

Softly, Victor said, "Tell me, or Mina will suffer like no one has ever suffered before. She will die very, very slowly, in absolute agony. Then I'll send my boys out to find your parents, and your sister. Do you want that, Colin? Do you *want* me to hurt your baby sister? Because I will. I'll do it and I won't feel the slightest qualm about it."

Colin raised his head to look Cross in the eye. "Do you have a Bible?"

"Don't try to frighten me with tales of eternal damnation. Just *tell* me."

"I need a Bible to tell you."

"I've memorized the Bible. Fifteen different editions. Where do I look?"

"King James edition," Colin said. "Revelation. Chapter nine. Verse two."

Victor sent a command to his memory to retrieve the quote, then paled when he realized what it was.

Laurie asked, "Victor? What is it?"

Victor recited, "And he opened the bottomless pit; and there arose a smoke out of the pit, as the smoke of a great furnace; and the sun and the air were darkened by reason of the smoke of the pit."

Colin stared at Victor. "The bottomless pit. The Chasm. And your weapon, your missile... that's what creates it. It tears the Earth apart. It's the end of everything, Victor. Even you. This is Armageddon, and you're its architect."

"They'll see us coming. And they're going to try to stop us." Stephanie Cord looked at Danny, Kenya and Brawn, steadying herself as the ChampionShip was rocked by turbulence.

Renata called back from the cockpit: "Steph's right. There are eight of them, plus whoever else Cross has on his side. They're going to attack hard, and fast."

Stephanie continued, "Our first goal is to get Mina and Colin out, if they're still alive. Secondary goal is that we stop Victor Cross by any means necessary."

"*Any* means?" Kenya asked.

"If we have to, we kill him. Are you OK with that?"

Kenya said, "If what you've told me about Cross is true… Because of him, I've already killed hundreds of people." She pulled off her gloves and looked down at her scarred hands. "Yes. I'm OK with it. He deserves to die."

"I hope it won't come to that," Stephanie said. "Cross murdered my father, but Dad never believed in like-for-like revenge, and neither do I. However…" Stephanie looked at the others for a moment. "I am willing to make an exception. Too many people have already died because of the Trutopian war, and if he does manage to rupture the tectonic plates, *billions* will die. All life on the planet could be wiped out."

"What about Cassie?" Brawn asked from the back of the ship. "We *should* have her with us."

"Lance says he has a different job for her."

Danny said, "So this is it. Five of us against eight of them. And two of us aren't even superhuman."

"We also have Mina, if she's still alive," Brawn said. "Plus we've got the armor. That does make a difference."

Stephanie said, "Danny, try out your new arm in fast-mode, make sure it works."

Danny looked down at his metal-covered hands, and flexed them. As Stephanie watched, he seemed to blur for a moment. "Yeah, it's working fine."

"It's stronger than your old one, and more precise. And it's much better protected because of the armor. You're going in first, Dan, as soon as we're in range. You've never used a jetpack before so we'll control it from here. That means you'll be in real-time. If you prefer, we'll set you down and you can run in fast-time." Stephanie turned to Renata. "What's our ETA?"

"Eighty-seven minutes."

"All right." Stephanie realized that her heart was pounding. She tried not to think of this as revenge for her father's death, but the thought kept surfacing. *We have to do what's right*, she told herself. *That's what Dad would have wanted.*

Mina woke up lying in her side, shivering, her stomach clenching and her head thick and dizzy. A voice said, "You're alive. You'll be all right."

She opened her eyes, but could see only a dark blur against a white background. "Where am I? Who are you?" Cold viscous liquid dripped from her face, and when she raised her hand to wipe it away, a sudden pain shot through her arm.

She blinked several times, and her vision began to clear. "Colin? Is that you?"

"No. My name is Shadow."

Mina coughed and tried to sit up, but her arms trembled and she collapsed back onto the cold hard ground. "I don't understand."

"We found you in Berlin, remember? For a few seconds you thought my brother Tuan was Colin Wagner. Then you saw his aura, realized it didn't match." Shadow was standing over her, leaning down with his hands on his knees. "But a few seconds was all Tuan needed. Remember suddenly feeling weak? That was him. He can steal energy and body-mass from others, take it into himself."

Mina frowned. She had a vague memory of seeing Colin approach her, then realizing too late that it wasn't him; his aura hadn't been quite right. Sometime after that she'd briefly regained consciousness to find herself being dragged through the air, too weak to break free. She remembered fumbling her phone out of her pocket to call for help, then the phone slipping from her numb fingers.

She looked around. They were in an enormous white-walled room, in front of a series of large metal-and-glass cylinders. The one behind her had been smashed open, its liquid contents already starting to freeze on the ground. "What *is* this place? Why is it so cold?"

"Northern Russia, a place called Zaliv Kalinina. We're in the heart of a hollowed-out glacier." Shadow straightened up. "Even at its thinnest point, the ice is five meters thick. Except for the hangar, because we need to be able to get in and out, right? But five meters is more than thick enough to block anyone from detecting us." He reached out a hand. "I'll help you up. C'mon, I don't bite."

Tentatively, Mina took his hand and allowed him to pull her to her feet. "Why do you look like Colin?"

"Like you, I'm a clone. I'm one of nine clones of Colin. We were created by Victor Cross."

Mina pulled her hand away from Shadow's, and stepped back. "No…"

"Tuan brought you here. Victor wanted you, you see." Shadow shrugged. "Turned out that none of *us* had what he needed. He thought *you* might. And also he wanted you out of the picture. Everyone thinks that Colin is the most powerful member of the New Heroes, but they're wrong. *You* are. And it's always better to disable your enemy before the fight begins, right? Except, maybe not *this* time."

"What are you *talking* about?"

"Your friends are on the way to try to rescue you and stop Victor from carrying out his plans. He sent me to kill you before they got here. You see, Victor didn't get what he needed from you either. So, anyway, I could have just killed you while you slept, but I woke you up because I'm kinda interested in seeing how you fight when you *are* prepared for it. I know you're very fast and very strong. You can read people's auras which probably allows you to anticipate what they're going to do. You're an interesting challenge."

"And you're an absolute *bonehead*," Mina said.

She teleported herself up to the gantry overlooking the room, and looked down at Shadow as, confused, he reached out and poked at the spot where she'd been standing.

How do I get out of here? She wondered. *If we are where he said, there's probably nothing but snow and ice for hundreds of miles.*

The gantry led to a closed metal door, and, with her fingers brushing the ice-cold railing in case her trembling legs gave way, and her breath misting in the air ahead of her, Mina made her way toward it. She could teleport herself to any point within a couple of miles, but this was a location she didn't know. She might end up materializing in the middle of a wall. Or right inside another person.

She pulled the door open and stepped through into a narrow, ice-walled corridor. *Focus!* She told herself. She reached out with her mind, sensing the locations of the other people in the area. Shadow was still on the floor of the chamber behind her. Somewhere ahead, four more, all with superhuman auras.

She slowly turned on the spot. *Eight... Eleven people*, she counted. Two of them were human, the rest superhuman. The humans seemed to be the safest option. One of them was a middle-aged man, the other was a clone who didn't seem to have any superhuman abilities. *No, wait... Is that Colin? His aura looks almost the same, but... If it is him, he doesn't have any powers.*

Mina walked quickly along the corridor, trying to build a mental picture of the interior of the base from the other people's movements. She resisted the temptation to teleport herself directly to the humans' location: three of the superhumans were with them, and the humans' auras showed that they were both incredibly nervous about something. *Nervous people have itchy trigger fingers*, she reminded herself.

She wondered if she should risk teleporting to a mile straight up—that way she'd immediately know where she was. *No, if this* is *the Arctic I'd freeze in seconds. And for all I know we could be more than a mile below the surface. How big* are *glaciers?*

Above her and to her right, two of the superhumans were moving. She gave them a few seconds, then teleported into their previous location.

It was a small, barely-lit room containing three bunk-beds. On the far side of the mostly-closed door, she could hear the superhumans talking. They both had Colin Wagner's voice.

The room smelled like sweaty feet and the floor was littered with piles of clothes: socks, t-shirts, underpants and jeans, none of which had been washed in a long time.

In a closet she found a fresh long-sleeved t-shirt, still in its packaging. A label on the package bore the name "Eldon" in crude hand-writing. Mina quickly pulled off her own damp shirt and replaced it with the new one. *Isn't there any sort of heater in this place?*

Rummaging through the clothes on the floor she found a pair of jeans that fit her around the waist, though they were much too long in the leg. She put them on anyway, and rolled up the cuffs several times. *Now there's got to be a way out of—*

She jumped as a siren blared in the corridor outside the room.

A man's voice panic-filled said, "Uh, danger! The girl is loose —if you see her, stop her!" There was a sharp click as the message ended, then, almost immediately, "And don't forget she's a teleporter!"

Chapter 25

Victor Cross turned away from Shadow without speaking.

"Look, I'm *sorry*," Shadow said. "It's just... I mean, I didn't think she'd *do* that. I thought she'd just fight!"

Colin said, "You didn't breed them for intelligence, then?"

Cross ignored him. He snatched up a walkie-talkie from the charging cradle, hesitated and then took another. "Zeke, take Wagner to the lowest level and stay with him. If he tries anything, kill him *twice*."

He ran from his office and made his way up the sloping tunnel, with Shadow following.

"Victor, please. We'll find her and we'll catch her. I'm stronger than she is, you know that. I'm smarter, too."

"Clearly, you're not."

They emerged from the tunnel into the main room. One of the boys—Nathan—darted across from one side to the other and jumped through an open doorway.

"I'll help find her," Shadow said.

"No, you'll stay with me. I don't want to give that little witch the opportunity to take me down. Shadow, do you know the phrase 'bitter disappointment'? Because that's what I'm feeling right now. All you had to do was shut off the airflow to Mina's pod. She'd have suffocated, and she'd now be dead. But you thought you knew better." He stopped walking and turned to face the clone. "I don't know if I'll *ever* forgive you for this."

Shadow's shoulders sagged, and it seemed to Victor that he was on the edge of tears. *Good. Let him cry, the little idiot. He could have ruined everything. As far as* he *knows, anyway.*

"I won't let you down again. Ever. I promise."

"Well. We'll have to see about that, won't we?" There was a brief movement on the edge of his vision. Something hiding close to the ceiling, among the support pillars. *There she is… How do I get her to come down?*

Nathan reemerged from the doorway. "She was just in there! Did you see her?"

"No," Victor said. "Nathan, forget her. Go help protect Evan. He's not superhuman, and if he can't get the payload into the rocket we've lost everything. Shadow, come with me."

They ran for the far stairway, and raced up, with Victor's feet pounding on the metal steps and Shadow flying after him. As he passed close to Mina's position, Victor deliberately kept his eyes focused ahead. *Good girl. Keep watching us…*

Victor unlocked one of the store-rooms leading off the upper gantry. "Keep a watch out for the girl." He stepped inside and stood with his back to the door, hoping that Mina didn't also have the ability to see through walls. He pulled open a metal cupboard and snapped the seal on a cylinder of gas, then threw one of his walkie-talkies inside before he backed out of the room.

To Shadow, he said, "OK, we're all right. The backup controls are secure. If she were to get in here and destroy them, it would set us back *months*." He looked around. "Locking the door's no good. She could teleport herself inside. Find something to put in front of the door. Something big enough to hide it. If she doesn't know that the room is there, she won't think to go inside."

Shadow began, "Yeah, but…"

"Just do it, Shadow!" Victor leaned over the rail and pointed to a large sheet of corrugated metal. "That. Bring it up here, hide the door with it. Come on! Quick!"

Shadow vaulted over the rail and dropped down to the floor below, grabbed hold of the heavy metal sheet and carried it one-handed as he flew back up to the gantry.

"Good," Victor said. "That should do it."

"I should just wait in there for her," Shadow said.

"And suppose she never *finds* the room? No, we're better off looking for her. We could do a room-by-room search, but that power of hers is too useful. She could be anywhere. The only way we're going to get her is if we can sneak up on her, and she can see our auras so *that's* not going to be easy." He gestured back down the stairs. "Come on. Time's fading fast."

In one of the base's narrowest corridors, certain that he couldn't be overheard, Victor quietly said to Shadow, "She was watching us, and listening. When she goes into the storeroom, the gas will overpower her." He held up his other walkie-talkie. "It'll hit her fast—you'll hear her falling. Then you go in and finish her off. Understood? No games this time. Just snap her neck." He frowned briefly. "No. Don't. A better idea has just surfaced. Take her to the hangar and wait there. The gas will keep her out for hours. Should be long enough." He pushed the walkie-talkie into Shadow's hands. "Don't let me down again."

Mina watched them go, then teleported into the now-hidden room. It looked like a storage room, with racks of shelving all piled high with boxes and crates. *I'm not seeing any controls...* She noticed a walkie-talkie on the floor and picked it. *Nice! Now I can listen in on them.*

She used the walkie-talkie's belt-clip to attach it to her jeans, and walked further into the room. *Ew, what's that smell? It's even worse than the boys' bedroom!*

Whatever the smell was, it was making her feel queasy. Her legs were still weak, and she held onto one of the shelving units for support.

Her knees buckled, and she collapsed to the ground.

The clone kept hold of Colin's upper arm as he led him down the icy corridors and into an empty room about the size of a two-car garage. The room's walls, floor and ceiling were crudely finished, with no attachments but a single low-powered bulb on the wall above the door.

"Cozy," Colin said. "What do you usually keep in here, Zeke?"

"Nothing."

"So we're going to just sit on the floor? We'll freeze."

"*You* might. Not my problem." The clone pushed the door closed. "Don't try to get past me."

"You know that Cross is mad, right?" Colin asked, pulling the blanket tighter around his shoulders. "If he destroys the world, where are you going to find food?"

"We don't really need food," Zeke said. "Just like you. Or like you used to be. It'll be a long time before your powers come back."

"I'm betting Cross needs to eat, though. How is *he* supposed to survive?"

"He'll think of a way. He's probably already thought of lots of ways."

"Yeah," Colin said, "but don't forget that he's still crazy."

"You're going to try to persuade me to turn against him," Zeke said. "That won't work. Victor built loyalty into us when he made us. Even *Nathan* is loyal, and he doesn't like Victor at all. But he'll do what he's told."

"You're not really people, are you? And that's not because you're clones. You're his pets. No, you're drones, like worker-bees serving the queen. You think that Cross cares about you, even a little bit? I doubt it. He hasn't sent a rescue mission to retrieve Roman. The only thing he cares about is himself."

"Is this really necessary?" Evan Laurie said to Victor. "Your plan failed, Victor. Just... Just quit. Call it a day." He turned away from the rocket's controls.

Victor looked up from his workbench. He had the Extractor connected to an oscilloscope and was testing its circuitry. "Could tighten this up a bit... What were you saying?"

"You know what I was saying. You can't destroy the world just because you don't get your way. Grow *up*, for crying out loud!"

Without looking, Victor pointed behind him. "Check the monitors. The kids will be in range soon. Got to tell you, this new guy running things in Sakkara is proving to be quite a challenge. He actually out-smarted me."

"What do you mean?"

"The attack on my father was a trick. And he knew I'd know that. The *real* trick was sending Colin."

"But we captured Colin."

"Right. And we took away his powers with this little toy and brought him right inside our top-secret base, which is now no longer secret. We did exactly what McKendrick wanted us to do. Like I said. He's a challenge."

"You think Colin has some sort of transponder on him? But

we searched him."

"I know… But we didn't look closely enough. He could have swallowed something. Or… No, that's it. A GPS strip implanted under his skin. Inside that cut on his head, has to be. They wouldn't be able to break Colin's skin themselves. So, yes, Colin's friends are on the way. Expect a lot of fighting. Our boys will win, of course." Victor leaned back and looked up at the ceiling. "Huh. McKendrick must have also figured that I'd have a way to neutralize Colin's powers. Clever thinking. Otherwise his plan wouldn't work. Well… No use crying over spilled milk under the bridge now. They're coming, and we'll deal with it. But it does mean we really need to step up the game if we're going to launch before it's too late."

Laurie sighed. "I never understood this. *Never*. You're playing with fire and you're wearing clothes soaked in kerosene, that's that you're doing. Colin was right. You're attempting to trigger Armageddon. What makes you think it'll work?"

"Because I'm smart enough to *make* it work."

Laurie looked out through the control room's windows, up at the enormous cylindrical rocket. "It's a one-hundred megaton nuclear missile… Victor, how are we supposed to survive an explosion that's strong enough to shatter the world's mantle and trigger a planet-wide tsunami of lava?"

Victor arched an eyebrow and asked, "We?" Then he smiled. "You should know by now to trust me."

"You're not going to detonate it, right? You're going to hold the world to ransom. That's what I'd do."

"I know that's what *you'd* do. That's why you're not in charge. I am going to detonate it. I'm going to punch a hole straight through the Earth's crust and set the world on fire."

"Why? *Why* do you want everyone dead?"

"Because screw them, that's why."

"All because your plan failed. You're sick." Laurie moved closer to Victor. "No, I can't let you do it."

Cross pried a fingernail-sized microchip out of the Extractor's circuit board. "You can't stop me. You're weak, Laurie. You always have been. You have a desperate need to be loved, to be needed, to feel important. That's why you stuck by me. But the truth is I don't love you, I certainly never needed you, and you're important only to the clones. You're a baby-sitter. That's all. An *au pair* with four masters' degrees that he never uses and an empty heart that will never be filled. You're here only because I didn't want to have to change all those dirty diapers."

Laurie threw himself at Victor, knocking him off his chair, sending him sprawling across the icy floor. "To hell with you, Cross! You... You..."

Victor got to his feet. "The truth hurts, huh? You sad little man. You don't have the guts to take control of your own life, so you followed me around like a puppy. No, you're like the sneering little kid who hangs around with the playground bully."

Laurie picked up the chair, and slammed it down on the computer's keyboard. Even before the shower of keys had settled, he was swinging the chair at the monitors.

Victor ducked toward the door as shards of plastic and glass flew across the room.

Laurie picked up the nearest computer and heaved it at Victor, who only barely dodged out of its way. "There! What does *that* do to your plans?"

"Nothing," Victor said. "Nothing at all. I finished most of my work hours ago. It's all automated from this point on. That code

I was just working on... It's a program to solve a four-dimensional Rubik's Cube. An amusement, that's all. Something to pass the time. Now, are you done with your rant, or is there more?"

Laurie pulled the chair free from the shattered monitors in a shower of sparks. "Your superhuman abilities are all inside your head. You're no stronger or faster than an ordinary man. What's to stop me beating you to a pulp right now?"

"What good would it do? When the missile launches, we're all dead anyway."

"It'd make me feel a whole lot better!"

"For a while, maybe. Put the chair down, idiot. You're embarrassing yourself. And also..." Victor reached out and opened the door. "Boys!"

Laurie dropped the chair, backed away further from the door. "You wouldn't..."

"Sure I would."

Eldon appeared at the door, followed by Nathan. Both of them had smudges of black paint on their hands.

Victor said, "Kids, uncle Evan is trying to kill Daddy. Now, don't hurt him. Just hold him so he can't do any more damage. Nathan, you do it. You're his favorite."

Before Laurie could react, Nathan had darted forward and grabbed his arm. Laurie knew there was no point trying to break free—Nathan had a grip stronger than steel.

"Your plan was insane to begin with, Victor. *Insane*. There's no other word to describe it."

Cross picked up the scattered pieces of the Extractor. "Tch. Now I have to start over. The plan will work, Laurie."

"No, it wouldn't. You just convinced yourself that it would

work because you wanted it so badly. Wanting something to be true doesn't *make* it true."

"It does when I'm the one who wants it."

Chapter 26

By carefully arranging the blanket Colin had managed to keep most of it around his body while also getting the lower edge folded into a strip he could sit on.

He still wasn't sure whether it would be better to be sitting in a corner away from the draft that gusted under the room's ill-fitting door, or in the center of the room furthest from the ice walls.

The clone had remained standing next to the door for a long time, but was now sitting down with his back to the wall.

Colin shuddered constantly and was finding it difficult to breathe. "Zeke. I'm dying here. Get more blankets or bring in a heater or something."

"No."

"Victor didn't order you to let me die."

"He didn't order me to let you live, either."

"Don't you care?"

Zeke shrugged. "Not really."

"*Victor* will care if I die. I'm sure he wants to know more about The Chasm. He'll punish you if I die without him finding out." Colin raised his head a little. "How *does* he punish you, anyway?"

"He tells us that he's disappointed. It's part of our programming to feel bad when he does that."

"What does it feel like?"

"It hurts. Not physically. I can't describe it. It just makes you feel rotten."

"That's called guilt," Colin said. "Aren't you curious about me, about my life? Don't you want to know about the real world, what life is like for ordinary people?"

"We don't have much curiosity about most things. Victor programmed us with everything we need to know."

"Everything he *wants* you to know." Colin shuddered again and tugged the blanket a little tighter around his shoulders. *Wish I still had the power to ignore the cold. I'd forgotten what this felt like.* "Hey, Zeke. I have two coins that add up to eleven cents. One of the coins is not a penny. How is that possible?"

"I don't know. I've never used coins. I don't know what denominations they come in."

"Oh. Right. Well, in America they're one cent, five cents, ten, and twenty-five. The one-cent coin is called a penny. So I've got two coins adding up to eleven cents, but one of them isn't a penny. Makes you wonder, doesn't it?"

"No. It's a trick."

"Yeah, but *how* is it a trick?"

The clone shrugged again. "Don't know, don't care."

There has to be a way out of here, Colin thought. *How can I trick someone who doesn't care about anything and has no sense of curiosity?*

Danny heard Stephanie calling his name, and he raised his head. He'd been thinking about the mission ahead, and what failure would mean. None of his thoughts had led him anywhere he wanted to go.

"Danny, it's time. We're fifty miles north of Zaliv Kalinina. It's solid ice down there—we'll fly you down, and you run." She handed him his helmet. "Your computer will show the destination projected on the inside of your visor. Just keep the dot in the cross-hairs, and you'll be on-target."

He held his breath for a moment. "OK."

"Right now we don't know the way in—search around. If you can't find an easy access point, come back. If you can, search the place top to bottom until you find Mina and Colin. Your helmet's cameras will be recording everything, but you won't be able to transmit it back to us until you switch to real-time. As soon as we get it, we'll come in after you."

"I'm ready."

Brawn said, "Good luck, little buddy. We'll see you in there."

Kenya nodded to him, and Stephanie slapped him on the shoulder. He looked toward Renata, at the ship's controls. She looked back for a moment.

She knows, he thought. *This isn't going to work, and she knows it. But we have to do it anyway. We have to try.*

He moved toward the hatch, and turned back. "Just one thing. I wish... I wish that we were normal kids, that we didn't have to do stuff like this. But, uh, I'm very proud to have you as my friends."

Again, he looked toward the cockpit. Renata looked back.

"Hey?" Danny said.

She replied, "Oh yeah."

"Cool." He lowered his helmet into place, and sealed it.

"What was that?" Brawn asked. "Did I miss something?"

Kenya thumped him on the arm and whispered, "You *didn't* miss your chance to win the 'spoiling the moment' award."

Stephanie opened the hatch, and the interior of the ship was instantly blasted with icy air.

Danny looked out at the howling, bleak landscape rushing past below. *Here goes...* He jumped, and for a few horrifying seconds he thought that he was about to die. Then he felt his jetpack burst into life.

He pitched forward, heels over head, until he was upright once more. He found himself being lowered toward the ground, as above him the ChampionShip continued on its way. It was out of sight by the time his boots touched the ice.

OK. OK. He forced himself to slow his breathing. *All right. I'm at the north pole. Or close enough. If I see a sleigh and flying reindeer I'm giving up and going home.*

He turned slowly from one side to the other, and back, watching the bright dot on the inside of his visor drift left and right. He centered the dot on the cross-hairs, and then slipped into fast-time and began walking.

Stephanie had told him that the ground should be safe, but it wasn't unknown for packed snow to disguise deep crevasses. "In case that happens," she'd said, "if your altitude suddenly drops, Razor programmed your jetpack to automatically activate."

"What if there's a blizzard?" Danny had asked.

"It's unlikely. The Arctic is a desert—it gets less than an inch of precipitation each year. The snow that *does* fall stays on the ground, because there's not enough sunlight to melt it, and freak winds can whip that up into pretty brutal storms. We should be OK, though. The weather's pretty good at the moment."

In the air, the ice had seemed flat and featureless, but he knew now that it was uneven, pitted with car-sized boulders and shot-through with long, parallel furrows that resembled a plowed field. The going was tough, and—to his mind—very slow.

But he was making progress. When he overtook the ChampionShip he looked back to see that the loose snow kicked up by his footsteps still hadn't settled: it was a thick column stretching back as far as he could see.

He trudged on, step after step, for what to him felt like several days. Often, he had to leap ravines or use the jetpack to lift himself over long, rocky outcrops.

The information projected on the inside of his visor showed him the distance he still had to cover, but Stephanie had told him that it was only an estimate, and could be out by as much as two miles on either side. "If you get close enough, you should be able to see some signs of activity," She'd told him. "The clones can get out, so there has to be a way in."

In the New Heroes' ship, Kenya Cho concentrated on her breathing. Slow deep breaths, in and out, in and out. It was supposed to help her feel calm, but right now all she wanted to do was give up and go home.

I shouldn't have come here. I shouldn't have joined these people. I barely know them, and now we're going on a mission that could get us all killed!

She glanced over toward Brawn. The blue giant was reading a paperback book that he cradled in his massive hands like someone holding an injured baby bird.

Renata and Stephanie were concentrating on the mission, quietly discussing tactics.

What do I bring to this? Kenya wondered. *I'm not strong compared to Renata, and I don't have Stephanie's experience.*

In Madagascar, and later in Africa, she had known what her role was in life: to help the helpless, to work to atone for her sins. Since she'd come to America, she had done none of that. She'd slept in a comfortable bed and ate good food, neither of which she felt she deserved.

Brawn looked up from his book and asked, "Quietly panicking?"

Kenya nodded.

"Me too. We all are. We're flying into the unknown and that's always scary."

"I don't know what use I'm going to be here, Brawn. I'll just be in the way."

He closed his book, and leaned back. "None of us are useless. At the very least, we'll be able to provide some distraction for the others. Even if that only gives them an extra second or two, that could make a big difference."

"Yeah, but you're... Well, you're Brawn. You're a *legend*."

Brawn smiled. "Hardly. Back before I lost my powers, sure, I was strong. Stronger than Renata is now, probably. But I spent most of my life in hiding, or in prison, when I should have been out in the world, trying to help people. I squandered my gift. Well, now I get to try to make up for that. We're here because they need us, Kenya. And that's a good enough reason for me."

"This man... Victor Cross. What does he *want*?"

"I don't know. And to be honest it wouldn't surprise me if *he* didn't know either."

"We might die today, Brawn."

"And we might live." He smiled again. "Does death scare you?"

"I'm not ready. I've done a lot of bad things. I've killed people—*hundreds* of people—and I don't want to die before I can make up for that."

Brawn put his book aside. "You can't. You can't ever make up for killing even *one* person. Every life you take also hurts everyone that person knows. You understand that, don't you? There's nothing you can do to redress the balance."

"I know that. But I have to keep trying."

Brawn nodded. "That's the right approach. What you did was wrong, Kenya, but you had no control over your actions." He pointed in the direction the ship was flying. "Cross, though, does have control. He chooses to kill. That makes him the bad guy. Trying to make amends for things that weren't your fault... that's what makes you a hero."

"Give up... yet?" Colin asked. He couldn't understand how his hands and feet were numb and aching at the same time. Earlier, he'd had the blanket pulled over his mouth and nose, and the moisture in his breath had turned to ice and frozen the blanket to his face.

Now, he was desperate to keep warm but unable to do anything but rock back and forth. He knew he had to keep talking: he was sure that if he fell asleep he would never wake up again.

Zeke had successfully proved himself to be the worst conversationalist in the history of the world. No matter what Colin said to him, the clone didn't seem interested.

"The answer... is a duck," Colin said. "All... right. Here's another... one. A man goes into a... a hardware store and he asks to buy... three hammers... OK? The store guy says... New regulations on the sale of hammers. I can only sell you... two hammers. The man says... fine. He pays the guy, and walks out... with three hammers. But... he didn't steal anything. How is...

that possible?"

Zeke sighed. "I don't care. Stop talking."

"Come on... Think about it."

"No."

"Because you're too... dumb to figure it out."

"He already had a hammer with him when he went in."

Rats, Colin thought. *Didn't think he'd actually* get *one of them.*

The door to the room was pushed open, and another of the clones leaned in. "Is he dead?"

"Hey, Oscar. No," Zeke said. "And he hasn't shut up once. Want to swap places?"

"Nah. Victor says to bring him to the hangar." The clone came into the room and looked at Colin. "Wow, he's cold. I suppose we should warm him up first, so he doesn't break if we drop him."

Zeke got to his feet and joined his brother. "Yeah, I guess so."

"How *do* you warm someone up?"

"We could pee on him?" Zeke suggested, and they both laughed.

Go ahead, Colin thought. *Right now I'll take anything that's warm.*

Zeke and Oscar reached down and took hold of Colin's arms, and lifted him up. He'd been sitting in the same position for so long that the blood rushing to his legs brought fresh waves of agony.

Danny was a little over a mile from his target when he realized that the furrow he was now stepping over was different to the others he'd encountered. Its edges were sharp and straight, and the trough bore a regular hexagonal imprint. *Tire track!*

Three yards ahead was an identical track. He looked to the left and right, along the tracks, but couldn't immediately tell which way to go. To the right, the tracks seemed to go on for half a mile or more. To the left, they stopped after a hundred yards.

They're perfectly straight... Who drives from one place to another without making the slightest turn?

He smiled to himself. *Trucks and cars aren't the only vehicles with wheels, idiot! Has to be the aircraft that Colin was chasing when the clones first showed up.*

So does that mean the plane landed there on the left, and then taxied to the right? Or that it started to take off from somewhere way off on the right and zoomed along this way until it was airborne?

Either way, it probably means that the base is somewhere on my right.

He took a few steps in that direction, then stopped. *Then again, the left end is a lot nearer. Makes sense to check that first.*

He followed the tracks to the left, and when he reached the end he realized that they stopped abruptly. *If the plane was landing or taking off from here, the tracks would get shallower before they disappeared.* He turned on the spot, looking for something—anything—that would confirm his suspicions.

Then he saw it, just in front of a towering outcrop. A line in the ice, no wider than a finger. He followed the line and saw that it curved smoothly around to the right. *OK. Interesting. Definitely not a natural phenomenon.*

And then he saw his own boot-prints leading up to the line, and realized he'd come full-circle. He stopped.

Huh. So the plane lands, taxis to this bit which sinks down like an elevator, like they have on aircraft carriers. How do I get in?

After a moment, he moved on. Even though he was in fast-time, he couldn't stay in one spot for too long, or he'd become visible to anyone watching. He followed the circle again, this time staying a few yards outside it. He walked in an increasing spiral, around and around, and was on his tenth lap when something caught his eye: another slight depression in the ice, this one also circular, but only a little over three feet in diameter.

He crouched next to it and began to scrape away the snow and ice. It wasn't long before his glove touched metal. It was a disc—a hatchway—and it was sealed tight.

So that's one *way in... How do I open it?* The hatch didn't seem to have any handles on the outside, or visible hinges.

Danny knew that his mechanical arm was stronger than the human equivalent, but he doubted it was strong enough to force open the hatch.

There's another way, he thought. He lay down flat on his belly, and ran the index finger of his artificial arm in a circle a few inches smaller in diameter than the hatch. He continued this, inscribing the same circle over and over, gradually increasing the pressure.

From his perspective, the job took hours, and he was glad that the mechanical arm didn't suffer from muscle fatigue. In real-time, it was taking only seconds—he hoped no one was watching.

But it was working: eventually the circle became visible as a groove in the metal, which made following the same path much easier. Then the groove began to glow. Red first, then orange, then yellow. When it was glowing white, Danny increased the pressure.

After a few more circuits, his metal-clad finger—which was by now also glowing—pushed through the hatchway.

He completed the last circuit and watched with satisfaction as the molten-edged metal disc slowly slipped through into a long vertical shaft. Inside, a steel ladder was bolted to a concrete wall.

Danny got to his feet and stretched for a moment, before climbing through the hole. At first, he was careful not to brush against the molten-metal edges, but then he realized that it wouldn't harm his armor.

His feet found the rungs of the ladder and he began to descend.

He had to stop every few rungs to wait for the falling disc to drop a little further: the shaft wasn't wide enough for him to climb down past it.

He counted as he descended, losing count after two hundred. *Man, this is a long way down.*

But finally the metal disc would go no further: it had reached the bottom of the shaft, landing on its edge.

He watched as, propelled by its great mass, the disc slowly dug its way into the ground, sending a lazy cascade of dust and rock fragments back toward him.

He stepped off the ladder, and looking left and right he saw that he was in a long, wide tunnel. Though the area around the shaft was made of rough-finished concrete, most of the walls and ground were ice.

Then he saw the crude sign affixed to the wall nearby. A hand-painted message scrawled on a long strip of cardboard: "Welcome, Daniel Cooper. Please follow the arrows."

Chapter 27

The tunnel walls were covered with hand-painted arrows and signs, all leading Danny into the heart of the glacier.

This is just creepy, Danny thought. *Cross* knew *I'd be first.*

The signs were crudely made, the handwriting like that of a five-year-old child, and Danny figured they had been made by the clones. He had already passed three of the Colin-look-alikes, frozen in the process of fixing the signs to the walls. One of them had been pushing steel nails directly into the ice walls with his paint-spattered fingers.

Now, the latest sign read, "Almost there! Around the next corner. But be careful."

Danny rounded the corner, and saw Victor Cross sitting in an ordinary chair in the center of a cavernous, mostly-empty room. Cross was wearing a thick padded jacket, gloves, and heavy boots. On the ground next to him was a thermos flask and what looked like a package of sandwiches.

At the far side of the room, close to the ceiling and suspended from heavy chains, was a black-painted aircraft of a design he didn't recognize. Above the aircraft was a large metal circular hatch—the same diameter as the circle he'd found in the ice.

Behind Cross a gray tarpaulin covered something large, and irregularly-shaped.

Surrounding Cross, embedded into the packed-ice floor, was a circular metal rail, thirty feet in diameter, and outside of it two more of the clones were crouched side-by-side. One was reading a scrap of paper, the other was in the process of crudely painting some words onto a large sheet of cardboard.

He approached the clones. The one with the paintbrush had so far written, "Danny—the circular rail marks a N"—in fast-time, Danny could see a single drop of black paint seemingly suspended in the air half-way between the paintbrush and the cardboard.

He leaned closer to the other clone and read the words on the scrap of paper: "Danny—the circular rail marks a Null-field. Remember that?"

Danny stepped back away from the circle. *Remember it?* He thought. *Yeah, I remember it.*

Two years earlier, in the abandoned Californian gold-mine that Max Dalton had been using as a base, the second power-damper—modeled after Ragnarök's—had been protected by what Cross had called a null-field.

Once activated, anything that attempted to pass through the null-field was instantly destroyed. It was an invisible, infinitesimally-thin shell in which nothing could exist. It was the ultimate passive defense mechanism.

He shifted to real-time, ready to switch back to fast-time if the clones attacked.

Victor Cross said, "... around the circumference of the rail. And do it *neatly* this time. You—" He stopped, reacting to the sound of the ruined hatch-cover echoing through the tunnels. "What was *that*? It... Ah. Don't bother, boys. Mister Cooper is already here." He smiled at Danny. "Long time no see. Gosh, I haven't seen you since, oh, since that time you killed your father."

Danny wasn't going to be drawn into that argument. "A null-field, Cross? Again?"

"I know. I hate to be repetitive, but it's the only thing I could think of that I knew would stop you." Cross leaned over and picked up a small fragment of ice from the ground. He flicked it in Danny's direction; it disappeared as it hit the invisible null-field. "Just in case you think I'm bluffing."

"I got through the last one."

"I know. You figured out that if you could see through the null-field, that meant light could pass through. And you actually managed to move faster than light. Not any more, though. A superhuman who loses his powers never *quite* recovers to full-strength. Would you like to know why that is?"

"No. If the null-field stops anything but light from passing through, then how come I can hear you? If it blocks the air, then that should block the sound-waves too."

Cross smiled. "Good thinking. There are tiny speakers embedded in the rail. So, about your superhuman powers. There is a rare form of energy that—"

"We know about the missile, Victor. We're not going to let you do it."

"You are." He reached behind him, grabbed one end of the tarpaulin and lifted it. "Look. It's your little pals Mina and Colin. Unconscious for the next few hours. You'll notice that they've been wrapped up in Mister Laurie's sleeping bags to keep them nice and warm. You attempt to interfere with the rocket and I'll push both of them through the null-field from this side. One at a time, and quite slowly."

"Why are you doing this?"

Cross let go of the tarpaulin and it dropped back over Mina and Colin's faces. "Hey, *somebody* has to destroy the world. Might as well be me."

Off to the side, the two clones were shifting their stance. *They're going to attack*, Danny thought.

Then Victor said, "Forget it, boys. He's too fast for you. Go and meet Danny's other friends instead. I figure if you follow his path back over the ice, you'll find them."

As the two clones rushed from the hangar, Victor said, "So. Danny. You and I need to talk."

"What would *we* have to talk about?"

"The future. And the past. But first... Kudos to your new boss McKendrick for being the first person in *years* to out-think me. I assume he's watching via the cameras in your armor?" Victor waved and smiled. "Hello, Lance. I'd threaten revenge against your loved ones, but you don't *have* any loved ones. Feel free to keep recording and desperately trying to think of a way to defeat me. It won't do you any good but, hey, it'll pass the time. Also, we're blocking any signals you might try to send to your people. Just in case you're wondering why they don't respond."

Cross looked back at Danny. "Mister Cooper... Do you know what you really are? You're the lynch-pin, the keystone. You're the nexus. Everything revolves around you. Like your real father, you are able to control time. You just haven't had the imagination to do much more than run really fast. Those visions of the future? They're not visions of what *might* happen. They're memories, rippling down through the time-lines. Everything that you have seen will come to pass. I know you've been worried, trying to figure out a way to change the future, but that's not how it works."

Cross stood up and stretched. He began to pace back and forth inside the circle. "Sometimes I wish I had your powers instead of mine. It would be nice to be able to fly like Colin or his brothers, or be practically invulnerable like Renata, but your power is the truly fascinating one. You're the god of time. Many years ago, before either of us were born, some quite clever people called The Helotry of the Fifth King decided that the world would be better off with a single leader, a long-gone superhuman called Krodin. You've heard the stories, yes?"

Danny nodded. "Some of them."

"Krodin was, apparently, the first superhuman. Extremely strong, very fast... and gifted with hyper-adaptability. Think of it as an immune system that worked on *everything,* not just bacteria or viruses. You could shoot him with an arrow, and it would probably penetrate his skin. But only once. The next arrow would find that his skin was suddenly a lot tougher.

"Despite that adaptability, Krodin seemingly died, thousands of years ago. His followers found a prophecy that they would one day discover a way to bring him back. They worked in secret, gathered their resources, waited patiently for the right time... And then the age of the superhumans appeared. Twenty-five years ago, The Helotry discovered a method to warp time to pull Krodin out of the past. It almost worked, but the time-line is elastic. You can stretch it and twist it, even fold it back on itself, but it *wants* to return to normal.

"The Helotry recruited a superhuman called Pyrokine. He could transform matter into energy... But there was so much more to his abilities than that. Like you, he was actually able to bend the physical laws of the universe. The Helotry used him to create a tunnel through time. But Pyrokine betrayed them. As he was dying, he used the last of his energy to blast Krodin back to his own time. At least, he *tried*. That didn't quite work."

"Brawn told me about this," Danny said. "Krodin traveled

back about six years. There were no superheroes around at that time powerful enough to stop him. He built his own empire."

"Right. A diversion from the main time-line. By the time Brawn and his friends were dragged into that reality, Krodin was on the verge of conquering the rest of the world. During those six years he had engaged in many battles, and so his hyper-adaptability had given him a resistance to anything that the would-be heroes could throw at him."

"But they still won," Danny said.

"They did. They used Krodin's own teleportation device against him. Of course, he'd already used it himself, and so therefore he was immune to its effects... But one of them realized that the teleporter works by picking an object from its current location and sending it to another. That works on a sub-atomic level. Do you know anything about physics?" Without waiting for Danny to answer, Cross continued: "Let's just say that every particle contains information on exactly where it is in the universe. It doesn't, of course, but that's an easy way to visualize the process. So instead of moving, say, this chair by picking it up and carrying it to its new destination, the teleporter simply rewrites the location values of each particle in the chair. It's suddenly over there, or wherever you want it to be. Clever, yes?"

Danny shrugged. *I could dig down, create a tunnel* under *the null-field, pull Mina and Colin to safety before he could even blink.*

But, no, he'll have thought of that. He'll have some other way to stop me.

Unless he's already guessed I'll realize that he's thought of it, and so therefore I won't do it in case there's a trap, and then he doesn't need *to have a trap because…*

Danny cut himself off. *You could go crazy trying to out-think this guy!*

"So the young heroes realized that if every particle contains information about its physical place in the universe, then that not only means where it is, but *when* it is. They aimed the teleporter to the exact location and moment that Krodin arrived in the past, six years earlier. At that stage, he had never encountered the effects of the teleporter and therefore it worked on him. That immediately set the time-line back to the way it had been, and most people never noticed. From Krodin's point of view, he was pulled out of the distant past, appeared briefly in a field somewhere, and then was transported to a rocky, airless desert. Mars."

Danny began to slowly walk around the circle. *There has to be a weak-spot. And if there's not, he's not going to stay in there forever, is he?*

"He's still alive, of course," Cross said. "Krodin's strongest power is his adaptability. He cannot die because his body automatically adjusts itself to compensate for anything it encounters."

"And you want him back, is that it?"

"I did, yes. Krodin was fated to lead the world. Not rule it. *Lead* it. Without him… We're a rudderless boat caught in a never-ending storm. The human race had such great potential. We wasted that on petty wars, pointless squabbling over land and material gains. In ten thousand years of recorded history, we have amounted to precisely nothing. Consider that, Danny. People are like children's building blocks. We can become anything the child imagines, but without a strong leader to build us into something greater, we are nothing but useless pieces of inert material."

"So you're going to destroy all life on the planet just because no one will play with you?"

Cross sighed. "You are so *dense*. No, Danny. Because as a race we have failed. We can keep trying to live with the results of our mistakes, and constantly make more mistakes as we go, building temporary solutions that only cause problems for the future... or we can hit the reset button and start again." He stopped pacing. "In time, the planet will recover, and new forms of life will emerge. It'll take millions of years, maybe billions, but the Earth will one day be home to another sapient race. Hopefully a better one. But... We don't *have* to go down that route. We have an alternative. *You* can fix everything."

"How?"

"Simple. You're the god of time. You reach back into the past and prevent Krodin from being taken in the first place. That's the *true* time-line, Danny. What we're living in now is no more valid than the alternative reality in which Krodin took control of the United States. You see, that's why there *are* superhumans. We're... like antibodies. The universe knows that something is off-kilter, and it created us to fight the infection. To make right that which is wrong."

Chapter 28

"Take them!" Renata Soliz screamed. She slammed her jetpack into full-thrust, arched her back to dart up and around the ChampionShip as one of the clones of Colin Wagner darted after her.

The display on her visor showed that Kenya and Stephanie were having a tough time escaping their own pursuers.

They've got to be faster, she thought. *If the clones even lay one hand on them, they're dead.*

The clone was only yards behind her. She had to fight the urge to lead him away from the ship—protecting it was her top priority right now. If she left then the others would attack it.

She had already taken down one of the clones, the first to attack. His colleagues had called him Warwick. He had launched himself directly at her, fists clenched, and if she'd been anyone else his punches would have snapped her in two. Renata had solidified her body just as he struck. The force of his blow knocked her more than a mile away from the ship, and he had chased after her.

She'd allowed herself to crash to the ground, to let Warwick believe that she was unconscious or dead. He had swooped in, coming down feet-first at great speed, aiming to slam her deep into the ice.

Renata had reached up, grabbed one of Warwick's feet in each hand, and forced them apart. At the same time she'd kicked up, shoving her boot deep into his stomach—while still holding onto his feet.

He'd collapsed to the ice, but recovered before Renata could press home her attack. She barely dodged a punch that, had it landed, would have pulverized the skull of an ordinary human.

The realization that Warwick was trying to kill her was as much of a shock as the ferocity of his actions.

She'd dodged a second blow, locked her hands around his wrists and turned them solid.

He'd struggled, screaming, trying to break free. His eyes were wide, specks of saliva spraying from his mouth and instantly freezing in the Arctic air.

She'd slammed his own fists back into his face, staggering him, then—still holding onto his arms—she kicked out at his chest.

He's stronger than me, she'd realized. *He's not going to quit!*

Warwick had grinned at her then. "Maybe I can't hurt you—but that just means you'll still be alive to watch me tear out your friends' spines!"

Renata had pounded his skull with her invulnerable fists until she was sure that he'd be out of the fight for several minutes. *An injured colleague is a double-distraction for the others*, she'd realized. *They'll see what I've done to him* and *at least one of them will lose time trying to help him!*

She'd left Warwick slightly twitching and bleeding into the snow and darted back to the ship—by which time the other three were speeding toward her.

Now, this second clone—Oscar—wasn't so easy to trick. He was faster than her jetpack could propel her, and more maneuverable, but didn't seem to be able to anticipate her moves. *No one ever taught them how to fight*, she realized.

She changed direction abruptly, heading toward Kenya who was zipping and darting through the air, her agile body twisting and spinning with fluidity and grace as the clone futilely attempted to grab hold of her.

"Kenya! I've got one behind me—switch!"

Renata steered herself at Kenya's attacker, and at the same time Kenya darted beneath her and came up directly in Oscar's path.

Renata crashed her fists into the other's face, smashing his nose, and immediately zoomed away, curving in a circle that brought her back to him just as he was recovering from the shock. A sharp jab to the side of his head sent him reeling, cartwheeling down through the air.

Somewhere behind her, Kenya was racing away with Oscar in close pursuit. Renata figured she had enough time to get to Stephanie, who had two of them chasing her.

Stephanie wasn't as agile as Kenya or anywhere near as strong as Renata, but she was an expert with the jetpack, and knew how to use the environment to her advantage. She kept low, darted around one of the massive boulders that littered the landscape, forcing the clones to split up, one coming from the left, the other from the right.

As Renata approached, Stephanie zoomed straight up from behind the boulder. The two clones crashed into each other in a tangle of kicks and punches, each one momentarily convinced that the other was Stephanie.

"Go help Kenya!" Renata shouted. "I'll take care of these two!"

The display on her visor showed that the ChampionShip was now only a mile from the base. *Almost there. A few more minutes. Hope we can last that long.*

*

In Sakkara, gathered around the screens in the Operations Room, Cassandra, Razor and Lance watched the video and audio feeds coming back from the ChampionShip, and from the cameras in the New Heroes' armor.

Razor said, "It's no good. Cross is scrambling all our signals and I can't figure out how. He could have set up a ring of white-noise generators around the base, but then how are the transmissions from the suits getting out?" He looked up at the other monitors. "The clones are toying with them."

"True," Lance said, nodding. "Cross pumped the clones' brains full of knowledge, but that's no substitute for experience. They're infants, remember. These guys have only been alive for a few months."

Cassandra said, "Roman's mind is a mess. If the others are the same, then they still don't really understand the difference between reality and imagination, or between right and wrong. That's how Cross was able to instill loyalty—he and that guy Evan Laurie are the clones' parent figures: they'll do whatever they're told."

"So what can we do to help?" Razor asked.

"We've done all we can, for now," Lance said. He turned to the screen showing the feed from Danny's armor. "What do you think, Razor? What can we do to get past the null-field?"

"There's no way to know without being there. Danny could go *under* it, but Cross will have thought of that."

Another screen showed an almost complete map of Cross's base, constructed from the data sent back by the sensors built into Danny's armor, and the information Cassandra had taken from Roman's mind. Lance tapped one point on the map. "So the missile's *there*... We could just tell Danny to go for it. In fast-time he'll be able to wreck it before Cross can even blink."

Cassandra said, "And then Cross would kill Colin and Mina."

"Yeah." Lance stroked his beard. "Tricky. There is a solution, of course. We let them die."

"No way," Razor said, jumping to his feet. "No *way*!"

"Relax, son, I'm just musing. Though you have to be prepared. It might come to that. The other problem is that we just don't know how the missile's payload is expected to work. An attack on the missile might be enough to trigger it… Clearly, Cross wants the payload delivered to a specific location—otherwise it wouldn't be a missile, it'd just be a bomb—but I reckon it's wise to assume we don't want it triggered at all."

Razor said, "So if we're going to stop it, we have to wait until it's in the air?"

Lance nodded.

"That's… less than ideal."

"I know. We have to gamble here… We have to take the risk that Cross will let the attack continue until the missile is ready to launch. Which by the looks of things won't be too far away. The alternative is to cut and run and hope that it doesn't work. I'm not a fan of that one." He paused for a moment. "But just in case… Cassandra, phone your mom. Don't tell her what's happening. Don't say good-bye or anything like that. Just tell her you have a few minutes to chat. Ask her about her day. That kind of thing."

"Because I might not get another chance?" Cassandra asked.

"Exactly." When Cassandra had left the room, Lance said, "You too, Razor. I know you haven't spoken to her in a while, but do it anyway."

The young man shook his head. "No, if I phone her she'll

know something's wrong."

"Hah, yeah, *that's* true. I don't know. Make it sound like you're asking her for something. Or…" Lance looked at Razor. "You could tell her you've finally met Hunter Washington."

"Who?"

"Your real father. Me."

Razor was still for few seconds, then he slowly turned to face Lance. "You have *got* to be kidding me."

"It's true. I even checked your DNA profile against mine. You're my son." Lance scratched at his beard and stopped when he realized that Razor was scratching his own. "You've got the same thing as me that makes you *almost* superhuman. Whatever it is, it has a tendency to bring us together. I figure that's why you and Colin found yourselves drawn to each other the first time you met. Same as with me and Paragon."

"So you're my real dad." Razor stared at him. "You picked a great time to finally show up!"

"Not *my* fault. I didn't even know you existed until Impervia contacted me and I started investigating everyone's backgrounds. Your mother and I didn't even have a chance. Max Dalton…" Lance stopped. After a moment's pause, he said, "It wasn't meant to be. I never saw her again."

Razor slumped in his chair. "Oh man…"

Lance smiled, and patted him on the shoulder. "Just call her. Go on. Tell her about me if you want. If you don't, it doesn't matter."

Razor wouldn't look at Lance as he left the room.

Lance moved in front of the monitors. "All right," he muttered to himself. "*That* was awkward." He turned to another screen, where Danny was still talking to Cross. *There has to be a way to get through to Danny. If we could figure out how he's scrambling our signals... I can still communicate with the ChampionShip, so the signals aren't scrambled at this end.*

He watched the screens for a few more minutes, and gradually became aware that he'd been avoiding an important task. He reached for the phone and keyed in a number.

The call was answered on the second ring: "Yeah?"

"Warren, it's Lance."

There was a tiny pause. "OK."

"Colin did it. The clones captured him, stripped his powers... And they brought him right into Cross's base. The GPS tag worked—we know exactly where they are. The fight's on. Our guys are doing OK, so far." As he spoke, Lance was typing on one of the keyboards. "Warren... I'm sending transport your way. Enough to get you all out of the Substation. The copters will take you to the peak of Denali, Alaska. Highest point in the USA. I've already got some people on the way to establish a base there. If things go bad—"

"No," Warren said. "We talked it over. We're staying. We've got a better chance of survival here."

"You're sure that's what you want?"

"Yeah. Lance, no matter how this turns out... If Colin dies, so do you."

"Back when you were Titan you were arrogant, but you never would have made a threat like that. But I understand... And I'll promise you this: If we win, and Colin does survive, I won't tell him how far you've fallen. He still thinks you're a hero."

"It's all on you now, Lance."

"I know. Warren, if this goes bad, this could be the last time we ever speak. So I want you to know that sometimes you can be a real jerk. But then so can I. And that's why I've always liked you."

Warren laughed. "Good luck, McKendrick."

"You too. Give my regards to Caroline and Vienna and the others." Lance ended the call, then made another. It was answered by Alia Cord.

"What's up, Mister McKendrick?"

"Not a lot. Just checking in. I hope you and Grant are keeping out of trouble. Oh, and stop ordering room-service, will you? We do have a budget, you know. Would it kill you to make your own sandwiches for lunch every now and then?"

Alia said, "Um… By the sound of your voice, things aren't going well, are they? We should come back. We already figured out why you left us here. It's because you think we're not good enough, isn't it?"

"Let's just say you're not quite good enough *yet*."

"But Kenya is?"

"She has ten times more experience than the two of you combined. Plus she's superhuman. Sorry, Alia. I know that's a blow to the ego, but I figure that hurting your feelings is less important than saving your lives. Stay there, Alia. Take the night off. Go to a movie or something. Enjoy yourselves."

"Oh man… It's *that* bad?"

Lance smiled to himself. *She's a lot more intuitive than I thought.* "It's worse."

"Mister McKendrick… Tell me what's happening."

"Right now, the New Heroes are all that stands between us and the end of the world."

*

Danny said, "You know, I can wait a long time. You think you're safe in there, but the fact is you're trapped. And you'll die when your missile detonates and floods the planet with lava."

"Except that the lava will vanish when it hits the null-field. I'll be safe."

"You'll be alone. Well, apart from Colin and Mina and the clones, if they survive."

"Danny, I'm so far ahead of everyone else I might as well be alone anyway."

"If you don't suffocate, you'll starve to death."

Cross shrugged. "I'm sure I'll think of some way to survive. But we don't want it to come to that, do we? You stop Krodin from being pulled through time, and it'll all be over."

"And how am I supposed to do that? Even if I knew how, I wouldn't. If I could reach back in time and change something in the past, I'd change it so that your parents never met. Without you, we'd all be a lot better off."

"You could do that. You could do *anything*. Buy yourself last week's winning lottery ticket. Go back to some time when you embarrassed yourself by saying the wrong thing to a girl you really liked. Pull Solomon Cord out of the past so that he was no longer dead. Fix it so that you didn't lose your arm inside my power-damping machine. Anything at all." Cross walked forward, stopping only inches away from the edge of the circle. "You're the god of time."

"So you keep saying. But I don't know *how* to do any of those things."

"It should be relatively simple. Concentrate on what you want to happen, and the time-line will flow around you, adjusting itself." He smiled. "You can remake the world any way you like, Danny. Whatever you want, you can have. And yes, you can even thwart my plans. I can't stop you."

"Then why are you helping me? Or are you just stalling for time?"

Cross laughed. "Stalling for time, that's a good one coming from you. Think about it. Concentrate on what you want most, and it'll happen. If you do it right. If..." He looked past Danny, and his smile grew wide. "No, you're right. I *was* stalling."

Danny turned around to see four of the clones entering the hangar. They were badly beaten, their faces and hands bruised and bloodied, their clothes torn. One of them was cradling his arm, which looked broken. The others were carrying the limp bodies of Renata, Kenya and Stephanie.

"Oh *look*," Cross said. "I won."

Lance swore and slammed his fist down on the desk. "No you haven't, you blasted psycho! Not yet! All right. You want to play hard-ball? *I'll* show you what a real fight is like!"

He picked up the microphone. "You there?"

"I'm here," Brawn's voice rumbled.

"Go."

Chapter 29

"They dead yet?" Cross asked.

Shadow threw Renata to the floor, and she tumbled to a stop in front of Danny. "Not yet. Thought you'd want to see it happen." He looked at Danny. "I definitely want *this* guy to see it. She broke Alex's arm and pounded the tar out of Warwick! We left him out there—I gotta go back for him."

"No, leave him. A wounded soldier is just something else to worry about." Cross turned to Danny. "You be mindful of this situation, Danny. Resist the temptation to attack. I've still got Mina and Colin here, remember."

Danny turned back to face him. "Give up, Cross. You don't stand a chance."

"What's wrong with you, kid? I've already won. My boys have beaten your crew. Their powers are gone. Shadow? Show them."

The clone held up a small hand-gun that resembled a toy. Its casing was patched together with duct tape.

"That's my Extractor," Cross said. "A handy fit-in-your-pocket version of Ragnarök's power-damper, with some improvements. We can target a specific person and drain their power without affecting anyone else. As you can see, it works. Right now, Renata and Kenya might as well not be superhuman. Same with Colin and Mina. Their powers will recover eventually, but until they do you and Cassandra are the only ones left with any superhuman abilities. The New Heroes have been utterly defeated. You're beaten."

"Not *all* of us."

"Oh, you have a hidden ace? I doubt that. You're forgetting who you're dealing with, Danny. I'm—"

Overhead, the ceiling trembled.

Cross took a step back, and looked up. "What was that?" Tiny particles of ice drifted down.

"Brawn, dropping from our ship."

"*He's* your last hope? Brawn's not even a superhuman!"

Danny smiled. "He doesn't need to be."

The ceiling trembled again, more violently this time, and Cross looked up again as a distorted gap appeared between the semi-circular hangar doors.

Danny shifted into fast-time, grabbed Renata's arm and dragged her across the icy floor to the relative safety of the corridor. He returned for Kenya, then Stephanie.

All three of them had been heavily beaten, their armor cracked and dented. But they were alive. *Have to find a way to wake them up. No, I have to deal with Cross first.*

Still in fast-time, he raced through the base, searching every room, hoping to find something he could use to stop the madman from carrying out his plans.

Lance had already warned him not to tamper with the missile, but he was sure there must be *something* he could do.

He returned to the hangar where Cross and the clones were still reacting to the slowly-widening gap in the hangar doors, and as he passed Shadow the clone reacted, and made a grab for him.

Danny jumped aside, and Shadow kept coming.

No! He can see me!

He remembered his battle with Colin, back in the Trutopian town. Colin had been fast enough to fight Danny to a stand-still.

I should have realized that one of them might have inherited Colin's speed.

Danny swung up an arm to block Shadow's punch, and the force almost knocked him off his feet. *He's not as fast as me, but he's a lot stronger.*

Danny grabbed Shadow's arm and pulled him forward, at the same time whirling around to slam the clone in the back of the head with his elbow.

Shadow countered the move by dropping to the ground and sweeping his leg out to collide with the backs of Danny's knees.

Silently, they fought. Danny's greater speed and strong armor put him almost in Shadow's league. Almost.

Shadow cracked the edge of his palm against Danny's artificial arm, but it did nothing more than dent the armor. Danny again grabbed the clone's arm, and this time he threw himself back, pulling Shadow over his head.

Shadow crashed into the floor, rolled onto his feet and lashed out at Danny's face with a powerful kick.

Danny tried to dodge aside, but was too late: the kick spent him spinning on his back across the floor, where he collided with one of the other clones, knocking him off his feet.

Shadow leaped after him, and this time Danny was prepared: he rolled to the side out of Shadow's path, grabbed the clone's ankles and at the same time activated his jetpack.

They skidded along the floor, heading straight for the wall, and at the last moment Danny let go and hit the jetpack's retro-burners, which stopped him almost immediately. Shadow slammed head-first into the wall, and lay twitching as Danny scrambled to his feet and ran toward him.

On the edge of his vision he saw a shape moving toward him,

coming too fast for him to get out of the way. The second clone —the one he'd crashed into—fell upon him with a barrage of kicks and punches.

One of the punches cracked his visor, and Danny grabbed hold of the clone's upper arms and spun him to the side, twisting the clone around to put him between himself and Shadow.

Two against one... Danny thought. *And it'll be worse if the other two realize what's happening. Have to keep the fight away from them.*

Victor realized he was backing away as he stared up at the hangar doors, and stopped himself before he crossed the circular rail.

The doors shook with another powerful, deafening boom, and now he could see a crack of daylight between them.

How is this possible? Brawn's stronger than a normal human, but only because of his size. *He's not a superhuman anymore!*

Into his radio he shouted, "Laurie—Sakkara must be still communicating with their ship! Ramp the signal jammer up to full power—blanket the entire area."

Another boom, then another. Cross yelled, "Stop him!" and the words had barely left his mouth when he realized his mistake.

Alex—despite his broken arm—and Zeke darted across the hangar and up to slam into the already-buckled doors. *No! They're only helping him to get in!* "Wait! Stop!"

Zeke hesitated, and looked back.

A massive blue fist burst down through the crack between the doors, crashing straight into Alex and sending him crashing back down to the floor.

Another giant blue hand forced its way through, grabbing hold of Zeke, and Cross now saw how this was possible.

Brawn pushed his way through the crack between the ruined doors, showering the hangar with head-sized lumps of ice that shattered when they hit the floor. He landed heavily, in a crouch, and looked around.

The giant spotted Victor. "You again."

Victor swallowed. *It's not fair! I didn't anticipate this! I wasn't* ready *for this!*

Brawn glowered, and began to stride toward him.

Powered armor, Cross realized. A tiny part of his brain was more impressed than scared. He knew that the biggest obstacle to creating effective powered armor was making it small enough for the average person to use. With Brawn, that was no longer a problem.

Chapter 30

Brawn pounded across the hangar floor, still holding onto the clone he'd grabbed. He stopped in front of Cross, and held up the clone, who was struggling to break free of the giant's grip. "Which one is this? They have names, right?"

"That's Zeke."

"How would you feel if I tore Zeke's arms from his shoulders?"

Cross shrugged. "Go ahead. I've got more of them." Cross tilted his head to one side as he looked at Brawn, as though he was examining an odd-looking bug. "You're not a killer, Brawn. Don't pretend you'd actually do it. Honestly. Look at this situation. *You*, trying to fool *me*."

Brawn spotted Renata and the others off to the side, but before he could investigate three other clones rushed at him, two on foot, one darting down through the hole Brawn had made in the ceiling. He spun to confront the one above him—the powerful motors in his armor greatly amplifying his speed and strength—and used Zeke as a club to swat the clone across the room.

One of the others threw himself hard against Brawn's leg, trying to knock him off-balance. Brawn reached down and locked his massive hand around the clone's head.

He kicked out at the third, but the boy dodged to the side, leaped into the air and came crashing down on Brawn's left shoulder.

The giant lashed out at the third clone with Zeke's still-struggling body, knocking him aside.

The motors in his powered gloves whined with the effort of keeping his grip on the two clones. The one he was holding by the head was digging his strong fingers into the armor, preparing to tear it apart.

"No you don't!" Brawn yelled. He swung his huge arms out to the side, then clapped his hands together with as much force as he could manage.

The clones crashed into each other, and went limp.

For good measure, he slammed them together a second time, then tossed their limp, unconscious bodies over his shoulders.

He advanced on Cross. "Your turn."

He almost hesitated: Cross hadn't run, he didn't seem to be armed, and Brawn knew he had no superhuman strength. *Why isn't he scared? What am I missing here?*

On the far side of the hangar, something was happening, but Brawn couldn't see exactly what. Fractures appeared in the walls, followed by small explosions of ice. Objects—old tools, metal pipes, chunks of ice—appeared and disappeared seemingly at random. Small fragments of cloth and chips of metal began to litter the room. As he watched, a splatter of blood shot out of nowhere and spread across the floor. *What is that?*

Victor Cross remained in place, standing next to his chair, in front of something covered with a gray tarpaulin, in the center of a large, circular metal rail.

Two of the fingers on Danny's mechanical arm were gone, torn away by Shadow. His visor had completely split open, and he was sure that his armor was cracked in dozens of places.

He fought on, always on the attack, doing whatever it took to keep Shadow and the other clone from getting to his teammates.

From his point of view, in fast-time, they had been fighting for hours. They had crashed from one end of the hangar to the other, over and over.

Shadow was relentless, and clearly smarter than his brother. Shadow would attack in a furious burst of energy, then dart away while the other clone took over and received the brunt of Danny's counter-attack. Of the three, Shadow was definitely taking the least amount of punishment.

Danny swung his fists, kicked, spun and jumped, but they kept coming. Every time he thought he had one of them beaten, the other would keep him busy long enough for the first to recover.

But they weren't used to working together: occasionally they collided with each other in their eagerness to get to Danny. He was sure that was the only reason he was still on his feet.

The unnamed clone rushed at him from the left, just as Shadow came from the right. Danny activated the jetpack and soared upward. Below, the clones only avoided hitting each other because Shadow turned his attack into flight.

In the air, Danny twisted around so that Shadow was hit in the face with the full force of the jetpack's blast—but it barely slowed him.

He darted toward the center of the room, dropped low, curved around the outside of the black circle, and zoomed between Brawn's armored legs. *C'mon, big guy—beat the living tar out of these creeps!*

With Shadow following him every inch of the way, Danny

curved back to the other side of the room where the unnamed clone was preparing to fly straight at him.

Danny dodged around him, made a sharp right and then kicked his feet up so that he flipped onto his back, reversing his direction. Shadow and his brother crashed into each other, slowing them for a moment, and Danny used the opportunity to head straight up, aiming for the black aircraft suspended below the ceiling.

He touched down on top of the aircraft for a second to gather his thoughts. *I can't keep this up much longer. If I could wake Renata... But how? In real time she's only been unconscious for a few minutes. And if she really has lost her powers again, she wouldn't stand a chance against them.*

Unless... Unless Cross wasn't lying about me being able to manipulate time.

He cast his mind back two years, to the moments before he'd lost his arm by phasing it inside Cross's power-damping machine. Colin had been on top of the machine, trying to tear his way inside while its count-down ticked off the last few seconds before it was triggered.

Danny remembered putting his hand on Colin's shoulder, somehow sensing that he might be able to increase Colin's speed. It hadn't worked. *I was still only learning to use my powers. Sure, I'm not as fast as I was then, but I've got more control. I could reach back in time to a few minutes ago and pull Renata out of the past. Take her from before they stripped her powers.*

He cut short his recollections as the clones spotted him and launched themselves after him, Shadow going to the left, the other to the right.

Danny waited until the last moment before leaping down from the top of the plane, hoping that the two were moving too fast to change direction.

He was about to reactivate his jetpack when Shadow's powerful fingers snagged his left arm.

Shadow jerked Danny back toward him, straight into his brother's flailing fists.

The first punch slammed into the side of Danny's helmet, knocking it clear off his head.

The second punch plowed into his chest, denting the armor so deeply that Danny could feel it pressing against his ribs.

The third punch caught him in the face.

In fast-time, there was no sound, but there was pain. Danny screamed in silent agony as the left side of his mandible snapped. He saw a spray of his own blood and pulverized teeth spread out, slowing to real-time as it lost the hyper-speed influence of his powers.

Another punch, this time to his stomach, doubled him over, exposing the back of his neck to the clones: the ideal target if they decided to kill him.

But instead Shadow threw him hard against the far wall. He struck it head-first, and collapsed to the ground next to Renata.

Weak, exhausted, and wracked with pain, Danny lost his hold on fast-time. The sound in the hangar returned as he saw Brawn, on the far side of the huge room, only seconds away from breaching the null-field.

He'll be killed! He tried to scream a warning, but the agony in his broken jaw was too great, and all that came out was a low moan.

Danny's vision briefly turned red from the blood dripping

into his eyes, and his head swam.

Brawn... No! Don't cross the rail!

He couldn't look away. Brawn continued to advance on Victor Cross.

God, no, please don't let it happen!

Danny's head grew heavier, and he knew he was about to pass out. He reached out and took hold of Renata's hand. He tried to concentrate on her personal time-line, to look back into her past. For a second he thought he saw something—a brief glimpse of Renata on a city street, protecting someone from a deluge of bricks and dirt—but then the image was gone. Every movement, every breath sent new waves of agony shooting through his body. *Please...*

Across the hangar, Brawn scowled at Cross as he approached.

Maybe he'll notice me here, Danny thought. *Maybe that'll make him stop.*

But Brawn kept walking.

He'd had a tough life, Danny knew. Gethin Rao's powers had kicked in when he was only twelve, instantly and permanently transforming him into a hairless blue giant. Hounded by the police and armies the world over, conned or framed or betrayed by almost everyone he met, Brawn had spent most of his life on the run, or in prison. *This is not the way it should end for him!* Danny thought. *He never had a chance for a normal life. That's all he ever wanted.*

Through the fog of pain, Danny felt his eyes begin to close, but he forced them to stay open. He didn't want to see this, but he knew that he must. Brawn was his friend. And even if they failed here, if Cross's plan to burn the world was successful, the giant blue monster was a hero.

He had a sudden memory—not his own—of Victor Cross stepping into the circle, thumbing a switch on a small remote-control device that activated the null-field. Outside the circle, Shadow or one of his brothers tested the null-field by pushing a metal spar over the rail; the end of the spar disappeared.

The vision cleared, and in front of him Danny saw Brawn hesitate, look down at the rail with a frown of suspicion.

And then, as Danny fell into unconsciousness, he saw clones all rush Brawn at the same time, crashing into him from the sides, knocking him forward.

No!

The impact threw Brawn over the rail.

The blue giant collapsed to the ground in front of Victor, and almost instantly pushed himself to his feet even as the clones were swarming over his armor, punching, kicking, desperately trying to keep him away from Cross.

Cross himself had pulled the remote control device from his jacket pocket, stared at it for a moment before he began to back away from Brawn. He stepped over the metal rail, then turned and ran.

Inwardly, Danny screamed. *No! I* could *have stopped him! He* was *bluffing!*

Danny blacked out.

Chapter 31

In Sakkara, Lance turned away from the screens to see that Cassandra and Razor had been watching from the doorway.

Razor asked, "What do we do?"

Lance couldn't think of a reply. *We're done*, he thought. *Brawn's not going to last long, and even Danny is out-matched by the clones.* "Suit up. Both of you. Prepare the Marlin."

"We'd never get there in time," Razor said. "And neither of us has any experience with the suits."

"You're not going to Zaliv Kalinina. You're going to Washington. In the event of a planet-wide disaster there's an emergency procedure that's designed to get the president and other important government officials to safety. There's a prototype aircraft that can reach a sub-orbital altitude and maintain it for months. You're going to try to ride out the storm."

"That wouldn't work," Razor said. "The volcanoes will be discharging lava with enough force to break orbit. And there's no way we'd be allowed anywhere near the craft."

"You'll fight your way to it. If you have to, force them to let you on board."

Cassandra said, "No. If Cross's missile detonates I wouldn't *want* to survive."

"Same here," Razor said. "Besides, the planet will be burning for thousands of years."

Lance nodded. "You're right, of course." He turned back to face the monitors.

*

Victor Cross walked out of the hangar, leaving the battle behind. He stepped over the unconscious bodies of the New Heroes and briefly wondered whether he should just siphon Danny's powers right now.

Best not, he decided. *He's too badly injured to be a threat. That broken jaw has* got *to hurt. When he wakes up I'll give him one more chance.*

Behind him the battle raged on. He briefly glanced back toward Brawn, and thought that he was doing remarkably well for someone without any real superhuman abilities. *Even I've underestimated him. He'll be dead in minutes, but still, that's impressive.*

Again, he looked at the remote control device in his hands. *So what happened? Why did the null-field stop working? When did it stop working?*

He'd designed and built the null-field generator himself, intimately knew every circuit, every microchip. It was infallible, designed to withstand even Colin Wagner's ability to remotely destroy electronic equipment.

He paused as he stared at the remote control, and felt a cold sweat break out on the back of his neck. *It's not switched on.*

Cross remembered turning on the device, remembered watching as Warwick had tested the null-field from the other side.

And he remembered demonstrating it to Danny Cooper by flicking a shard of ice at the field and watching it disappear.

It was on. It was working.

Danny did this. He changed the past so that I never activated the null-field. Incredible!

Victor shook himself, realizing that this was not the right

time for such speculation. He reassigned that chain of thought to a secondary part of his brain, and continued making his way through the base' corridors until he reached the missile silo. *It all comes down to this. Years of planning, of manipulating, lying, cheating, stealing and killing.* He sighed. *Wonder what I'd be doing now if I was a normal person? Mowing the lawn, probably. Ordinary people are obsessed with the condition of their turf.*

Out of breath, bundled in his thick parka with the hood up, Evan Laurie descended the last few steps of the gantry, with Nathan following close behind.

"It's done," Laurie said to Victor. "All the checks are green. It's ready."

"Yes. Good work. Excellent. But I don't trust you not to mess up. Check it all again."

"I'd tell you that I'll hate you forever for this, but there's not going to *be* a forever, is there?"

"Not for you, certainly. Nathan? Your brothers are in the hangar fighting Brawn. It's quite spectacular. You might want to go look, or even help out." He inclined his head back the way he'd come. "Go."

Nathan took off at a run, and Victor watched him go. "Still doesn't like me, but he has no choice but to obey."

As they walked to the missile's control room, Laurie said, "I wish I'd never met you. I wish you'd never been *born*."

Victor laughed. "If wishes were horses, glue would be a lot cheaper."

"There's still time to stop this. There *will* be more superhumans. Or you could create a new batch of clones. Or you'll find a way to build a physical teleporter like Krodin had and not have to hope for a superhuman who can do it."

"The technology in Krodin's alternate universe was a *century* ahead of ours, at least. I can't wait that long."

"So instead you're going to destroy the Earth. Can't you see how *insane* that is, Victor?"

Cross began to climb the stairs to the control room. "I keep telling you, Laurie. I can see *everything*. I plan for every eventuality."

"You know what you remind me of? The cat I had when I was a kid. Sweet little thing. Used to swing out of the curtains, and sometimes he'd climb all the way up, walk along the rail, and sit on the top of the open door waiting to ambush my dad."

"What a great story. And such a refreshing change to hear one mercifully free of relevance."

Laurie said, "And with that, Victor Cross proved once and for all that the only thing he *truly* loved was the sound of his own voice."

Cross stopped on the stairway, and looked back. "What?"

"You actually look offended!" Laurie grinned. "Wow. I managed to hurt your feelings. Well, now I don't mind so much if I *do* die today. Anyway, the point is that now and then the cat would make a leap from the couch to the armchair, or from the counter-top to the table, and he wouldn't quite make it. He would then instantly drop to the ground, lick his paw and rub it over his face. And he'd sit there with an expression that seemed to say, 'That was what I meant to do.' That's *you,* Victor. You like to think that everything that happens is part of your great plan, but the reality is that you're just navigating your way around a series of disasters. Being a genius doesn't exempt you from being a fool."

"Hah. I think you'll find that—"

"Before the Trutopians picked Colin up in Romania, where was he going? Did you think to ask him before you knocked him out?"

"Shut up, Laurie!" Cross pushed open the control room's door.

Laurie followed him inside. "You don't know, do you? That must be eating you up inside. There's information you need, but you don't have it and don't know how to get it." Laurie stood at the window, looking out at the missile. "And *this* monstrosity... You want me to tell you what this really is? You can't get your way so you're throwing the biggest strop in the history of the human race." He turned back to Victor, and pointed at the missile. "*That* is a tantrum. And you are a child."

Victor brushed fragments of plastic and glass off the seat before sitting down in front of the replacement screens. "So... No luck hacking your way into its mechanisms, then?"

"What?"

"Yeah, I see it here in the code. You tried to hide a subroutine that would send the missile to where it would do the least amount of damage. Tch... Look at that. Sloppy. Evan, that's *not* the most efficient way to compare a value against a list of numbers. With every loop, you're checking the number and then looking to see if you've reached the end of the list. That's two tests you're doing for every number. Look." Victor began typing on the new keyboard, aware that this wasn't the time for a programming lesson, but unable to stop himself. "This is what you do. You add the number you want to find to the *end* of the list. Then your loop only has to check the numbers until it finds the right one. You don't have to worry about running off the end of the list because you *know* you're going to find it. If the one you've found is the last one on the list, then it wasn't on the *original* list, so you mark it as 'not found'."

"Good lord, you really *are* insane!"

"No, look…" Victor picked up a pencil and grabbed a sheet of paper from the printer. "If you've got a list of, say, ten items to search, then—"

Laurie bellowed, "Enough! I understand the principle!"

"Then why didn't you use it? That's very disappointing."

"In the name of all that's good, Victor, look at what you're doing! You're on the verge of wiping out the human race and you're peeved because the code I wrote to sabotage your plans isn't efficient enough!"

"Right," Victor said, nodding.

"Don't you see? You're losing your mind."

Cross pointed at the screen. "Yes, but if your code was better written it would be twice as fast, and my diagnostic routine might not have found it. Your shoddy programming has prevented you from saving the world. So *now* who's the fool?"

"Still you, Victor. Still you."

In the hangar, Brawn was almost surprised to be still on his feet, still fighting.

The clones of Colin Wagner were strong and infuriatingly fast, but Brawn had fought alongside—and against—the most powerful superhumans the world had ever seen. He knew how to fight dirty.

There were seven of the clones, and normally they'd be almost impossible to tell apart. But now, with their torn clothing and wide range of different cuts and bruises, Brawn was sure he knew which was which. And the orders shouted by their leader, Shadow, helped him to work out their names.

Alex was the one with the broken arm. Brawn liked it when he was attacking because all it took was a swift kick to that arm to send the kid running away screaming. *Brat still keeps coming back, though,* Brawn thought, *got to hand it to him. He doesn't quit.*

Shadow had a shattered nose and blood all over his uniform, and he was the one who most bothered Brawn. He was at least as strong as any of his brothers, and he was sly. He tended to attack only when Brawn was dealing with the others, darting at him from behind.

Brawn knew what Shadow was doing: he was saving his energy. *He's going to let them wear me down, then he'll swoop in at the end to finish me.*

Eldon and Oscar rushed at Brawn from the left, with Eldon on foot and Oscar in the air. Brawn let them get within arm's reach then jabbed his fist at Oscar, pulling it back at the last second as the clone ducked down to avoid the punch. He crashed into Eldon and the two of them ended up in a squirming tangle at Brawn's feet.

Brawn kicked out at them, the toe of his massive metal boot catching Oscar in the small of his back. The force of the kick sent them skidding away across the icy floor.

Nathan came next, leaping down from the ceiling's support beams. Brawn snatched him out of the air and held tight, his fingers around the clone's throat. As Nathan struggled to free himself, Brawn was struck in the chest by Shadow, who darted away almost immediately.

Tuan attacked from his right side. Flying in low and fast, he locked his arms around Brawn's left calf and pulled back, trying to topple him. As he did so, he seemed to be growing larger, more muscular, and Brawn felt himself weakening.

Brawn bashed down at him using Alex as a baton. Their heads cracked together with a sound so loud that even Brawn winced. *Man, that's gotta hurt!*

Tuan was knocked aside, but Alex stretched out his legs, bracing them against Brawn's armored chest.

Brawn could clearly see the strain on the kid's face as he tried to tear off his arm.

He opened his hand and Nathan half-fell, half-flew to the ground.

Then Zeke and Alex and Eldon were rushing at him at once, from different sides. *I've got to even this out a bit!*

He knew what he had to do. Reduce their numbers as quickly as possible. He focused on Zeke and Eldon, allowing Alex to come within grabbing range, then spun around and took hold of the clone's broken arm.

Alex screamed as Brawn hauled him up into the air and violently shook him. "Don't like *that*, do you, punk?!" The clone squirmed and kicked. *Jeez, he's still too strong for me!*

Brawn noticed a flicker of movement off to his side, and spun around, holding Alex up as a shield.

Shadow crashed into his brother, and darted away again.

Nathan launched himself at him again. Brawn ducked to avoid him, dropped to one knee and slammed Alex into the ground. He pivoted himself up on the hand still holding the clone, and came down hard putting all of his weight into the other fist. It struck Alex in the groin, and he screamed louder than ever. Brawn hit him again in the same spot, while increasing the pressure of his grip on Alex's broken arm.

The clone collapsed, passing out.

Good. One down.

Shadow came next, for once attacking when there was no else to act as a distraction. Still holding onto Alex, Brawn threw himself to the side, rolling onto his back, swinging his arm up to crash Alex's limp form into Shadow's side.

Shadow hit the ground hard, and was in the process of rolling to his feet when Brawn charged at him, slammed into him shoulder-first, pinning him to the ground.

Brawn threw Alex aside and pulled back his fist, but before he could strike he found himself being pushed up: Shadow was lifting him into the air.

Oh man... I hoped they wouldn't think of that.

The others attacked all at once. Two of them grabbed onto his legs, another two took hold of his arms.

He tried to jerk his arms free, but they were holding on tight. Then the one on his right arm—Nathan—squeezed hard enough that Brawn heard his armor crack.

On the ground, looking up at him, Shadow sneered. "Got you now, you over-sized freak!"

The remaining clone, Oscar, limped over to join him. "*Kill* him, Shadow! Tear out his throat!"

"No, that's too good for him. Without his armor Brawn's just a human, regardless of his size. Fly him out of here and strip the armor off him. You go with them, Tuan. Find a nice spot and crack the ice. Drain as much power as you can from him, then dump his sorry butt into the sea. Let him freeze to death before he burns along with the rest of the world."

Tuan flew up ahead of his colleagues, and opened the

warped hangar doors. The chamber was flooded with a shocking rush of freezing air, and the clones continued to rise.

Brawn struggled and roared as they carried him, face-down, out into the sub-zero temperatures. His already-blue skin turned darker as Tuan flew around him and, piece by piece, tore away his armor.

Far below, through the hangars' circular opening, he saw Shadow striding toward the New Heroes.

Cassandra felt her stomach churn as the lop-sided footage from the camera in Danny's discarded helmet showed Brawn being carried away.

"That's it," Razor said. "Brawn was our last chance."

Lance glowered at the screen. "Not quite. Cross hasn't anticipated our next move."

"What?"

"Not what. Who." Lance turned to the girl on his left. "Cassandra."

"Me? What can I do from here?"

"It's time to read some minds."

"Lance, they're four thousand miles away!"

"True. But distance shouldn't be an obstacle. You're superhuman. Most of the things you people think of as limitations are only limitations of the imagination. You *believe* that you can't reach that far, so therefore you can't. For the first nine months after Colin's powers kicked in he believed he wasn't able to fly, so he couldn't do it. Most superhumans only discover their powers by accident. Why do you believe that there's a maximum radius to your mind-reading ability?"

"Because I've tested it. And superhuman minds aren't easy

to get into, especially the clones."

"I'm not talking about the clones, or Victor Cross, or any of *our* superhumans. I'm talking about Stephanie. She was never a superhuman, so she hasn't lost anything. You know *her* mind. Wake her up."

Can I do it? Cassandra wondered. *Stephanie's tricky to read.* She stretched out with her thoughts, slipping past the anxious minds of Razor and Lance. Out into the world beyond Sakkara.

A mental map begin to form, a lattice dotted with human minds throughout the region. To the west, a huge cluster of minds in Topeka drew her toward them, but she resisted. *Further*, she thought. *Further.*

North, into Nebraska. Each mind she encountered pulled her toward it, drawing her away from her intended course.

She opened her eyes, and looked at Razor and Lance. "It's working... But there's so many people. It's getting harder to steer away from them."

And then she glanced at the monitors and saw the globe of the Earth, and realized that there was a better way. *Why am I sticking to the surface? It's shorter to go* straight *to Zaliv Kalinina, and easier—there's not going to be a lot of minds underground.*

She visualized her power as a spear, piercing the Earth in a straight line from Sakkara to Cross's base.

"Almost... Yes. I can sense their minds above me. Cross is... His mind is huge! Lance, it's like a whole *city* of people inside his head. Most minds are simple, a large cluster at the center, with threads radiating outward. Cross's mind has *dozens* of clusters."

"Can you read his thoughts?" Razor asked.

"It's too complex. I can't even see where to begin."

"All right," Lance said. "Concentrate on Stephanie."

"I see her."

"Wake her."

Chapter 32

Stephanie Cord opened her eyes. She was lying on her back, staring up at a beam-crossed ceiling far overhead. At the top of her vision—behind her—was a high wall cut from the ice.

A voice inside her head said, "You're awake—good!"

What? Cassie, is that you? I told you I don't like people poking around in my mind!

"Don't move. Just listen."

Stephanie's skin began to crawl as Cassandra explained what had been happening. When she was done, Stephanie asked, *So what can I do?*

"Try to wake Renata and Kenya. Danny's injuries are too much. He's unconscious—leave him that way. The others... Steph, get out of there! Shadow is coming for you!"

Stephanie squeezed the fingers of her right hand against the pads inside her gloves that controlled her jetpack. The instant she felt herself move she pitched her head and torso forward so that her jetpack pushed her up against the wall at an angle rather than straight into it.

With her jetpack scraping the wall, its edges cutting long gouges into the ice and the heat of its exhaust evaporating the particles into mist, Stephanie soared straight up, cut the thrust before she hit the ceiling, then darted away from the wall, zipping in and out between the support beams.

"He's following you," Cassandra said.

Yeah, that's the point. What do I do now, Cassie?

"Lead him away. I'll try to revive the rest of the team."

Will do. Stephanie checked the fuel gauge—she had a little over half a tank left. There was more fuel on the ChampionShip, but that wasn't much use to her now.

Maybe it is, she thought. She dropped low and aimed for the far side of the room, all too aware that Shadow was right behind her.

Cassandra said, "I think that fighting Danny and Brawn has taken a lot out of him."

Forget about me—wake the others! Stephanie zoomed up, aiming for the open hangar doors beyond the suspended aircraft. As she passed the craft she reached out and grabbed one of the chains.

Her jetpack still pushing her on, she swung around the chain and Shadow shot past her, moving too fast to adjust his speed before he passed out through the doors.

She carried the movement through, going full-circle, emerging from the hangar just as Shadow was darting back in.

Stephanie steered toward the ChampionShip, knowing that out here speed was more important than agility. Shadow would catch her within seconds.

On her left, she saw Brawn struggling as he was carried by four of the other clones, with a fifth standing on his back as he tore the giant's armor apart. She resisted the instinct to go to his aid—it was essential to stop Shadow first.

On the far side of the ship its main hatchway was open. Stephanie swooped under it and in through the hatch, snagged one of the two spare jetpacks—its reassuring weight told her that its fuel-tanks were full—and zoomed back out again just as Shadow plowed straight through the ship's hull.

Clutching the spare pack tightly to her chest, Stephanie flipped the auxiliary ignition switches on its side.

It burst into life, dragging her faster through the air, the exhaust from its powerful jets scorching the paint from her armor. It began to tremble violently in her arms, but she clung on tight.

The readout projected onto the inside of her visor showed that she was leaving Shadow behind. That was not what she wanted. *If he gives up chasing me, he's go after the others!* She began to flip the switches on and off, hoping that the pack's sputtering, sporadic thrust would convince Shadow that it was malfunctioning.

He began to catch up.

Come on, little closer... Closer...

At the right moment, when he was only yards behind her, she pulled open the refueling inlet on the side of the spare jetpack and let go.

The pack crashed into Shadow just as the exhaust from her own jetpack ignited the fuel.

The force of the explosion sent Stephanie shooting forward, tumbling head over heels, and by the time she righted herself all she could see behind her was a thick ball of orange fire.

Did I get him?

Shadow came screaming down out of the fireball, his uniform burning away from his blistering skin in a thick trail of smoldering ash. He plummeted to the ice, came down hard, rolled to a stop, and lay still.

Stephanie kept moving, arcing her path toward Brawn and the others. She had no idea how she was going to help him. Dealing with one of the clones had been hard enough. Five more would be impossible.

If I can get them to chase me one at a time... There was a second spare jetpack on the ChampionShip.

Doubt the same trick will work twice, but maybe it doesn't need to. Maybe there's another way to get them away from Brawn.

Cassandra shook her head. "I can't wake any of them. That thing they were zapped with has completely messed them up."

Razor said, "Get inside Cross's mind, then. Or, no, try Laurie's."

"I've already tried Laurie. He's like Brawn or Impervia—I can't get in. Some people it just doesn't work with."

"Possibly one of the reasons Cross chose Laurie as his partner," Lance said. "Keep trying, Cassandra. Don't quit. Whatever happens, never quit."

Cross turned away from his monitors. "Looks like Shadow's out of the game for now. Pity. I've invested a lot in him... Hope he recovers. If he does, send him to me, not back into the fight. How are our other kids doing, Laurie?"

"Warwick's still down. In fact, he hasn't moved since Renata engaged him outside. I've got a bad feeling about that. He might be dead. *Your* fault—you should have sent one of the others to help him. Alex's got a broken arm and, well, emotionally he's having a bad time. He's not used to pain. None of them are. Tuan, Eldon, Zeke, Nathan, and Oscar are dealing with Brawn."

"And Cord's daughter is still out there. Tell the boys to drop Brawn. He's not much of a threat without his armor. Tuan and Zeke are to take care of Stephanie, and order the others back here. They're to make sure that Cooper doesn't try anything clever."

"What about his friends?"

"They're human now. They're no threat. Let them live."

"Why? Another sudden change of plans?"

"No, the same plan it's always been. You just don't know all the pieces." Victor checked the status of the missile. "That's it. All locked and loaded and ready to go." He turned slowly in his chair to face Laurie. "Well? Aren't you going to ask me why I'm not launching it yet?"

"I honestly don't care any more. I can't stop it, can I?"

"No. And the reason I'm not launching yet is—"

"Don't care, not listening. You're insane and we're all going to Hell for what we've done. Even if we don't go through with this, we're going to Hell anyway. We killed people, Victor. We're murderers."

"I prefer to think of it not as killing, more as *pruning*. Helping the human race to flourish by thinning the herd." He grinned. "You can't make an omelet without shooting a few eggs, right?"

In the hangar, Danny refused to allow the pain in his broken jaw to get the better of him. He had woken a few minutes earlier, his entire body wracked with agony every time he coughed.

The blood on his face and neck had frozen solid, and it had taken all of his strength just to roll onto his stomach. He couldn't stand up, or even switch to fast-time.

He had checked Kenya and then Renata, and almost cried with relief when he saw that they were still alive. But he hadn't been able to wake them.

Now, he was crawling on his belly to the center of the room, toward Mina and Colin. His mechanical arm was useless. It dragged limply behind him as he pulled himself forward with his left hand.

Every movement was torture, every breath of the freezing air sending needle-sharp twinges through his lungs. He knew that if he could turn his head enough to look back, there would be a trail of rapidly cooling blood behind him.

I'm going to die today. Very soon, probably. If the loss of blood doesn't finish me, the cold will.

He stretched out his left arm again, placed his gloveless palm flat on the sub-zero floor, and pulled. Another few inches closer to his friends.

Let them still be alive, please. Let Mina wake up so she can teleport the others to safety.

His outstretched fingers reached the freezing metal rail, and he used it to pull himself forward a little further.

I'm a fool. I believed Cross when he said there was a null-field. I saw him throw that piece of ice at the field and it disappeared, but that must have been a trick. A hologram, maybe. I should have tested it myself. But I was scared—I knew what a null-field could do so I allowed my fear to control me.

All of this is my fault.

He heard voices from somewhere above, but couldn't raise his head to look. He stretched out his hand again. Another few inches. The tarpaulin covering Colin and Mina was only four or five feet away now.

The voices came closer, three people talking, and they all sounded like Colin.

Then one of the clone's voices echoed loud around the hangar. "Look at that. He *is* still alive."

"All that blood. *I'm* not cleaning it up."

"Me either."

Danny saw three pairs of boots land side-by-side in front of him.

"What do you reckon he thinks he's doing?"

"Getting to the girl and Wagner." The clone dropped to his hands and knees in front of Danny, and lowered his head, peering right into Danny's face. "That what you're doing? Man, your face is a *mess*, Cooper."

The clone got to his feet, and said to his brothers, "Hey, check *this* out. This'll be funny."

They moved out of Danny's field of vision, but he didn't care. He stretched his arm out once more, and his fingertips touched the edge of the tarpaulin.

Then he felt strong hands around his ankles, and he was being dragged back across the floor, over the metal rail, back toward the wall.

His ankles were let go, and his feet thudded against the ground, sending a fresh shockwave of pain shuddering through his body.

The clones laughed. "Aw, and he was so close!"

Danny stretched out his arm again, pulled himself forward another few inches.

Chapter 33

Stephanie Cord wondered what her father would have done in a situation like this, if he was being chased back and forth across the top of a glacier by two superhuman clones who just would not give up.

Dad would have used his grappling gun or found some other weapon, and he'd have faced them, not run away.

Stephanie didn't feel that taking on the clones head-on would be a wise move.

Fuel's running low. What do I do? If only there was somewhere I could hide from them for more than a couple of seconds!

But this was the Arctic, in summer, which meant few hiding places, and no true darkness at night.

Then she passed over a dark shape on the ground, a large irregular patch of red and black, and it took her a few seconds to realize that it was Warwick, the clone Renata had encountered first. *Well,* he's *dead.*

She zoomed away in a wide curve, and the pursuing clones followed.

They must be getting tired, she thought. *They seemed to be a lot faster earlier.*

Ahead and to her left was a large cluster of twenty-foot-high boulders, scattered like giant marbles spilled from a bag, and Stephanie steered toward them. She zoomed around to the far side of the closest boulder and immediately slowed to a stop and dropped to the ground.

Seconds later the clones came charging after her. Looking

up, she saw one indicate to the other that they should split up to search.

As soon as they were out of sight, she reactivated her jetpack—the fuel-gauge was now worryingly close to the red line—and raced back the way she had come, flying no more than a yard above the ice.

When she was close to Warwick she shut off the jetpack and allowed her momentum to carry her forward, dropping lower and lower, until she skidded to a stop right beside his body. She tried not to look at his face—it was like seeing Colin dead. She knew she was going to have nightmares about this for a long time, if she lived.

The clone was on his back, frosted-over eyes staring up at nothing, covered in a mess of his own blood and gore. She didn't feel anything for him that resembled pity, but she wasn't sure whether that was because he—or one of his brothers—had murdered Butler Redmond, or because she found it hard to think of them as real people.

As she slid her metal-gloved hands under Warwick's broken, frozen body, she realized that wasn't a fair thought. Mina was a clone, and she was definitely a real person.

Come on, move faster!

Renata had hit Warwick so hard, and so often, that he had been forced down into the densely-packed snow, creating a body-shaped depression. He was frozen to the ground, glued down by ice-blood, and it took all of her strength to roll him onto his side.

They'll be back here any second! Move!

When she'd raised the clone's body high enough, she slipped into the shallow depression and let the body collapse back on top of her.

Less than five seconds later, she hears her pursuers coming back, searching for her.

She hoped they wouldn't want to look too closely at the body of their dead brother.

Brawn was sure his left wrist was broken. Fractured at the very least. The clones had dropped him onto the ice from a height of at least a hundred feet.

He'd landed on the sloping side of a shallow crevasse which slowed him down enough that the fall didn't kill him, but it had still hurt.

He stooped to pick up another chunk of his ruined armor. This one was the cuff of his left glove, crushed and torn beyond usefulness. He threw it aside and kept walking.

So far, the only intact piece of armor he'd found was his left boot. He felt almost foolish trudging across the frozen landscape wearing only his shorts and a single boot, but that was still better than shorts and *no* boot.

He was, in a way, thankful that the clones had torn off his armor as they carried him away from the base, because the chunks of discarded metal were a trail for him to follow back.

The next piece he found was his chest-plate. It, too, had been badly warped, the lower edge torn and jagged, but the shoulder straps were still intact, so he put it on anyway. It was icy to the touch and made him feel even colder than not wearing it. *It'll warm up soon*, he told himself, more out of hope than faith.

So now I've visited both *ends of the Earth*, he thought. *Not many people can say that. Or would want to.*

The Antarctic had seemed a lot warmer, a quarter of a century ago. But Brawn had been superhuman then, his skin almost impervious to the cold. Now, his fingers and toes were numb, and he was trying not to breathe too much because the freezing air tore at his lungs and threatened to bring about a coughing fit.

Keep going, man. You did it before, and you were only a kid. You walked hundreds of miles across the Antarctic in the worst blizzard the continent had seen for years. You can do this.

Something small and dark ahead caught his attention. His helmet. He broke into a run and scooped it up. It seemed to be mostly intact, but the visor had been shattered. He put in on anyway, hoping it would stop his ears from getting frost-bite.

Then something else caught his eye: something moving on the horizon.

He realized too late what it was: two of the clones, zipping back and forth, searching for something or someone.

Before he could find a hiding place, they spotted him, came zooming toward him.

Oh man... They're really going to finish me this time.

Heck with that attitude, Gethin! You held your own against Krodin, and Daedalus. In New York you defeated six of the most powerful superheroes single-handed. You can take these two little punks!

Just need to focus. When you haven't got a weapon, what do you do? Find one.

Or make one.

He slipped the chest-plate's straps from around his shoulders, gripped them with his right hand, holding the chest-plate in front of him like a shield.

One of the clones took the lead, putting on a burst of speed. He dropped to a height of eight feet, increased his speed again, came thundering toward Brawn with enough force to plow through a mountain.

Brawn crouched a little, braced himself with his left leg behind him and all his weight on it. He kept his make-shift shield in front.

The clone showed no signs of slowing down.

A fraction of a second before the clone crashed into him, Brawn dropped to his knees and slammed the shield at his attacker. The torn, jagged edge of the chest-plate caught the clone under his chin, and Brawn held tight as the clone passed overhead

The jagged edge bit deep, raking along the clone's body, tearing open his skin from his neck to the pit of his stomach.

The clone's screams echoed across the barren landscape, stopping only when he crashed to the ground far behind Brawn.

Victor returned to the hangar to see three of the clones watching Daniel Cooper feebly attempt to crawl across the floor to his friends. "What's this?"

Eldon looked up at him. "We're taking bets on how far he gets before he passes out again. Or dies."

"Go find Laurie. Tell him to get the medical kit. There are five syringes of morphine. We need it to ease Danny's pain. You two, help him up. Lift him onto the chair. And be gentle."

When they had lowered Danny into the chair, Victor said, "Brawn and Stephanie Cord are outside doing serious damage to your brothers. Deal with them. But find Shadow first. If he's alive, bring him in."

Victor hunkered down in front of Danny, and showed him the Extractor. "Danny… This is your last chance to save the human race. You know what I want. Visualize Krodin's time-line. Concentrate on it. Reach back… Follow that time-line, trace it from the present into the past. Right back to when he was taken by The Helotry. The stories say that it looked like he was consumed in a pillar of fire. You have to prevent that from happening."

His voice barely a whisper, Danny said, "Can't."

"You can. You already *have* changed the past, Danny. I clearly recall activating the null-field, we both saw it in operation, but somehow it was never switched on. *You* did that. Now… Krodin's time-line. You can do it."

"Hurts too much… can't reach back."

Cross jumped to his feet and yelled, "Laurie!" To Danny he said, "Concentrate… I'll get the morphine. You won't be in any pain. You can… Look, just stay alive!" Cross ran from the room.

In the cockpit of the ChampionShip, Stephanie leaned over the pilot's chair as she desperately tried to get the radio to work. "Sakkara, come *in*. We need help!" The only reply was static. She switched to the emergency channel. "Anybody… Mayday, mayday. This is an emergency!" Again, only static.

Stephanie stepped back from the cockpit.

I'm the last one standing. I could take the ship and get out of here… And then die anyway when the missile detonates.

She dropped into the pilot's chair and unlocked the controls. The constant hum from the engines increased a notch as she guided the ship high into the air, away from Cross's base.

*

Brawn clutched the wounded clone tight to his chest, one arm around his neck, the other pressing on the side of his head.

In front of them, the other clone was hovering.

"Just one push," Brawn said. "And his neck is broken. He's already cut up pretty badly, so don't think you can get around this by waiting for me to succumb to the cold. He'll die before I do. What's your name?"

"Oscar."

"Well, Oscar, your little buddy here is bleeding to death. I don't mind that because you all deserve it, and because his blood is hot. But I'm sure your boss wouldn't be happy to lose another one of his pets. So back off." He took a step forward, and the clone backed away.

"Good boy. We're going back to your base now. You can kill me there instead, where it's warm."

Danny raised his head a little as Victor Cross slowly walked back to him.

When Cross had left the room, Danny had tried to wake Colin and Mina by nudging them with his feet. Colin had stirred once, but remained unconscious.

"Uh... Bit of bad news on *two* fronts," Cross said. "You're going to have to ride out the pain unaided, because there's no morphine. My colleague Mister Laurie has used it all." Cross fell silent for a moment. "Pity. I was getting used to having him around. And he would have liked what's coming next."

"D... D...?" Danny tried to ask.

"Dead? Yes, he is. Injected himself with all five syringes. Which is quite an impressive feat when you think about it because after the first couple he should have been so spaced-out he wouldn't have the strength or the interest to use the rest of them." Cross looked down at his feet, and again fell silent.

He's upset because his friend killed himself, Danny thought. *Maybe he's not completely inhuman after all. Maybe I can use that to—*

Cross raised his head again, smiling. "Ah, got it. He inserted each syringe one at a time but didn't press its plunger. Then when they were *all* in, he pressed all the plungers at once. Another mystery solved. So, Danny... Time for you to get to work." He knelt down in front of Danny. "Concentrate."

I'll concentrate all right, but I'm not going to do what you *want.* Danny fought to ignore the pain in his broken jaw as he allowed his sense of time to expand.

"You can do anything, Danny. Reach back. Pull Krodin out of the past, like The Helotry did. But go to a time *before* they grabbed him. When they did it, they damaged the time-lines. But you're the god of time. The universe created you so that you could make things right. It tried first to give your father that role, but he failed to understand what was required because he didn't have anyone to guide him. The task has now fallen to you, and you have *me* as your guide. You can manipulate the past any way you like, without side-effects. Danny, you could even take Krodin from his time *and* leave him there. Do you understand what I mean by that? Split the time-line into two streams, one where Krodin stays where he is, the other where he's pulled out of the past. You can do *anything*."

Danny felt as though a door was opening in his mind, and he allowed his consciousness to step through. He saw himself as he was now, slumped in a chair in an icy cavern, wearing battered armor that was covered in his own frozen blood.

He slipped back further, and was rocked slightly by a sudden rush of images. The most painful memories were strongest and brightest. The death of his father. Losing his arm inside the power-damping machine. Working at hyper-speed as he used a scalpel to cut into Renata's stomach to remove a bullet. Watching Solomon Cord's body being brought back to Sakkara.

But there were good memories, too. Seeing his baby brother in hospital the day he was born. The discovery of his powers. Sitting on the floor of his bedroom with Colin and their friend Brian as they read through piles of comic-books.

The first time he and Renata kissed.

The memories came rushing at him then, all at once, overwhelming him.

Danny remembered everything. So many memories, and most of them not his own... His parents being introduced to each other by a mutual friend. His father racing back and forth across the planet, desperately trying to bring the cure for The Helotry's plague to the entire human race. Victor Cross as a teenager, walking through a courtyard on a bitterly cold night with fireworks in his pocket and a gallon of gasoline in his backpack.

He saw Lance McKendrick, not more than twenty-five years old, playing poker with a deck that contained fifty-eight cards. He saw a silver-clad young woman wielding an ax in one hand, a sword in the other. He saw Solomon Cord standing in a remote field, staring up into the air with an angry expression, holding on to two broken leather straps as his first prototype jetpack disappeared into the sky.

He saw his younger brother Niall dressed in black rags, racing through a brick-walled corridor as he carried a two-year-old child in his arms.

He saw Colin Wagner ripping open a metal sphere and releasing a wave of energy that washed over Renata and failed to restore her powers.

He saw a man—a teacher—speaking in a room full of oddly-dressed people, while the wall behind him showed pictures of Colin, Renata, Brawn, Stephanie, Mina, Cassandra and Danny himself.

He looked through the eyes of a man staring into a mirror and seeing a woman in the reflection.

He saw Max Dalton's dead body lying in rubble. He saw Evan Laurie crying as his trembling hands fumbled with the clasp on a red plastic medicine box. He saw Victor Cross's missile launch, the force of its exhaust shattering the glacier.

Roz Dalton as a young woman on a deserted street, talking to a hungry dog. His own mother, heart-broken, unable to cope with the knowledge that the man she'd believed was her husband for eleven years had been an imposter. Brawn, fighting for his life against Titan, Energy and others. Solomon Cord, stripped of his armor and thrown from a helicopter.

Too much, Danny thought. *I can't... I have to focus on one thing, not everything.* He looked at Cross. "You..."

"What have you seen, Danny?"

"Everything. You. The Chasm."

"Colin quoted the Bible, the bottomless pit... But I know that was a lie. That was McKendrick, trying to freak me out. Payback for me getting Roman to quote the Bible to him. What is The Chasm?"

"A... hole. An emptiness. A void."

His teeth gritted, Cross said, "What does that *mean*?"

Even if I knew, I wouldn't tell you, Danny thought. All he knew of The Chasm was Victor's obsession with it. "It... It's something you won't know, ever, if you launch that missile."

Cross rocked back on his heels. He looked disappointed. "But that's a *lie*." He pulled the Extractor from his pocket. "You had your chance." He pressed the muzzle of the gun against Danny's forehead.

No! Danny thought. *I have to do something—anything!* His mind raced through his memories, through the visions he had just seen, desperate for something, anything, that would help.

One image leaped out to him, but he didn't know why. He grabbed onto it, focused, concentrated. He felt the change begin to happen.

And Victor Cross pulled the trigger.

Instantly, the images were gone, only vague traces remained, and as Danny Cooper passed out he knew that the last chance to save the human race had been lost.

Chapter 34

Victor stepped back away from Danny's slumped, unconscious body. "So close."

He turned around. Behind him, two of the boys were carrying Shadow between them. His skin was scorched and blistered, his uniform almost completely burnt away.

"How is he?" Cross asked.

"Alive, but only just. Brawn's out there. He has Zeke hostage. He's wounded. Oscar is there too."

"Take Shadow to the gantry. Right to the top. Tell Oscar to get back here, to forget about Zeke. Then lower the plane. It's already fueled and prepped, just get it down. When all that is done, meet me back here."

As the boys carried Shadow out of the room, Cross returned to the circle. He pulled the tarpaulin away from Colin and Mina. "Kids, playing in an adult's world. How did you *think* that this was going to end? Did you honestly believe that you would win? I've been ahead of you every step of the way."

He absently twirled the gun around on his index finger, and turned to look toward Renata and Kenya over by the wall.

"And you, Ms Soliz... You were my favorite."

Victor strode across the hangar floor, and made his way to the control room.

Evan Laurie's body was slouched in the chair, his left sleeve rolled up, five empty syringes in a cluster at his feet. Victor tipped him out of the chair and keyed the missile's ignition sequence. Then he disabled the software that jammed the communications to Sakkara.

He set up a link between his radio and the communications console, and left the room. As he strode along the corridor, he said, "Hello, Sakkara. All the lines are clear. You may speak freely."

Lance McKendrick's voice said, "You're a *dead man*, Cross. I'm going to strangle you myself!"

"No, you're not, McKendrick. Is Cassandra with you? Put her on."

Cross visited his office long enough to collect his prepared backpack, and briefly looked around. *Not forgetting anything? Good.*

Cassandra's voice said, "I'm here."

"Hello Cassandra. Guess what? Not counting my little genetic creations and a certain prisoner in The Cloister, you and I are now the last two functioning superhumans on the planet. That makes us extra-special. How do you like that?"

"Not much." A pause. "Mister Cross, please, don't launch that missile."

"Oh. OK then. Consider the launch aborted. See? All you had to do was ask politely."

Lance said, "Cross, you're insane. How are you going to live on a destroyed Earth?"

"Oh, that's simple. Suspended animation. I'll wake up when the planet is once again conducive to human life." Victor climbed up the missile's gantry. "Hold for a second, please." He lowered the radio's volume control and raced up the remaining five flights of metal stairs.

Shadow was sitting on the top level, with his back leaning against the rocket. He lifted his head as Victor approached. "Hey, boss."

"Hey yourself, Shadow. Stand up."

Shadow grabbed the rail and hauled himself to his feet.

"Wow. Paragon's little girl really did a number on you, didn't she?"

"It wasn't all her," Shadow said. "A lot of this damage is from Cooper and Brawn. But I'll recover."

"Of course you will." Victor reached out past Shadow and pulled down on a handle set into the missile's plating. A three-foot-square hatch slid open. "In you get."

Shadow stared. "What?"

"In. There's room, trust me."

Shadow climbed into the missile. "But... I'll die."

Victor raised the radio to his mouth. "You hear that, Lance? He believes he's going to die, and he's getting in anyway. Gotta love that loyalty."

"Cross—"

"No, shut up. My turn now." He crouched down next to the hatch. "Comfortable? All right, Shadow. This is it. Out of all your brothers I disliked you the least. And now you've got one more job to do for me. The screens will tell you everything you need to know once you're in the air." He patted Shadow on the arm. "It's been fun, kid, but this is where we part company."

Victor straightened up, and sealed the hatch. Far below, something deep inside the missile's engines began to rumble.

He charged down the stairs, taking them three at a time. He vaulted over the last rail and raced for the corridor.

"Ignition in two minutes, Lance. Exciting, isn't it?"

"We've alerted the Russians, the Chinese... Everyone! That missile of yours is going to be blasted out of the sky!"

"No, it won't. It's going to be fast, and it's got a very nifty scrambler that will render it invisible to any other missile. Plus it's got the best avoidance system in the world. Shadow. Right now, the missile's computers are feeding my boy everything he needs to know about piloting it."

Cross ran into the hangar and saw the five clones gathered in front of the black plane. Nathan was unhooking the last of the chains. "Nice work, boys. Daddy is very pleased."

"What do we do about the New Heroes?" Tuan asked.

"Nothing. Leave them. They're finished."

Nathan asked, "But what about Zeke, and Shadow and Roman and Warwick?"

Victor shrugged. "Who cares?" As the ground began to tremble, Victor climbed onto the plane's wing, and dropped his backpack into the cockpit, then leaned in and activated the plane's systems. "Warming up. Good." He took a last look around. "All right, kids. Welcome to the end of the world." He smiled. "Gather round, gather round."

The clones clustered around the wing of the plane, and looked up at him.

"So. You've all been exemplary students." He removed the Extractor from his pocket. "And here's your prize, my little Pinocchios. You get to be *real* boys. For a little while." He pulled the trigger, and as one the clones collapsed to the ground, and lay still.

Victor climbed into the cockpit, and lowered the canopy. He pulled on the helmet and linked the plane's radio to the base's communications. "Still with me, Sakkara?"

"We can hear you," Lance said.

"It's been fun playing with you. If I had a conscience, I'd probably feel bad about all those lies I told. Like... well, there's no point in confessing now, is there?" Cross pulled back on the joystick.

The plane rose. Even over the roar of the plane's vertical thrusters, he could hear the deep rumble of the missile's engines.

He looked up. The hangar's circular opening was directly overhead, a growing circle of blue set into the ice and metal of the ceiling.

All systems are in the green, Cross thought. He glanced to the side—a huge vertical crack had appeared in the hangar wall, and it was growing fast. *And we are clear...*

The plane continued to rise. The chains from which the plane was usually suspended were swinging back and forth now, the entire ceiling trembling and shuddering.

Any second now...

He looked up. With a deafening roar the missile rose into the air, gathering speed, then the steam clouds rushed out, blocking everything above.

"And we're off," Cross said into the radio. "Missile's in the air. Boy, are you people in for a fun ride."

As the plane emerged from the circular opening Victor briefly looked around and saw a quick flash of blue against the roiling clouds of steam. *What? I shouldn't be able to see the sky yet...*

Something hard and heavy crashed onto the plane, covering the canopy.

A huge blue fist was raised, and came smashing down, shattering the glass.

Victor Cross's scream was cut off as Brawn's hand locked around his throat.

Chapter 35

The plane bucked and rocked and it was taking all of Brawn's strength to hold on.

He was thankful for the steam generated by the rocket's exhaust melting the glacier—it meant that he couldn't look down and see how high they were above the ground.

"Set it down, Cross!" Brawn yelled.

Victor Cross's eyes were wide with fear, but he shook his head.

Brawn squeezed tighter. "I mean it! I'll crush your neck into paste! Set it down!"

Again, Cross shook his head.

Right. Brawn thought. *That does it. I don't care if we crash, as long as this piece of filth gets what's coming to him.*

He let go of Cross's neck, and instead grabbed hold of the joystick, and ripped it free of its moorings. He dropped it into Cross's lap. "*Now* try flying the plane!"

In the ChampionShip, Stephanie Cord slammed down on the controls, sending the craft shooting forward. "Come on... Faster, faster!"

The ship's radar screens showed that Cross's missile was already half a mile into the air.

"Still not as fast as we are," she muttered, "but it's accelerating."

She checked the screens again. Directly behind the ship, the missile was riding on a thick white column of exhaust fumes that stretched all the way back to the glacier.

A collision-warning light began to flash. Stephanie ignored it.

Her eyes constantly flicked between the radar display, the monitors, and the controls as she banked the ship a little to starboard, then—satisfied with the ship's trajectory—she rested her hand on the throttle.

The missile was three hundred yards behind the ship.

Two hundred.

One hundred.

Fifty.

Stephanie pulled back on the throttle and the ship juddered with the sudden deceleration.

Then she jumped from the pilot's chair, and threw herself out through the open hatch, triggered her jetpack and shot away from the ship.

She flipped over in the air, looked back to watch the explosion as the missile collided with the ChampionShip.

"Yes! Take *that*, Victor Cross! You don't mess with Solomon Cord's little girl!"

Get a grip, she told herself. *Don't hang around here—there might still be time to get the others out.*

She darted down, following the missile's exhaust trail, and saw Cross's plane emerge from the steam clouds.

Brawn was sprawled across the front of the craft. It was weaving and rolling, clearly out of control.

"Nice going, big guy," Stephanie said, grinning. She adjusted her course, and swooped in to land alongside Brawn. "Need any help?"

"Go get the others—they're still in the hangar!"

"What about you?"

"Forget me—the glacier is collapsing. Get the kids clear!"

The steam was beginning to condense into snow as Stephanie dropped down through the hangar doors.

Colin, Mina and Danny were closest, but Renata and Kenya were in greater danger: the floor around them was cracking, falling away in car-sized chunks.

She zoomed over to them and grabbed Renata's arm with her left hand, Kenya's with her right, and dragged them up and out of the crumbling hangar. In the air, she could see that the glacier was collapsing from the southern side—she flew half a mile north, and set them down.

She raced back to the hangar—and the low-fuel warning light began to flash inside her helmet. Danny and the others were still safe for now, but the clones... They were piled in a bunch almost directly beneath the hangar doors. *I can't. I can't leave them to die.*

One at a time, Stephanie carried the unconscious clones to safety.

Each time she returned to the hangar, there was less of the floor and walls remaining—and the low-fuel light was flashing fast and faster.

Now only her friends were left. Colin was groaning, trying to sit up. She dropped down next to him, grabbed his arm. "Come on, hold onto me! I can't carry you all at once!"

Colin pulled himself away. "No—Danny and Mina. Take *them*."

"We don't have enough *time!*"

Colin screamed, "Do it, Steph! I'll be OK—get them out of here!"

She grabbed hold of Danny and Mina with her aching arms, and said, "Col... I'll come right back, I promise!" She zoomed out of the hangar once more, and left Mina and Danny with the others.

She was half-way back when she realized that something was missing. Something was wrong. She looked up.

"No..." Far above, past the thick black cloud that was all that remained of the ChampionShip, a long, steady vapor-trail told her that Victor Cross's missile was still flying.

Forget that! She told herself. *Deal with it later. Get Colin out! Move!*

Stephanie rocketed forward, and was within a hundred yards of the hangar when her jetpack sputtered and the emergency fuel tank cut in and she began to descend.

It had only enough fuel to allow her to land safely.

"No, please..."

Stephanie dropped as close to the ground as she could, but didn't touch down—she wanted to stretch out the emergency fuel right to the last drop.

Then the jetpack cut out completely, and she hit the icy ground hard and fast. Before her skid even slowed to a stop she was up and running, racing for the edge of the hangar.

She was fifty yards away when she saw the cracks radiating from the circular opening.

Forty yards away when the edges began to crumble.

Thirty yards away when the entire hangar roof collapsed in a blinding cloud of snow and ice.

Brawn yelled, "Come on, Cross! You can do it!"

"Shut up! I'm working as fast as I can!"

Brawn pressed his forehead against the fractured canopy and looked in. Cross had stripped the torn wires from the ruined joystick and was desperately trying to jury-rig a way to control the plane.

"You're supposed to be a genius—get it done!"

"Almost... Hold on..."

Brawn watched as Cross twisted wires together, pulled others free and strung them from one instrument to another.

The plane banked abruptly to the left, and Brawn felt his grip begin to weaken.

"We're both gonna die if you can't do it!"

"I said shut up! I don't work well under pressure!"

"*Learn!*"

Something sparked inside the cockpit, and Cross yelled, "Got it! I can only control the altitude but—"

"Set us down!"

The plane began to descend.

"I don't know where we are, where we're going to end up," Cross said.

"Who cares, as long as we don't end up flat! Not that it's going to make much difference, when your missile lands."

"It's not a missile," Cross yelled back. "It's a rocket."

Brawn paused. "What?"

Stephanie backed away from the slowly crumbling edge of the crater, staring down at the devastation. As she watched, thousands of tons of ice slowly collapsed down on Cross's base, crushing everything. Shards of ice as large as ocean-liners crashed and shifted against each other with deafening cracks and booms.

I was too late. Too slow. I should have got Colin out first. I should have left the clones to the end.

Another chunk of ice broke off from the edge, and she took a step back.

"Pretty spectacular, isn't it?"

She turned to see Colin standing behind her.

"Man, I thought it was cold in there. Out *here*? Wow."

"I thought you were dead!"

Colin shrugged. "I climbed out."

"What? *How*?"

"There were all these chains hanging down from the ceiling. Remember when your dad was teaching us to climb the ropes in the gym? I guess I must have learned *something* from that."

She rushed at him, pulled him close. "Don't ever scare me like that again!"

"Ow, Steph, your armor's cold. We should get out of here. Where did you bring the others?"

Stephanie pointed to the north. "That way. We have to walk, though—my fuel's gone. Hold my hand. Don't let go."

"Will do," Colin said, smiling. "I don't want to *ever* let go."

Chapter 36

"You have been found guilty by a jury of your peers of committing heinous crimes so numerous that a complete list would keep us here for several more days. Do you have anything to say to the court before I pass sentence?"

"I do," Victor Cross said, looking around the court room. "I can't have been found guilty by a jury of my peers because I don't *have* any peers. Everyone in this room is a moron compared to me." He looked at the judge. "You especially."

"Are you done?" The judge asked.

"Actually, no. What you people fail to understand is that—"

"You're done."

"No, I—"

"Bailiff, if the defendant speaks again, you have the permission of the court to silence him in any manner that pleases you. Victor Cross, I sentence you to a term of not less than four thousand years penal servitude, without the possibility of parole. You will spend this time in solitary confinement, without access to any form of technology more advanced than a butter-knife. A *plastic* one. Take him away."

The New Heroes gathered in Sakkara for what Colin knew would be the last time in a long while. They were in the gymnasium, where Brawn was packing away the last of his few belongings.

Danny walked up to Colin. His neck was in a brace, and there was a line of fresh stitches along his jaw. "You OK?"

"Yeah. You?"

"I've been better." He grinned. "Ow. Hey, we get to have

normal lives for a while, until our powers come back. That'll be interesting."

"How are the new teeth settling in?"

"They feel really, *really* weird! But considering the alternative, I'm OK with that."

They walked over to Brawn. "Where are you going to go?" Colin asked.

"Home, first, to see my ma. Visit my dad's grave. Then..." he shrugged. "I don't know. I'm thinking I might go back to school."

"Well, *that* sounds like fun."

"Yeah. Just hope I don't get bullied."

Danny laughed and then said "Ow!" and clutched at his jaw.

Brawn said, "And let's hope that all the bad guys don't find out that you kids are powerless now. Still," the giant added, shrugging, "we saved the day. Stephanie knocked Cross's missile off-course and out into space, and the world was saved. Well, I say 'missile' but Cross insisted that it was a rocket."

"Same thing," Danny said.

Colin frowned. "Yeah, I guess." He looked up as someone approached. "Hey, Raze. We're gonna need a whole new bunch of armor until we get our powers back."

Razor gave him a thin-lipped smile, and said, "I know. But someone else is going to have to make it. I'm leaving."

Brawn said, "Ah, you're *always* leaving."

"This time I mean it." He patted the bag slung over his shoulder. "I'm all packed and there's a copter on the roof waiting for me. I'm going in, like, two minutes. I've done my bit, guys." He tilted his head toward the door. "C'mon, walk me up."

They started for the door, then Razor turned back to face Brawn. "Sorry, big guy. Forgot you can't come this way."

"That's OK," Brawn said. His giant hand completely swallowed Razor's as they shook. "It's been an honor. I'll see you again, right? We'll have a big reunion, or something."

"Count on it. Take it easy, man," Razor said as he walked backward toward the door.

In the corridor, Danny said, "Razor, you could take your mother to the Substation and both of you could live there. That way you could still work for us."

"That's what your dad suggested, but, nah, I don't think so. I helped save the world, now I have to go do my own thing. I've got a job lined up."

"You? A job? *Really*?" Colin asked.

"Yep. At the runaways' shelter in Jacksonville. They've got an opening. It doesn't pay much, but... Hey, even ten bucks a week would pay better than this place!"

As they emerged onto the roof, Razor paused. "Aw, what's *this*?" A small crowd was clustered around the waiting copter.

Warren Wagner approached him, shook his hand. "Good luck. You drove me crazy half the time, but we'll miss you. Caroline said to give you her love. You ever need us, just call. Oh, and Josh Dalton told me to tell you that when you get to Jacksonville, you're to check your bank account."

Razor frowned. "Bank account? I don't *have* a bank account."

"Seems you do now," Façade said, patting Razor on the shoulder. "Looks like you got paid after all."

Then the hugs came: Renata first, then Stephanie, Alia, Kenya and—deliberately holding back to the end—Cassandra.

Grant threw Razor a clumsy salute, and grinned. "I owe you one, Razor. If it wasn't for your armor, I'd never have made it."

Renata said, "We *all* owe you. The whole *world* owes you."

Razor turned in a slow circle, then looked at Colin. "Lance?"

"Sent his apologies. Said he had something to do. But he'll be in touch."

Razor nodded. "All right." He gave Danny a friendly punch in the chest. "You look after Renata, OK? If you don't..."

"I will."

"And I want an invite to the wedding."

Renata blushed and glared at Razor, and Danny blurted, "What? Now wait a second..."

Razor laughed and threw his bag into the copter, then reached out his hand to shake Colin's. "Take care, little buddy. I mean it."

"You too," Colin said. He looked down at their clasped hands. "Hey, remember the day we met?"

Razor laughed again. "Yeah. Seems like a lifetime ago."

They both grinned. Razor let go of Colin's hand, hesitated for a second, then pulled him close, wrapping his arms around Colin's shoulders. "Never had a real brother, but if I had..." He slapped Colin's back twice, and stepped away.

Façade climbed past Razor into the copter. "All right, enough with the good-byes. Daylight's wasting, kid. Let's go."

Razor nodded to Colin one last time, then jumped up into the copter. "Hey, can *I* fly it?"

From the cockpit, Façade's voice floated back, "*Can* you fly a copter?"

Razor replied, "I don't know—I never tried."

The crowd stepped back as the copter's engine whined and the rotors began to turn.

All too soon, the copter lurched into the air, and within minutes it was nothing but a dot on the horizon.

*

Lance McKendrick stood in front of Victor Cross's impenetrable prison cell, a perfect cube four yards long on each side, made of eighteen-inch-thick transparent aluminum. The cell was situated in the center of the Cloister's courtyard: Cross could be seen at all times.

The only gap in the walls was a four-inch diameter hole, set close to the floor, through which the guards could pass Cross's food and water, and he could pass back the small waste-bucket. On hot days, with the sun baking down on the cell, Cross could be found lying on the floor, his face pressed against the hole, gasping for breath.

Victor walked up to the glass wall, and stared out. "Knew you'd come, McKendrick."

"Of course you did. You know everything. You're a genius." Lance tapped on the glass. "How's that working out for you?"

"It's not over. You think you've won, but I'm playing the long game."

Lance began to walk around the cube, peering in at Victor as he did so. "Just tell me, then. What is your ultimate goal? What do you *want,* Victor?"

"What do *you* think I want?"

"You want to be the best. The smartest. And you want everyone to acknowledge that." Lance pulled a thick-nibbed marker from his inside jacket pocket, and began to write on the cell's glass wall. "And I thought *I* had an ego problem. Your actions killed almost a million people, harmed countless others, threatened to wipe out all life on the planet... why?"

"Now, Lance, you know by now that the supervolcano thing was a ruse."

"I figured that," Lance said, nodding. "Something to keep the New Heroes away from your rocket. They couldn't risk getting close to it in case it detonated. A deterrent designed to buy you enough time to persuade Danny Cooper to change the past. But even on the edge of death, Danny's will was too strong for you. You failed." Lance stepped back from Cross's transparent prison, and admired his work. In large, neat letters he had written, "Idiot In A Box."

"There's always a back-up plan."

"And what is that?" Lance asked.

Cross grinned. "I *could* tell you, but I really don't want to spoil the surprise."

Epilogue 1

Four months after the trial of Victor Cross...

Shadow fixed the mask to his face and unsealed the hatch, then stepped out onto the almost airless desert. Overhead, the sun was small in the orange-tinted sky.

His boots kicked up brown dust as he walked toward the thin, bronze-skinned man sitting cross-legged on a large flat rock.

In the ancient language the ship's computer had taught him, Shadow said, "I'm a friend. I've come to take you back to Earth."

The warrior stood. He arched his back and flexed his muscles. "What is your name, boy?"

"They call me Shadow."

"Shadow. I like that. My name is Krodin." Then he nodded. "I knew. I knew that this was not the Earth. This is another place. Another world."

"And another *time*," Shadow said. "Four and a half thousand years since you were taken from Alexandria."

"Alexandria... Where once I ruled." They began to walk back toward the craft. "And I will rule again. I am Alpha and Omega, the beginning and the end, the first and the last."

Epilogue 2

One year after the trial of Victor Cross...

Kenya Cho raced through the burning forest, her tears carving paths in the dirt and soot that covered her scarred face. She was almost thankful for the fires: the flames illuminated the thick clouds of smoke, throwing back enough light that it almost compensated for her poor night-vision.

The soldiers were close behind her. A whole Viper squadron. They were hunter-killers, given full authority to use any means necessary to stop the rebels. Somehow they had learned where Kenya's people were hiding, and rather than waste time tracking them down, the Vipers had chosen to burn them out.

I'm not going to make it, Kenya thought. *They're driving me this way because they have someone waiting at the other end!*

Ahead, the flickering light of the fires showed a small crevasse in her path. Kenya increased her speed and jumped. She somersaulted in the air, silently landed in a crouch in a small clearing, rolled onto her feet and kept going.

"Sarge, I see her!" A voice called out from her left.

"Don't move!" A second voice yelled. "You move, you die!"

A black-clad soldier threw himself at her, and Kenya dodged to the side then slammed her elbow into the back of his neck as he passed her. The soldier's gun flew from his hand: Kenya threw herself after it—and was within inches of grabbing it when a large, thick-soled boot kicked it away.

They were on her in seconds, grabbing her legs, dragging her back to the clearing.

"Get her on her feet!"

One of the soldiers grabbed hold of Kenya's hair and hauled her upright.

"Resisting arrest." A man with sergeant's stripes on his uniform stepped up to her, and Kenya flinched.

No, not him!

Sergeant Antonio Lashley grabbed Kenya's chin with a leather-gloved hand and roughly pushed her head back. "Now that's a nice find. Kenya Cho. Well, we got your pals. Every one of them. They're dead. We gave them a chance to surrender, but they figured resistance was the best option. When are you freaks gonna learn? You *don't* resist us. If you resist, you die."

"You can't do this! This is America!"

"Not any more. America was just an idea—and it's an idea that's gone now, wiped out just like half the planet." Sergeant Lashley pointed to the symbol on his shoulder; a blue eye inside a golden sun. "What's left of the Earth belongs to Krodin."

"We'll stop you!"

He planted his out-spread hand on her face and pushed her back—two of the soldiers caught her arms and dragged her forward again. "Pathetic," Lashley said. "There are so few of you punks left we could waste the lot of you with one clip!"

Kenya glared at him, her teeth gritted. "*Someone* will stop you."

The sergeant laughed. "Who? There are no more heroes. There's just us." To his men, he said, "Take her. Find out everything she knows before you kill her. She was working with Cooper's cell; hurt her until she talks. Then *keep* hurting her. Record everything. Cross is going to want to see it. Maybe she'll tell us what we need to get the rest of these rats out of their tunnels and into the open." He looked around. "The rest of you stay sharp. There could be more of them about."

The soldiers marched away, dragging her backwards over the rough, cinder-strewn ground. She looked up to see the sergeant smirking at her.

"Someone will stop us. Hah. Good one," Lashley yelled after her. "You so-called New Heroes are only making things worse for everyone. When are you going to accept that Krodin is the only power now?"

And then the soldiers dragging her suddenly stopped. The sergeant was staring at something beyond her.

With some effort, Kenya twisted her head around to look.

Fifteen yards away, the air was glowing. A sphere of orange light. It flared briefly, and disgorged a human figure onto the ground before it faded.

Lashley rushed over, stopped when he was next to Kenya. "What the...?"

The figure straightened up, silhouetted against the burning forest.

Kenya squinted, trying to make out the features. The flickering firelight showed a polished steel helmet, metal gauntlets, a glimpse of sweat beading on dark-brown skin.

The sergeant yelled, "Open fire!"

The soldiers let go of Kenya to use their guns. She ducked down, and ran.

The gunfire was quickly replaced with screams, then Lashley yelled, "You? That's not possible—you're *dead*!"

A final, brief scream, then silence.

Kenya knew she should run and keep running, but something drew her back to the clearing. She crept slowly, silently, through the smoldering forest, and saw the strange warrior crouched among the dead bodies of the Viper squadron.

On the ground, not more than a yard away from Kenya's feet, Sergeant Antonio Lashley stared at her through dead eyes. The rest of his body was quite a distance from his head.

The armored warrior straightened up, and slowly looked around.

Who is *that?* Kenya asked herself. The armor wasn't familiar —it seemed cruder, less advanced than the armor worn by the members of Team Paragon.

Every other superhero—powered or otherwise—was either dead, imprisoned, or a long way from here.

But I know them all… So that means … Kenya could hardly bring herself to even entertain the thought. *No. It's impossible.*

She moved closer. "Are you… Are you Paragon? But you were *killed*."

The stranger turned toward her, and now Kenya could see a lot more clearly.

"No," the woman said. "I'm not Paragon." She looked around again. "What *is* this place? How did I get here? And these men… Why are they wearing Krodin's symbol?"

"I'll tell you everything I know. But… Who *are* you?"

The woman wiped the blood from her sword and returned it to the scabbard on her back. "My name is Abigail de Luyando."

Michael Carroll

www.quantumprophecy.com

The New Heroes / Quantum Prophecy trilogy:
The Quantum Prophecy / The Awakening
Sakkara / The Gathering
Absolute Power / The Reckoning

The Super Human series:
Super Human
The Ascension
Stronger
Hunter

E-books:
The Footsoldiers
Flesh and Blood

Limited-edition short-story collection:
The New Heroes: Superhuman
(Includes "The Footsoldiers" and "Flesh and Blood")

For more information, see the Quantum Prophecy website:
www.quantumprophecy.com

or the author's website:
www.michaelowencarroll.com

Made in the USA
Lexington, KY
15 October 2016